Rumors & Whiskey

THE WHISKEY WOMEN SERIES: BOOK 1

VICTORIA WILDER

Bloom books

Published by Bloom Books, an imprint of Sourcebooks
1935 Brookdale RD, Naperville, IL 60563-2773
(630) 961-3900
sourcebooks.com

Cataloging-in-Publication data is on file with the Library of Congress.

Printed and bound in the United States of America.
LSC 10 9 8 7 6 5 4 3 2 1

For you, the brave one. The hard things you've survived don't define you.

But, damn, they've shaped you.

This story is about life after something massively altering. It's about looking at bravery from a new perspective. It doesn't have to be bold and loud, sometimes it's quiet, lingering there all along. And then sometimes it takes someone else to make you realize just how much of a badass you are.

If you need someone on loan for that last part, then I'm happy to introduce you to the Crowne women…and Julian Colton.

ALSO BY VICTORIA WILDER

The Bourbon Boys

Bourbon & Lies

Bourbon & Secrets

Bourbon & Proof

Whiskey Women

Rumors & Whiskey

A NOTE ABOUT *RUMORS & WHISKEY*

I'd like to welcome you to Rumor, Tennessee! This is the first book in the Whiskey Women series, and while this romantic suspense is a work of fiction, there are some heavy subject matters that you should be aware of before diving in.

The following is a list of potential triggers that are not meant to be spoilers or tropes, but rather a warning of what's inside if you feel more comfortable knowing before diving in:

Death, murder, descriptions of torture, kidnapping, use of weapons—specifically knives and sharp self-defense tools, loss of a parent (off page), captivity, torture, body dismemberment, PTSD flashbacks, physical violence on page, references to domestic violence, cannibalism, grief, discussion of sexual assault (off page), drugs without consent, destruction of fragile male egos, vulgarity, and descriptive sexual content.

PLAYLIST

PROLOGUE

It's been one-hundred and twenty-two days since I've heard the sound of my own voice.

"Isn't he clever, Professor?"

I don't answer. Ignore the question. Stifle the fear that rises unwanted in the back of my throat, threatening to come out in the form of a plea or scream. Quiet is smart. If I'm anything anymore, it's smart.

"Am I misreading things?" I want to remember who said that, but I can't.

"Professor?" He chews, trying to get my attention. Clicking his tongue, his mouth tips up in his version of a smile—a perverse smirk laced with false emotions. "Isn't our new friend the most clever? Aside from you, of course."

Don't blink. I maintain a stoic gaze and motionless, unwavering posture. I will not speak or answer. Feigning disinterest in this disruption will make him enjoy it less. I'm not brave. I *hate* him. The way he entered just now, though, is anything but usual—out of breath and seemingly disheveled. As much as I try to keep my expression impenetrable, he knows that despite my best efforts, I've noticed the large body he's dragged inside, in plain sight and not stowed inside his black leather rolling bag.

My mother would be fucking appalled knowing I'm choosing to be silent. But she'll never know. I blink back the blurred tears that unexpectedly swell in my eyes. It happens every time I think about her. I block out images of Stevie and Jo. If I allow myself to remember the last time we laughed until we cried or yelled until we laughed, I will die. If I soften, even a little, he'll know.

He slowly sharpens his filleting knife along the rough leather hanging between the shelf and metal table. I can see flecks of dust kick up around him from the desk lamp as he drags the smooth edges back and forth. My chest tightens with every scrape and scratch. It reminds me of an old park seesaw—creepy or comforting depending on the memory surrounding it. Much like here—a small rectangular space that for some might be a luxury, but for me, it's a nightmare.

"Professor," he tuts like I'm being silly for being silent. Again, he smiles, his crooked front tooth escaping just enough to show how pleased he is with my predictability. That tooth is one of many imperfections that would otherwise seem mundane on someone's face. A man I would have never looked at twice. Ordinary on the outside in every way. But inside, he's the kind of monster I never prepared to encounter. *"You are my most prized possession, Professor. So smart and beautiful. What makes you think I'd ever let you go?"*

It's been one-hundred and twenty-nine days since he's had me. After the first seven of those days, I learned that he liked screaming and begging. His pants bulged when I pleaded for him to let me go. He smiled, petting me like I was his fucking pet. I screamed so hard and so loud it burst a blood vessel in my eye and made my throat burn for nearly a week. That was the last time. Above everything, I'm smart enough to recognize that my pain was fuel, a turn-on for him.

When he cut along my skin, I didn't scream. Instead, I bit the inside of my cheek to disperse the pain. I clenched my fists and breathed only through my nose. Screaming and pleading were encouragement. He craved it, so I denied him of it. He likes to play and taunt as if I'm his special brand of entertainment. I never liked entertaining people, that was my sisters' and mother's arena. My highs came from learning and teaching. Researching, testing, and waiting. I took comfort in being the one people underestimated but who always outperformed.

I swallow the tangy-false sweetness of my spit. It's a reminder that my last sip of water was nearly two and a half days ago. It's been just under three days since I've eaten the food he laces with some form of barbiturate. Lethargic movements in exchange for not dying of hunger. I miss the way it feels to have my belly full and pants tight.

Stop it, Wyn. I grind my molars, snapping away those feelings.

A shiver rolls up my back and through my body, anchoring my anger. It's the only emotion I allow myself to focus on. Tempers are the unmistakable signature of being a Crowne. I know I'm going to die in here, but I'm not going to make it easy. Or rewarding. When he kills me, I will not give him what he wants. I think only about the things I can control now. Being quiet and obedient is my method. He doesn't restrain me anymore, and I wonder if it's carelessness or just that he knows I've accepted my fate.

Control in chemistry is about creating a baseline for the variable being tested. I'm the control now, not the variable.

Moments like this, when something ugly and evil is a glance away, I think about my favorite ways to apply what I've learned. The processes that led me to my academic career. I think about whiskey. The taste of it, yes, but also the process of making it—the head, the heart, and the tail. Three components that came off the still, but only one worth keeping. *I want to be the part worth keeping.*

"You've wandered into something, friend, that I don't think you quite comprehend," he says to the still-breathing body. "But you will." The pitch of his voice is elevated, like he's readying to show off. I hate knowing that this is where I'm going to die and that his voice is the last one I'll ever hear.

My eye catches on the blood draining from a discarded limb in the far corner. As usual, nausea rolls through my sweat-slicked body. I never met its owner. Not officially, at least. She looked a lot like me. Similar build, the same color hair, cropped short like mine had been when he first took me. I hated that haircut the moment I watched the stylist start drying it.

I cycle through the things that comfort me. The smell of burning oak. The first taste of whiskey when it's ready. The way charcoal smooths out its bite and how barrels can change the chemistry completely, helping it become something new, something better. I mix up the order sometimes, but I think through each process and dissect what could be done to bend "the rules." As soon as my mind drifts to who taught me, I redirect. I can't allow that—it'll have me unraveling. Instead, I shift course. Frozen honeydew melon balls in pink lemonade make me think of summer. Summer rolls into the picking of a banjo. It's a Pavlovian thought that tricks my mouth, making me salivate, picturing smoked meats and tangy barbecue. I stifle my instant curiosity about what it feels like outside right now.

I clear my mind again as he parades a new person into the snug space. It's the second person he's brought here—wherever "here" might be. The first, I thought, was only here to scare me. To show me what he planned to do to me next, but it was like he wanted to impress me. I recognized the act of it—the posturing and flaunting. My experience was only with intellectual sophomores with overzealous five-year plans in my chemistry lab, or a cocky graduate student who cared more about hearing himself speak than the response he garnered. Someone finding my opinion of them important always felt strange. But this is entirely different—watching the inner workings of a monster unfold and trying to remain unaffected. Other people's opinions of me had always mattered—maybe too much. It's the only part of him that I can relate to—caring how someone else sees your accomplishments or lack thereof. My indifference now, however, is a performance that I'm banking my life on. He won't see approval from me, or disgust. The moment he sees it, he'll have won. I won't give him that satisfaction. Ever.

Regardless of how many ways he enjoys toying with me—the way he cut parts of me and then sometimes ate them, I never got sick over it. I play over and over in my head the one thing my mother always said to me when life got sticky: "You're a Crowne, Wyn. Start acting like it."

A sliver of light catches my attention as it bleeds beneath the pull-down metal door. That's new. A foot above it, the lever that locks the door is perpendicular to the floor. It's not locked.

He made a mistake.

His shoes make a scuffing noise—the only warning to look away from his error as he turns toward me. I shift my focus straight ahead at the same crack along the dark-gray cinder block eye level from where I sit and to the right of the metal door. As he opens the small, rectangular case from his bag, I can see the pleased-with-himself smile he has plastered on his long, thin face. I keep my tongue resting on the roof of my mouth and take measured breaths in and out of my nose. I ignore how he grows more and more amused, rubbing his hand along the bulge in his pants just as he turns toward his newest "guest" with a scalpel. "There's something so pretty about decolletage, don't you think, Professor?"

I don't answer. I don't look. The last "guest" he brought in here, he had slowly sliced the skin that rested along her collarbone. He said, *"It's just like peeling an apple, Professor."* When I didn't answer and tried to keep my eyes from watering, he asked, *"Did none of your students ever bring you an apple?"* As if that was why I struggled to keep tears from falling and not the meticulous violence playing out in front of me.

He tsks, like I've given him a response. "I hadn't planned for it, but when the world decides to deliver," he pauses, "you take."

A grunting sound echoes, deeper in cadence than what I've become accustomed to hearing. It instantly registers that his newest guest is not another woman.

I glance over just as he says, "I've always admired men who grew too quickly. That's all that makes up an Adam's apple—rushing to grow bigger than the body is ready. But it's lovely when it protrudes like this." He smiles at me, knowing he's got my attention.

I messed up because I catch him smiling.

I shift forward and look at the sliver of light again. I messed up...but so did he.

The latch isn't pulled closed. The door is not locked. He isn't this careless. His guest hadn't been planned. It was reactionary.

Within the same handful of seconds of realizing this, a loud thump echoes off the wall, and the crunch of bone rings out as two bodies hit the floor. The monster and his newest, quite large and very much still alive, guest. Grunts and yells steal my attention back to what's happening just feet away from where I sit. My hands shake as I glance at the sliver of light again, and then back to the chaos of both men wrestling for purchase on the floor. But it's the gruff voice that cuts through the chaos and knocks the smarts back into me.

"Go!" he yells as he pins the monster.

I stand, my legs barely holding me upright, heart pounding so fast it makes me dizzy.

There's another grunt and the sound of flesh being ripped.

My mind made up, I shuffle forward, bend over, and grip the latch. *Be brave.* Pulling up the door, bright white light blinds me. I squeeze my eyes shut just as a deep voice bellows, "Go! Wyn. Runnnnn!"

CHAPTER 1

Wyn

Present

TECHNICALLY, I'M NOT DEAD. BUT it fucking feels like I'm on its doorstep when my heart stops for what feels like a power ballad after being startled awake by a rapid succession of closed-fist knocks. I suck in a breath, sitting up. My left arm is asleep from the awkward angle it's been draped on the toilet paper holder. My cheek is sore, nearly numb from the cold marble sink it was resting on.

"Are you alright in there?" a woman's voice calls out, followed by another hurried knock on the other side of the door. I stand too quickly, shifting in front of the mirror, rendering me lightheaded as the haziness blacks out the edges of my vision. I squeeze my eyes closed and take a slow breath. When I exhale, I lean against the sink, elbows locked straight as I stare at my reflection.

"Fucking brilliant," I whisper sarcastically, confirming that I look as great as I feel. Smudged mascara, nothing left of my long-lasting lip stain except a line edging my lips that somehow makes me look paler than I should for late August, and a nice little same-day hangover headache lingering just behind my right eye socket. I turn my head and spot a crease along my cheek. I rub my fingers along the indentation, trying to erase the evidence of my mid-party power nap.

"All good," I singsong, like it's totally normal for a woman in her mid-thirties to get tipsy and then sleep it off in the bathroom. "I'll be right out."

What time is it? I turn over my phone to check—Fuck me. Blinking hard, I focus on the blurry glow of 1:26 a.m. Below it, there's a wall of texts from my sisters in response to the rescue request I sent nearly two hours ago.

WYN:

I need a ride.

STEVIE:

I got pulled into covering at the bar tonight.

STEVIE:

Jo, will you go pick her up?

JO:

I am literally next to you watching you text this and there's a crowd stacked 4 rows deep of drunks and cranky bikers. Neither of us is going anywhere any time soon.

STEVIE:

Text mom.

JO:

Again, do you need your eyes checked? She's on the shot swing.

I wasn't going to text my mother anyway. The last thing she said to me was that "I'm always so predictable." I told her she was a narcissist, to which she replied, "At least I'm not boring." I swallow the guilt of hating her again.

STEVIE:

Sorry Wynnie. Go a little wild, call a rideshare.

JO:

Come to the bar before you go home.

JO:

A bachelor party just walked in and Stevie has that ready-to-stir-some-shit look in her eyes.

I sniff out a laugh. I missed them more than…I look up, trying to coax back the tears from falling. I should go to the bar. I didn't like leaving after an argument—life's too short, despite wanting to flip Lu Crowne off regularly. I thought I'd never see any of them again, never mind hear them laugh or listen as they continue to make the most ridiculous life choices. And then, by some karma-level turn of events, life threw me a curveball. Again.

A shiver runs across my skin and settles low. Goosebumps track up my arms, but it's not from nerves or panic. It's the kind that has my cheeks warming and thinking about a different place. An entirely different life. *About him.*

Swiping to the rideshare app, I find that there isn't a car available for at least thirty-five minutes. *Superior timing, Wyn.*

I turn the faucet on long enough to mimic handwashing, dip my wrists under the cool water, and then press my palms against my cheeks. My face is flushed, and the lingering buzz will give me just enough courage to pretend like this didn't happen.

"Wyn," my boss's voice calls out. Tonight's host and head of the university's chemistry department knocks again, just as I swing open the door. "Are you alright?"

Giving her a smile, I say, "Your wife's spritzers were too good." Smiling and playing off the fact that I just took a nap in her half bath, I add, "I'm so sorry if I wandered for too long."

She flaps her hand at me like that was a wild thing to say, and then loops her arm with mine. "Not at all. There were so many people here, I feel like I barely had a chance to talk with you. I thought you'd left, and I wanted to say again how thrilled I am to have you back."

I didn't think I'd return to work. At least not right away. But small counties have an impeccable way of rolling out townie news like thunder from a summer storm. Quiet at first, and then fast, furious, and without invitation. Before I could consider the audacity of declining, I had my position at the university back—tenure isn't taken lightly in academia, and damn did I work my ass off for it. So when tonight's host said, "Wyn, we're going to throw a little welcome back party in your honor," I was appreciative. But now, I can't get out of here fast enough.

I smile and awkwardly wave at my boss. She leans in for

a hug, just as I raise my hand. Turning on my heel, I tell her, "Lovely party," as I side-eye four of my colleagues playing an intense game of Catan in the dining room. Two of our department secretaries linger in the foyer, speaking quietly about something or other. I give them a smile and half wave as I keep walking, trying to avoid being pulled into whatever it is they're gossiping about.

The moment I step outside, it's like an open-handed slap of skin-slicking humidity. My blouse sticks to my lower back, as if sweat was readying itself to flee from my pores as soon as I remembered it's August. I hated it and missed it all at once. I tilt my chin up and close my eyes, hoping for a wave of relaxation to wash over me. I should've opted for a maxi dress instead of my typical work attire. I'm not sure what it is about chiffon and tweed that says, *well-respected chemistry professor* to me, but it works. I slid into the clothes and persona as if I had never left—like memorable armor, or a mask. Right now, though, I want breathable cotton, the less the better.

I work my fingers through the first two buttons of my blouse before I hear a deep voice cut in from my right. "Thought you left, Dr. Crowne."

I practically choke, shuffling to my left. "Holy fucking shit," I rush out. My mouth tilts up into a smile as soon as I realize I'm okay and who it is. "Reed," I say on an exhale. "I didn't see you there."

"And I didn't know you had such a colorful vocabulary, Wyn," he says in an amused tone. His gaze flicks to the sharp weapon gripped in my hand. Catching me off guard isn't safe for anyone.

I glance down at it. A matte-black metal cat head with finger-size eyeholes where my middle and ring finger fit snugly, and razor-sharp pointed ears that protrude perfectly to puncture skin with the right amount of force.

As I shift my weapon into my back pocket, he passes me my phone that fumbled to the ground when he caught me off guard.

The rideshare app displays the abysmal arrival time just as it buzzes, and then powers down, turning black and flashing the dead battery logo. "You've got to be kidding—"

"Come on, I'll give you a ride," he says in that warm country drawl of his, nodding toward a black Porsche Cayenne.

From afar, Dr. Reed Andrews looks like an upgraded version of the man I once knew. Instead of golf polos and baggy cargo pants, now he wears a crisp white Oxford button-down and well-fitted suit pants. His sandy-blond hair is short and nearly buzzed at the sides, with tousled waves impeccably styled along the top, and his smile is kind above a cleanly shaved jawline.

"That's yours?" I ask, smirking at the car he's moving toward. I've always looked at those fancy cars and thought: Someone's trying a little too hard.

He smirks right back. "Jealous?"

My eyebrows pinch as I laugh out, "It screams finance bro, or at the very least, *I won my fantasy football league three years in a row.*"

"Two years." He chuckles, knocking on the roof of it. "Want a ride?"

"It's fine," I say, waving off his offer. I wasn't sure how I'd feel seeing him again. Everyone I knew moved on with their lives.

I clear my throat again. "I'm living in Rumor now, closer to where my family lives. It's a bit out of your—"

"Wyn, I don't mind," he says, leaning on his open door with a soft smile. "I've been out that way plenty of times, and I've got nowhere else to be at this hour. I'm a bit of a night owl." Looking at his phone, he taps away at the screen.

I need to get out of this heat, and my head already hurts from the lack of something greasy. I'll have to let at least one of my sisters know I got home safely. And maybe Lu is still wrapping up at the bar—she owes me an apology.

I nod, making my way down the front stairs, thinking about how this is the second time tonight Reed's managed to rescue me.

"Isn't that clever, Professor?" my colleague asks.

The smile I've been faking falters. My fingers tingle, and a cold chill runs up my spine and down my arms.

Don't pass out.

"Prof-professor?" another voice stutters, and nausea takes shape.

Four pairs of eyes study me, trying their damndest to politely ignore the fact that I had been on a leave of absence that had started as a missing persons case nearly three years ago. And despite being back, having to only share that my case was confidential and I was unable to share more, a part of me feels like I don't belong here anymore, that this part of me is still missing. I had my job again—it's a luxury, truthfully, but my desire to dive into work, the passion I had for it, didn't follow me home.

"A published article from that long ago should not still impact grant distribution…"

I maintain a tight-lipped smile, trying to ignore the audacity of that remark, along with how bored I am. Did I used to enjoy this? I spent years working and studying to practically erase any signs of my origins. It's what I'd always wanted—difference and distance. But now, it feels more like a punishment than an achievement.

"Dr. Crowne?" my colleague in the center prods. "Are you alright?"

I shift my weight to shove down the panic. My chest burns from holding my breath, and the lack of oxygen is making me dizzy.

Breathe. In and out. Say something.

They glance at each other as if I should have something prolific to say in response. It's been years, and all it takes is a combination of two words to trigger me. I'm stronger than this.

The lead scientist of the chemical engineering department adds, "The reentry program grants you've been able to secure already are really quite—"

"Remarkable," a deep and familiar voice cuts in.

I instantly exhale the breath I'd started holding again and smile at him. A friend, and for a brief moment, something more. Reed flexes his superpower—making everyone feel at ease.

He gives me a wink and a smile. "Brava, Dr. Crowne," he adds with a teasing smirk. Flirt. *He's one of the only teaching assistants, better known as TAs, who didn't flounder in his first graduate year. Instead, he could command a packed lecture hall with grad students who were his own age. Just another reason I wasn't surprised to find that he was hired as full-time faculty while I was gone.*

"Put in the address," Reed says as I click my seat belt and look at the brightly lit console. "You can charge your phone there, too, if you'd like." His head tips to where there's a wireless charging pad.

When he glances at the screen and where I've typed, he asks, "The Whispering Fool?"

"I want to see if my sisters are still there before heading home," I say, knowing they'll want a status update on my whereabouts. They were both more concerned about me, now that they knew. At least the pieces I was able to tell them. I watch the campus lights off to the left blur past. I used to enjoy the luxury of living this close to campus. But now, I crave space. I want to be closer to the home I missed.

I look over at Reed as he focuses on the road. I know he spent some time with my grandmother after I disappeared. He was always thoughtful and present; it's one of the things that made him feel comfortable. "Birdie said you came around a few times after I..." I struggle to find the right word. "Left."

He glances at me, and I feel the need to add, "Thank you for that."

He simply nods, nothing more. Maybe an old friend wouldn't be the worst thing to have right now. I considered him that, some time ago. We were more than colleagues, friends who respected each other, and then briefly crossed that line. Reed has an easygoing, all-American vibe about him—an athletic, an academic, and a rule-follower. Reed was, and still is, the opposite of the type of men I grew up around—rough around the edges and bleeding masculinity as thick as their facial hair. Motorcycle club members and blue-collar boys, who rarely regarded women as anything more than a good time. I naïvely thought all men who looked like that believed the same-minded small things. And I didn't want anything that resembled the lifestyle I grew up around.

Settling isn't the right word, and I liked Reed, but he used to feel so comfortable. And back then, it was nice to have someone look at me the way he did after a long day and a late night in my office. But now, I know the difference between an attractive friend and attraction. When I glance at Reed again, I think to myself, *you never felt right, not like it did with* him.

I lean against the door, propping my chin on my fist as I look out into the dark. My mouth feels suddenly dry, I try swallowing, and my face heats as I play with the worn, brown leather cuff on my wrist. I crave someone I'll never see again. A shiver runs along my skin as I recall the scratch of a beard along my neck. Clearing my throat, I focus on where I am, and the person I am now. It's only ever going to be a memory, a fantasy that I can call on when I need it.

Reed turns on the radio and flips through news talk on satellite, pulling my attention back to this car ride and out of my head.

"Are you still packing lecture halls?" I ask him teasingly.

He smiles, looking ahead. "The novelty of being a young teaching assistant isn't in my favor anymore," he says.

A familiar voice talking about whiskey and crime comes through the car's speakers, interrupting.

"Wait, stop on that one. It's Stevie's," I say as he scrolls past my sister's widely listened to podcast. I smile to myself, loving hearing her. I've been listening to her podcast for longer than she even knows. It was the only thing that kept me connected to my family, to this place, and back then, I was convinced I'd never set foot here again.

"*The Distilled Truth*," Reed says, glancing at the center of his dashboard. "She's causing a bit of an uproar at the university. Lots of interesting opinions…"

"She's always been good at making people pay attention," I say proudly, then shift the conversation back to work. I haven't spoken with him much since I've been back. "Do you plan to use a teaching assistant for the fall semester?" I ask. Immediately realizing that was a poor choice of words, I close my eyes.

His lip kicks up, and he glances at me. "The last assistant I had, decided to leave mid-semester. It caused a bit of noise, and it left the graduate program a little messy. But yeah, I'll probably use one," he adds. "You were lucky with me; I was post-doctoral when I assisted you, much more mature than some of the graduate students coming through the doors now."

Needing some fresh air, I crack open the window. I look out at the dark shadows that fly past—trees backlit by the moon that barely wants to peek through the night.

Our drive hugs the river after only a few exits on the highway, and just as the view of it starts to get lost behind the tree line the Welcome to Rumor sign comes into view. It's only a twenty-minute ride from campus, not too far from Nashville, but tucked away enough that people need to be looking to find it. It's a small town that lives up to its name. It's where I grew up, where my family lives, and where I wanted to return to.

I spent so much of my life longing to feel close to my family, but needing distance. Growing up a Crowne wasn't for the weak or sensitive. My family's business thrived, while our reputations were dragged through too much mess to ever really come out seeming clean. Distance felt necessary. Then I felt too far.

I click the button to roll the window down farther, and the warm breeze blows in the savory smells of earth and herbs that linger in the air here.

Dry dirt kicks high under crunching gravel, painting his shiny black sports car with a film of dust as we pull into the oversize parking lot. The standout bright neon sign is dark now, but it's still big enough to read. The Whispering Fool is the kind of bar that encapsulates all the things I didn't want for my life—a beacon where most of the nasty rumors about the Crowne women began. And every woman from my grandmother to my youngest sister fueled those rumors in varying degrees of bold displays of careless and crass behavior. A bar that's as much of a show as the life I'm trying to fit back into.

Out of the corner of my eye, I watch Reed look over to me twice. It's why I wanted to avoid too much silence.

"You can ask, but I'd rather you didn't," I tell him, assuming the typical questions will start any second now. Specifically, ones like, *Where have you been? Are the rumors true?* Or my favorite: *How could you have done that to your family?*

"I didn't say anything," he says. "Your family never stopped believing you'd find your way back to them." He leans along the armrest between us. "I'm just happy you did and that you're alright."

Am I alright?

With one hand draped along the steering wheel and the other still on the center console, he smiles, and while it's comforting, there's a part of me that doesn't want to hear what he's going to say. "You look good, Dr. Crowne."

I bark out a laugh. It's smooth, I'll give him that.

"What? You do. You seem…different. But it suits you."

I am different.

"I'm not inviting you for a nightcap, Reed," I say with my hand on the latch for the door, quirking my eyebrow at him.

He shakes his head. "That wasn't where my head was, Wyn." But he smiles once more, like my proclamation isn't at all surprising, but rather reassuring. "Just glad to see you're good… that we're good."

I don't know what we are, but the reality is that I've been avoiding him since I returned.

When I lean down before closing the passenger door, he meets my eyes through the still-open window. "Grab a coffee with me this week?"

I simply nod and smile as I grab my phone from the center console, charged enough to turn back on finally.

Quiet settles as his car pulls away. I look around the empty parking lot of the bar—this place was probably rowdy as hell little more than an hour ago. Birdie's always been adamant about a midnight closing time. Anyone who tried to linger any longer, she had no problem hoisting her shotgun up to rest on her shoulder as my mother would so eloquently deliver the line: "You don't have to go home—at least not alone—but you sure do have to get the fuck outta here."

Even though the neon sign by the road and the one above the door are dark, there's still a light on inside. I tilt my head back and take a glimpse at the big moody sky, with its deep grays and purples, deciding just how much rain it wants to dispense.

I whip my head to the left at the sound of movement over the gravel. My stomach sinks, feeling instantly unsafe. On instinct, my hand moves to my back pocket, where I put the sharp-tipped key chain I stay completely still, waiting and listening. The sounds of rushing water from beyond the riverbanks that loop halfway around the property, the chirp of bullfrogs, and the intermittent sounds of cicadas singing out in the ebb and flow of their calls. But that's it, nothing else. And yet, I *feel* it.

I've been hunted before. I know what it feels like to be watched and timed. The crawl of someone's attention rolls along my damp skin, as if it's powering me up. I know better than to wait and see—waiting only gives them time. Time isn't something I'm interested in giving up any more of.

My hair whips across my face, blinding me for a few seconds as I react quickly. I don't think about where I'm heading; I only know I need to get far away from where I just was. Taking long strides, I glance along the darkened side of the old building. Nothing's there except a tire lying in the grass, no cars or bikes left in the lot. Not a straggler or drunk passed out in the weeds.

Shit.

I pull my phone from my purse and glance up at the double doors to the bar, stepping inside. Finding Birdie's number, I press call. The red glow from the sign that reads Sinners and Goddesses Welcome bathes my path as I move along the entryway. The overpowering smell of bleach tickles my nose. It should smell like stale beer, smoked barrels, and a hint of lavender from mixing bleach with Fabuloso. It's the only way to get this place fresh again before the next day, Birdie would say. Only, there's nothing floral or nostalgic lingering in the air now.

Something isn't right.

The second I enter the main room, there's enough light for me to make out filled garbage bags, a caddy with cleaning brushes, solutions, and putty knives. But it's the thick pieces of cloth piled on the floor, absorbing a deep, dark red liquid that had spilled out and pooled in a spot right in front of me that has every hair along my arms raising as a sinking feeling settles low in my gut. In a panic, I take a quick inventory of what else shouldn't be here—equipment I've never seen, jugs of unmarked liquid, a pile of shredded clothes, and a pair of men's work boots neatly placed next to it.

Stepping back shakily, I'm careful not to make any more noise than I already have. My body vibrates, remembering the way danger feels when it's too close, the way it slithers just before it strikes, tearing everything apart. I take another step back the way I came. *Don't panic.* And another. Quietly, I take three more steps back.

On the fourth ring, Birdie answers. "Wyn? It's late, honey. You alright?" she says faintly from the phone. My foot hits the threshold, but before I can respond, a heavy arm wraps around me like a vise against my ribs, trapping both of my arms at their sides. I can barely suck in a breath before a hand covers my mouth. I bite it, but I can't catch the palm; instead, I taste latex. Frantically looking as the bar's doors come into view, I try screaming, but only a gut-clenching groan escapes. I'm held so tightly, my back pressed against a bigger, stronger, and taller body that barely budges even as I try thrashing out of its grip.

The deep voice grits out, "Calm down."

"Fuck you," I try shouting, but it comes out pathetically stifled.

He adjusts his hand along my mouth, still covering it and pinching my nose at the same time. *Shit.*

"I said. Calm. Down," the low, deep voice repeats.

I stop moving, but my mind races for a way out of this. I've learned to follow directions the hard way. The scars on my palms and along the left side of my body burn in my subconscious.

I hear a muffled calling of my name from the other end of the phone that's been kicked into the dirt and gravel of the parking lot. *Birdie.* "Wyn? Wyn, sweetheart, are you still there? Where are you?"

It's an interruption that works as a distraction. He moves us closer to where the phone lays, out in the open, under the night sky. His hand moves a fraction away from my mouth, his wrapped arm loosening slightly, enough to allow me to let go, exhale from my gut, heavy my limbs, and drop. Deadweight.

I never hit the ground. It's not enough. Instead, something pricks the base of my neck, then a stinging burn follows in the same spot.

No, no, no, no, no.

I know what it feels like to be stuck with a needle. I'm being drugged. Shadows quickly drench the outline of my field of vision like an old movie vignette. "No," I try shouting again, but it doesn't sound as loud as it should.

I move fast enough that I loop my fingers into my back

pocket, and with the little energy I have, I raise my hand out and come down as hard as I can on his thigh.

"God. Fucking—Fuck," he groans just as my arms become as heavy as my legs. But he doesn't drop me or hit me. He gently places me on the wood-planked floor. Being drugged doesn't feel freeing. It's panic held in a soundproof box. I try to even my breathing. Placing the tips of my thumb and middle finger together, I raise them to my mouth. The whistle I try for is pathetic. There's no way it'll be heard. I hold on to consciousness for as long as I can. I take in every detail I see—a worn-in cowboy boot the color of the whiskey I just bottled this morning stepping beside my head, and in contrast to the stark-white shiny plastic-like pants that mold to a large, looming form. I blink and take in the white PPE coveralls, the sleeves of it tied at his waist. I fight to keep my eyes open. No shirt, a bare torso leading to shoulders, each capped with—

That can't be possible.

Dark shapes that look like paper airplanes turning into birds as they move to the center between his shoulder blades. Words and then a compass below it. His hair is pulled back tightly at the nape of his neck. I look at his hands and see one brown leather cuff fastened to his wrist, peeking out above his black latex glove.

"Julian?" I rush out as quickly as my lips allow.

He turns immediately toward me, steps closer, and towers over my weighted body. If it weren't so dark in here, I'd see hazel eyes studying me.

I know it's him.

But he doesn't say my name, or anything in return. I only hear the sound of blood rushing in my ears.

The only thing I know, with every fiber of my being, is

the person who made me feel something again, the charming stranger who I haven't been able to scrub from my memory, a jeweler who made me smile, who made me feel lighter and more confident, who moaned the dirtiest things I've ever heard, is somehow here, right now. And he lied. Again.

CHAPTER 2

Naomi

10 months ago

"I'M GOING TO NEED A shot of your whiskey and an ice-cold IPA."

I glance at the clock above the jukebox. Sure enough, it's quarter past seven, and it's within a fifteen minute window that I can expect the same request every night.

"Dammit," Boss mumbles from his stool. On an exhale, he adds, "Thought we were in the clear tonight."

"Wanna say that while you're looking me in the eye next time, fucker?" Viv says as she sidles up to the bar. She has more attitude than most people know what to do with. And that's saying something, considering where I grew up and the people who raised me, but Viv has the kind of energy that makes you hate and love her all at once. It doesn't help that Boss used to be married to her.

I give her a nod as I pull a frosted pint glass from the cooler. "Rough day?"

She hums to herself before she starts rambling off a roster of all the ways people are the biggest problem with the great state of Montana. The audacity of tourists stopping to take pictures of her bison, and how her new horses are stubborn as all get-out.

This bar is the opposite of the one I grew up around. It's slow and quiet. We work at a comfortable pace, and there's an easy layout, where I know every exit and can see every place a person could enter. The predictability of happy hour visitors and theme days like trivia, football, and the newest, podcast flight nights, puts me at ease. It's a small part of the world, where everyone tells it like it is instead of gossiping behind people's backs. The one thing I don't miss from my hometown is the rumors.

"You can't tell me there's a single brewery in all of this big, beautiful country that makes an IPA as good as those boys down near Missoula."

I give the regular a small nod, but I wholeheartedly disagree. While IPAs are nowhere near my favorite, there's a small craft distillery up in the Northeast that makes some of the best beer my near-perfect palate has ever tasted. But I don't share that. I don't need to be asked more questions. There isn't much I can share about myself that doesn't stretch the truth. I can also understand loving something because it's local. Hell, I grew up in a household that rooted for local everything.

"Be right back," I say, moving toward the small galley kitchen. It isn't that kind of place with a menu, but we have some decent snacks. "Shit," I huff out, looking down at the scrape along my elbow as I pull out a bottle. The textured wood paneling is a hazard sometimes, but it fits the vibe of the establishment. The seventies are preserved here in a way that's familiar and homey. Seats peppered around the bar have been refurbished in a green leather that wouldn't be my first choice, but somehow, it works. And the metal lamps perched at each end of the bar add their own shadowy flair. I liked it the moment I stepped foot inside. Even the taxidermy bison head that hangs with intention along the back wall, watching over everyone.

There's some version of a watchful eye over every bar—it's good for business, and for karma.

"You wanna know how many people used to come into this bar, Naomi?" she asks as I make my way back in front of her.

Sliding the shooter of specialty whiskey into her waiting hand, I ask, "Before me, or—"

"Three," she interrupts, chasing the shot with a swig of the pale beer. "I don't know which one of you idiots," she says, turning on her stool, "decided to tell people about this place, but it continues to piss me off."

"Oh yes," Boss deadpans. "Let's be pissed that there are *more* customers." He waves at the air in front of him like he's swatting a fly. "Don't listen to her, Naomi. It's when she stops complaining that we all need to be concerned—"

She flips him off as she takes another chug of her beer.

He returns the gesture, just as the bell above the door rings as it's shoved open.

I take a glance around and see more seats filled than when I first started working here. Shuffling down to two regulars, I refill their pints, listening to the few words they exchange about the latest hike in feed prices.

It's been two years of pouring drinks where the median age is around fifty-five years young. Folks wandered in here after a long day despite it not being much of a destination, but Montana towns near here aren't bustling cities; they're small in population and vast in land. Everyone needed some place to come and feel seen every once in a while.

"Viv, tonight is busy because it's podcast night," Boss says as he scribbles something in his sports book. Glancing at me, he adds, "A true-crime podcast coupled with a whiskey tasting is better than dumb-ass trivia nights. It's a great idea, Naomi."

I smile to myself. The first time I heard it, I dropped an entire bottle of tequila, and it shattered all over the linoleum floor. It was a suggested podcast after my playlist hit the end. I recognized her voice right away. My sister's tone was always a bit sweeter than mine, and when she was fired up, she talked faster than her Tennessee roots typically suggested, and got plenty of people's attention.

"I dare you to tell me one whiskey blend that won't feel more elevated after you've distilled it in a second finishing barrel," Stevie said. I frantically scroll through my phone with blurred vision from the tears in my eyes and see a picture of my sister. Reading through the podcast description, I find her YouTube channel with the recorded podcasts and nearly 1.3 million subscribers. The Distilled Truth *was named as one of Spotify's top twenty-five podcasts of the year and was described as a fresh take on true crime with a "whiskey woman" as a modern-day sleuth and recorded in the heart of Tennessee.*

"The podcast starts in about ten minutes," I tell Viv with a smile. "Want me to pour you a whiskey flight?"

I don't hear her answer as I do a double take at the man who just took a seat at the bar. Swallowing roughly, I bite back the way I want to smile and try not to linger my attention. *Who the hell is that?* I turn toward the bottles stacked high behind me and blow out a slow breath. There aren't too many new faces around here, and when there are, it's always cause for concern. But when I turn back and see his eyes on me, it's not concern that I'm feeling. *You're smarter than this. Get it together.*

Anyone who I haven't met before, walking into the bar, makes me anxious. A product of losing time and trust, or maybe just a survivor's penance, but Boss and Viv have been here a long time and know how to handle people wandering in. *They're brave.*

Boss is well aware of him too. "Haven't seen you here before, young man. What brought you to this fine establishment? The music?" he asks, looking at his refurbished jukebox. "Maybe the tasty bar snacks?" He nods to the half-empty bowl of popcorn in front of him. "Or did you hear about our podcast and whiskey flight Thursdays?"

The serious look on the newcomer's face breaks as he smiles at Boss first, and then looks back at me, as if I'm the one who asked. "Sounds like a good time. But I just got a little turned around when I got off the interstate. Not many signs for where I am right now." His brow furrows.

That's the idea. Where we are isn't on any map. It isn't supposed to be found.

"What's the name of this place?" he asks casually, glancing around the bar.

I look at Boss just as he clears his throat. People coming around and asking questions is never good—there are rules. But Boss decides to keep it light, since the handsome stranger doesn't seem threatening.

"The bar has no name. No name means we get to choose a name each week, and the owner of that name drinks for free," he explains while pointing to the blackboard behind the bar.

The stranger adds, "Someone down in Missoula mentioned a ranch out this way in Hideaway." Looking at me, he asks, "Ever heard of it?"

He shouldn't know that name—and whoever told him about it is stirring up trouble.

I don't want to even acknowledge the question, never mind answer it.

"Nope," I lie as I shake my head. The taste of it sours my mouth. "But there are quite a few ranches around here, if you were looking for an authentic Montana experience, I'm sure you could find one." I smile sarcastically.

"I wasn't, but now I'm curious. What does an authentic Montana experience look like?" he asks.

I turn toward the bottles and glance at Boss, making sure I'm not doing anything wrong. He doesn't look up. Instead, he carries on writing in his sports book. I know I answered how I'm supposed to, but it's the first time anyone's come right out and asked about the place I've called home for the last couple of years. If something was off, Boss or Viv wouldn't seem so relaxed.

He pulls out his phone and starts typing away—there isn't much service out here, but he busies himself with something as I playfully say, "You know, that's a great question. Why don't you tell me what you're looking for, and we'll see if we're thinking the same thing."

"I can almost guarantee we're not thinking exactly the same thing," he says as he looks up from his phone, his eyes locking right onto mine. A hint of mischief shines in his gaze and across his lips.

My heart stutters, my body suddenly feeling hot all over. *What the hell am I doing?* Flirting with a stranger isn't a smart move. *Why the hell isn't Boss stepping in here?* Quickly, I turn toward the end of the bar and move to fill up the empty pints waiting. I work through the things I can control as I take a deep breath. Like knowing how many steps to the exit—*fifty-two*—the exact location of the shotgun Boss has behind the bar, nestled between the Arbor Mist and Zima bottles. I roll my ankle, reminding myself of the switchblade I have tucked inside my left boot. I list off the rest of the precautions I've taken, like the steak knife taped to the toilet in the bathroom, and the taser stuffed behind the fire extinguisher strapped to the wall between the emergency exit and the office. *Breathe.* It's all there, I assure myself. *I'll use them if I need them.*

When I finish, I turn back and take in his dark brown hair, half pulled back into a knot. Long hair on men always looks messy to me, but on him, it more than works. *Do I like messy now?* The only thing I keep thinking about is how it would feel between my fingers. A short shadow of a beard surrounds lips that have tipped into an almost smile. His arms drape forward, fingers clasped loosely together on the bar. The rings on his fingers and the worn leather cuffs along each wrist earn a second look.

Viv's voice cuts into the podcast that's playing over the sound system. "You do realize that the names you keep picking don't belong to people who actually come here?" she says with an eye roll, looking up at the board with this week's name written across it. "Never met a Julian in all my six decades."

"You mean seven decades," Boss corrects.

She flips him off as she tilts the empty bowl in front of her. "Ah, fuck. Please don't tell me there's no more popcorn, Naomi."

"Julian isn't an uncommon name," I say, plucking the rest of the half-empty popcorn bowls from around the bar.

"It's a little feminine." She scrunches up her nose. "Not a single cowboy or farmer I've met has a name like that," she mumbles out. Close-minded and judgmental sounded the same, regardless of where I found myself.

"You say feminine like it's a bad thing, Viv. I grew up thinking that there wasn't anything more beautiful than women and the things we're capable of." I liked Viv, depended on her even, which means I don't let her get away with shit comments like that.

"How many times do I need to go over this?" Boss pipes in.

"It's a random name generator, so I don't have anyone," he says, pointing at her and three others listening in, "pissed off and accusing me of picking my friends' names out of a hat."

She ignores him, waving her hand in the air before she reaches for her pint.

I pour my popcorn into the three empty bowls, catching the scent of the rosemary I dried and ground up with sage. Tossing herbs on popcorn is entirely underrated. Depositing the freshly filled bowl in front of her, I catch the handsome stranger still looking at me.

He's wearing the hell out of a black long-sleeved shirt that fits rather nicely across the expanse of his chest to each shoulder and down his biceps. His build is imposing—thick and defined. Even sitting on the other side of the bar, he's tall, but his presence feels bigger than most of the people who come in and out of here.

It was my mother, sometimes my sisters who I thought too aggressively objectified the men who passed through their bar. But right now, I'm trying to determine the difference between objectification and appreciation. The size and stature of a complete stranger, not to mention the closed-off but curious vibe he's emanating is making my face flush and my pulse race.

"Stevie Crowne here," my sister's voice cuts in and plays over the Bluetooth speakers placed around the bar, instantly taking me out of my own head for a minute, and I smile at the fact that she'd be nudging my arm about this guy, making sure I noticed him. *"I hope you're ready to hear about some of the best tasting whiskey you can buy for twenty-bucks and the cold case that's finally reopened because of coordinates scribbled across a twenty-dollar bill that led to multiple bodies found in the Pacific Northwest. This is* The Distilled Truth.*"* I pause the episode, knowing I still have

some whiskey flights to pour for the few folks participating in tonight's tasting.

"Decided if you're going to stay?" I ask, putting down a cocktail napkin in front of him.

He meets my eye for a moment and gives me the smallest tip of his lips. It's not a smile, but something close. "A podcast and whiskey flight sounds good." Clearing his throat, he leans forward, elbows on the bar. "I should probably clear up a few things first." He reaches around to his back pocket. "I'm not a farmer or cowboy," he says, taking out his wallet and sliding his ID across the bar. I'm not sure what he's referring to until he adds, "You're right about that." He turns his head towards Viv.

No way.

Viv's resting bitch face blooms a little pink as her eyes dart to mine, wordlessly saying, *You've got to be shitting me.*

Boss starts laughing from the end of the bar, watching Viv eat her words.

The stranger's eyes connect with mine, holding me in place and making it nearly impossible to break away, never mind breathe. Looking down, I focus on the Oregon ID of Julian T. Colton. Born in the same month as the one we're in, only thirty-eight years prior. Organ donor. Eye color: hazel. I would argue it's prettier than that—more green with only a few flecks of brown. height reads six foot three.

He looks around at Boss, Viv, and then back to me when he says, "What do I get for having my name on that board?"

Viv barks out a laugh before answering, "You drink for free."

"All night?" he asks with his eyes on me.

With a smile, a bit of inflection, and a twinge of confidence, I answer, "All night."

"With that kind of time…" he trails off, glancing down

at his phone. He swipes at the screen and leans forward again, fitting it back into his pocket. "What do you suggest?" The eye contact only lasts for a few seconds, but I'm brave enough to meet it. It's when he shifts his attention down, to my lips, that I falter.

Instead of answering like the confident woman I'm pretending to be, I turn away, pulling the bottles of whiskey for tonight's flight. With my back to him, I swallow down my nerves and say, "We offer a whiskey flight every Thursday. It's been curated to match each week's episode of *The Distilled Truth*."

"That's creative. Are you more of an expert on whiskey or true crime then?" he says, rotating the ring on his left pointer finger.

I used to watch my mother do this like a goddamn professional. I've never been good at it. Flirting, for me, always meant being quiet, paying attention, trying to best or one-up whomever I found wildly attractive. My sisters somehow inherited the effortless gift. But that skipped right over me. This, however, feels easier. Maybe it's for the simplest reason that I have nothing to lose. No past to tell, no future to plan, no rumors to navigate. I thought that maybe I was too broken now to feel attraction again. Or even want to flirt. *Apparently, I'm not so broken.*

"I could tell you a thing or two about whiskey," I tell him, tipping the first bottle I lined up in front of me. "True crime, not so much." *Best to avoid topics around truth and crime.*

I lean forward, resting my elbows on the bar in front of him, mimicking his earlier posture. "If there's something you want that's not on the menu, I can make it. You can have whatever you want as long as it's behind the bar."

"Anything I want, hm?" he asks with a subtle quirk of his eyebrow as he moves a fraction forward. *Jesus Christ.* I want to cover my face and snort out a laugh, but it's the way he smiles at me that has me pausing my self-deprecation. "Alright then, you choose. I'll have dealer's choice."

If he only knew what that got him in some bars—one, in particular, that took that request to its limits and made one helluva show about it.

I reach for the metal shaker, and it hits the ground with an exaggerated clang. *Brilliant.*

Viv smiles at me, sensing that I'm feeling all sorts of out of my comfort zone, and pushes her empty shot glass forward. "It's a three-finger kind of day, Naomi. Hit me with another." As particular as both Boss and Viv are, they take their roles here seriously, and I'll forever be grateful for that. Equal parts protectors and therapists, among other things.

I pull the bottle of whiskey again and pour her shot to the rim. It's enough to shake me out of my head and focus on a task I've done plenty of times.

"Since you're technically lost, are you passing through or planning to stay?" I ask Julian, looking over at him again and holding up the bottle.

With a tilt of his head toward the bottle, he says, "I wouldn't mind staying if you tell me a little more about what you're pouring."

I rub my lips together, trying to play off my smile and not geek out too much. There are two things I understand and know more about than most—catalyst reactions in organic compounds, and whiskey. Most of the time, I'm shoving this kind of information at customers, and they couldn't give a damn. So I start with what most distilleries start by saying. "Every bourbon is whiskey—"

"But not every whiskey is bourbon," he finishes, and it has me noticing the way his scruff is meticulously groomed right at the jawline, and the black ink of a tattoo peeking out just below the neckline of his shirt. I survey the things that make this man seem different from everyone else. Rugged but polished around the edges. His hands are clean but callused, the kind of strong hands that have seen a hard day's work, just not the kind this farm town is known for. Large hands and corded forearms always seemed like a cliché attraction, but I'd be lying if I said I didn't want to see what they would look like on me—touching, playing…

I clear my throat. *What the hell was that?*

"I know some bourbon boys. I've heard them recite those rules plenty of times," he continues with a smirk. He isn't posturing or trying to mansplain anything to me. *And fuck, is that a turn-on.*

A smile tugs at my lips as I pull out another few shot glasses—one to add to each of the flights I'm pouring, and then a clean shaker. "Whiskey, as you know, is a little different. Those differences are based on where it's made and how it ends. Where I'm from, *women* know whiskey."

He cuts in, "And where exactly is that?"

My eyes dart up, finding him looking at me in a way that's sincere and not predatory, and it makes me want to answer truthfully. "Small town you've probably never heard of before." I turn to Viv and ask, "What was that saying about the devil you're always spouting?"

Without missing a beat, she says, "The devil's greatest power was making everyone believe she didn't exist." Of course, she gave me the wrong quote.

"Not that one," I say, chuckling as she sticks a clove cigarette in her mouth and holds open her palm for me to pass her a book of matches.

Boss points at her without looking up. "Outside."

She huffs, stands, and mumbles, "Asswipe."

He flips her off.

I shake my head and focus back on Julian, who's equally amused by the two of them. When he shifts his attention back to me, I correct the quote I was referring to. "What I was expecting her to say is that 'the devil is in the details.'"

"Ah," he says. "I'm very fond of details." His eyes never leave mine.

A rush of confidence buzzes through me as he listens so intently, his weight shifting forward just slightly enough that it feels like he wants to be just a little closer. I clear my throat, trying to recall where the hell I was going with this. *Whiskey, right.*

"There are *some* whiskeys that are just as nuanced and need to follow strict rules, like bourbon. But even more so..." I pause, knowing I'm entering dangerous territory with this next fact. "Tennessee whiskey. All Tennessee whiskey is bourbon. But not all bourbon can be Tennessee whiskey."

I pull my bottle from the middle shelf. Its logo, a fox head wrapped around the letter *F*, is prominent. If anyone knows anything about expensive bottles, they'd assume I'm about to do a tasting with a two-hundred-dollar bottle of small-batch bourbon. I recycled this one because Foxx Bourbon also made beautiful bottles for their delicious bourbon. It didn't get made in Tennessee and it didn't get filtered through sugar maple charcoal. But it's *my* whiskey. I tied a piece of thyme and a dried vanilla bean around the neck of the bottle—the notes its drinkers will hopefully find as they taste.

Whiskey has stamina; it evolved and could change. That's the beauty of it. There are still rules if you're going to make, bottle, and sell it. But those rules gray out at the end for whiskey. It has the luxury of being finished in all sorts of ways. Time matters, but it doesn't define it. And time is something that I have a lot of now. I would've preferred it to happen in a barrel, but I'm not in any position to be particular.

"Typically, when people think of whiskey, they assume a bar like this would only offer Jack, Jim, or Johnny." I smile as I grab the small kitchen torch and light it, pulling a few dried pieces of rosemary from the bouquet perched next to the rest of the garnishes. I light each one, blow them out, and then place them beneath each of the turned-over rocks glasses we use as makeshift tasting glasses. "But tasting flights are a great way to show off how much more is out there," I say, sliding the first tasting toward Julian.

As the podcast plays in the background, my sister talks about the way flavors can be just as powerful when they're smelled as when they're tasted. It's something we've talked about countless times.

"It's all about manipulating the senses and tying those to things you're familiar with," she says. "Which leads me into this next case, one that feels more about trust than deception. Countless women are subjected to this kind of behavior every day. While plenty of my listeners are men, this is a reminder for the ladies; the easiest way for someone to take your control is to manipulate your power to say no."

I watch him tip the glass to his lips and take a small sniff first before sipping. Why do I find that so intensely sexy? I shift my weight and try to ignore the way my cheeks feel like they're on fire. *I need to get a fucking grip.*

Julian doesn't bother covering his smile, whether it's from watching me or the drink he just tasted. Regardless, a little spark of pride lights in my chest and turns into something much more arousing as it makes its way between my thighs.

A few customers hold up their glasses, and I hear, "Naomi,

that's some damn fine whiskey," and "I'm going to need another pour of that one." But it's Julian's hum after taking a second taste that has me preening. "Might have just tasted my new favorite thing."

His words work their way into somewhere I didn't know I needed. It feels better than the way everyone else compliments me. And I can't seem to look away from him as he runs two fingers back and forth along his bottom lip. And quietly, almost to himself, he says, "So, she likes praise."

All over again, my pulse quickens, my cheeks instantly warming, and I can't help but search for a visual of what that would look like from him. At the thought of all the ways he might praise me, what I'd do to earn more words that would make me feel something I haven't given myself permission to feel before, I squeeze my thighs together.

"She likes tips too," Viv interjects from her stool.

Boss chimes in, "Highest tip of the night earns a reading, too."

Julian's eyebrows raise. "Are we talking poems, tea leaves, tarot?"

"Palm," I correct. I'm barely good at it, despite the efforts of the woman who taught me. If she saw me now, she'd swat at me and tell me to *take my time and do it right*.

He throws down a hundred-dollar bill. "Pour one this time for both of us, and I'll let you tell me all about my future," he says, keeping his eyes on me as he tips the glass back slowly.

I can't help but bark out a laugh. "Let me? I think you mean, beg me," I say, raising an eyebrow. "A hundred dollars seems pretty desperate, Julian."

"I never mind a little bit of begging," he says, tipping his empty glass toward him. "And yeah, I'm feeling pretty desperate."

My stomach swoops and lips part as I try to decipher how I'm supposed to respond to that. What would that look like? A man like him begging someone like me for what he wants? Goosebumps run up my arms at the flash of such a dirty fantasy. I glance at the abandoned ingredients and decide to shift back to the actual request.

"It doesn't really work that way," I say as I use a sharp knife to cut open a vanilla bean stalk. Slicing the tip of the knife through the dark, paste-like insides, I swipe it along the edge of the glass. I lift it to smell, close my eyes, and allow the savoriness of the thyme and sweetness of the vanilla bean to remind me of home. When I open my eyes and find him watching me, it doesn't make me uneasy—it does the opposite. It has me audibly exhaling.

"Don't leave me on the edge of my seat like that, Naomi," he teases. Leaning on his elbows, he says, "Tell me how it works, then." The lilt of his voice is coaxing and calm, almost as smooth as the liquor I just poured.

The podcast episode fills in the blips of quiet, so I doubt anyone's listening too closely. I've been offered plenty of drinks from customers before, and while Boss says he doesn't care, I've still never had one while working. Until tonight. I pour two shots of the whiskey I infused into two rocks glasses, both with a swipe of the vanilla and thyme paste along its edge. As I slide Julian his glass across the bar, he opens his hand, palm facing up.

Be brave.

Glancing down, I lean my weight onto the bar's edge. "It depends on how much you're willing to believe. Palmistry has deep conflicting origins, but it all derives from the assumption that fate exists, and that those fates, if interpreted correctly, can be adjusted."

I run the tips of my fingers along the worn leather of the

cuff on his wrist. It's wide enough that it extends almost to the base of his palm.

"May I?" I ask, with my fingers lingering along its edges. I'd like to see the lines beneath it too.

His closed-mouth smile comes with a nod as I begin unsnapping its two gold buttons. "I like this," I tell him, grazing my fingertips along its stitched edges.

"Made it a long time ago, but it's still one of my favorites."

"You made this?" It doesn't look like a weekend craft project.

"This one too," he says, pointing to the other wrist, and then running his fingers along the rings on his opposite hand. "And these."

"Do you do this for a living?" I ask with a smile, and he nods. "You're a—"

"Jeweler, goldsmith, designer, among other things. But yes, I do this for a living," he says with almost a shy smile, like there's more he's not saying.

"I would not have guessed that about you," I say as I run my fingers across his open palm again. I don't particularly need to touch him, but it would be a shame not to.

"What would you have guessed?" he asks. He glances down at where I'm touching.

Brushing two fingers along the width of his hand, I quietly say, "Something far more dangerous, morally gray. Until you started talking, you were very intimidating."

He sniffs out a laugh. "You're right; maybe you're not very good at this telling-my-future thing." He starts to sit back, pulling his hand away to play with me, but I catch his wrist and pull him back toward the bar. My smile falters as my eyes lock with his. I guide his hand back to where it was and I brush my fingers from his wrist to his now extended palm.

His Adam's apple bobs as he looks at where I'm touching. The playfulness of his attention seems suddenly more serious, more curious. This should feel like an innocent exchange, but there's something about our closeness that seems quite the opposite.

"Your dominant hand is the path you're on." I send a pointed look to the hand that's holding his drink. "While your nondominant is the path you were born to take. The way it was explained to me is that every line can have a meaning, but they can be interpreted differently. It's not so much about telling you your future, but it's about putting the possibilities into words and then interpreting them however you'd like."

He looks up at me, his gaze lingering on my lips again, and it feels like it's struck a live wire. Any part of me that hadn't already been aware of his proximity is well informed now. *What is it about this man that makes me want to keep talking?*

I look at the glass he's palming, and with as much confidence as I can gather, I abandon the topic of palms and futures, and ask, "Do you like it?"

I watch him try to bite back a smile that feels loaded with more than just a simple yes or no. And instead of words, he shifts even closer, moving the glass up to his mouth, presses it against his lips, and tilts it for another sip. The small hum that rumbles from his throat makes my stomach swoop and instantly wets my panties.

I lick my lips. *What would it feel like to kiss a stranger?* I've never done that before, gotten lost in lust with someone I only just met.

He shifts his weight forward and leans into the bar, closer to me, his cheek nearly brushing mine as he quietly says, "You were right."

I tilt my head to look at him, questioning what he might be referring to.

"It's in the details," he says, his words like a caress before he stands and steps back. With one last searing look at me, he pulls his phone from his back pocket as the vibration buzzes in his hand and quickly raises it to his ear.

Then, he's grabbing his coat from the chair and moving toward the door. I'm stuck in a daze, wondering if he'll stop and turn, maybe even tell me he'll be back. He's leaving so soon, seemingly out of nowhere. I know that makes me seem eager, borderline pathetic for a woman in her mid-thirties, but truthfully, who the fuck cares? It's been far too long since I've felt anything other than anxious or angry.

When he's through the doors and headlights flit across the frosted front windows, I finally snap back to reality and step down the bar to fill another pint for Viv. I glance at the spot where Julian had just been, and that's when I see it. Dark brown leather. The bracelet cuff that I'd taken off of him. He never put it back on.

I grab it off the bar as I move past and out the front double doors. Plumes of white opaque air puff out in front of me, with no sign of anyone except the few trucks parked and Viv's horse standing, tethered to a post at the far end of the lot.

Looking down, I run my fingers along the soft, worn leather. It's one of those moments that feels like something is different now. It's a shaken-up and invigorating feeling of seeing myself as something other than the outlier, the victim, or the survivor. I drape the leather along my left wrist and take in a deep breath, exhaling as I snap it closed. Whatever that just was, attraction, connection, or just some conversation and flirtation with a perfect stranger, there's been a shift within me, and damn, it feels good.

CHAPTER 3

Naomi

7 months ago

"YOU'RE CUT OFF, HANDSOME," I shout over the fired-up cowboys who keep yelling in disagreement. It only took a few months for the podcast that's streaming through the speakers to pull in a new crowd of very opinionated locals. True crime paired with whiskey flights isn't novel, but rather genius, according to Boss, and it's been keeping the bar packed every Thursday without fail.

"Oh, come on, Naomi," the burly rancher huffs out as I clear the empty tasting glasses.

I wink as I slide the water in front of him. "Where we going, cowboy?"

He takes a gulp, and then adds, "You can't tell the distinct difference between Jim Beam and Johnny Walker. The stuff Stevie just went on about doesn't taste any different, and nowhere near as good."

I smile every time I hear my sister's name. "I'm going to have to disagree with you, but I love that you were willing to try it."

His older brother next to him throws down the cash to cover tonight's tab. "Cutting you off was my call," he says, nudging his brother. "That was some damn fine whiskey. Not as good as yours, but I still enjoyed it." He winks at me and then taps the bar. "I think the kidnapper is someone they know." This is always the most fun—hearing what they all think about the flights I pour once the podcast is over.

"Naomi," Boss calls out. "Got any more bottles of Japanese whiskey under there?"

As I crouch down and reach for the last bottle beneath the bar, Viv forces out a loud, cackling laugh. With a clap of her hands, she says, "I'm out twenty bucks! Never thought we'd see you around here again."

But it's a deep, smooth voice that responds with, "I like being underestimated," that has my breath catching.

Julian.

I smile to myself before standing to face him.

He came back.

Hazel eyes roam up my body until they lock with mine. His hair is still long and half pulled back, scruff meticulously trimmed, and his stature seemingly larger and more imposing than my late-night imagination dreamt up.

"Hi," he says slowly, and with a smirk. "If you're still pouring, then I'll take one of those flights. Maybe cash in on the palm reading you owe me."

Pursing my lips, I tilt my head. "Hm. It's pretty busy on podcast nights. Not sure you'll be able to top the highest tip..." I say teasingly.

"Yeah, ante up, pretty boy," Viv says through a laugh from the other end of the bar.

I give her a wide-eyed, knock-it-off look, and then turn

back to Julian as he settles on his bar stool. "The palm reading is only good for the highest tipper of the day—not one from sixty-four days ago."

It's been just over two months since Julian walked into this bar. And I've thought about seeing him again—though, *fantasized* might be the better word. I hadn't been able to shake the atypical probability that maybe the universe was finally doling out some good karma my way.

"Naomi," Julian says with a playful lilt, "sixty-four seems—"

"Wildly specific?" I cut in, smiling and squinting one eye.

"I was going to say, not as long as it's felt," he corrects, shifting his weight.

Did he really just say that? My stomach whirls at that, and my cheeks heat instantly.

"I'm surprised you found your way back here."

His eyes stay on mine as he says, "I was always coming back. Just took me a minute."

My arm pauses from moving toward the bottle I was reaching for, unable to suppress the smile those few words pull out of me. I've never been this woman—the kind who gets too excited at attention or overly eager for a guy to show interest.

His body language and the way his eyes don't leave me feels damn good, and so incredibly overwhelming. *Don't shy away from this.*

Julian rubs along the back of his neck, looking nervous and maybe like he's working through something. "I've been listening to the podcast that was just playing. I'm still stuck on the one about the missing people down in Tennessee."

My shoulders tense at hearing the place I used to call home. I glance at Boss, who meets my eye for a wordless exchange. Something like: *Be cautious. We don't know this guy.* But what

Boss doesn't know is that I did a little bit of online sleuthing after Julian left.

"I was partial to the one about the stolen paintings and how they've been discovered," I say, trying to shift the conversation away from anything having to do with my past.

When I glance back at Julian, his eyes are on me. "I have some friends in the art collecting world—savages, the entire lot of them," he teases.

Art and collecting is a world that he's intimately familiar with, though.

"If that's how you describe your friends," I say, shaking my head, "I'd hate to hear what you think of your enemies."

All it took was a shameless internet search to discover that Julian Colton is a bit more than the jeweler he mentioned being in passing during his last visit. He underplayed the fact that his pieces are considered fine art. "Exquisite" and "prolific" were mentioned a few times in varying articles. He's a celebrated artist, and his work is more than sought-after; it's praised and widely known. He has installations in galleries all over the world, and his name is connected to a couple of high-profile actresses who attended Met Galas multiple years in a row, wearing statement pieces from jewel-encrusted gowns to headpieces. Every single item was stunning.

"You sound like her," he says, making me stop what I'm doing for a moment. "The podcast host—similar ways you say certain things. Where did you say you were from again?" he asks.

I raise an eyebrow. "I didn't," I answer. Surprisingly, there isn't an ounce of hesitation in my response. "I don't know that you've earned those details just yet."

If he tried the same method of searching for me, he would've come up with nothing. There isn't a single social media account, pictures, or registered party history. It's not because I haven't accomplished remarkable things or taken countless pictures of drinks and food once upon a time. There's an explanation as to why none of that existed; I just wasn't willing or able to share. Just like there isn't a *Scientific American* article that features the breakdown of sugars in organic compounds and how it relates to the whiskey and bourbon industries. Naomi Nash wouldn't be listed in its byline or referenced as a spotlight speaker at the National Symposium of Organic Chemistry in Nashville a few years prior. The same way there wouldn't be any grants or countless hours of research attributed to the same name that had its own impact on the organic chemistry community.

"And what would I need to do to earn those details?" he asks. a smirk playing on his lips.

Why am I so focused on the way he licks that bottom lip?

The sound of the jukebox kicking back on and the familiar crooning of Boss's latest additions shakes me enough to focus back on the task of making the drink in front of me. "I'm not in the business of oversharing and making it easy." When I lift my eyes and look at him, I add, "What fun would that be?"

Holy shit, who are you right now? I've opted for a quiet, uneventful life. Accolades don't matter, and I've learned that the painful way. And while the bulk of my family have been hopeful romantics, I never saw myself that way. I preferred rational pragmatism. But this, with him, is fun. And while being a realist now means that the probability of finding a physical, intellectual, and emotional connection with a person would be almost impossible. I look at the way he's smiling at my comeback and wonder if maybe something physical could be enough, even for only a short while.

The limitations are not because I'm broken, though I am,

it's because the details about my past and where I've chosen to remain need to be kept secret. Naomi Nash is simply a bartender in the middle-of-nowhere Montana, living on a ranch that doesn't exist on any map or GPS system. I'm meant to be easily forgotten. And yet, the way this man's arms are crossed over his chest as he watches me pour out three fingers of whiskey into a smoked and chilled glass makes it all feel like bullshit. Julian Colton is looking at me as if he didn't forget me the same way I didn't forget him—or the palm reading he was promised.

His attention moves a fraction lower, settling on my lips, and then landing on my wrist. I realize what he's looking at, and my face heats, slightly embarrassed, hating that I've only taken this off to shower.

"You forgot something," I say quietly, bringing my fingers to the gold snaps that hold the leather cuff in place.

As I move to take it off, he says, "I didn't. It gave me an excuse to come back here and flirt with the beautiful woman at the bar." He covers my wrist with his hand. "Leave it. Looks better on you."

I swallow, not sure what to do with any of this—the compliment, the embarrassment, his gentle touch—hell, even how he looks as good, maybe even better, than I remember. *Put those brave pants back on, Wyn!*

He's all charm as he lets go and lingers closely. Leaning on the bar, he runs his thumb along the scruff lining his jaw, and I can imagine even in certain crowds, he'd be considered arrogant or even presumptuous, but there wouldn't be a single person who could argue he has a presence and sex appeal that leaves an impression. What Julian has is learned, maybe even refined, into what I imagine is a hell of an experience.

I look down at the leather before I meet his eyes again. "It's a smooth move, Julian Colton." I give him a genuine smile as I say, "And you're right, it does look awfully good on me."

His eyes track down to my lips for the briefest moment and it makes my chest flutter.

I want more of this feeling. I want to keep smiling over small talk and flirt as if it's for sport. I glance up at the clock that hangs just below the bison. *The Distilled Truth* playback ended more than three hours ago, and the crowd that packed the place has dwindled down to just a few. During the night, I wrote down the flavor notes of the flights of whiskey, and as I look at the tally of what people enjoyed most, I smile.

Pulling a sticky piece of popcorn from the bowl between us, I dip it into the huckleberry jam. I almost hum at how delicious the sweet and savory mix so well.

"This one might be my favorite," Julian says, pointing to the tasting glass in front of him.

He leans forward and turns around the piece of paper where I've written down the flavor profiles from tonight's podcast tasting flight. He reads through the details of which are balanced and which ones linger, the spice and char, the legs and the body. My scale of color and rating. Smiling, he slides it back to me. "That's the perfect-sized piece of paper for a cross wing."

Suddenly, it looks like he just got hit with something, and it prompts me to dip my head so his eyes can find mine again.

With an understanding smile, I say, "Now you've piqued my interest. You have to tell me what a cross wing is."

Clearing his throat, he gives me a tight-lipped smile. "A paper airplane."

I slide the paper across the bar, back to him, wordlessly telling him to show me what he means.

He takes the paper and folds it lengthwise first, and then again in the other direction.

It feels like he's working through something that I don't have the privilege of knowing, considering we're practically strangers. Maybe it's why I feel the need to ask, "What are you really doing in Montana?"

He pauses his movements for the briefest of seconds, and then continues folding the corners and tucking them inside so that the shape of the paper is entirely different now. "My first time here, I was looking for something." Leaning his elbows on the bar, he looks up at me.

"And did you find it?" I've never been good with lingering curiosity. To me, there's always some kind of answer or explanation.

He clears his throat again, looking like he's weighing how much or exactly what he wants to say. "Yes." At that, he smiles, and my stomach sinks, knowing what he asked when he first came in, but I exhale, relieved, when he adds, "And no." He looks back down and folds the corners again. "I lost my dad a few years back—"

"I'm sorry to hear that," I interrupt.

Nodding once, he pauses, and then quietly says, "Thank you." Holding up the folded, half-completed airplane, he adds, "Used to make these with him. Feels like I've been looking for something or other ever since he left."

"I know the feeling," I say with a heavy sigh.

His eyes dart to mine at that confession. The comfortable quiet that lingers for a moment bursts when he reaches forward and runs the tip of his thumb along the corner of my mouth. The lightness of it doesn't make me flinch like I would've expected. It feels like kindling in the form of a gesture. With eyes locked on mine, he licks that same thumb, and then, without missing a beat, he says, "This is the first time, in a long time, when I've just stopped and looked at what's in front of me."

I search his hazel eyes, letting the truth of his words settle between us, and try to determine if it's the insinuation or just plain attraction that makes me realize I've done the same.

The typical loop of music lingers throughout an almost empty bar. But it's the sound of Viv and Boss mindlessly singing along to Tina Turner as she belts out the irony of what love has to do with it that has Julian and me turning our attention to watch. Both of us almost snort out a laugh.

The change in mood has me reaching for the bottle of whiskey he liked and pouring out two shots. I slide one toward him and then take mine in a slow and steady sip. I want to enjoy the burn of it, give myself a minute and let it coat whatever bits of nerves still reside from the "old me," and embrace the kind of woman I'm starting to feel I might like.

Julian gives me a knowing smile as I watch him drain his shot, tilting his head back and giving me a peek at the way it works down his throat. I have a rather aggressive urge to lick and feel the scratch of his scruff along my tongue. My attention lands on the neckline of his shirt first, and then the peek of black ink at the base of his neck just as it curves. "Be careful, looking at me like that, Naomi," he interrupts.

My face heats immediately. I look back up, finding him watching me now. *Be brave.* "Still interested in letting me read your future?"

He quirks an eyebrow and says, "Thought you said it was more than just futures."

I run my thumb along the edge of the leather cuff, thinking

about the way it feels against my skin, how I wouldn't mind his hands in its place, holding me where he wants me while I—

"I can almost see your dirty thoughts play out with the way you're touching and looking at that thing," he says, low and slow.

My stomach swoops at his boldness. He absolutely just called me out. "I have no idea what you're talking about," I respond in a playful tone. "But you gave me this—" I hold up my wrist and show off the cuff. "I'll pay for it with a palm reading."

Viv gives me the side-eye and then glances at Julian. I can almost anticipate what she's going to say just from her body language alone. She loudly whispers, "I can think of a few other ways to pay him more handsomely..."

Eyes widening, I bark out a laugh. "Viv!" I jokingly grit out through my teeth as I look at Julian who's wiping his palm across his mouth, trying to cover his laugh. She didn't need to say a damn thing; I've already made up my mind. I've been numb for so long, and I've been playing it safe. I want to feel something again.

I pour out another two fingers of whiskey just as Boss ducks under the bar. He tips his chin toward where Julian's sitting and says, "Go. I've got it."

I try keeping my face neutral as I move around to the same side of the bar and next to Julian. Lifting myself up onto the bar stool, I sit sideways, tip the glass to my lips, and take a sip, letting myself enjoy it for a moment. My skin feels warm, and I'm very aware of the way he's watching me. When I hand him the same glass, he tosses back what's left and then grabs onto the leg of my bar stool and drags me between his legs.

My breath catches. Swallowing the way that move just made me feel, I cross my legs and glance at his hands. "Show me," I demand.

He does as I ask and lays both, palms up, on the bar.

As I've been taught, I evaluate what I see first. I paid attention last time he was here to his dominant hand—right. That will be his present and future. His left is the path given or inherited.

I observe the length of his fingers in relation to his palm, take in the mounds at the base of each finger, and then brush my fingers along the center of his left hand. My heart rate kicks up, and I feel like the sound of it has to be as loud for him as it is for me. I blow out a slow breath. *Be brave.* My fingertips trace over the two rings he wears—one on his pointer and the other on the middle. The metal isn't smooth; it's raised and looks like it's been intricately cut.

"Am I making you nervous, Naomi?" he whispers.

"Shh," I bite back with a laugh, my hands trembling slightly as I move my fingers along the deepest line of his palm. "But yes, you make me nervous," I say honestly, looking up through my lashes. "I think you already knew that." Running my touch up the length of his right hand to the tips of his fingers, I graze the rough calluses that protrude along each. I wonder what other parts of him feel like and if he's wondering the same about me. He lets out a short, low hum, and instantly, this changes from struggling to concentrate on a palm reading to focused foreplay.

Large hands, warm skin, and the way I'm so turned on by this simple, G-rated contact that it makes me realize how touch starved I must be.

"I can't tell if what you're seeing is good or bad," he says jokingly.

I smile and move my touch across four deep-set lines.

"How did you learn how to do this?" he asks, watching me as I move my fingers along each indent and line.

I hesitate for a moment, deciding how much he gets to know. Attraction is one thing, but sharing about a life that I miss will make this feel more intimate than I planned. He watches me and waits, giving space for the silence I've let linger from his question. *Be brave.* "My grandmother believed and practiced all of it—palms, crystals, astrology." I let out a small laugh. "And of course, tarot," I say, trying not to get too lost in any memories. I smile when I think about the rumors that she leaned into and let fly—she was, or rather is, a force of nature. And while I didn't agree with the way my mother and grandmother chose to lead their lives, I still hated how judgmental the world could be about what others chose to put their beliefs and energy into. "Palm reading, out of all the things she'd practiced, seemed like the most practical, so she would talk to me about it in her garden. She'd always tell my sisters and me that we were so different despite so much of us being the same."

"How so?" he asks.

I think about the things that made us stand out, the parts we shared that made me feel good. "Green eyes," I say, smiling. "We each have award-winning personalities, but we also have the same shoe size. Shared a big, fat love of heels and boots." It feels wrong talking about them out loud like this, like I'm sharing too much of myself with someone who hasn't earned the privilege.

Shaking my head, I try to come back to the present with him. "I think that's why I liked all of that—palm reading, astrology, and tarot. Everything's up for interpretation, but..." I run my pointer along his deepest-set line. "I appreciate the idea that it's not all predetermined or that we don't inherit a life we don't want." I lower my voice and lighten the moment. "And it's a fun party trick that'll sometimes score me a really thick tip."

"Jesus Christ," I hear Viv rush out as she heads for the door with a clove cigarette hanging from her lips. "You said thick tip..." She shakes her head like I'm killing her.

My gaze whips back to Julian, slightly mortified, but he just widens his eyes and smiles at me with amusement.

Biting my lip, I draw my finger along the center of his life line when he asks, "Does this tell you anything about the incredible woman I've just met? Or why talking with her has me feeling like I don't want to go anywhere else?"

I release a shaky breath. Maybe he's just handing me a line, and maybe that's even better. Allowing whatever this is to play out. Attraction? Desire? And not read into it any more than that. I can't think of the right word for what this feeling is as I brush my fingers along each line of his hand, so instead I finish the task I've started and read.

"This is your heart line," I tell him. "It's the deepest one, and there's no deviation, which some might say means you connect with people and you love deeply. Are you married?"

He tips his head down, trying to find my eyes. When I glance up at him and smile, he asks, "You can't see the answer?"

Shaking my head, I look back to his palm and brush my pointer along the center line again and trace the mounds that are typically called Venus and Jupiter. "Eyes up here."

I look up again, eyes on him as he requested.

He smirks, another low and pleased hum coming from his throat that feels as if it rumbles through my limbs and settles at my core. "I wouldn't be sitting here with you if I were married, Naomi."

I swallow, already knowing that in my gut and so distracted that I don't know what I'm seeing in these lines anymore. "It could be assumed that you will have one great love of your life," I say, then, with a twinge of joking sarcasm, I add, "No pressure." But then I sway slightly closer and exhale the breath I didn't realize I was holding.

"Just one?" he asks jokingly. "You said it's all up for interpretation, so what do you think that line really means?"

"Beyond the luxury of loving someone, I understand what it feels like not to be in control over any of it. So I would say, this line means wherever you focus your love for something or someone, you'll do it without hesitation. Fully focused and in control." I laugh at how opposite that sounds from the life I'm living.

"Why is that funny?" he asks quietly, smiling as he stares at my lips.

On a sigh, I answer, "That must be nice."

His fingers move slowly, grazing mine as he asks, "Which part? To feel in control? Or to let go of it?"

The idea of both has me squeezing my thighs in response. What would that feel like? To take control and then to lose it, with him.

He looks down at his fingers, curving them upwards and drawing them along my palm that's been hovering above his. On an exhale, his gaze travels back up, and the confident man with the cocky smile slips as something vulnerable settles across his brow.

A wave of panic rushes through me—there's no leaving here with him. He can't know that the ranch he asked about when he first stopped in here is where I call home. Maybe this is where it ends. Soft touches and a fantasy to play out later.

"You can't come home with me," I say quietly, hating how much I'm enjoying the way his fingers tease along my palm. I focus on the way his lips tilt up as if what I've just said is amusing.

"I don't remember asking if I could," he volleys back. "But I like that you're thinking about being alone somewhere else with me." He leans in, close to my ear, and the scruff of his beard scratches along my cheek, sending a shiver throughout my body. "What would you do with me?" His lips skate along my earlobe. "To me?" he breathes. "For me?"

I swallow audibly, breathing faster as he pulls back. Grabbing a rocks glass, I pour a finger of whiskey and toss it back. I don't taste a thing, only the welcome burn of courage that travels to my chest, offsetting the thrum of anticipation at what I'm about to say.

You're in your mid-thirties, single, and wildly attracted to this man. Woman-up, Wyn.

Closing my eyes, I stand from the bar stool. What I'm going to say could lead to the bravest thing I've done in a long time.

He watches and waits, like he knows what's coming.

With one more steadying breath, I tilt my head toward the dimly lit hall across the bar and say, "Then, there's something I'd like to show you."

CHAPTER 4

Naomi

The red glow of the exit sign is enough light to see him follow as I look back over my shoulder. My stomach flutters, and sheer excitement courses through my veins. *Who do I think I am right now?* I've never put myself in a situation where this would be on the table. My sisters? Probably. My mother? Most definitely.

I didn't wake up this morning and think to myself, *I'm going to hook up with a stranger at the bar today.* I've absolutely fantasized about all the ways I could enjoy the man looking at me as he grabs my hand, stopping my steps. I just haven't considered it becoming a reality, never mind seeing him again. He steps closer, and I catch the faintest smell of mint and something masculine and warm as his body presses against mine. It sends a shiver through me that shuts off any further internal questioning. *I want this.*

"What did you want to show me?" he asks, leaning in, his words vibrating along my skin as one of his hands moves to my hip.

"I lied," I say, taking two steps back.

Eyebrow quirking slightly, he takes one step forward.

"I don't think I mind," he says with a smirk as he continues to slowly follow me.

Why does his height make him even sexier?

"Tell me something that isn't a lie then," he says as I move back a few more steps.

"I searched for you," I confess. My back hits the wall next to the exit, and the coolness from the door's draft seeps into my skin. "I searched your name to see who you are and find out more about…you and what you do."

"You must have liked what you found, considering you didn't tell me to get lost when you saw me tonight," he says, seemingly amused by this.

"It's impressive—your art, the things you've made, what you've accomplished. No social media. Plenty of pictures of you at events and red carpets with models and a few celebrities."

"Clients. All the pictures you likely found were of people who paid me for my work," he says, like he doesn't want me to get the wrong idea. Lifting his hand, his fingers cuff the dark strands of my hair behind my ear and then linger as they move down to the cropped ends. He rubs the piece between his thumb and forefinger. "Did you find what you were looking for, Naomi?"

I keep my eyes locked with his, trying to read his reaction, but he gives me nothing. There's no smile or teasing tone this time.

"No." I swallow, tipping my head back. "Not everything." What I don't say is that I wanted to know that his presence was a coincidence and not trouble. But instead, I settle on something trivial that I remember. "Your middle name. It only listed 'T' as the initial. What's your—"

"It's just T," he answers and shifts closer, cutting off my

question. His fingers let go of the hair he'd been playing with, and on their descent, they graze along my shoulder, brush down my arm, his knuckles ghosting the side of my breast. The light touch leaves tingles in its wake, and I look back up at him, my head pressing into the wall I'm up against. He keeps watching the path he's drawing, his knuckles now brushing against the waist of my jeans. The lightness mixed with intention spikes my pulse and has me holding my breath, wanting more.

"What does T stand for?" I ask as I exhale, my voice coming out too breathy for the topic we're discussing.

The corner of his mouth tips up. A beat later, he says, "It was a line from a movie. A woman asks a man what the T stood for, and he said *trustworthy*. My mom loved the movie, and my dad loved my mom, which awarded me with that letter as my middle name."

I smile at the story. Tilting my chin up, he brushes his thumb along my lower lip, rubbing away whatever was left of the saltiness from the popcorn earlier. The look in his eyes as he does it is downright hungry.

"Trustworthy," I say softly. It's a big word for what this is, but maybe it's exactly what I needed to hear. *When will there be another moment like this in my life?* My fingers flex. I want to feel him. I'd have to be crazy to do anything other than lean in and take exactly what I want. Plenty has been taken from me.

I touch the front of his shirt, curling my fingers into the soft ribbed cotton, and pull just enough to encourage him closer. His mouth tilts up at the corners, revealing the sexiest smile. The lines along the edges of his eyes crinkle, and I catch a glimpse of a dimple pinching inward beneath his facial hair. It's the last detail I see before he's too close to focus on anything other than the fact that he's going to kiss me.

Lingering a breath away for a moment, he waits for me. But I'm finished waiting. I brush my lips against his, gently testing and waiting for him to follow. And whatever it was that held him back, snaps. His hands frame my face, fingers tangling in my hair as he tilts my neck and angles my mouth exactly how he wants it.

The spontaneity of what I started transforms into something deeper, more purposeful. Julian's lips press and taste mine, warm and wet, moving with a natural passion that draws a moan from my throat and has my body coming to life. His tongue seeks entry with a simple swipe as I open eagerly until we find the other's pace. It's a deep and languid roll between lips and tongues. His body presses flush against mine, and it feels heavy, safe, and wanton along every one of my curves. I'm practically buzzing with need. My legs feel weak, and my pussy tingles as his tongue plays with mine. Fingers flexing, I fist his shirt tighter, unable to get close enough.

This is how a woman should be kissed.

His arms wrap tighter, and his fingers grasp onto the material of my shirt. He hums an encouraging sound that unlocks a new level of confidence in me. I move my body, shifting and switching our positions. His ass hits the door to the small bathroom, shoving the door open. Backing into the edge of the sink's counter with a thud, he leans me back so he can flip the light on. His smile and light laugh against my lips is warm and sultry, making me smile in return. I've never gone from turned on to laughing and then back again with such ease. His hands roam down my body and the feel of it throws my center of gravity off-kilter. One of my hands grips along the neckline of his shirt and the other threads into his hair, pulling him close as his lips trail down my chin and across my jaw. He kisses me again and it's dizzying, a haze of desire and fucking need. I pull back, breathless.

He watches and waits, glancing around my face and then moving his gaze down to my chest. "Deciding how brave you want to be?" he asks playfully.

I lean away and take a step back. I've already decided. I know what I want; I just want to remember every single detail of this moment. The space is so small that it only takes one more step for my back to hit the door, closing us inside. Sex in a bar bathroom feels dirty. In another life, I would've judged someone for it, called it trashy, but right now, that judgment is thousands of miles away.

Be brave.

I flip the lock.

"Take off your shirt," I demand.

He doesn't raise an eyebrow or even smile. Instead, he reaches his arms back, hands gripping the material behind his neck, and in a blink, his shirt is off and discarded next to him. In the reflection of the mirror behind him are tattoos that run along the caps of both shoulders, continuing down and across his back—paper airplanes turning into birds and drawings that look like blueprints with lines and details that would take time to read, and between his shoulder blades, a compass with four main cardinal points. *Beautiful.*

"I showed you mine..." he says as he leans on his hands braced on the edge of the sink, elbows locking straight and watching as I drink him in.

I toy with the hem of my shirt, remembering the parts that I hate. So much of me is different now than before. Then, it was a soft tummy and a lack of self-esteem, but now it's scars from a story I don't ever want to tell.

I'm in charge.

I slowly shake my head and let go of my shirt.

A low hum escapes his throat. "You won't let me see you," he says, registering what I'm telling him. Nodding once, he runs his thumb along his lip. "I'll have to use my imagination then. I'm already thinking about what you'd look like bare and sweating beneath me, Naomi." His eyes trace the length of my body before he asks, "If you won't let me see, will you let me touch?"

"Please," I rush out, sounding needy.

His hand comes up along the side of my neck while the other wraps at my waist, slowly pulling me back into his orbit. The brush of his mouth along my neck lulls my eyes closed. Another shameless moan escapes me, and I tip my head slightly to the right, giving his lips better access. His teeth graze along my pulse point, sending a shiver down the front of my body and coiling at my center. I know I must be soaking my panties now, my breasts sensitive and breaths labored. I've never been so eager and turned on like this, not with anyone.

His fingers toy with the button of my jeans. "How long?" he asks. On his next breath, before I can respond, he adds, "Until someone comes looking for you, how long?"

"Minutes, maybe?" I say breathily, just as a knock hits the door.

"Taken," Julian calls out.

"Is this okay?" he whispers, nipping at my lower lip, gliding the zipper of my jeans down.

"Yes," leaves my mouth like a plea.

He shifts behind me, adjusting our bodies so that my back is to his front.

I nudge my ass back and watch our reflection in the mirror as his mouth tips into a smile. Knowing what this is doing to him—the hard press of him and how the tiniest bit of friction has him humming in approval—injects a heady mix of confidence and lust into my veins. The low vibrating buzz of the fan is the only sound covering what we're doing in here and masking it to whomever was just standing outside that door. I widen my legs to grant him better access. "More."

It's the only direction he needs as he grips the waistband of my jeans, shoving them down my ass and thighs.

I gasp, taken off guard by the sudden movement.

He palms my ass with a throaty growl as he squeezes. A little thrill zips through me as he kisses along my neck as he comes back to his full height, the look on his face showing his hunger for me.

I lean my weight against him, watching as our dirty fantasy plays out. His fingers tease into the waist of my panties while his other hand pulls the neckline of my shirt to the side. Sending a wave of arousal right between my thighs, his teeth graze the curve of my neck. He growls next to my ear, watching along with me as his fingers move below. Breath rushes from my mouth as two of his fingers tease along the lips of my pussy. "Is she feeling needy?" he whispers quietly, and goose bumps trickle across my skin. His head lowers and his nose moves to the crook of my neck as he takes a deep breath. On his exhale, one finger glides into me. "She's so wet, isn't she?"

I exhale and nod as I watch his hand between my legs.

"I've never wanted to watch someone come more than I do right now. Will you do that for me, Naomi? Will you let me fuck you with my fingers?" His lips roam along my neck as his finger pumps slowly in and out, running through my lips and to my clit and back again. "Will you come all over them for me?"

I can't hold back the whimper he pulls from me. My eyes

close, head tipping back against his shoulder as he keeps the same pace.

"Are you telling me you want more?" he asks gruffly.

"Yes," I whimper. "More."

His fingers move away.

I shift, opening my eyes, but before I can protest, he grips the sides of my jeans and tugs them down farther.

Another double knock hits the door. Our eyes meet in the mirror, and he calls out, "I said, someone's in here."

Without wasting any more time, he reaches down between us, his hand gripping along my ass and then lower. His wrist twists and then two fingers glide through me, spreading the lips of my pussy, back and forth before he moves higher, grazing my clit on the second stroke. It makes my mouth open, and the smallest hum vibrates in my throat. I haven't been touched in so long. And not like this. I can't remember it ever feeling this good.

He pulls me tightly against his body, my back pressing from his chest to his hard length confined by his jeans. Taking all my weight, one of his arms wraps beneath my breasts while the other teases along my clit. The way his skillful fingers work me over as he holds me tightly feels like he's taken complete control. *Goddesses, I love it.*

Raising my arm up to pull his lips closer, my fingers glide into his hair as he kisses along my neck.

His teeth graze along my skin as his touch skims along my opening before two of his fingers slide inside. My eyes flutter closed for a moment to enjoy the stretch and fullness.

"Fucking beautiful," he whispers softly, and it has me feeling lightheaded. I open my eyes to find him watching me in the reflection of the mirror. His mouth tips up on the right side, knowing all too well what he's doing to me.

I look down and watch as I ride his fingers. It sends a rush through me, and I can't help but feel turned on by the reflection of us, being able to watch what we look like together right now. He shifts as I lean back and hold him close. Moving his other hand down between my thighs. Without faltering, his fingers find my clit as they spread my arousal in slicked, slow circles. I've touched myself this way plenty of times, but with him, it's unpredictable and feels like I have permission to let go.

"Oh god," I moan as pleasure builds and my skin flushes hot. "I need—"

"Me to make you come?" he cuts in. "That's it, soak my fingers. I want you dripping down to my wrist."

"Oh god." I'm unable to catch my breath. Between his fingers and words, I know I'm going to come so hard. "Yesss, please," I plead. I want this feeling to linger and crest all at once.

His fingers never waver on my clit, the steady pace and pressure like a masterclass in erotic persistence. I hold him closer. His lips on my shoulder, his beard scratches along my skin as he adds a third finger.

My fingers grip into his hair while my other hand presses against his, adding pressure and watching the reflection of all of it play out in front of me.

He practically growls as he says, "The sound of you on my fingers..." His lips brush along my neck, eliciting another shiver. "So damn wet and tight. Listen to the way your pussy's making such a mess for me."

The fullness mixed with his words is exactly what I need to push me right to the edge. Mere moments of this, his teeth nipping my neck, his dirty words ghosting my skin, and a weightless tingle begins behind my knees.

"You're going to come for me, aren't you?"

A desperate whimper and dazed nod are all I can respond with.

"Go ahead. Let me feel you grip my fingers nice and tight. Show me how pretty you look when you come, Naomi."

My eyes snap open to see our reflection just as my orgasm crashes through my body like a goddamn awakening. As my pussy contracts and grips his fingers relentlessly, I cry out, trembling against him, our eyes never leaving each other in the mirror until I've ridden the last wave of euphoria. Eyes closing on a heaving breath, I fall and *fucking* die a little in his arms.

His lips trail along my shoulder and neck as awareness finds me again. I want *more, more, more*. An orgasm like that deserves more than just shifting clothes back into place. I turn to face him, just as another knock hits the door, followed by a muffled, "I gotta piss," and we both share a smile.

"Two minutes," Julian calls out as he shifts his fingers from between my legs and then lifts them to his mouth. When he sinks the digits between his lips and hums with pleasure, my brain explodes. *Is this really happening?* My pussy flutters like she didn't just come harder than she ever has.

I swallow as he lowers to his knees, reaching for my panties and pants that are pooled there. He leans in, and his face buries between my thighs. I hear him take a deep breath of me, and then he slowly licks up my center.

I can't help but shudder at the sensation and try to chase it as I roll my hips forward. My mouth opens, no sounds coming out other than the rush of breath that he's stolen from me.

When he pulls back, his beard is shiny, and he smiles up at me. "I could spend hours savoring this sexy cunt of yours, Naomi." He nips at my thigh as he guides my panties and jeans up my legs.

My face is already heated, but the way he speaks to me with such palpable desire makes another ripple of lust buckle my knees.

As he stands, he shifts the hard-on that's tenting his pants and scoops up his T-shirt from the floor. He turns, giving me his back, and I'm rewarded with a closer glimpse of the artwork that's drawn there. I can't help but reach out and trace the compass and coordinates at the center. Out from there are shapes of small birds and paper airplanes—some shaded in black and others just outlined. *Beautiful.* He pauses, letting me touch.

He wouldn't know, considering I left my shirt on, but I have tattoos along my back too. I never wanted tattoos, but it's one of the many things that's different about me now. I needed something that was pretty on my skin when I arrived here. I wanted something to offset the ugliness that lingered. Where his are black and gray, taking up the expanse of his entire back, mine are bright and bold. Pinks and greens and golds run up my spine. Tattoos of the flowers I remembered from my grandmother's garden. I didn't want to see them every day, but I wanted to know they were there and that I could look at them when I wanted.

I finish righting myself, and without overthinking, I say, "I don't want this to be over." Turning around, I watch as he runs his hand along the back of his neck, weighing his response.

"Neither do I," he says, moving toward me, claiming my lips in another kiss. His arms wrap around me, hands wandering, making me feel the most wanted I think I ever have. I'm drunk on this man—this stranger. I don't care if it's because I've been celibate and healing, or in doing so, I've realized just how lonely I've always been. This moment feels too good to stop and dissect or explore the deep-rooted whys.

I smile against his lips as he kisses me. His tongue tastes like me, and I think about how much I'd like mine to taste like him. Moaning, I nip at his lower lip.

With a lazy smile, his lips press to mine again before he asks, "Where did you come from?" He doesn't wait for my answer as his mouth moves lower, lips gliding below my ear as he grazes his teeth along my pulse point.

I unlock the door and twist the knob. "Small town," I say with a small shrug. When he lifts his head, I lean forward and kiss him again, seemingly unable to stop. "Somewhere I doubt you'd know."

He ghosts his fingers back and forth along the slip of skin above the waist of my jeans. The hum and vibration of the fan, the quieting of my heartbeat, the way he's touching me—all of it is soothing.

We both shift into the hall, with me walking backwards and him forward, as if he's leading. My back reaches the wall between the fire extinguisher and the open office door. *Where do we go from here?*

His hand frames the side of my face as his thumb brushes along my jaw. Smiling and looking as dazed and disheveled as I feel, he looks up and over my shoulder as he says, "I want more time. Come with me."

The reality is, I can't bring anyone to where I've been staying. It's been a moot point up until now. Feeling safe and starting over have been the only plans I've had for the past few years here. Even if it's just to his car, it would be more time. And I want more. I finally look up, not ready for this night to be over, and notice the way his body goes rigid before he says, "You lied."

He looks inside the office and moves away from me. It takes me a moment to stop smiling and realize this door shouldn't have been opened. It's Boss's space for filing paperwork, keeping track of newcomers, and making calls.

My body tenses as silent alarms trigger.

"You said you'd never heard of Hideaway," Julian says, staring at the map of Montana behind the desk.

Four yellow Post-it notes are stuck on various places, and one of them is placed at exactly two miles from where we're standing right now. It's marked Hideaway Ranch.

Nervously, I glance down the hall, my heart racing for a whole different reason now. "That's not—"

"I had a feeling you knew more," he cuts off my lie as he turns to face me.

"You what?" I ask, instantly angry. "So...you were using me?" I say quietly, almost not believing what's happening. "Who the fuck are you?"

He doesn't answer, eyes only narrowing as he searches mine.

What the hell have I done? I take a step back. "You lied. You weren't lost," I rush out. This is bad.

There's one rule I have to follow. One that must stay in place not just for my safety but for too many others. I don't have time to question why he wants to know or if he means any harm.

He steps closer, making me take one shaky step back. This time, the choreography of our movements is blanketed with an entirely different mood. Quickly, I step just past the threshold of the door and back into the hall, sliding my palm against the wall, reaching the cutout where the fire extinguisher hangs.

"Get out," I warn as I feel for the grip of what I have hidden.

Stepping closer to me, he says calmly, "I'm not looking to hurt anyone. Just—" His words cut off when he feels what I have in my hand that's now pressed to his groin. "What's in Hideaway?" he still asks.

"Nothing."

Glancing down, he holds his hands up in surrender. "Then why lie, Naomi?" He looks down at the weapon in my hand.

"Says the *liar* who just tried seducing me for information," I bite back.

"*Tried* to seduce you?" he says, his eyebrow quirking in question and pissing me off further.

I dig the taser into his groin.

"Fuck," he breathes out. "If I was a threat..." He doesn't finish his thought. Instead, he moves too fast for me to register what he's doing. The taser is knocked from my grip, clanging to the floor just as he shifts around me, pushing me so that my body presses up against the wall. With my arms somehow twisted behind me now, he gathers my wrists into one of his hands. He leans into me with his full weight, holding me there so I can't move. As I'm about to shout for help, his hand covers my mouth.

My pulse spikes. Panic slamming into me so violently that I feel dizzy.

"I'm not going to hurt you," he says next to my ear, almost like he's pleading with me.

I try making a noise, but I'm shaking and can't make a single sound.

"Naomi," he grits out.

I want to tell him, *"Nope, sorry, that's not right. That's not my name, asshole."* I want to hang onto my wits and not crumble at what's happening. I glance around as my nerves ratchet, my whole body now vibrating with adrenaline. Where's the person who kept knocking? *Fuck.*

"Listen to me," he says through a clenched jaw. "I'm not interested in causing trouble. I'm just looking for information, but you lied to me, and now I really want to know what's in Hideaway?"

He doesn't realize how complicated his question and my non-answer just made all of this.

"Shit," he mumbles, stepping back slightly and letting go of my wrists. "Tell me what will make you stop panicking. Please." He turns me around and looks over my body. "You're shaking. I'm going to lift my hand away from your mouth. I promise, I'm *not* going to hurt you."

It takes me a second. *Breathe.* "Leave," I mutter as strongly as I can. A tear stupidly falls down my cheek, and I swipe it away, hopefully before he can spot it. *Be brave.* "Forget you were here. Forget whatever this—" I cut myself off. "If you're not looking for trouble, then leave. And forget."

"Naomi, you alright?" Boss shouts from the end of the short hallway.

Before I can even answer, the weight of Julian disappears just as abruptly as the door to the emergency exit opens. He glances back at me one last time before he walks through, regret and confusion playing out across his face.

What the hell did I just do?

"Naomi?" Boss calls out again.

I swallow repeatedly, feeling like I might throw up. My clammy hands tremble, and I breathe in through my nose, holding for *seven, six, five, four, three, two.* Get it together. *Exhale.* I remember the protocols. I shove down any emotions that are lingering. *This isn't just about me anymore.*

When I look back up, I'm as focused as I can be, my panic still on the precipice, but I can deal with that later. As I'm rushing down the hall, Boss meets me in the middle. "What happened?" he asks, reaching for my shoulders.

I step back, not wanting anyone to touch me. "I messed up," I tell him as my eyes blur with tears. "I need to make the call. And you need to head to the ranch. Make sure I didn't just get everyone—"

"Already on it," Viv says, speeding past the hall entryway. "I've got Peaky saddled outside; I'll get there faster. I knew I didn't like that fucker!" she calls out, moving through the bar.

Boss is already moving and tosses me my burner phone from behind the bar. "Call it in, and I'll give the ranch a heads-up before Viv gets there."

With my heart pounding in my ears, I hustle back to the office and close the door behind me. I flip open the phone to the only number programmed on it. It only rings twice before she answers.

A loud breath blows out, and then the sound of jazz music echoes in the background before she says, "Talk to me, Wyn."

I clear my throat. "Bea, I messed up." I don't bother swiping at the tears that finally fall.

"Are you in danger?" she asks, immediately following up with, "One-word answers only right now."

I squeeze my eyes closed. "No."

"Good. If that changes, you hang up and do as you've been instructed," she directs.

I'm nodding, as if she can see me. There are protocols and rules for staying here. The U.S. Marshall who brought me here made everything crystal clear, and I've broken one of them, or rather, the only one. *Keep this place quiet. If anyone asks, Hideaway doesn't exist. It needs to stay that way.*

"Is anyone else hurt?"

"No," I tell her through more tears.

"Is anyone on their way to the ranch?"

I shake my head, slamming my eyes shut. "No. Yes." I let out a frustrated breath. "Viv just hauled ass out of here."

"Good. She'll take it from here, then." I hear the click and zip of a lighter. Bea sucks in a breath, and on the exhale, she says, "Now, tell me what happened."

CHAPTER 5

Julian

Present

"Fuck," I grit out, finishing the last steps and starting to run down my list. This never should've happened. I'm so fucking distracted. The second my knee hit the dusty gravel, my hands shook as I brushed a piece of light brown hair away from her face. It's been months of looking without so much as a hint as to where Naomi went. I have people who are very good at finding things searching for me too, but it was like she never existed. And now, she's right here, in a crime scene where she doesn't belong.

I couldn't forget the beautiful liar, never mind move on. I couldn't shake off the way it felt talking with her, the way she looked at me, how she felt in my arms, on my lips, and tasted on my tongue.

The plan was to find Hideaway and get some answers. Manipulating attraction to get what I needed had never been an issue for me. Spending some time with a beautiful woman at a bar was straightforward enough, and I was intent on helping find out all I could about a place that was important to a friend. So, when I went back again, I wasn't expecting the tables to flip the way they did. She smiled at me, like she'd been waiting for the day I'd show up again, and I fucking forgot what the hell I was supposed to be doing there.

And then I saw it, in plain sight on a fucking map.

Weeks later, I finally understood why she lied. Hideaway is a place for witnesses and survivors of extremely violent crimes who still aren't safe to live and heal. It made sense that when I went back again to see her for a third time, I was greeted with a shotgun. She wasn't anywhere in that bar, and I stayed parked outside for a handful of days and asked a few people when they were leaving if they had seen Naomi. *"She picked up and moved, I think."* She wasn't there anymore, and Boss and Viv weren't going to tell me a single fucking thing. It's haunted me ever since.

But now, here she is, walking into the middle of a job. We're thousands of miles from where I first saw her, kissed her, and watched as she came all over my fingers. I shake my head, tilting it back to look up at the angry, gray-purple sky. "Fuck," I breathe out. Thunder rumbles low in the distance, as if the weather's saying, *Indeed, Julian. Fuck.*

I rip off my gloves and pocket them. It's the quickest cleanup I've ever done. Efficiency takes time, but I know I don't have that luxury—not now. I glance at her propped along the side of the building. *I hurt her, and I could've done worse, goddamnit.* She stayed out here while I finished the task I'd been interrupted doing. I didn't need any other traces of someone inside the bar, not if I was going to properly clean it all.

Brushing my fingertips along her cheek, my gaze travels the length of her. She looks different. Her hair is lighter, a few strands escaping from where it was twisted up high. Her clothes look like she's either just come from a library or an archeology site in the 1920s And while it isn't the vibe of the woman I met in Montana, it's still her—different but the same. Plush lips with an exaggerated bow, high cheekbones, and I'd bet everything I have that if she opened her eyes right now, I'd see the deepest emerald greens staring right back at me.

I do a double take when my eyes pass over her hand. She's wearing the leather cuff…I can't decide if I'm relieved to have found her or pissed off that there's another lie wrapped around it.

"What the hell are you doing here, Naomi?"

The pulse in her neck moves with measured beats, but that's the only movement. A hefty sedative will do that to someone. She won't be stirring for a while. The thought churns my stomach.

Gathering her in my arms, I lift her up off the ground. My stopwatch timer sounds off, making me groan. They wanted this all cleaned by sunrise. That timetable gave me less than five hours after I landed. The body wasn't cold, which meant they texted before he was dead—it isn't typical for the jobs I'm used to handling. This was planned and premeditated. *A full set* means a complete cleanup, from the body to its surrounding areas. On my drive over, the last text I received read: *The situation got messy.* The contact for this job has been in our files for more than five decades, but they haven't called the burner in a long time—nearly three and a half years ago now. If I hadn't held on to my father's books, I wouldn't have recognized the name on the initial message. *Crowne.*

The click of a cocked and loaded shotgun has me stopping all movement. *Fuck me.*

"You better pray to whatever or whoever you believe in that

she's going to be okay," a woman's raspy and measured voice says from behind me.

Not authorities, but the clients were expecting my father to be here—not me.

"You called me here." I turn my head, still trying to shield an unconscious Naomi from whatever happens next. "Get that gun off of me," I demand.

The woman lowers her sawed-off shotgun slowly as I turn around with Naomi limp in my arms. Curly silver hair whips around the woman wildly in time with her billowing blue overcoat as the breeze kicks up around us. Her glare traces my body and then my face before she says, "You're his son." Lifting her chin, she shoves her shoulders back, trying her best to harden herself. She falters slightly when I catch the glassy shine of tears in her eyes. Clearing her throat, she adds, "He's gone then?"

I nod, unable to share much about what happened to my dad, even if I wanted to. I don't know this woman, but I also don't know the exact circumstances surrounding my father's death. It's been more than three years, and the details—where he was found and his cause of death—remain sealed in confidential files. Even his autopsy was redacted when it was delivered by the FBI. All of it had me asking more questions. I'm still not satisfied with the minimal answers I've been given. My father and I have done plenty of jobs for government organizations, but everything should've been off book. The expertise they required shouldn't have been stored in any databases. It's what Dad required when he answered those requests. If his death wasn't connected to something we did, it wouldn't have been the FBI delivering the news of his death. I hated not having answers.

She walks closer, reaching toward the woman I'm still holding.

I flinch and step back.

"That's my granddaughter you're holding," she says pointedly, taking another step closer, making sure she's still breathing. "Wyn," she says under her breath. "What the hell were you doing here?"

I look down at Naomi again, confused by what this woman is saying about her. "What did you say her name was?" The last time I saw her, she was angry and threatening me with a taser, but we were in a bar near a place meant to hide people who weren't safe, and her name was Naomi there. *She wasn't just there to look out for the people in Hideaway; she was hiding.* I swallow, hating how much that unsettles me, knowing that whatever drove her there couldn't have been anything good.

The old woman looks back up at me with a furrowed brow. "I'm assuming she saw what you were doing?" she asks gruffly, ignoring my question.

My stomach sinks—she was *never* supposed to see this or know this part of me. I give her a nod to answer.

"Ugh." Throwing her head back, she mumbles, "Goddesses. Can this get any more complicated?" She points up at the sky. "Never mind, don't answer that."

Who the fuck is this woman?

She takes a grounding breath and looks around us, nodding like she's just made up her mind. "Alright, Mr. Colton, what'd you drug her with? And how long until she wakes?"

"Equivalent of a horse tranquilizer. So ballpark, eight to ten hours. I don't typically think about someone's downtime when I'm concerned they've walked into something they're not supposed to. Usually, I eliminate the issue..." I shove down the thought of what could've happened if I'd grabbed my gun and silencer instead of the syringe. A wave of self-loathing washes over me.

She looks toward the entry to the bar and asks, "If the job is all set, then you can follow me."

It is now, but when I arrived, there was more than just a body and a pool of blood on the floor. The smears along the side and top of the bar were signs the deceased had struggled. After the body was removed and dealt with, I worked inward. It's the things that can't be seen or flecks of DNA feet away from the deceased that'll end up identifying the person, perpetrator, and possibly even the time of death. That's where I like to start.

The closet next to the office had a bottle of Clorox and another of Fabuloso, so I used those around the entire place as if it were the usual nightly clean after the enzyme solvents—it needed to look like I was never here. That was when I heard the car door. The concentrated area of blood was still being absorbed. It's always the last place I focus my attention on. The body removal is the first. I packed my deodorizing fogger into my trunk and watched from the shadow of the building's exterior as a woman walked inside.

"Carry her up to the house. You look strong enough," she says, her eyes tracking down and then up the front of me. "Follow the path along there. And then you and I are going to have a cup of tea while you answer a few more questions. I'll meet you at the front door to my home. Please be gentle with her." She turns her back, and then hustles to a quad that's parked off to the side. It roars to life seconds later, and I haven't said a fucking thing.

I wasn't going to just disappear, not now. My plans changed the moment I heard her say my name. The hike up to the house isn't easy, but the path is lit, and the woman's waiting for me at the front door as she promised.

This was supposed to be an in-and-out job. Maximum of

twelve hours, and then I'd mark the end of one family legacy, allowing me to focus on the other. And I could go on searching for the woman who's now limp in my arms. *Fuck.* I hate how my training has put me on autopilot, to the point I did this to her. I tend to zone out and focus on the single task of cleaning and disposing, and then erasing every trace of violence, and my presence. I didn't get a look at her, only that she was someone who shouldn't have been there.

Sweat drips down my torso as I round the front walkway, and the older woman greets me with a cold stare, leaning against the front porch baluster of her Victorian-style home.

"You're bleeding," she says, like it's an inconvenience to her. Before I can even respond, she turns away and walks through the open front door. "Bring her inside. I have a chaise in my solarium where she'll be comfortable."

A steel-gabled roof and turrets make the place seem opulent, brimming with as much character as the woman in a bright blue velvet housecoat. I move through the dimly lit home and down the hall that deposits into an eclectic kitchen. Tipping her chin up and nodding toward her left, she says, "Through there. I'll be right behind you."

I do my best to place Naomi down gently on the long, plush lounger, but her head lulls back, and seeing her like this makes me feel like the scum of the earth. Hating that this is the way we've been brought together again, I push a piece of her hair off her face. The dim lights around the room serve as uplighting to the lush greenery throughout as I straighten and take a deep breath. It's cooler in here, but the air is damp with humidity. Windows reflect the light, making it feel more like a greenhouse.

"That is my oldest granddaughter you so valiantly carried in here," she says upon entering. "I'm Bernadette Crowne, but you may call me Birdie." She deposits the tray with a teapot and cups on an empty, gold-embellished bar cart to the right of an ornate wingback chair. "Sit," she demands as she pours a cup of tea.

When she offers a cup to me, I hold out my hand and say, "I'm good, ma'am. No thank you."

She sniffs a laugh to herself, like something is funny about that. "Like I said, it's Birdie, not ma'am. And you see, Mr. Colton, this isn't a nice gesture from an older woman." She looks over at her granddaughter. "As you can imagine, we've found ourselves with a little problem—"

No shit.

"And I need to figure out how best to proceed." Tipping her head, her gaze drops to the dainty teacup that hovers between us. "First, you're going to sit, then drink the tea that I've prepared, and then you're going to answer a few more of my questions."

I look over at the beautiful woman laid out in front of me, and then back to Birdie as I take a seat and sip the putrid-smelling drink. "Alright," I resign. I'll answer her questions and expect a response to a few of my own.

After a few quiet moments as she leans against the wall, her arms crossed in front of her, on an exhale, she asks, "How long?" She swallows and clarifies, "Since your father passed?"

"A little over three years," I say, clearing my throat.

"Sam." She whispers my father's name as her hand covers her mouth.

Shifting in my chair, I tell her, "I thought I had shared the news with everyone. My apologies that it took so long for me to tell you."

Birdie bats away a tear and raises her chin. "He was a good man."

I nod. There wasn't a single detail that I could find that said otherwise. Dad liked to manipulate the rules. His morals skewed differently from what was typically considered right and wrong. But she's right; at the core of who he was, he was a good man.

"I think a part of me knew." She shifts, crossing her feet at the ankles "We had a bit of a streak for a while. I've been dealing with things in my family, and I hadn't realized how long—"

I glance at my watch. If I was going to leave, I would be talking to air traffic control right now, not a woman who's likely far more dangerous than she appears. My goal was to wrap up this part of my life after tonight. I wanted something more than having to keep secrets from people. I glance at Naomi. The idea of having someone I shared everything with only works if I'm actually able to share everything. The cleaning business doesn't allow for that—my father learned that the hard way.

"Birdie, I'm going to need you to lose my contact after tonight."

She gives me a tight-lipped smile. There aren't any further questions about it. That's always been a part of this business that I respect—the stakes are high, and it leaves little to no room for emotions and opinions.

"If that's what you prefer," she says with a nod. "I would like to know exactly how much of the mess my granddaughter had a chance to see." She holds up her finger as I take another sip of the tea, and then adds, "But first, let me see your palm."

CHAPTER 6

Wyn

A CHILL WORKS ITSELF DOWN my spine. *"Or am I misreading things?"* I suck in a sharp gasp at the memory, not wanting to open my eyes.

The smell of rosemary lingers as I take a steady breath. *One.* I always felt safest when I smelled the pine-like sweetness. *Two.* Another breath in as I anchor to the nostalgia of that smell from a youth that was never quiet or calm. But it was safe. *Three.* The oil from its needlelike leaves on my fingertips when I stopped to appreciate the small bushes outside of my mom and Birdie's house. *Four.* The way it turned from a floral to more of an earthy scent when it was dried and hung from the kitchen windows. *Five.*

I flex my fingers, and where I'm lying is plush and soft—velvet. A heavy, almost lethargic-like feeling lingers in my limbs as I shift slightly, and my breathing halts altogether. *No! I can't still be there.*

I have to open my eyes and make sure. I glance around, only to find blurred shades of pink and deep burgundy. Bloomed peonies are peppered around a spread of lush greenery. I dig my fingernails into my palm, hoping my mind isn't playing tricks on me. *Try to remember the last thing you saw.* The bar. The blood. Julian. I sit up fast, trying to take a full breath, but it's shaky. *Don't panic.*

"Finally," a deep voice exhales from the other side of the room.

Nearly jumping out of my skin, I scan the space, careening back against the plush velvet pillows stacked behind me. I squeeze my eyes closed and brush my fingers against my lips. *This can't be right.*

"Julian?" I say, in utter disbelief.

"Naomi." he says, sounding groggy. "Or is it Wyn?" With a humorless laugh, he adds, "Hard to figure out which one is the lie."

"What the hell are you doing here?" I say in response, realizing that he is, in fact, sitting across from me, shirtless. Everything from before this comes back immediately. Lifting my hand, my fingers brush over the still-tender spot where he pricked me on my neck with a needle.

His eyes move around my face, and then my body, as if he's worried. "Are you alright?"

"Am I alright?" I parrot back, lacing it with sarcasm. "You stuck a needle in my neck and drugged me." I try to tamp down the rush of panic I'm feeling all over again.

He tips his head back with a heavy breath. "To be fair, I didn't know it was you."

"I'm not sure how that's supposed to make me feel better," I mutter.

"It isn't," he says, then immediately adds, "Just tell me you're okay. You should've woken up a while ago."

He shifts in his chair, and that's when I notice the white

gauze wrapped around his leg—the exact spot I shoved my handy feline weapon into.

"Hope that hurt," I rush out with narrowed eyes.

He follows my line of sight. "That's not very nice," he says teasingly. "I forgot that the last time we were together, you pulled a weapon on me too."

"The last time we were together, you—" I cut myself off. I remember everything that he and I did when we were together. I hate that my thoughts even wander there. Clearing my throat, I say instead, "Maybe remember what I'm capable of the next time you're anywhere near me." I shove off the small blanket that was draped around me, blinking away the wave of dizziness and trying to get my bearings as I swing my legs to the floor. Taking a steadying breath, I stand up. My pulse races and my skin feels overheated as I sway when I stand.

"Easy," he says softly.

I try glaring at him, but I end up doing a double take, noticing the opaque plastic zip ties wrapped firmly around his wrists and bound to the arms of his chair. Then, looking closer at the way he's sitting—rigid and legs spread wide. His ankles are bound with zip ties to the front chair legs in the same way.

"Woke up like this." With a small shrug, he glances at his wrists, fingers wiggling. "Quite a while ago, actually." He stretches his neck, and I catch a glimpse of his tattoo. "Birdie asked some questions, and I started feeling...tired." He looks down at his bandaged leg, and then back up to me. "I'm still not sure if I passed out from losing too much blood from the puncture wound you so kindly gave me, or if it was the bitter tea your grandmother demanded that I drink." That charming fucking face of his shines up at me, and I feel bad for hurting him. Then he smiles, almost like he knows exactly what I'm thinking, and it makes me not regret it at all, and that instantly pisses me off. I lean into this feeling and decide not to question why I'm not more scared than angry right now. *Oh right, because he's zip tied to a chair.*

I shift my blouse and fix the button that's come undone, when I look back at him, he's watching every single move I make. *Of course, he's as handsome as I remember.* His hair is a bit shorter, but half pulled back and still long. My fingers flex in memory of what it felt like to drag them through those dark strands. Dammit, I can feel my face heating as I remember how he felt pressed up against me, inside me, all over again. Shaking my head, the way he lied comes to the forefront, the way he used me to get what he wanted... *What is he doing here?*

"I would very much like to get out of this..." he trails off, looking at where his wrists strain, as if I'm going to fix that for him. "Can I get a hand?"

I don't think so. I flip him off instead as I move toward the arched doorway.

He laughs to himself. "I went back."

His words have me stopping mid-step, and I turn back around. "Where?" I ask, even though I know where he means. But I'm not even sure if I want to hear the answer.

"It's been seven months, and I still—" He cuts himself off, and my heart flutters traitorously at what he was about to say.

I tilt my head back and the light coming in from the windowed roof isn't telling me much about the time of day. There's condensation blocking any decent view of the yard, but the brushstrokes of honey yellow and the faintest pink in the sky almost make it look like a sunrise, except the sun doesn't rise on this side of the house. My stomach sinks, thinking about how long I've been unconscious.

When I look back down, he's staring at me, studying me.

Why do I feel it all over when he looks at me? I try to harden myself, taking in the situation in front of me—a very large and handsome man, whom I fucked around with once upon a time seven months ago, is tied to the chair. And while he's not a threat at the moment, I need to understand what I walked into last night. I run my fingers beneath my eyes, wiping away any black that may have lingered. My skin feels like it's been basking in a sheen of sweat for far too long.

He continues his thought before I can get my head on straight. "I went back about a month after our night in the bathroom—" He stops what he's saying again, aggressively trying to yank his wrists free before giving up with a frustrated groan. His voice turns quiet, expression gentle, as he asks, "What the hell are you doing in Tennessee, Naomi?"

It's not Naomi. My eyes water instantly. If I answer, it'll open the floor for more that I won't answer. I bat away the only tear that falls. I don't trust him, and I know whatever I walked into at the bar last night was something violent. I need to see that my mom is okay, and I need to find my grandmother.

"Where are you going?" he calls out after me as I move up the three steps and out of the warm room. He thought sharing details would convince me to untie him. *Not a chance*. I need to find my grandmother.

The sound of the chair dragging on the floor echoes out. His tone changes as he shouts, "Untie me right *fucking* now."

The house is big and bold, old and lovely, much like the matriarch of my family. This is the place I've always felt safest. My mother moved me and my sisters here after our father was gone. It's still one of my favorite places in the world, from the sitting room to the garden. The memories that linger here kept me company when I needed them.

"Birdie?" I call out as I weave through the mudroom that connects the solarium to the kitchen. When I turn the corner the smell of baking bread hits me.

"Oh, thank all that is good," Birdie says, her hand splayed on her chest across the front of her navy-blue caftan with chiffon scarves draped around her neck. "You're alright. I've been so worried."

I rush across the cool terra-cotta tiles as she meets me halfway. She wraps me in her arms, her stacks of bracelets clanging together as she does it. Her curly gray hair is pulled back and up high with only a few streaks of the dark strands she used to have left. Holding her this way reminds me that time hasn't stood still—she's still strong, but so much older, it seems. She takes a deep breath, which prompts me to do the same.

You're safe.

I blink away the fresh wave of tears and try to piece together exactly how I got here. Worry instantly blankets me, recalling the blood on the floor of the bar, before I'd been drugged. "Is Lu—"

"In the dining room," she cuts me off. "Your mother's fine. No need to worry, sweetheart." She pats my hand, looking past my shoulder, where chatter carries. "Everyone's in there havin' supper."

My grandmother is one of the most confident women I've ever known. People only need to see her to feel it or even absorb some of it. It's in the way she moves, slow and steady. The lilt of her voice, measured and kind. Like she's thought about every possibility and person in her presence before they've even greeted her. Birdie's a force. I know she has secrets. There are too many rumors and far too much town gossip about Bernadette Crowne for all of them not to be rooted in some kind of truth. But she is, and always has been, the steady part of mine and my sisters' lives.

She returns to the bowl of salad she'd been mixing, and without even sparing me a glance, she asks, "Is our friend awake in there too?"

I steal an olive from the small dish next to her. The salty brine makes my mouth water and erases the taste that lingered from hours of being passed out. It also has me remembering the list of flavors on a piece of paper he turned into an airplane months ago. "Awake and tied to a chair," I answer.

"And you know him," she says it like she already knows it's true.

"What's he doing here?" I shake my head and close my eyes, trying to recall the details. "What happened?" I ask softly. "Someone was hurt at the bar? What I saw—"

"You don't know what it is you saw, Wynona," she says curtly. "And while I'm still trying to understand how it is you're acquainted with him, Mr. Colton is here at my and your mother's request." Her bracelets jingle as she moves around the kitchen. "He is tied to that chair, however, because he went ahead and drugged my oldest granddaughter," she says, matter-of-factly. "I felt it was only fair that I kept him there until you woke up. A little taste of his own medicine." She shrugs a shoulder. There must be a horrified look on my face because she wafts at the air in front of me as she tries adding logic to the situation. "He should be thanking me; I bandaged up that nasty gash in his thigh." Tipping her head to the side, she winks at me. "Nicely done, by the way. Smart to have a weapon on you. I noticed the ones you've strategically placed at your house and the bar, too. Perhaps a habit you picked up while you were away."

While my sisters knew that before I returned home, I was in witness protection, Birdie and my mother didn't. Only that

I had been a part of something difficult and that it was confidential. I don't need either of them looking at me with pity. Or worse, thinking that they could've done anything to change it.

Birdie shifts around the room, pulling a cutting board and bread knife. Taking a sharp left with the conversation, she says, "He's very good-looking..."

I scoff a disbelieving laugh. I always expect comments like this from my mother, but not Birdie. What the hell am I supposed to say? *"Yes, I agree? I flirted with him when I was living another life?"* or *"Yes! And he finger-banged me in a bar bathroom once. Highly recommend."*

"You're only laughing because you agree, don't you?" She smiles, adding, "I love hearing you laugh again." She continues slicing up a steaming loaf of sourdough, probably unaware that I haven't said anything. "Where was it you said you met him?" Birdie is good at most things—cooking and cross-stitch, growing gardens, reading palms and tarot, but she excels at getting people to tell her what she wants to know.

"I didn't say," I say, shaking my head.

"You can trust me, you know. I know there's more, Wyn."

"I think I deserve to know what's going on and why I just woke up in there...with him." Swallowing a huff, I fill a glass of water from the sink.

"Oh, is *that* what you think?" she says to my sass, raising an eyebrow.

Tipping the glass to my lips, I overhear loud and conflicting conversations carrying on from the next room. *"I'm telling you; it was bigger than a baby's arm..."* and *"There's no reason why a piece of art should ever cost that much money..."*

Birdie piles slices of still-warm bread into a basket, taking her time with what I'm hoping is going to be an explanation.

The sweet smell of yeast from the bread shifts slightly more savory as the meatloaf and coleslaw linger from the next room.

The kitchen is the same as when my sisters and I were kids, sans a few upgrades. The long, centered island, where Birdie would always set up a Saturday morning waffle bar. Crystals and frosted glass pendants hang in the window over the sink, and at certain times of the day, like right now, the way the sun shines in the sky hits them just right and bathes the entire room in prisms that carry a warm, comforting glow.

I pull out the pins that are still holding my hair in the now messy twist from last night's party—it's the best feeling running my fingers along my scalp. My hair is past my shoulders now, and I like it longer. The highlights brighten the brown, and it makes me feel new again. The last person who played with pieces of my hair is tied up in the next room. They were darker and shorter then. *I almost hate how much I enjoyed his fingers in my hair and the way he moved me to get a better taste.*

"Come on. Give me something. What exactly is Julian here for, Birdie?" I run my fingers along the leather cuff on my wrist. "Was that a dead body?" I whisper.

She lets out an audible exhale, like my question is inconveniencing her. "You walked into a situation, Wyn. A situation that you weren't supposed to—" Her words stop abruptly as she looks toward the doorway, and at the man who's now filling it.

"Are you fucking kidding me?" I breathe out as I watch Julian casually lean against the doorway as if he wasn't just bound to a chair. His feet cross at his ankles and arms cross over his chest, and I know I'd only reach his shoulders at best, even in his current position. "How the fuck did you get out of those zip ties?"

"Not my preferred way of being tied up," he says to me, wiggling his eyebrows.

I tug at my blouse and move my hand behind me, trying to hide where he's staring. "I already saw you're still wearing it." His lips tilt to the side, like he's pleased that I haven't taken it off—a leather cuff that doesn't fit, but I still wear it every day anyway. He tosses my switchblade onto the counter—the weapon I had stashed away inside of my boot. "I didn't want to miss this conversation."

Dammit, how did he find that?

"Ah, just the man we were discussing. And how is it that you know my granddaughter, Mr. Colton," Birdie says, ignoring the weapon that just collided with the butter dish.

Instead of looking at her, his focus stays locked on me when he answers. "I'm not sure I can really say that I *know* her." He tilts his head just a fraction.

Son of a bitch.

"The version of her I thought I knew wasn't residing in Tennessee. She dressed much more casually. And her hair was different—dark, almost black, cut short." He points to his jawline.

Birdie starts to say, "Wyn, your hair was—"

"Naomi," he cuts in as he limps through the entry into the kitchen. "She told me her name was Naomi."

It feels like the universe is playing some kind of fucked-up joke right now.

Birdie quirks an eyebrow at me again. "Interesting behavior coming from you. This is more in line with something your mother or sisters might have done." Her mouth twitches like she's amused before she shakes her head. "Giving a man a different name," she says under her breath.

Standing straighter, she sizes him up. It's a power move that I've witnessed plenty of times throughout my life—if there's any truth to be found in this room, it's that Birdie's always the one in charge. "There's a shirt over there for you, if you'd like." She glances at me. "Although, none of us are complaining if not." A chuckle slips past her lips when I widen my eyes at her to cut it out, and she grabs her basket of bread, moving toward the dining room. "I see the appeal," she says, leaning into me, before heading through the arched doorway.

Gritting my teeth, I ignore that comment and say, "I need you to finish telling me what that was last ni—*Birdie*!" I call after her, but she's through the doorway and done with this conversation, apparently.

When I glance back at him, there's a tiny smirk dancing along his lips, and I know he heard her not-so-quiet commentary.

There are layers of lies that hover between the two of us, yet he knows more than most should about me—where I had been, and even more, intimately. I struggle with what to say as he watches me and comfortably allows the silence to linger. *I hate it.* Clearing my throat, I grasp at the first thought I have as I stare back at him. "You cut your hair."

"You're an entirely different person," he volleys back as he limps closer, reaching the other side of the island between us. Leaning forward, he rests his elbows on the counter and waits for me to say something more.

I push my shoulders down and fist my hands on my hips. "Observant. Yes. But you can start," I grit out. "Tell me what you're doing here."

"Is that how you think this is going to go?" he says in a teasing tone that makes me want to slap him—*definitely not kiss him*. "You might want to ask your beloved grandmother the answer to that one."

"You're dangerous." I cough out a laugh. I've thought about

this man too often. "I can do a lot of things, but apparently knowing who I can trust—"

He shakes his head and laughs like this is funny, cutting me off. "You're a beautiful liar," he says, erasing the playfulness that's been on the edge of his words. "And I know why you had to, but—" The way he looks at me now feels intrusive and overwhelming.

"I'm a liar, but so are you," I breathe out, shoving past him and through the doorway, down the hallway, and toward the dining room. If there was another way to leave, I would've chosen it. The last thing I want is to be catapulted into family dinner.

"Auntie Wyn" my nephew, Nash, yells out, stopping me in my tracks and causing everyone to look my way. *Shit.*

"Wyn, you better sit that pretty ass next to me right now," my brother-in-law, Theo, says.

"Did you ditch the nerd party and go on a bender?" my sister Stevie asks. Eyes widening, she takes in the mess of my appearance. When she reaches my bare feet, she looks at her husband. "Please ask her where her shoes are, Theo."

"Wyn, where—"

Stevie cuts him off. With her eyes closing with exasperation, she says, "Where are my favorite Tecovas, Wynnie? You will not get back the chartreuse Manolos if you've lost my favorites."

I give my sister a look that says, *Now is not the time.*

"She looks like she just got a nice railing, honestly," my mother says, as if this conversation needs interjection. "Are you feeling rested, Wynona?" she asks with a smirk playing on her red-slicked lips. "Or well worked?"

That gets her my leveling glare. *Nice, Mom.* I know she has to be clued into the fact that I was just passed out in Birdie's solarium for hours. It's a packed room with more faces than the usuals sitting around the table—because, of course, this moment needs an even bigger audience.

On the other side of my mother is my Uncle Tommy, who quietly observes the chaos around him. My father's brother has been putting up with our family for my entire life. He made it his business to step up into the role our father stepped out on.

Next to him is my youngest sister Jo, as she adds, "Nobody cares about the boots right now, Stevie." She smiles at me like the damn Cheshire cat, knowing all too well that she's going to badger me for details about what our mother is talking about later.

My sisters are good at getting details. But nobody at this table knows everything—only the pieces I've allowed. Stevie and Jo are aware of what happened to me, the abbreviated version, but they don't know the timeline of it all. Julian knows the woman who built herself up and landed as someone else entirely. But now, in the aftermath of it all, there isn't a single person here who knows my entire story. It's safer that way.

Next to Jo is Jameson Bishop. My brother-in-law's father and someone I know my sister trusts. Having a contact within local law enforcement is protocol for returning from WITSEC, and Jameson now leads the county sheriff's homicide team. He knows the formalities, the details of what the U.S. Marshals and authorities filed about my case. He never asked why I didn't return sooner. It's one of the things that's always been likable about Jameson; he observes and rarely judges.

"You alright, Wyn?" he asks, brow pinched.

"She's fine," Birdie says from the head of the table, sipping casually on a glass of red. "Got swept up with something or..." she pauses, seemingly to search for the right word. "Someone."

And as if she summoned him, Julian walks up next to me with his hands casually slung into his pockets, his hair swept into a half-up man bun, wearing a too tight T-shirt with The Whispering Fool logo splashed across the front of it. Goose bumps fly up my arms at his proximity. He's tall and broad, which adds to the appeal, along with that sexy, smug look framed by his meticulously managed facial hair. A current of warmth runs through me and settles at my center.

Theo stands up and starts a slow clap. "Wyn, on behalf of all of us…"

"Jesus, Theo," Jameson says to his son, trying to cover up his amusement.

But both of my sisters join in with the clapping and exchange wide-eyed looks.

Stevie turns to Theo and mouths, *What the fuck?*

I know! he mouths back.

Everyone's attention is on Julian when he says, "I am, disappointingly, none of the things Birdie just listed off, but it is nice to meet you all." With his hand to his chest, he says, "Julian."

"My name is Nash Thomas Crowne. And I like your hair," my nephew chimes in. "Did you do that bun yourself, or did my mom help you? She's really good at hair."

"Thanks, baby," Stevie says to him, and then raises her eyebrows at me.

"She was going to be a hairdresser," Nash says over a mouthful of meatloaf. "That was after she was a country singer, but before the bar entertainer."

Jameson, who's usually fairly quiet when he comes around, sniffs out a laugh.

Stevie isn't going to let that go. There's something about Theo's dad that sets her off like nobody else. "I'm sorry, is something funny about a woman changing her career to suit her lifestyle?"

"Dad..." Theo tries to get his dad to hold back, but Jameson keeps his attention on Stevie when he says, "I just hadn't heard the term 'bar entertainer' before." He winks at Nash.

"I'm not sure you would know what entertainment looked like even if it was naked and prancing right in front of you."

My mother claps her hands, because obviously there wasn't enough attention on her.

"Next to me, handsome," she says, patting the empty chair I started moving toward.

Why are she and Birdie allowing Julian to join family dinner?

I rub at my forehead and close my eyes, trying to navigate the varying levels of shit I've been dealt today. The last thing I need is my mom reading between lines, the way she so stealthily does. It annoys the hell out of me that she seems more impressed at the insinuation that I was with Julian than when I had earned my PhD.

"Not so boring, after all, apparently," she says to me with a side-eye, drumming up a reminder of the argument we had last night.

I might kill her.

"Lu," Tommy says with a shake of his head. He tries to be a buffer, but Tallulah Crowne can be a real asshole when she wants to be. My mom knows exactly how to wield her weapons. She declared to my sisters and me at a very young age that Crowne women have superpowers in the form of great tits, snarky wit, and a knack for speaking truths with facial expressions alone. But now, I don't think she knows what to say to me. A part of that is my fault, for not trusting her with all the details of what happened to me when I was gone. The truth is, I'm not sure she'd be able to handle it.

Before Julian moves to sit, he says, "Nash, it's nice to meet you, man." He holds out a fist for Nash to bump. "To answer your question, I did my hair myself." Then he nods to me. "But your Aunt Wyn likes to play with it. Mostly mess it up," he says with an audacious fucking smile on his face as he glances back at me.

Both of my sisters' eyes go wider than they already were. Wordlessly asking, *What the hell is happening?* I curl my lips in and just shake my head, trying to keep it together.

Julian shifts his body closer, I flinch slightly as his hand finds my waist. I've gotten better with being touched, but along my left side, it's still a sensitive spot. A phantom pain any time something brushes against it. He must notice because he lets go almost immediately and instead just leans close enough to whisper, "You have so much explaining to do."

Dammit, the way he says it makes a shiver run through me.

"Wyn, are you just going to stand there?" Birdie asks, even though every seat in the room is taken.

"Wyn, you can have my seat. I need to head out anyway," Jameson says as he wipes his mouth with his napkin and stands.

"Jameson, I feel like it's been too long since we've all been able to have a meal together. When will you be back?"

"I should be leaving tonight," he says, looking at Nash, and then Theo. "I have a case that's been keeping me on my toes, but the sheriff called my team in, so I might be here a day or so longer."

Birdie turns her attention to Julian and feels the need to add, "Jameson is a homicide detective for the county sheriff's department." She raises her glass to Jameson. "Very busy. We enjoy his company whenever we get the chance."

"Nash," Jameson says to my nephew, circling the table and holding up a fist for him to bump. "Love you, kid."

"Can you please butter this for me, Sonny? You do it the best," Nash asks him. So instead of moving toward the door like he planned, Jameson shares the chair with my nephew. Nash looks at the side of his head and says, "You have more grays now than last time."

Jameson only nods trying to keep from smiling as he helps butter his roll.

"My mom says gray hair just means that—"

"Bah bah bah," Stevie cuts in. "Nash, out of context, it's not a good idea to repeat the things I ramble on about."

Jameson turns to look at her, eyebrow quirked just slightly. "Now I'm interested, what does gray hair mean?"

Theo snorts out a laugh as Stevie tries to find words. It's rare that my sister is left speechless, but my nephew has gotten good at calling her out lately.

There's history there, more than my sister's willing to share, but I know her relationships with the Bishop men are complicated.

"Dad, when's the next guys' night?" Nash asks, moving on.

Theo leans over to ruffle his son's hair. "We'll make sure it happens. Just need to coordinate it with your mama when she's busy or working at night."

"Mom, aren't you working tomorrow?"

And I don't even realize I'm smiling as I watch the exchange until Stevie claps her hands at me. "You can have guys' night whenever you want, baby. Speaking of work... Wynnie—"

I glance at Julian, whose eyes seem to have stayed on me. But I ignore it and shake my head at my sister, knowing what she's going to ask.

"Don't say nooo," she says dramatically, throwing her head back.

Jo rolls her eyes and proceeds to ignore all of us while she keeps eating.

"Jo, tell her that we need another set of tits behind the bar," Stevie adds.

"You literally just said it. I'm not repeating it."

I smile at Stevie, but then Jo adds, "Wyn, if you're not busy, I wouldn't mind the help. Aside from one of the shot girls always calling out sick, and then our newest bartender disappeared and just stopped showing up, I can never catch time off."

Stevie exhales and glares at Jameson. "Missing people is quite the trend around here."

"Technically, not my department," Jameson says without interest. He glances at me, knowing all about my missing persons case.

When I look over at Birdie, she's having a quiet exchange with my mother. For as loud as this dinner table is, there's plenty unsaid.

Jo kicks her feet up on the table. "All of my inspiration has been coming at night, which really is incredibly inconvenient if I want to duck out and paint. There's no one to cover for me. Wyn, do me a solid here?" She takes a bite of her piece of bread. "I know you hate bartending, but—"

"Huh. You hate bartending?" Julian leans back, seemingly entertained by this family dinner.

I close my eyes, just as the chatter from the room goes quiet. *Fuck me.*

"She's a fantastic bartender," Julian adds, crossing his arms.

If I could make him shut up right now, I would.

CHAPTER 7

Julian

"I'm sorry, but this is the first time we're meeting this guy, right?" The sister with the wild bold-red hair—Jo, I think—asks rhetorically. She has the same green eyes and high cheekbones as Wyn, but with a "fuck off" attitude. She looks at Wyn, and then at Stevie, the boisterous one, before she adds, "How is it possible that someone I've never met is telling us something as wild as our sister, Dr. Wynona Crowne, an organic chemistry professor, is actually also '*a fantastic bartender*'? Since when, Wyn?"

"Doctor?" I ask, looking at Wyn as she shifts and fidgets in her chair. The way she glances at Birdie, and then Jo, looking for a lifeline makes it clear that there are pieces colliding here that she wasn't anticipating. The biggest one of them being me. She hasn't lied only to me. But what I was called out here to do before she walked right into the middle of it makes me realize how much is being kept from her as well.

"Plot twist!" Stevie interjects with a laugh. Her voice sounds familiar, similar to Wyn's, but…I've heard it before; I know I have. "Julian," she says with obvious amusement. "Our sister has been holding out on us if this is true." She crosses her arms and throws Wyn a leveling glare. "You are *absolutely* helping me tonight."

Wyn shakes her head, face flushed, clearly ready to get the fuck out of here.

"You're the podcaster," I say, finally realizing why her voice sounded so familiar. I look at Wyn, though, as I smile knowingly and add, "*The Distilled Truth*."

Stevie laughs, delighted, holding up her glass. "I knew I liked you. So…" She takes a sip of her wine. "Does this mean you're a true-crime fan or a whiskey snob?"

"Maybe a little bit of both now." I clear my throat, deciding to play a little. "I was at a bar once where they played your podcast every week, and the bartender would curate whiskey flights to complement the whiskeys you would review before each case breakdown."

In my periphery, I notice the detective, who decided not to leave, is quietly observing, making me realize how out of my depth I am. *Fucking great.* There are layers of why this job has become more dangerous than I ever anticipated. Every part of my gut is screaming to get the fuck out of here. Except when I look at Wyn again, her green eyes are on me, still trying to figure out why I'm here in the same way I'm trying to do with her.

I need to talk to her. Alone.

"I know there's a lot of listeners, but that's—" Stevie takes a second, eyes tearing. "That's pretty amazing to hear. Where was this bar?"

I glance at Wyn, who looks about ready to throw something at me with the way she's glaring. So I shake my head. "Can't remember the name." And technically, it didn't have one.

"Why are you here?" Lu interrupts from my side. "We were expecting your father."

I sit back in the chair, trying to get my bearings on the swift change in conversation and tone. Out of everyone at this table, I have a feeling she might be the biggest wild card.

"Lu," Birdie says firmly with a swift jerk of her head—calling her off. "Not here."

Lu ignores the warning and smirks at me. With a singsong tone, she bites into a piece of the bread that Birdie had been cutting and says, "A quiet one." She looks down at my lap and then back up, eyes trailing slowly all the way to the top of my head. "Good-looking too."

I meet her glare, remaining quiet so I can figure out exactly what kind of trouble these women are capable of doling out. The fact that I was just tied up in the back greenhouse is being ignored, either because this is a common occurrence, or because she didn't know. Lu's hair is darker and short, the way Wyn's was when I met her as Naomi. There's no mistaking, though, that all these women, regardless of their different styles, are related. I didn't notice at first, but each of them has deep-green eyes and high cheekbones. Individually beautiful, but in the same room, it's the kind of beauty that intimidates and ruins plenty.

"Who was the last one you brought to dinner?" Lu asks Wyn.

Wyn squints at her mother, her nervousness drifting into something more annoyed, or maybe even pissed. "What are you doing, Lu?"

She shrugs her shoulders, grabs her glass of wine, and says, "What? The last one you brought to dinner was exceptionally dull. Then he came back again two times after you, well, went wherever it was you went." At that, she takes a gulp of her wine. "Not sure who invited him," she mumbles. I watch the three sisters all look at each other, silently exchanging a full-blown conversation.

Wyn sits back in her chair, relaxes the grip she has on the arms of it, looks her mother square in the face, and lies. "The details of my se—" She detours the word when she sees Nash listening. "Spicy life, Lu, are none of your goddamn business."

Her sister, Stevie, snorts out a laugh, while Jo just smiles, crossing her arms and watching her mother choke on Wyn's words. I don't know the dynamic, but I'm a quick learner, and I can't help but want to praise Wyn for standing up for herself.

I usually don't mind silence, but I don't want to have to answer any more questions, especially from the detective who hasn't stopped paying attention. "You have a beautiful home," I say, shifting my attention to Birdie. But she was already watching me stare at her granddaughter.

"Thank you, Julian," she says with a tilt of her lips as she butters a piece of her bread.

The house mirrors its owner—layers of character and a labyrinth of detail. From the velvet drapes and gold metal vines that part them at the center to the walls that are bathed in busy, rich-toned wallpaper that, on a closer look, I realize has a pattern of women dressed as goddesses, some naked or wearing flowers as stars and constellations swirl around them. *Fitting.* The eclectic taste could feel gaudy in some circles, but the artistic part of me respected their taste and style.

Wyn moves next to where Nash sits, and I try listening to the conversation.

"I told her it was a bird, Auntie Wyn," he says very seriously. "And then Dad said pterosaurs are dinosaurs, which he's wrong about, because it has 'saur' in its name." He rolls his eyes. "They're not listening to me. Will you please tell them?"

Wyn smiles at him, and I swear it hits me harder than I expect. *Fucking hell.* "I didn't know that either, but I think Uncle Tommy has some books all about dinosaurs in his library. Maybe we can find one and show them that you're right."

"I sure do," the older man next to the detective says. "Wyn, you remember all those books we used to drive the librarian nuts over requesting. What was that old battle-ax's name again?"

I don't realize I'm staring again until Lu nudges me. I miss the rest of what they're saying when Lu decides to start a side conversation with me. "She is beautiful, my oldest daughter. Isn't she?"

Clearing my throat, I move my full attention to Wyn's mother as she leans her elbow on the table, propping her chin on her fist. In a lower tone, she adds, "Though she doesn't know it. The parts you can't see are even more intriguing when it comes to my daughters." She looks around the table, and it makes me wonder why the hell she feels so inclined to say any of this to me. Until she pats my arm and quietly adds, "My girls are my entire world, which is why I'd like to request that you get the hell out of here. I don't know when you would've had time to romance my daughter since you arrived, but we both know why you came here."

What she doesn't know is that Wyn is the only reason I haven't left yet. That, and being drugged and tied to a chair.

"That's how I know you," I hear as a snapping finger clicks. "You're Julian Colton," the woman with the auburn hair in the chair across from me says, slapping the table. She laughs as if she just won a prize at the realization and looks around at the rest of the table. Gawking at Wyn, she says, "You just forgot to mention that you know someone who's had work in galleries and on red carpets?"

Wyn glances between me and her younger sister. "I haven't

seen Julian in a little while. I haven't really thought about mentioning it."

I swallow and hate the way her words fucking hurt. She's all I've been able to think about.

Jo waves her hand in front of her, like she's annoyed at her sister's lack of a real response, and focuses back on me. "You designed the emerald-encrusted bustier and that..." Her hands move in a circle above her head. "And the gold crown thing that everyone went crazy for during the Met Gala last year."

"Jo," Wyn scolds.

Jo mouths, *What?!* holding up her hands like she's unarmed.

People don't tend to recognize me for the work I've done, unless they're a part of the art world in some way. I've had a few higher-profile clients who my father wasn't thrilled about taking on, but the work was too unique to pass up.

Stevie and Theo start scrolling on their phones, likely looking for what she's talking about.

Nash asks, "What's a boost-yay?" He looks at Birdie, and she tries to describe the garment to him. Then she looks to me as she says, "Jo does all of our design work for our business. She paints sometimes too."

"She makes the prettiest paintings," Nash adds. Leaning forward, he whisper-shouts, "She says mine are just as good, but I know pretty when I see it." He shakes his head. "Mine are *not* pretty the way hers are."

"Painting is challenging," I say to Nash with a smile, and then whisper loudly, "I'm terrible at it."

"Would I have seen your work anywhere?" I ask, turning my attention to Jo.

She's already shaking her head before I've even finished. "Not that kind of artist."

"Julian is a big deal," Wyn interjects. I almost take it as a compliment until sarcasm dances around her words when she adds, "Makes me wonder what he's doing in our small town to begin with." She raises her eyebrows at me in challenge, as if I'll actually answer her. She doesn't waver, looking me in the eye. She's not the kind of woman who backs down. The gash in my thigh aches at the reality of that.

Alright, if she wants to play, I'll play. "You're forgetting how we met, darling," I say in a low, teasing tone.

"Please tell me this is something salacious," her louder of the two sisters interjects.

Theo leans forward, elbows on the table, chin resting on his closed fist. "Feed me with something that's not as boring as an online hookup or at a fucking farmers market meet-cute..."

Wyn locks eyes with me and then smirks. "He drugged me," she says, tipping her chin up in the air.

Birdie chokes on her wine.

Wyn's mother starts laughing next to me.

"That's not—" I mutter under my breath as the rest of the table erupts. Closing my mouth tight, I shake my head. I can't believe she just said that.

Wyn's uncle looks at me like he's about twenty generous seconds from trying to kick my ass, his chair sliding loudly on the wood floor as he starts to stand. "Wyn?" I don't doubt he's waiting for her approval to throw a punch.

"Thomas," Lu says, trying to calm him or maybe set him off; it's hard to tell.

Theo points to his son. "Earmuffs, dude."

Without missing a beat, Nash stuffs another bite of meatloaf into his mouth, and then covers both ears.

"While we all love a juicy story, Wyn..." Theo starts to say.

But it's Jameson who sits with his arms crossed, observing, and shifting from being a part of this dinner and into his detective role. "Theo, come on," he says, annoyed and almost reprimanding. When he looks back at me, it's Wyn who he addresses. "Wyn, I've been told there are reports coming in too frequently lately, and while it's not my department, if this is true..."

Fuck my life.

But Wyn answers over whatever her sister was saying. She looks at her uncle first. "I'm okay, and I shouldn't have said that." She shakes her head. "But that's what it felt like," she says, trying her hardest to backpedal.

Birdie just sips her wine, watching her granddaughter lie. Because I absolutely drugged her, but for some reason—and one I'm hoping has everything to do with how she wants to see me again too—she tells the men who looked seconds away from beating my ass that it was a poor choice of words.

"It was a bit...like I was in a daze, or like we—" She stops and looks down at the leather cuff she's still wearing and smiles. Glancing quickly my way, she shakes off whatever she was planning to say. "We met a while ago, and I'm still not sure how I feel about seeing him again." Her eyes are glassy when her attention lands back on me. It makes my chest ache. "Things got heated last night, and now it just feels like an inconvenient coincidence that we ended up in the same place again," she says with an exhale.

Her words feel like a slap across the face. *Inconvenient.*

A succession of quick knocks sounds at the front door right after the doorbell rings out.

Jo stands, circling the table. "I've got it."

"Julian *fucking* Colton," she says, turning her head left and then right, almost in disbelief. "Damn, big sister. Total opposite of your usual type."

I'm dying to hear this. "What type is that?" I whisper.

Wyn's glaring eyes meet mine, and I can't help but smirk at her. The twinge of jealousy that's seeping through my veins of her having "other types" is only covered up by the fact that this dinner is a fucking shit show. "Can we talk for a minute?" I ask her.

Before she's able to answer, Jo interrupts, lingering in the threshold of the room with another woman. "Birdie? She's asking if she could have a chat with you?"

Wyn's arms cross as she observes for a moment just as the young woman with glasses sees her and holds her hand up in a shy wave. "Good to see you, Dr. Crowne."

Who the hell is that? This house is nothing if not unpredictable.

"Birdie, I'm so sorry, I tried to call," the girl rushes out. "I didn't want—"

Birdie cuts her off with a click of her tongue. "No apologies necessary, honey. Glad you're here now. You can head through there, and I'll be right behind you." When the woman walks down the hall that we had come in from, Birdie looks to Wyn and says, "I'd love it if you could find a few bottles for me, Wyn. I have to chat with my friend." Humming to herself, distracted for a moment, she then comes back to what she was saying. "I hadn't realized she was a student of yours."

"Andi is a TA for our department," Wyn says simply.

"Ah, that makes all the more sense," Birdie says with a nod. She glances at Lu, one of their many silent exchanges I've noticed just in the time I've sat at this table, before looking back at Wyn. "There are a few clients who I'd like to offer something very special to when they arrive."

"Wine or whiskey?" Wyn asks.

"Something of yours might be nice. Bring it to the bar for

me?" She raises her eyebrows, pulling attention to the fact that she was drugged and slept it off in the same clothes from last night.

Wyn smiles at her grandmother, stands from the table, and brushes past me and mumbles, "Let's go."

I push my chair back and do the same, and the sound of it gliding against the wood floor has everyone's attention. "I'll help," I say.

"She's more than capable of getting what she needs on her own," Lu says as she sips her drink, kicking her legs up and blocking me from following Wyn. "You can stay right here."

I stop and look down at her legs brushing up against mine. "With all due respect, ma'am—"

"Ma'am?!" she scoffs.

"Lu, let him go," Birdie says. And just when I think she's going to ignore the matriarch of their family, she lets me by.

I don't say anything more; the dynamics in this room are far too complicated for me to figure out right now. I'd like to tell Lu to fuck right off, that I've done what I was asked to do, and my time is no longer their concern. But I have a feeling it would be wasted words. And at the end of it, she's still Naomi's—Wyn's mother.

And my interest lies with her, the woman who's hightailing it as fast as she can away from me. *Fuck.* She's already out the front door and taking a path down the side of the house.

"Wyn," leaves me as soon as my foot hits the front porch, but she's turning the corner of the gravel pathway and moving out of my sight. Once I make it to where she turned, the bar from last night is a mere fifty feet ahead, and Wyn hustles just past the main entrance, along the side of the building.

At dusk, this place is a helluva sight—the parking lot filling up and plenty of noise coming from the bar that was eerily quiet in those hours just before dawn. Right now, cicadas ring out almost as loudly as the music pouring from the double doors of the bar every time they open.

An entire day had come and gone, and the only thing I had to show for it were bruises around my wrists and a bandaged leg, slowing me down a bit. At least that wasn't ignored. I'm almost certain she could've sliced something deep and dangerous with that fucking weapon.

Smokers take drags and blow smoke in conversation as I pass by. Harleys and Ducatis line the sides of the building, , and a party bus parked in front delivers a laughing horde of women in matching black dresses. Two female bouncers, who look like they've never backed down from a fight, give me judging glances as I rush past. The Whispering Fool is already lit and loud with neon lights and plenty of people angling for a good and rowdy time.

"Wyn," I call out, louder and deeper, but she doesn't stop. She doesn't even look back. "Naomi!" I yell, and that at least has her looking over her shoulder.

"Well, hello handsome," one of the women from the bus says as I shove by. *"What's the rush? Come buy me a drink!"* I hear behind me.

It takes only a few painful jogging strides to hit the edge of the gravel and down the small riverbank toward the footbridge that Wyn is nearly halfway across. "Why are you running away from me, *Naomi*?" I call out to her.

She doesn't slow. "Not running, asshole, just have things to do."

"Asshole? That's not very nice," I say loudly over the rushing water.

Finally, she stops when she reaches the incline of the riverbank. "Not nice? You fucking tricked me in Montana—" She pauses like there's more she wants to say. "And then you drugged me, Julian," she says, but it's the way her voice falters and how she's looking at me that makes me feel like I want to take it all back.

I rub along the back of my neck, knowing I can't change what happened here, but I can apologize for it. "I'm so sorry—" I bend so that she'll look at me. "If I'd known it was you last night, I never would've done that. Trust me when I say that I would never hurt you, not like that—" I take a step towards her, and she takes one back, but I know she's working through the things I've just said. "I mean it. I'm sorry."

Tall grass moves with the little bit of breeze a late summer night will allow. The last thing I want is for her to be scared of me. And right now, it feels like she might hate me a little. I need her to know that I'm not going to do anything to hurt her. I shove my hands into my pockets, because what I really want to do is to feel her wrapped up in my arms again. I stopped asking myself why I couldn't seem to stop thinking about her or why it felt so easy to be around her. Instead, I decided that, after this job, I was going to find her. And now that I unintentionally have, I've already fucked it up.

I tilt my head back, closing my eyes, thinking about all of the things I want to ask and hope to hear.

"I know," she says in a whisper. I forget what she's even responding to when her fingers glide along the side of my face and rake into my hair. The unexpected touch has me exhaling and hoping like hell that I'm not imagining it.

I keep my eyes closed, basking in the way it feels to be touched by her again. "Tell me something that isn't a lie?" I say on a breath.

Her fingers fall away. "You first."

CHAPTER 8

Wyn

"I've been looking for you," he says, swaying closer. The deep current of his voice is as distracting and smooth as the warm river roaring behind him. I wanted to touch him, glide my fingers through his hair and forget why this isn't smart. Watching his eyes close like he's been craving the touch as much as I had is what has me remembering myself. I close my eyes as the smell of oak and mint mingle in the air. I shake my head. I'm smarter than this. The red fucking flags that parade ahead of this man are too blatant to ignore.

With my heart pumping, I turn away from him and move toward the distillery, ignoring the fact that he's following right behind me.

I like that he's not so quick to give up.

I glance at the movement along the riverbank. "You may want to step up here; there're alligators who feel very territorial living in that river."

He tips his chin up, eyes on me. "Can we quit it with the bullshit now?"

"Nothing bullshit about being eaten by a prehistoric reptile," I say, turning my back to him.

"Amphibian," he says. "Alligators are amphibians."

"You're very wrong. They're reptiles." I squint my eyes closed and shake my head, frustrated. "You know what? I don't care. What exactly do you want, Julian?" I ask in a huff as I shove open the sliding barn door to the distillery.

"You're not serious," his words echo as he follows me once again.

When I left Montana, I made an agreement. To return to the life I had before—it was safe for me now—but I had to forget where I've been for the past three years. I couldn't talk about it or be in contact with anyone. It's for everyone else's safety, not mine. Make up a lie, embellish the truth, whatever it would take to preserve Hideaway, Montana as the safe haven it was built to be. It had been that for me. A place for people who survived the worst, but who still need to hide and be protected. I left Montana and every person who knew me as Naomi behind, including Julian Colton.

How am I supposed to tell him to leave, when the last thing I want is to see him go? I've been trying to feel like myself again, the old me who worked hard and earned my place. But nothing has felt right, not since I've been back. Not until right now...

I look around the open room, trying to find my bearings and swallowing down how much this place makes me feel more like myself than anywhere else too. I count the barrels stacked two high, three wide, with space for more all along the right and far back walls. The workspace in the center is the most polished and professional component of all of this. A small lab that I built a long time ago, when making whiskey was the most interesting thing about me. All of it was barely touched in my absence, and ready for when I returned. My Uncle Tommy's doing, most likely. He would listen to me talk about atoms and orbitals or the basics of hybridization and bonding—even if he was bored out of his mind. And then we'd make some sort of mash or try a different flavor combination. *"Doesn't matter what you nerd out on, Wyn. Just means you're passionate about something."*

"You have a distillery," Julian says slowly, almost like he's awestruck. "Your whiskey. The flavors you bottled and made, that wasn't just a small hobby to pass the time…"

I stop to flip off the vents to cool the mash that was starting to turn over in the large steel vats and then pluck two bottles from what I bottled up earlier this week.

"It was that. Still is, really," I confess. I don't understand why I feel the need to be so forthcoming with this man.

"This is where you live? Where you're from," he concludes as I turn, practically colliding into him with how close he's standing. He plucks one of the bottles from my hands and reads the flavor profile handwritten along the ribbon waxed to the neck.

The way I'm trying to appear unaffected is blatantly ignored, like he isn't going to play these games with me. I hold my breath, not wanting to give him anything. If I do, I don't trust myself to not tell him everything. And that's too risky.

"Whatever it is you think you want from me, I'm not interested. I don't know you," I mumble through my lie, then add with a little more strength, "I barely remember you."

When his eyes meet mine again, my stomach flips.

"You're going to tell me that you don't remember me? The lines on my palms? The way you studied the curve of my hands and the length of my fingers?" He bends lower when I look away to force me to look him in the eyes again. "Does that mean you've forgotten the way you came all over them too?"

He went there. This fucker. I try not to react, but he saw my lips part. There's no mistaking the way I swallow or how my pulse quickens at a flash of memory, one I've replayed countless times in my mind, wanting to remember exactly the way he touched me and teased me.

"I haven't." His words are slow and smooth when he adds, "The way it lingered on my fingers long after I left you."

My face heats as tingles travel between my legs as if his imagination is touching me.

"My mouth is watering remembering it now," he says with a small hum.

I huff out a breath. "What do you want me to say, Julian?" My brow furrows as I think over his words. "It wasn't that for me." I tilt my head condescendingly, trying to hurt him. I *should* be scared of this man, but I'm not.

He takes a step closer, rubbing the silk bow of my blouse between his fingers. "Dr. Wynona Crowne," he whispers, like he's trying to get used to saying that name. It's annoying how good it sounds when he says it. His gaze follows down the front of my blouse, and while I'm going on far too long without a shower, I'm at least thankful I'm wearing my version of armor. The respected professor, who has her act together and isn't on the cusp of a panic attack, is far easier to play with my high-waisted trouser pants, a wrinkled white blouse, and black silk tie. It's a far departure from the jeans and fitted T-shirts I wore when I tended bar in Montana.

He tugs on the tail of my tie as he whispers, "I like this."

I swat his hand away.

"It just doesn't feel like you."

"And you think you know me well enough to know what I *feel* like?" And the second it comes out, I regret it. The innuendo and the very real possibility that he's a little bit right make my cheeks warm and lips part. *Dammit.*

His lips curve up into a knowing smile.

I lift my chin and shove down my shoulders. "You're not going to *romance* anything more out me," I say with as much confidence as I can muster.

"Romance?" He sniffs a laugh. "That was romance to you?"

"Don't talk to me like that," I bite back, more softly than I intended. I clear my throat. There isn't any space to be vulnerable with this man, so I bristle myself, take a small step back, and add some distance as I put my hands on my hips. "Call it whatever you want—romance, intimacy, manipulation…I'm not falling for it." I don't let him interrupt, asking what I want to know, even as my pulse hammers at the thought of his answer. "Tell me why you're here, and don't lie to me."

When he moves a piece of my hair out of my face, his finger brushes along my jaw, and I shamelessly sway closer. I'm touch starved and disappointing myself at a masterful rate at the way I haven't added more distance between us. This feeling I have when he's close, it's the same now as it was months ago.

He looks me in the eye when he says, "I didn't kill anyone." I feel relieved the moment I hear it. It's an assurance I need, because I, for some reason, believe him. But still, it doesn't explain why he's here.

Before I can say anything, my uncle's voice calls out from the far side of the distillery. "Wyn, you alright over there?"

I turn toward Tommy as he grabs his work gloves, taking long strides to us. My Uncle Tommy is one of the only reasons things work around here; not to mention, my place looking more like a home than a forgotten, rundown barn. He also made it his business to teach me as much as he knows about making whiskey.

My mother waltzes up behind him. "She's fine. Aren't you leaving, Mr. Colton?"

He smiles at her, and I know full well just by his body language that him leaving is more like her idea. "I actually saw a bed-and-breakfast on my way into town—"

"The Rackhouse," Tommy chimes in. "That's my place. And yeah, there's a room for you."

"I thought your business was done here?" Lu puts her hands on her hips and looks at my uncle. "Thomas, I actually *don't* think there's any room at the B&B right now."

Tommy crosses his arms and levels an annoyed look at her. "Lu, don't pretend like you aren't keeping tabs on what goes on over there."

"Quit flattering your fragile ego, Thomas," she bites back.

While there's always been rumors swirling around my family, Tommy stays out of most of them. My mother, however, is the centerfold of many.

The name Tallulah Crowne is Rumor, Tennessee lore that picks up every few years when someone either becomes a widow or gets divorced. When I was sixteen, my English teacher went on a bender and showed up to school still wasted on pinot grigio, carrying on about how Lu Crowne was the kind of good time she was missing and it was her pleasure to watch her work her *magic*—whatever that meant. That was a fun one to try navigating as a teenager, trying to understand why I should care if my mother was a lesbian like Greta Cooper called her, or if I should be more concerned about why my English teacher went from married to a widow shortly after that.

"First of all, sexuality is fluid, so you can tell Greta Cooper to go fuck herself before she starts throwing out preferences as if they're bad words. And second, your English teacher is having a hard time,

and if people would stop judging and start opening their tiny minds, maybe they would stop gossiping about the parts that aren't important," Lu said, pointing to her chest.

My mother glances at me, sizing up the situation in front of her. I know how much she hates not knowing everything. "Don't get lost out here," she says to me as she gives Julian a full-body scan, from his legs to his head and back down again. "Birdie is expecting you to bring those bottles," she says to me, seemingly unaffected as she glances at her wristwatch. "Her clients are arriving shortly."

"Don't let the door hit you on your ass on the way out," my uncle says under his breath as she leaves the way she came.

"Get off my property, Tommy," she croons from the pathway outside.

My uncle sniffs a laugh to himself. His thick gray 'stache tilts as he adds, "She's the fucking worst." When his eyes meet mine, he says, "Sorry, Wyn."

Tommy and my mom have been like this my entire life. Hot oil and cold water. He's never been married, taught me more about the things I've grown to love than anyone else—aside from Birdie. He's one of the toughest men I've ever met, and he does it without trying to posture or prove something. If I could've picked my dad, he would've been my choice. But that's not how it works.

My uncle looks at Julian with his calming smile. "Plenty of vacancy," he says in a not so quiet whisper. "Wyn, I don't know what's going on between the two of you, but if you'd rather he leaves, then I'll rescind the invitation." I can feel Julian's attention on me, but I ignore it.

"I don't care," I lie.

With a nod, he gives me a kind smile before looking more

seriously at Julian. "Whatever you're wrapped up in with Birdie and Lu, keep her out of it," he says, pointing at me. "Wyn doesn't need to be anywhere near the viper's bullshit."

If Tommy only knew the things I've been wrapped up in, the things I've seen and survived…

"Fuck yourself, Thomas," my mother singsongs from outside, where she was obviously lingering and eavesdropping.

"My favorite pastime, Tallulah!" he shouts after her, eyes rolling as they come back to Julian. "You can follow me over there now, if you'd like."

And instead of saying anything more, Julian gives him a respectful nod. Then his eyes land back on me as he steps closer. "Looks like you'll know where to find me." His hand wraps around my bent elbow as he quietly adds under his breath, "We are nowhere near done here."

Swallowing roughly, I feel out of sorts as I watch him walk away.

I'm still wearing the same clothes from a day ago, I was drugged, I'm almost certain there was a dead body at my family's bar, Birdie and my mother are very much involved, and the man who cleaned it up is also the same one I never thought I'd see again.

I rub along the leather cuff fastened to my wrist. *Breathe.* Out of all those things, the one I hate the least is him.

The Whispering Fool has always been in its own class. If you were to throw together the chaos of a roadhouse like the Swayze movie from the '80s, with a small-town watering hole, a college stop at the end of a crawl, along with the music and hype of a cowboy bar you'd find on Broadway in the heart of Nashville, then you'd come close to describing this place. It may have started as a stain on the sweet Southern vibes of a town like Rumor, but it's evolved into something so much more. When people mention Tennessee, they know of three places: Nashville, Memphis, and The Whispering Fool.

I glance up at Ralph, The Fool's talisman, the head of an alligator that lived along the river surrounding this place. Birdie used to say he looked out for us and died of old age or maybe indigestion. He's been decorated over the years; sometimes, it's a seasonal string of Christmas lights, or a top hat for the New Year, but he always has bras hanging from his half-open mouth.

I've spent more energy avoiding this place than I should have. I hate how much I let other people's opinions shape so much of me. But the truth is, this bar was, and is, my family in a nutshell. It's almost funny that now, in my mid-thirties, after so much time fighting for space from it and my family, I live across the river, within walking distance.

"Ladies and gentlemen," Jo shouts over the microphone, her ass perched on the trapeze-style shot swing that's gliding through the air above the crowd hooting and hollering below. "Shot swing shots are seeerrrved!" she croons as she leans back. Her fishnet stockings and tight black shorts leave barely anything covered to the gawking crowd beneath. Long red hair flows behind her as she scoots back on the swing's bar, dropping her body from sitting to hanging upside down. "Show me those pretty throats, ladies, and open for your goddess."

Anyone who would see this for the first time would bark out laughing at the audacity. But they listen. More than two large groups of women disperse throughout the crowd, opening wide, tongues out, as my baby sister pours out her premade shot swing special of the night all over them.

I skirt around behind the bar and off to the side, waiting for the chaos to subside so I can make my way up the spiral staircase and toward Birdie's lounge. Her sign is lit, which means she isn't seeing anyone just yet.

As soon as Jo sits back up on her swing, and at least half the crowd is doused, "I Touch Myself" kicks in over the speakers. I count about eight motorcycle club members and a smaller crowd of men, who look like they're on a longer-than-planned after-work happy hour, shift their attention to my other beautiful sister. It's impossible not to smile when Stevie's smiling. She has that way about her—charming and disarming. Her dark hair is pulled back in a bubble braid that looks like a faux-hawk snaking halfway down her back. She stomps her boots in time with the beat and is instantly flanked by two young bartenders. When I take a look around the sea of people, enraptured by the spectacle, I spot Gina and Gail standing on each side of the double doors, just waiting to haul some assholes out. They are, and always have been, late-night crowd control.

There are plenty of feminist practices that my mother and grandmother lean into, and Birdie's firm about keeping this a women-owned and women-run establishment. There would never be a man behind that bar pouring drinks, at least not while the name Crowne is on the deed.

"Professor Crowne," someone shouts from behind me. It would be just my luck to be recognized by a student while being back here for the first time. *Shit.*

Slowly, I turn around, and I can't help the relief that follows at who I see. A laugh bubbles from my lips as I hold my hand to my chest. "Dr. Reed Andrews." I glance behind him, curious about who he might be with, but the only people around him are a few young college students and a trio of guys working up the nerve to talk with them. "What are you doing here?"

"Might ask the same of you. You never seem to wander into this place," he says, leaning closer and shouting over the crowd. Looking at the two bottles of whiskey I'm holding first, and then at me, he quirks an eyebrow.

At almost exactly the same time, Stevie whistles loudly, and the large gold bell next to the vintage pinup girl poster sounds off. "Some fool ordered a Dealer's Choice. And since there are multiple Crowne women in the house tonight, you get your pick of who serves it."

Jesus Christ.

"Dr. Crowne..." Reed teases as he watches me shift around to avoid being spotted. "What are you doing behind that bar?"

If he only knew how much I preferred it to being in front of a class. But I shake my head. "Just an errand for Birdie," I say in response, trying to keep it light. "She knows you're here? She mentioned wanting to have you again for dinner." I try turning my body so that Reed is blocking me now. If Stevie spots me, she'll make a spectacle.

He smiles. "I'm going to get going."

"What are you doing here anyway?" I cover my mouth quickly. "I'm sorry, that's none of my business."

He shakes his head. "Had a drink with a friend." Glancing around at the crowd, like he's looking for someone, he holds up his hand to wave as he moves toward the doors. Shouting, he adds, "Don't get into too much trouble." He winces the moment my sister starts shouting from her perch on the bar.

I give him a wave and a smile as Stevie yells out, "Rub those nips and get ready to feed me some tips, boys!!!" I move from behind the bar and up the spiral staircase toward the second-floor balcony. Birdie does her tarot and palm reading up here. Sometimes she'll do these things at the house or join her garden club. When I reach the top, it's the perfect view to watch as Stevie kneels on the bar top as a man tilts his head back, face up in front of her. She pours a shot of tequila down his throat, and then leans over him with a lime wedge from her mouth, passing it from between her teeth to his waiting lips and lingering there with a more than heated kiss.

Chuckling to myself, I shove through the small crowd waiting outside the drawn curtain to find my grandmother enjoying music of her own pouring through a small speaker while shuffling a deck of tarot, a Philly blunt hanging out of her mouth.

I raise my eyebrows at her. "Getting warmed up?"

"Stop pretending you're a prude, Wyn." She holds the joint out to me, but I pass. "It's from my garden," she adds. "And *we* need to have a conversation."

"Your bottles," I say as I place them in front of her. "And yes, we do."

"Good. Now, cut the deck," she says, putting her tarot in a stack in front of me, as if I'm here for this right now.

"Nope." I cross my arms. "Tell me what I walked into last night."

With a sigh, she leans back, placing the blunt into a small jar next to her and covering it. Seconds later, a small flame encapsulates the roach and what's left is just a jar filled with white smoke. A party trick she's done for plenty of people over the years, and as much as I'm trying to remain stoic, my grandmother is my person. The steady. The magic of this family. "You first," she says as her bracelets jingle down her arms and fingers intertwine at her lips.

Birdie knows there's more to the assumptions that something awful happened to me.

"The place where I was before I came back..." I shake my head and take a breath. "I knew him. Well...I didn't know him," I correct. "Met him." Clearing my throat, I keep going. "Julian knew me as someone else. And as it turns out, we're both liars, and now he's here. But the mess I saw him cleaning up before he stabbed me with a needle is a little more concerning, don't you think?"

"Dramatic," she interrupts under her breath with an accompanying eye roll.

"Birdie, yes. A dead body is a little more important than some guy."

"Is it?" she asks. "Wyn, there's so much you don't know. And I'm not going to sit here and have you assume that I'm the only one who's keeping the truth close." She has a point. "Your mother needs to be involved in this conversation. But I want you to know that there is no unhearing it, so please think about whether you really want to know about the things that happen around here, or if you prefer, you can simply chalk it up to serendipitous timing in seeing Julian again."

I open my mouth to respond, but I'm not sure I know what I want just yet. I keep thinking about what Julian said to me, that *we're nowhere near done,* and I hate—or maybe love—knowing he's right.

A buzzer goes off, signaling her night of fortunes and fun are primed and ready. *Holy hell*, my mother was extreme and over the top, but it was very evident where she got that streak.

Changing the subject back to the reason for coming here,

I say, "This one would meet the three-and-a-half-year standard for being a straight Tennessee whiskey—" My words halt, I didn't think about what that timing would have meant when I chose this. Birdie wanted to know what happened to me, and this was the last blend I made before I was taken. The barrel it came from was marked with the date, and unknowingly, I found myself on a freight train three days later, heading up the coastline and into the grips of a monster. *Breathe. You're not there anymore.* I nod toward the bottle and run my fingers along the wax seal. The smooth texture keeps me present. "It's a really smooth sip. Even better than I would've expected."

"I already know it's good, my darling. Maybe you'll finally believe it's good enough to focus on doing it full time?" she asks. The question settles in my gut. I know all of the details of how to make it, but the practicalities of just starting a business like that seems overwhelming and impractical.

I take a steadying breath when I say, "We've been over this; I have a doctorate. And a job that I worked really hard to make sure I could have—"

She cuts me off, "Yes, I know all about that word that's so special to academics—*tenure*. As if you shouldn't ever do something else just because you worked your ass off to achieve something great." She shakes her head with a huff. Birdie rarely comes right out and says things like that. She usually figures out a way to tell her opinion as if it's mine. "I'm in a shit mood tonight." Flicking out her wrists, she flips a card over so it faces me.

"It's alright," I say with a warm smile. "Want to tell me why?"

With another eye roll as her answer, she shifts and says, "It's Five of Cups, right?"

I give her a smirk and nod. "Negative focus, I knew it." She flips it back into her deck and starts shuffling.

It's the one card in the tarot that feels the most ominous at first glance. It's riddled with negativity, but it's the card that reminds the person who turned it to hunt for the silver lining.

"Ignore me, Wyn," she says as she shakes her head and shuffles. Her bracelets clang as she does it. I love that sound. "Send in the short blondie wearing the blue dress," she adds.

I move around to her side of the small coffee table and kiss her on the cheek. Rosemary and citrus mingle in the air and on her skin. "Love you."

Her fingertips brush down my forehead and over my eyelids as I shut them. A simple gesture she's done to my sisters and me since we were little. I take a deep breath, grateful for moments with her.

There have been times in my life when I knew whatever I chose next would change the direction I was heading, like a forked path that I was forced to go left or right. I know, as I walk down the spiral stairs and tell the blond in the blue dress to go talk to my grandmother, that I want to know all of it. Everything I've missed about being a Crowne. The things I've been too jaded to embrace.

I'm done with being in the dark.

CHAPTER 9

Julian

"HOW'D YOU SLEEP?" TOMMY ASKS as I come down the back stairs and into the kitchen. I'm not used to anyone asking.

"Great," I lie. I was exhausted, but it took me forever to fall asleep. I kept running through the details of last night's dinner, the side conversations happening without words, and how the hell I'm going to convince Wyn that she can trust me. I watched her sleep for so damn long in that solarium, anxious about what would happen when she woke up. *Fuck, this situation is complicated.*

Moving around the stark white kitchen, it's bright and a far better morning than waking up tied to a chair. Its stainless-steel appliances reflect the morning light coming in from the windows. It's polar opposite from Birdie's place. "May I?" I point toward the coffee pot. He gives me a nod.

The Rackhouse Bed-and-Breakfast is as simple as it comes. Upon first look, I might guess the owner is meticulous, maybe leaning into clean and modern, but after walking through the space, it's more like Tommy just didn't have a plan for it. Most of the decor was white or navy, the fixtures seemed basic too, but the pictures that hung throughout were incredible. Old posters that had been repurposed and mimicked classically recognized art. I noted a few modern pieces in the stairwell and an intricately painted mural on the ceiling of the library when I had a look around last night.

"Uncle Tommy," Nash yells as he comes rushing in from the side door. "Oh, hi, Julian." He stops and waves, extending a fist for me to bump. Behind him is Stevie, who's carrying a dino backpack and two grocery bags.

"Thanks so much," Stevie says as she swipes away on her phone with her free hand. She does a double take at the cup I'm holding. "No, no, no." Pulling a carafe of iced coffee from the refrigerator, she plops it in front of me. "If he made that, I wouldn't drink it."

"I heard that," Tommy says, watching as Nash unloads his backpack with dinosaur figurines.

"Good," she says, sending him a playful yet pointed look, making Tommy chuckle. "I made the cold brew. It's safe and doesn't taste like burnt paper. It's good, I promise."

"Not much of an iced coffee guy," I tell her as I take a sip out of the hot mug. I try not to cringe at the way it does, in fact, taste like something burned at the bottom of the pot.

She sucks in a dramatic breath. "Do not let Wyn hear you say that; otherwise, whatever it is that's going on between the two of you will be done," she says sarcastically as she cracks a tray of ice and pours out a cup of her cold brew coffee.

"How does she take it?" I clear my throat before I add, "Wyn, and her iced coffee? What's her preference?"

A big, wide smile takes over her face, and she lifts a hand to cover it. "I feel like I'm about to play an integral role in you sweeping her off her feet here." She claps like this is exciting information, the level of excitement a bit aggressive for this early in the morning. "Okay, most of the time, she'll do a splash of cream and three sugars. Sometimes four sugars. We're Southern girls, we like to really crunch our sugar when we're drinking. Same goes for sweet tea," she says with a wink. "Anyway, if you can't handle the cold brew and happen to wander into town, you might want to try Moonie's. It's one of our favorite spots."

"Thank you." I smile.

"There, right there, the interested questions and the smile." She points and squints her eyes. "You're charming. You went ahead and hopefully charmed her pants off." She leans closer and whispers, "Don't stop, keep going. She deserves a good one."

I'm not sure I'd be considered a good one if Wyn's sister knew what I was brought here to do, but in the short time I've been folded into this family, it's felt good. I like to sit back and watch, observe people. It's always challenging to get too close. The few friends I have know about my hand in my family cleaning business, the favors that are given and taken as payment, and the more public life I lead when designing jewelry. But I haven't been to massive family dinners or folded into the nuances of people's relationships like this. I'd be lying if I said I didn't like the idea of being a part of it. I understood why Wyn came back here when she could, I would have missed this too.

"Is that Nash I hear," another voice says from behind us.

Nash runs toward him and yells out, "Sonny!"

When I turn, it's the detective from dinner.

Fuck, I'm usually much better at knowing my surroundings.

Shoving through the double doors from the screened-in porch, Jameson takes off his aviators and crouches down with arms open to greet Nash.

If cops had poster boys, my guess is *that* guy was one of them about twenty years ago.

He greets me with a handshake. "Julian," he says, nodding once. "Tommy said you were staying here too. Didn't realize you were sticking around. Thought you might have just been passing through."

"I'll be here for a while," I say, glancing at Stevie, who's smiling at me like she knows something I don't. The truth is, I *should* be on my way out of here. The minute I step foot outside, I should get in that truck, call in a flight plan, and get the fuck out of this town. Complicated usually means dangerous with the life I've led. But there isn't anything waiting for me back at home. I have friends in numerous places and work that I can do almost anywhere. And I had planned to find *her*. I've been alone for a long time, even when my dad was still alive. I've been gliding through life, enjoying what my talent allowed for me, but from the moment I left her, I wanted to find the woman who made me feel something. The one I couldn't stop thinking about. And now I have. Yeah, I'm not fucking going anywhere.

"Where's Theo?" Jameson asks.

She tips her head back to the ceiling as she mumbles, "It's too early for this shit." When she looks at him, she says, "I don't know; I'm not his keeper."

"Just his wife, though, right?" he bites back, trying to speak more quietly when I look at him. "I was just asking where he might be today and why you're dropping Nash here."

She smiles, like what she's about to say is going to be sweet. "Theo was tied up," she smirks. "And I have a podcast I need to record, but you already knew that. I am, after all, practically doing your job for you."

I sniff out a laugh that has both of them looking at me. Leaning against the counter, I cross my feet at my ankles. I glance at Jameson, and while he's not the kind of guy people would want to piss off, I'm finding their exchange a bit entertaining and can't help myself when I add, "Whether or not you're doing other people's jobs for them, you're pretty damn good at yours and hunting down information. Entertaining while sharing it, too."

She's smiling from what I've said when she looks back at Jameson. "When's the last time someone said you were pretty damn good at your job?"

He runs his hand along the back of his neck, trying his damndest to keep himself in check. "I'm a homicide detective, not a shit stirrer, so you're not doing my—"

She crosses her arms. "Do you have any idea what's going on in the department you're a part of?"

He crosses his arms, and under his breath, mutters, "Here we go again."

Stevie doesn't stop though. "I know you were MIA for a long-ass time, but seriously, Jameson? Sexual assault allegations aren't being followed through on, there are *dozens* of missing persons, and those are just the violent-like crimes alone..."

"I don't need to hear this right now. I've got a case that won't close, a serial..." He pauses and takes a breath. "I've got a lot on my plate. And to top it off, a missing deputy."

"Oh, so a missing cop is more important than—"

"I'm not in charge, Stevie. I have to do what I'm told. I know it's a novel idea to you. Deputy Billings has a helluva reputation, too, and I wouldn't mind focusing my attention where it should be, but like I said, I need to follow what my boss asks of me. So, I'm in town..."

I focus on what Nash is doing as soon as I hear about the missing cop. "Dinosaur fan?" I ask him as he starts lining up a parade of figurines.

The chances that the body I cleaned up is exactly who the detective and the entirety of the Rumor County Sheriff's Department is looking for has me feeling nauseous. *Fuck my life.*

Nash empties the rest of his bag and gives me the side-eye. "I *said*, the Quetzalcoatlus is a pterosaur, which means it's not really a dinosaur."

Focusing back on him, I ask, "I thought they were all dinosaurs."

"Technically, dinosaurs can't fly, so anything that flew during the Jurassic or Cretaceous period were just flying reptiles," he says as he moves the pterosaur in a flying motion above the line of herbivores.

"I have a few more we can paint later, Nash," Tommy says from his spot at the kitchen table. Nash's eyes light up when he looks at Tommy, who starts helping him. And though Tommy is his great-uncle I remember looking at my dad like that as a kid—he always made time for me. "Auntie Wyn said that you have some books in your library about dinosaurs. I need to show my mom and dad that I'm right about pterosaurs."

"You could look it up on my phone and show them," Tommy offers, but Nash is already shaking his head.

"Not as reliable. A book would be better," he says, and I can't help but crack a smile.

I glance over to Stevie, who just swatted Jameson's hand away from pointing to a spot on her neck, quieting the back-and-forth between them.

When she notices my attention, she says, "Yeah, I know. Kid blows my mind regularly." She looks back to Jameson and adds, "You're welcome to spend time with him any time you want to grace us all with your presence—"

"I thought you were running late," Tommy says to her. "Go. I got him." Waving her off, he looks at Nash. "Want to help me in the workshop? I've got a project I need to finish and could use another set of hands."

She drums her fingers on the counter and says, "Alright, Nashie baby, I'm off to make the world a greater place."

Jameson makes a sound that has her casually flipping him off as she rushes out the door after kissing Nash's head.

"Julian, want to join us?" Tommy asks. "There're some tools you might know a little something about. Belonged to an old friend, hasn't been here in a while, but you might put them to use. If you're going to be here a bit longer, that is."

I pour out the rest of the coffee in the sink and place the ceramic mug into the dishwasher. "I'll be here a bit longer," I say to him. "I'm going to stop in town, see if I can get my hands on some materials." My inbox and missed calls from galleries had been piling up for a while, but I haven't felt inspired to do anything original for a long while now. My creative well dried up when my father passed, then ten months ago, I walked into a bar and met a woman. And it woke up something in me again. I've been so focused on finishing out the favors owed from the cleaning business that making something beautiful has been the last thing on my mind. And then I woke up this morning and thought maybe it's time to shift focus again. The bed-and-breakfast isn't far from the main strip of what's considered downtown Rumor. Tommy advised that I take a walk instead of drive. The way my shirt is sticking to me as sweat slicks my back, I know that from now on, late August in Tennessee means that I drive.

I glance at the dark-green train car and the gold lettering along its side: Moonie's Coffee and Pies. The bell on the door chimes loudly, and an older man calls out, "Take any seat that's open." When I move to a seat at the end of the counter, he does a double take. "You look just like your father," the man with the gray handlebar mustache says from behind the counter. His hunter-green polo shirt with the popped collar and Moonie's scrolled across the left side matches the small space.

I look around me, because I know he can't be talking to me. My father had clearly been to Rumor a few times, but he never would've lingered long enough to be seen somewhere like this. He's probably rolling in whatever afterlife he's in right now, watching me stick around for over twenty-four hours after a job. I run my hand along the back of my neck and tug at the length at my nape. "I don't think you're talking about me or my father, friend."

"Sure I am. Last name is Colton, right?" He flips over a coffee mug in front of me and holds up the freshly brewed pot.

I pause, before giving him a nod, signaling for him to pour. The name *Mickey* is embroidered in cursive along the left chest of his shirt.

"Oh, I never forget a name or a face." He nods slowly. "Yeah, your dad was an early morning customer. I was never sure if he was coming or going. Took him a while to say much, but he mentioned you a few times. A son who had more talent on his worst day than he ever had on his prolific ones," he says, pointing at me. "I always assumed he was here for someone instead of something," he says, shrugging a shoulder. "But rumors stayed mostly quiet about him."

What the fuck, Dad?

Mickey doesn't need to know the real reason my father was

here, but it was always for someone. Specifically, someone who was killed, and whomever did it needed him to clean it up. I never knew the origin of most of my father's or grandfather's colleagues; how they determined the acceptability of lines being crossed. At the core of it, our family chose the idea that the lines of right and wrong would always be deeply gray and widely blurred. It was how the jewelry business began—my grandfather would sometimes do a favor for a favor, but often he'd need to be paid for his "expertise." Fine jewelry became his currency. And the Colton men learned how to flip what we were given into something different, sell it, and live comfortably.

A few people have taken seats around the small counter as the man comes back, interrupting my thoughts. "People don't come to Rumor for very long. They tend to either grow up here and stay or simply pass through. And once they leave, rarely do they come back."

A bald man with round eyeglasses chimes in. "Except the oldest Crowne girl. She came back, alright."

Wyn.

"Where was she?" I ask, despite knowing *exactly* where she was.

"Dead, apparently," Mickey answers.

I can't help but laugh at that. I take a sip of my coffee, but when I look back up around the counter at each of them, their faces are dead serious. It tracks with her being in Hideaway.

Mickey shakes his head and runs his fingers through his handlebar 'stache. "That's not an exaggeration. Her family didn't believe she was gone for good, but the town held a vigil for her along the green. She was a missing person, and then most assumed she was dead. That all happened over the course of a year, maybe. And then two more after that, she shows up…not dead."

Pieces are starting to make more sense, but with it comes a whole new host of questions. I needed to see Wyn, but I really needed answers from Birdie. She had been expecting my father, and truthfully, I needed to understand how often he was coming out this way. Repeat jobs were one thing, but for someone to recognize me because of my father is a whole other story.

A small round cake covered in strawberries and a thick cream slides in front of me.

"That right there is an original Moonie's pie," a woman with a slicked-back black bun says just before she stalks through the swinging doors to the kitchen. *Luna* is embroidered along her shirt.

"Thank you, ma'am. Looks delicious," I say, digging right into it.

"Not to be confused with the disaster that is known as the Moon Pie. Heathens stole our thunder..." she calls out. "It's not even a pie; it's a glorified s'more."

The bald man at the end of the bar mumbles, "Here we go..." He takes a sip of his coffee. "Y'all don't need to shit all over a Tennessee legacy. They didn't steal nothin'—"

"Fuck off, Fred," the other two say in unison.

They remind me of the banter at the bar in Montana, and that has me thinking about the woman who smiled to herself every time her friends volleyed their conversations.

"I'm just telling my new friend..." Luna pops her head out from the kitchen. She leaves an opening for me to add my name, and before I think better of it, I say, "Julian."

"Julian has never been here, which means the man deserves a little bit of an education."

Mickey's mustache shakes in amusement before he says,

"My sister is passionate about our legacy. I'm sure you can understand that."

"I know a few things about family legacies," I say before taking another bite.

Mickey tosses a dish towel over his shoulder and says, "Family legacies are important. My family had its ugly bits, but I don't regret a single day standing by my sister and running this place with her."

"You can't still be stuck on Moon Pies now, can you?" A woman with a watered-down New York accent sidles up to the counter next to me. "You're new." She crosses her hands on the counter and adds, "I'll have a mimosa, Mickey." Holding up her fingers, she pinches them together. "Just a splash of juice in this one."

The mustache tips up to one side as he pulls out the same ceramic mug that I have and pours her a cup of regular coffee. "Cora," he says. "Regular or decaf?"

I run my hand along my mouth, stifling the smile.

"Prosecco or Moscato," she breathes out. "Either will do."

A moment later, a small dish of individually packed creamers slides in front of her, along with sugar packets. "Cora Billings, we're fresh out of mimosas."

"Bloody Mary?" she asks hopefully, and the lightheartedness of it is entertaining.

Mickey crosses his arms over his chest and shakes his head.

"Fucking small towns," she mumbles under her breath, and a part of me can absolutely agree. "I hope you're not planning to stay in this one too long. The brunch beverage selection is bullshit."

"Cora, are you drunk?"

She holds her hand up in front of her mouth, opening her eyes wide. "Drunk brunch is the only way to brunch."

I turn to her and say, "What was your name again?" I'm almost positive Mickey said her last name is Billings. *The "missing" cop's wife.*

As if on cue, she hiccups, then smiles at me. "I think it can be whatever you'd like for it to be, handsome."

Jesus Christ.

"Do you want me to call Stan?" Mickey asks.

"Stan will not be coming to the phone right now. Thank goddesses." She shifts closer to me. Yellow splotches peek out from beneath her right eye, like a bruise is finishing healing. "Plus, my new friend was just about to tell me his name, weren't you?"

I shift on my stool and flash her a smile. "Julian Colton," I tell her.

She pats my forearm. I can imagine there's more to this woman's story. The fading bruises and mid-day inebriation could all have innocent origins, but I know now that the body I erased, the reason Birdie and Lu Crowne brought me here, was not just a cop, but also this woman's husband.

"Well, Julian Colton, I'm Cora Billings. Now tell me, what brings you to our small town?"

CHAPTER 10

Wyn

"One of these days, I'm going to convince my big sister to join me on an episode of The Distilled Truth.*"* Stevie's voice echoes loudly over my speaker. I smile, knowing my answer to her question: Not a chance.

I shift my weight back and forth in front of the notes projected on the front wall. I need to make sure I didn't miss anything on these starting equations—my graduate students will be all over me if I do. Taking a step back, I lean on my desk as I suck down what's left of my coffee. I used to always be eager to get here early, tackle my own research before lesson plans when the campus was still quiet, but I can't focus.

I've forgotten what it's like dealing with eager students in organics. I want it to feel the same as before. I want the adrenaline to kick in. I want to feel that rush of admiration students had when they realized the work they were capable of making happen. That excitement when a theory can be experimented and proven like the curriculum plans. Grants and published articles used to have my pulse racing in the best way, but now…

I huff out a breath, frustrated. Feeling like this isn't part of the plan. This should be the easy and natural part of returning to Rumor. Everything in this place is the same as *before*. Everything except me.

Stevie's voice shoves my internal spiral away. *"The needle isn't moving on any of the missing persons cases in my neck of the woods, either. I walk through the Rumor County sheriff's station and see another person listed, and let's not get me started on the number of sexual assault complaints that do not line up with arrests or warrants in this part of the county."* My sister has never been one to let dust settle. The moment something doesn't work in her favor, she's ready to dive in with tweezers and figure out what went wrong.

Stevie's managed to merge two things that would make people around here, and just about everywhere in this country, listen to what she had to say—crime and whiskey. And while it started as a passion project, a way to siphon questions that she wanted answered, and a way to deal with losing me, she's built a helluva following for herself. A business that could keep her from having to do shifts at the bar if she wanted. But she was in her element there, a focal point, and of all the things that my sister was good at, being the center of attention is the winner. She's like our mom in that way.

She doesn't know I listened, or that I had made it a big deal in the small place I called home for a while. But she'll probably never really understand what hearing her weekly meant to me, especially during a time when I thought I'd never hear or see anyone from my family again.

I pluck an earbud out of my ear and glance toward the door. It's early, and the weekend, but now that the sun is up, there's finally some movement around campus. I slept like garbage. I tried to numb my emotions the moment my body hit the mattress, but Julian made a home at the forefront of my mind. I wanted to march over to The Rackhouse, knock on his bedroom door, and finish what we started. He said we're nowhere near done, and I agree. I want the answers that'll make me feel like someone knows me. The way I felt when I saw him again, how it felt to have him near me… I shouldn't, but I want more.

And since I'm not interested in lying to myself, despite everyone else, I know that if I went there, I wouldn't have left without feeling his hands on me again. So I came here instead. I tossed and turned for too long and watched the shadows of my ceiling fan move like a metronome, until I did what I always have done—found distraction in my work.

"Thought I might find you here," a calming voice says from the doorway to my office. I know the tone before I turn to see Reed leaning against the frame. One hand slung into the pocket of his navy chinos as he eats an apple. The smile he flashes at me used to feel flirtatious but now seems more concerned than anything else. "How long have you been working?"

I glance at the clock on my laptop—8:30 a.m. So, for more than three hours now, but I decide on saying, "A little while."

"I tried to get into my office, but I left my key card somewhere and can't seem to find it," he says, looking behind him at the empty hall from where he just came. "If you're not in the middle of something, want to duck out and have some breakfast with me?"

I exhale, more loudly than I intended. The last thing I want to do is unload any of my feelings on Reed, but maybe some food and a break wouldn't be the worst idea.

He shifts, crossing his hands over his chest. "Are you doing okay? Feels like something is off—at the cocktail party, you looked like you were about to have a panic attack. And when I just came in here now, you looked about ready to throw your laptop clean across the room." He smiles, asking more gently, "Or am I misreading things?"

Misreading things…

"I'm sorry." I pinch my eyebrows and quickly shake my head. "What did—"

"Let me buy you a coffee and a bagel, maybe some grits too."

I'm overthinking everything. I nod. "Coffee sounds like a good idea." I slide my laptop into my bag, flash him a smile, and slip my shoes back on. "I'm meeting my sisters in Rumor a bit later this morning. Feel like hitting Moonie's with me?" I ask with a more genuine smile.

"If it ends in a cup of coffee and some time with you, then yeah, I'm game."

Rumor might be considered a small town in Tennessee, but I always thought it felt so much larger than the population or the size of its downtown footprint.

The trees that line our version of Main Street are so old that their roots make for a bumpy ride as we park along it. I throw on the parking brake and glance down at the cemetery that connects to the church at the bottom of the hill. The county sheriff's department is opposite of the direction we're walking, running along the far end of the green. While I'll be the first to admit that my town isn't quaint and cute by most small-town standards, it's always felt like it has a big personality.

A few things feel like traditions here—a farmers market on Saturdays, the drive-thru in the winter, and Rumor's garden club that's usually held on Birdie's property, despite most having no problem bad-mouthing my family whenever the mood strikes. There isn't a cute coffee shop with trendy drinks either. We have Moonie's, an old train car that crashed off the tracks during prohibition, and nobody had bothered clearing. It was an old, repeated story about the train that ran through this part of the state, the only one that brought booze in and out without consequence. Until someone caught wind, tried to steal what was inside, and it ended up derailed and burning.

"I'm just brewing another pot now," Mickey says as Reed and I step inside Moonie's, taking a seat at the tightly packed counter. He always looks like he's smiling with the way he tips up the edges of his thick mustache. "Give me two minutes, and I'll bring you both a cup."

"Mind if I ask you something?" Reed questions once we've both settled into our seats.

I take a look at the small printout of today's specials, and my mouth waters at the sight of their savory Moonie Pie—short ribs and grits quiche. "Depends," I answer him mindlessly.

He laughs, like I'm joking. "Alright. Then maybe I can start small and then see where that takes me."

I smile as Mickey pours out two cups of coffee in front of us, seemingly not listening, but I know this town far too well to know that he's clocking every word.

"What was it like?" Reed rushes out.

My throat runs dry. "I'm not sure what you—"

"Transitioning," he clarifies. And still, it takes me a beat to wade through my own trauma to hear what he's really asking.

His eyebrows raise as if I should know what he means. "From associate to professor..."

My shoulders sag on an exhale, and the steel rod that held my posture feels like it's giving way for me to breathe.

"To be inside this department without really caring what others think." He leans closer, and I let the question settle. There's something about his tone that feels condescending.

"What do you mean?" I ask.

"You came back, after deciding you needed some time to reflect, and plenty of people have things to say about it."

It's the only explanation I was willing to share when I returned to town, yet hearing him say it back—*time to reflect*—he's making it seem like our colleagues believe I went on a self-discovery trip.

"I'm fucking this up," he says with his boyish smile.

I give him a reassuring smile and touch his forearm. "You're not. It's okay."

"All I'm saying is…I'm impressed. You were gone, then came back from—from, wherever you went, and now you're jumping right back in as if no time has passed at all."

I know the rumors about what happened to me are all over the map—from dead to eloping with a stranger. I told Reed, along with most people at the university, that I'd needed time away and that the rest was personal. None of it even came close to the truth, and I didn't want to add another lie to the mix, so I kept it vague.

My phone buzzes inside my bag, and when I pull it out, seeing it's from a number I don't recognize, my nerves kick in.

UNKNOWN:

Are you on a date?

I glance up and look to my left, only to see a few folks focused on their breakfasts. When I look right and past Reed, I find hazel eyes locked on me from the other end of the counter.

Julian. He swipes at his screen, and my phone buzzes again. *How did I not notice him when we came in?*

WYN:

Sorry, wrong number.

I try biting back a smirk after I send it, feeling relieved that it's him and that he's still here. He wasn't lying when he said we weren't done…

"Last semester, there had been a nasty accusation, and it's been an ongoing issue," Reed says.

I haven't been listening, so instead of asking him to repeat himself, I just nod and add, "That all sounds fairly disruptive." I try to *not* look at the end of the counter and focus on whatever it is Reed is going on about.

"That's exactly what it's been," he says, just before holding up his hand for something from Mickey.

My phone vibrates in my hand again.

UNKNOWN:

I know you just saw me, Crowne. Let's not play pretend. Unless you're into that...

I swallow the flood of emotions that hits me all at once. That fucking flutter in my chest—and I know it's excitement at seeing him unexpectedly, and the stubborn part of me wants to stifle down and ignore it on principle. My cheeks warm at him using my last name like that, while my alarm bells sound off at the nagging reality of what he's capable of.

"Would you like anything else?" Mickey asks.

But before I can even answer, from the other side of the counter, Julian calls out, "I'll take a coffee to go, Mickey." He stands to his full height, walking towards the door, and us. I slightly shift away from Reed as he continues talking, not having caught on to any of what my attention has shifted to. There was a time when I read into every word the young teaching assistant said to me, but right now, I only catch every few.

"All I'm saying is, I couldn't find you." Reed clears his throat. "And then you didn't come back. I was afraid that you were going to think…"

I take one last look at Julian, who's standing next to me as he pulls cash from his back pocket. It's impossible I ignore the way he smells like oak and mint or how impossibly tall he seems as I sit low on a stool next to him.

"We're okay," I tell Reed, trying to pay attention to the man I came here with and not the one stealing my focus. "Hey, Mickey, any chance I can get some slices of pie to go?" I ask, leaning forward. I need something sweet, and even more so now, I need this breakfast to end and go talk with my sisters.

"Sure thing, Wyn. What kind?"

I wave in front of me. "Surprise me."

"Wyn," Reed says, a little more quietly when he realizes who else is listening.

Like he just remembered something, Mickey snaps his fingers. "You know," he says to Julian, looking at me briefly as he slices into the oversized pie. "If you haven't gone yet, The Whispering Fool is a spot where you might find some faces who'll remember your father."

I'm stuck staring and instantly curious that Julian would have talked about his personal life with Mickey Moonie over coffee.

Mickey tilts his head toward me. "Birdie Crowne met him here a couple of times. They were close." His mustache tilts in a friendly half smile, completely oblivious that we already know each other, that Julian is well aware of who my grandmother is. "Wyn here is her granddaughter."

When Julian's focus shifts from Mickey to me, I feel it fucking everywhere.

"That's really helpful," he says in a measured tone. "Where did you say The Whispering Fool was again? I'll have to stop by."

CHAPTER 11

Wyn

"There's no way anything is going to survive out here," I mumble to myself.

Water siphons through the hose and the makeshift irrigation system at a glacial pace. It was an awful idea to take on a garden project at the end of the summer. And now, looking around at the mess of overgrown grass and weeds, I second-guess my plan of trying to build this all on my own. I thought this was brilliant. Tackle the outside once the inside had been renovated. Tommy runs the B&B, but he's a carpenter by trade, so all of the things that needed to be done to turn this place into my own were done in record time. The garden, though, has always been something I wanted to do on my own. I thought it would be cathartic, give me a sense of purpose in the summer months when life is usually slower and quieter, but all I can hear right now is the suctioning sound of water busting through rubber and midafternoon insects berating me for being really fucking bad at this.

Don't cry. It's just dirt and water. I blink back the ridiculousness of my emotions and blow out a breath. Maybe a meltdown in a pathetic-looking garden is on par for the kind of week I'm having.

"Has Birdie seen this?" Jo calls out from the double doors off the back of my studio. I whip my head around as she pulls the sunglasses perched on her head back down over her eyes and surveys my yard. "This looks worse than before… somehow."

I bark out a laugh and wipe away the tear that somehow escaped. Jo isn't one to gloss anything over, and I love her for it. My youngest sister is shamelessly blunt and wildly confident, but I know how soft she is at her core.

"Birdie came over and helped me plant a few of the rosemary bushes when I first started renovating," I say, dragging my palms along the bandana from my back pocket. My bare feet squelch along the freshly drenched dirt as I weave my way back toward the paver walkway I installed myself. "Those are the only two things still alive"—I glance at the potted plants that are in dire need of shade and water—"and they're barely holding on."

When I came back to Tennessee, the house I'd been renting was no longer mine. Most of my things were either in storage or taking up space in Birdie's house. Coming back meant starting over, *again*. There have been so many starts and stops, and this time has felt even more dizzying than the last. When I passed this old barn at the edge of my uncle's property, I didn't overthink all the reasons why it wasn't a good idea, I asked him if I could rent it. Of course, he said yes. I looked at this run-down structure for my entire life, and I always imagined what it could be if someone took care of it. *I* wanted to take care of it.

"Do you remember the ducks that used to live in the pond

across the street?" Jo asks as she tries smelling the bunches of wildflowers that are probably the only pretty thing out here—and another weed.

I pause, thinking back to when we were kids. It wasn't really very quiet or easy in our house, but getting lost outside always felt good. "You mean the one's Mom said would be great as duck l'orange?"

"God, she's such a bitch," Jo says with a heaved sigh, and it has me barking out a laugh.

"What am I missing!?" Stevie shouts to us from her car. "You're not allowed to have fun until I get there!"

"Just reminiscing about how mean Mom was about the ducks," Jo shouts back to her.

Stevie chuckles. "Ah, yes, our mother…a real fucking Snow White."

The level of asshole our mother is capable of being has always been one of our ways of connecting. I'm not sure what that says about us as siblings or daughters, but when you grow up with Tallulah Crowne as your primary example of responsible adult behavior, there are only two ways to go: lean in and endure, or throw yourself as far away as possible. Stevie and Jo chose the first, and I took the second route, yet somehow, we still find common ground in half loving and half tolerating the woman who raised us. Thankfully, it was Birdie who kept us grounded when Lu was living her most destructive life.

I can't help but wonder if my sisters know what I walked into the other night. What our mother and grandmother might be involved in. I don't have it in me right now to broach that topic with them.

"I need meat and cheese right now," Jo says, moving toward

the patio doors. "Stevie, I swear, if you didn't bring shoes this time, we're going to your place to get them."

"Have no fear, my bitchy little sistah," Stevie calls out in some atrocious British accent. She walks to the back of her car and pops the trunk. "I have the shoes!"

I shake my head and laugh as she hoists two very large garbage bags out of her trunk.

"Did you seriously put eight-hundred-dollar stilettos into a Hefty bag?" I ask, wiping my feet off and stepping inside my place.

I hold the door for her as she shoves inside. When she drops them, she says, "Don't be a snob. Who gives a hoot how beautiful things arrive, as long as they arrive. Right, Jo?" Stevie says, giving Jo a side-eye.

"I stopped listening when the truffle cheddar entered my mouth," she says over a mouthful.

Stevie drags her eyes from my feet to my top and then back down again. "I'm glad you're in a good mood. It's the perfect time to tell you that you're officially on the schedule with us this week."

I glance at Jo. *I'm absolutely fucking not.* "I already said no to that. I have a job. And it's *not* at The Whispering Fool."

Jo smiles wide. "Everyone could use a little mad money, Wyn. I mean, we have a semi-expensive obsession," she says, pointing to the garbage bags in front of our sister.

"Oh, come on, Wynnie," Stevie says, cocking her hip and dumping a garbage bag filled with clothes and shoes onto my floor. "And according to the very delicious looking man at dinner, you're a great bartender. Hmm, should we elaborate on that? And by *we*, I mean you."

I furrow my brow and skirt around the kitchen island to my

fridge, pulling out the latest cake Lu delivered. I never thought I'd eat cake again, but now I eat it every damn chance I can.

"Wouldn't mind a little detail about that one, if you're feeling up to it," Jo says as she slathers a piece of bread with Brie and honey.

I take a bite of the jam cake and the chopped pecans with the brown sugar coats my mouth, instantly making me feel better.

Stevie flops her body on my bed across the open room. "What if we resort to begging? I would like to both have you pouring drinks alongside us *and* witness the most dirtiest of details about exactly what kind of bartending skills Julian experienced," she says, propping her chin on her fist.

"Begging doesn't work with me, you know that," I tell her.

"Does it work when he does it?" Stevie covers her mouth, and then says, "Wait, no, he's so much more BDE. I bet he's a make-you-beg-for-it guy."

Jo sniffs out a laugh, knowing full well I'm going to cave. "BDE?"

"Big Daddy Energy," Stevie says. "Or Big Dick Energy. Depends on the vibe, still trying to figure out Wyn's guy."

Jo looks at me, raising her eyebrows.

"Jo, really, we're in our thirties; do I really need to educate you on BDE? And stop derailing the focus of this discussion."

Yeah, she's on fire today.

"You're unhinged, you realize that, right?" Jo says as she rounds the pile of clothes and shoes.

"I'm very self-aware," Stevie answers, turning her attention to me and rolling off the bed to get closer to where I'm standing and enjoying my cake. "Wynnie, I will take you off the schedule if you tell me. I need to know what the hell went on with you and Julian."

The reality is, I'm going to talk to my sisters about all of it, regardless.

Jo sucks in an audible breath that has Stevie and me turning to look at what she's pulled out of the bag. Holding up a vintage pair of Jimmy Choos that I thought had been lost, she says, "YOU had them this whole time! You sneaky slutbag."

Stevie cackles, and then sticks out her tongue. "I'm older than you, which means I get dibs on the good ones." She glances at me. "I want the Manolos and Tecovas."

Jo buckles the straps of the black pumps and kicks her legs up high before she stands. Walking over to the full-length mirror in my bedroom space, she admires them. They really are the sexiest heels I've ever seen. In the reflection, Jo looks at me.

"I don't know who you are." She points my way. "The whole professor vibe is a flex. I mean, you're a badass for basically telling Mom to shove it after she called you stupid your senior year in high school. But having an obvious fling with a semi-famous artist feels like a whole new level of badassery I don't think we've accounted for." She winks at me in the reflection of the mirror and adds, "You, more than anyone, deserve blips of good and happiness, Wyn. And maybe that's with a sexy jeweler…"

I cross my arms over my chest, shoving down the emotion that surfaces at hearing her say that. I want that too. And there's a part of me that wants to be behind that bar with them—it's not who I was, but maybe that doesn't matter.

"Oh, I'm almost certain that Wyn has an entirely different side that we've never had the pleasure of seeing before," Stevie says, moving over toward my wardrobe. When I look over at Stevie again, she's pulling out a pair of jean cutoffs and chucks them on my bed, followed by a pair of Louboutin booties I thought I'd never see again.

My jaw drops. "You had the booties too?!" I shout at her.

She shrugs her shoulders, then gets back to it. "Where do you think they met?" she asks Jo.

I send her an exasperated look, eyebrows raising. "Remember when you wanted me to call you out for being a dick?"

Stevie throws up her middle finger and pretends to uncap it as if it's a lipstick container, drawing her middle finger around her lips, and then pretending to put the cap back on when she's done.

When Jo barks out a laugh, I point at her. "You too."

Her mouth snaps shut, just as Stevie whines, "I'll tell you what I've been hiding if you give us even the tiniest detail."

"What else have you been hiding?" I ask point-blank.

"You first," she says.

I cut her off right there. "Fine. Julian and I fooled around in a bar bathroom in Montana, and I haven't been able to stop thinking about it since."

They both stop what they're doing and look at each other, speechless. The truth is, this isn't the life I left. My sisters and I weren't close. Not like this. We had our childhood together, growing up in the same house, and living with our mom and Birdie was something we shared. It shaped us differently. Three and a half years ago, I barely made it to family dinners, never mind late-afternoon schmoozing and shoe swaps. It's been seven months since I wandered back here, and I promised myself long before that, if I ever saw them again, I would make our time together count. Maybe that means leaning into the things I want instead of trying to fit a mold that I've long since outgrown.

They both haven't said anything. "You've seen him," I say, blowing out an exaggerated breath. "How am I not supposed to have fantasies about him? I mean, have you seen his hands?!"

Both slack-jawed, they instantly start laughing in agreement.

"I fucking knew it." Stevie carries on cackling. Her demeanor changes seconds later, though, from sheer excitement to something far more dangerous, like one of her brilliant ideas is brewing.

I flap my fingers forward at Jo. "You two can fight over the Choos. Give me the boots. I'll pour drinks tonight, but from behind the bar, not on top of it."

They both look at each other again like I've just shared the world's most incredible news. This time, I'm the one chuckling. To be fair, they've been trying to get me back behind the bar since I quit very aggressively the week before I submitted for graduate school.

"Now, start talking, Stevie. What have you been hiding?" I prod.

"Okay, maybe hiding was overselling it, but I did see your guy when I dropped off Nash at The Rackhouse. It's like a boys' club over there with Jameson staying too." She opens the refrigerator, looking for something. Pulling out a jar of olives, she opens it and plops one in her mouth. "He totally slipped about another missing person case."

My stomach sinks at hearing it, and it has me wondering if it's connected to what I stumbled into at the bar the other night.

Stevie adds, "There are so many, and not a single lead. I could dedicate an entire podcast season just to missing persons in our county alone. Like, what the hell is in the water here?"

"Limestone," I deadpan as I open the doors to my wardrobe.

"Obviously," she says, knowing her fair share about whiskey. Limestone in the water here is one of the many things that makes Tennessee whiskey so damn smooth.

"I get the runaround any time I ask about cold cases. And

don't get me started on the sexual assault rumblings on your beloved university campus."

"What sexual assault rumblings?" I ask, snapping my attention to her fully, stopping from looking through my display of shoes.

"Don't get her going on this," Jo whispers loudly. "She won't stop."

"It's only rumors at this point, because our county sheriff's department isn't doing shit about it. Any of it. It grinds my gears." She pops another olive into her mouth, then flops onto the bed. "Give me something good to focus on instead, Wynnie. I'm dying for a little hook-up story, some juice to keep my spirits up, please please please tell me the details of this bathroom tryst?"

"Are you hormonal?" Jo asks her with a quirked eyebrow.

"All the fucking time," Stevie groans out dramatically. "I'm living my best life in a loving, platonic marriage. I'll take what I can get."

Stevie and Theo's relationship has always had gray lines and curious roots, but they stay together and would go to bat for each other in a minute. When she's ready to talk about it, I know she will.

"Here," Jo says as she tosses me the boots. "Can I ask you another question?"

I glance up at her as I sit to put them on. "You can."

It's one of the deals we made when I came back—to ask before asking. Stevie blows past remembering that one most of the time, but Jo doesn't. She stared at the scar along my side in horror after the Summer Solstice party Birdie had thrown and I told them that they could ask.

"News flash," Stevie interrupts. "That was more dessert than

brunch, but I'm not mad about it. Here. If we're staying in the same place tonight, then it's a sleepover, and sleepovers equal matching pajamas, or being naked, depending on the parties involved." She laughs, throwing a wadded-up ball of pink plushy fabric at my head.

I stand up, and without thinking, take off my shirt, but before I'm able to shed my pants, they're both staring at the jagged, protruding scar. It isn't pretty, and it never would be, but it's healed. The phantom pain happens less often now—the memories of how it was made never truly leaving me, but muting more as time goes on.

"What happened, Wynnie?" Stevie asks as tears track down her cheeks. I hate seeing her like this—both of them crying over something I didn't want to think about ever again, let alone talk about.

I clear my throat to hide the emotion that's threatening to surface. "If I share this, it stays with us. Only us. I don't want Mom or Birdie knowing any of it—not until I'm ready."

They look at each other, silently agreeing that they can do that—keep a secret if it means making sure I'm okay.

"We promise," they say in unison.

And they've kept it. My sisters know what I survived, that the monster I escaped is dead and that meant it was safe for me to come back home. But they didn't know where I had been while I healed. They didn't know that it took me so long to come back.

"You said Montana, so that means you met him while you were…" Her question drifts off.

"Healing," I tell her. They couldn't know about Hideaway. It's the one place that has to stay out of the conversation. There are still people there, because it isn't safe for them anywhere else. "I was working at a bar. We flirted and he showed up a couple of months later, and we fooled around in the bathroom." I smile, thinking about how that makes me sound—so out of character with who I used to be. Or maybe it's more like me now. *I wasn't Wyn when I was with him.* At least not the one everyone in Rumor knew. "But I never thought I would see him again."

"But he's here now," Jo says.

"He found you," Stevie says, like it's romantic.

He said he looked for me, and while I want to believe that, I know I'm not what brought him here. "What if that's not the entire story? What if it was a strange coincidence that brought him here, but I don't want it to be?"

Jo furrows her brow. "There's always more to every story, Wyn. You know that. And I'll remind you of one very important truth." She looks at Stevie and then back to me as she raises her chin. "You're a Crowne, Wyn. We believe in what we want. If you want to flirt and have fun, be serious and fall hard, or just forget it all, then do it. What's stopping you?"

CHAPTER 12

Julian

Muffled roars of motorcycles echo ahead as I pull into one of the few spots left in The Whispering Fool's parking lot. I spent the rest of the afternoon hunting down materials for a piece I wanted to start working on, and trying to convince myself that staying here isn't as dangerous as it seems. Between my conversation with Mickey and the mess that is Cora Billings, I want to understand exactly what Birdie and Lu Crowne are doing and with how much frequency in this town.

The door to the bar is flanked by an intimidating pair of women, their arms crossed, keeping a roped-off line at bay. It's a crowd that's starting to curve around the side of the building. There's a handful of men, similar in height and build as me, wearing leather cuts that show off the location of their motorcycle club, plenty of others who I wouldn't remember, and groups of women peering at me as I bypass all of it and head straight for the doors.

"Nope," the tall woman says as I approach, holding her hand up in front of my chest. It hovers inches from touching me. I look down at it, then back up to her as she says, "You wait in that line, just like everyone else."

I flash her a smile.

"Still nope," she says, monotone.

I sniff a laugh. "Alright, would it help if I told you I'm a family friend of the Crownes?" I ask, glancing inside at the sea of people gawking at the bartenders who dance on the bar. I didn't realize it was going to be as lively as this.

"Do you have a reading with Birdie tonight? Is that it?" the other bouncer asks, holding out her hand for what I assume is my ID. I wanted to speak with her, so I say, "Yes?" as I pull it out of my wallet and clear my throat. *I'm usually a better liar.* I'm off my game here—have been since I woke up tied to that damn chair.

She looks up at me with a questioning glare. "At least some of these assholes put in an effort when they're lying to my face." She smiles sarcastically. "Back of the line."

When I move to put my ID back, I slide her a folded-up twenty-dollar bill. She holds it up, glancing at the line that's at least fifteen people deep. "I see you've dropped a hundred dollars under your shoe right there. Might want to pick it up."

I can't help but smirk at her as she watches me reach into my pocket and pull out a hundred. "This the one you saw?"

Plucking it from my fingers, she nods and opens space for me to fit through the threshold of the bar. "That'd be the one."

Last time I set foot in here, there wasn't a living soul until Wyn walked in. But now, the chest-pounding beat of drums hits me the moment I step inside. The Whispering Fool is nothing like the bar in Montana. Hell, I've been to plenty of places, from roadhouses to speakeasies, but this place isn't like those either. This is something all its own.

The same drumbeat repeats, now with the stomping of feet on top of the bar to amplify the song's intro. The band in the corner of the bar brings in the violin next, and "I'm Shipping Up to Boston" starts to echo, with yelling cheers throughout the bar as most join in.

An alligator head sits prominently above the bar, with a variety of lace and satin garments draping from its mouth, acting as this place's centerpiece. From there, it's an eclectic mix of bold neon signs and oversize pieces of art, from an Andy Warhol print to a reimagined Monet donned in spray paint and glitter. The place is a vibe with the lights on. Green plants fill corners as vines creep along edges and ledges, and even the ceiling is peppered with oversize florals and chandeliers that hang from its wooden beams. There isn't a single spot in here that feels untouched or ignored. It'd feel alive even without people packed inside. The creative part of me flexes, effortlessly inspired by everything I'm taking in. There aren't too many faces focused on the band, however, because the real entertainment of this place is absolutely the women whose last name is carved into the front of the massive bar they're perched on.

It's the same spot where a dead man was slumped on the floor.

Looking around some more, I notice three of the men in leather cuts who walked in after me are now speaking with Lu Crowne as if they've known each other their entire lives. Her head tips back in a laugh as she pulls a bottle of Jack and shows off a long pour into a row of shot glasses.

The crowd is a melting pot of people—drunk couples making out, random trios who look like friends, four girls with matching sashes draped over them that read *The Party*, and handfuls of men who range from cowboy wannabes in cutoffs, to bikers, to businessmen in khakis and loafers who look like their bourbon tour took a wrong turn. If this place was in Nashville or New York—hell, even Miami—I don't think it would stand out, but this feels like a spectacle in a town as small as Rumor.

A crew of university students stands starstruck, staring up in awe of the woman gliding around the top of the bar on roller skates. She's all confidence in her cutoff jeans shorts and a cropped shirt that has a picture of a rooster on the front and, when she spins, a lollipop on the back. Stevie Crowne commands the rest of the room while she double-fists two bottles. The youngest sister, Jo, calls out numbers and points to the crowd who raise their hands to bid on something. With a steadying stance, she launches small balls of fur with a slingshot into the crowd.

I stand in the back, leaning against the only empty pillar, entertained by the dopamine kick that is this establishment.

The balcony railing glows pink, and the vibrant neon sign above the arched ceiling looks like a classic-style tattoo of an ornate crown with a cursive font written across it—*Whiskey Women*. I glance around again, hoping to see Wyn somewhere. I came looking for Birdie, but now that I'm here, there's only one person I have any desire to lay eyes on.

"First time, right?" a voice asks from beside me, smirking when I turn to look at him and nod.

Theo leans against the other side of the pillar. He passes me a cracked-open can of a craft lager without his attention ever leaving the woman gliding around the bar on skates.

"Is it always like this?"

He takes a sip, mulling over the question at first, and then chuckles. "Yeah, most nights. But Thursday through Saturday are the wild ones. Wait until Lu gets on the shot swing." He tuts. "That's when shit gets a little unhinged."

"What are they auctioning off?" I ask, slinking my hand into my back pocket and taking a drink of my beer.

Barely covering his laugh, he holds his fist in front of his mouth. "Oh, Julian, my man." He claps his hand on my shoulder. "Just fucking wait. Honestly, my girl is hot as fuck, so I get the hype. But the crowd goes wild for all of this. When you add Lu, Stevie, or Jo to the equation, people will pay a pretty penny to be slapped around and poured out cheap shots."

Movement toward the side door, and then someone smoothly sliding beneath the bar, grabs both of our attention. *Wyn*. I got the impression that she didn't set foot behind that bar, that she might be the sibling that doesn't fit in with her family and their antics. What she was wearing the other night screams the polar opposite of what she's wearing now. I'm not sure which one I like better. The tight black jeans that hug her perfect heart-shaped ass are giving at least a half a dozen men and two women a helluva show, while her tight white T-shirt reminds me of what she wore when she was "Naomi."

"What's going on with you and my sister-in-law?" Theo asks curiously as we watch her pour pints from the row of beers on tap. She fills orders that her sisters call out without so much as turning to get paid for them.

"More than I'd like to share," I tell him honestly. There's a helluva lot that's gone on between us, but I'm nowhere near understanding any of it.

He tips his drink back, takes a swig, and says, "I can respect that."

I watch as Wyn moves behind the bar, her longer, light brown hair pulled back off her face, showing off those high cheekbones and deep green eyes. The shape of her is damn near mouthwatering, but when she smiles, I'm brought right back to the night I kissed her, touched her, watched her come so fucking hard I nearly had myself.

She laughs when Stevie rolls by, and again, even harder when she and Jo see something at the same time and widen their eyes at the other. She's focused as she pours, her body moving effortlessly, like she could handle every single order on her own. No fear or hesitation, it's such a fucking turn-on. When I realize that I've been staring, a black-and-white stuffed cat bounces off my chest. My reflexes have it in my grip, stopping it from falling to the floor.

Theo laughs into his beer like he knows something I don't.

"I don't want this," I say, holding it up for him to take.

Theo shakes his head, smiling like he just won the lottery. "I'm so fucking happy I stopped in before heading out."

"You travel a lot for work?" I ask him over the riff of Pat Benatar warning off heartbreakers.

"A bit," he answers as he looks up at the few people moving across the balcony. The walkway runs along the upper part of the right wall and looks more like a fire escape that was built inside instead of out. I follow his line of sight to the people waiting outside of a sheer red curtain that's billowing in and out with whatever's making the air move up there.

"How long have you and Stevie been together?" I ask him, trying to understand the dynamic. I'm too fucking possessive. I don't know that I would be so calm and cavalier watching my partner flirt her ass off all night.

He tips his drink at her just as she rolls along the length of the bar, bending at the waist to deliver the pints that Wyn keeps pouring. "She's been in my life for almost as long as I can remember.

I think the word 'together' can mean different things to different people," he says with a side-eye. "We're married. We're raising Nash together, and when I'm in Rumor, their place is mine too. We're our own kind of family." He winks, and then salutes me with his bottle before tipping it back. "But she loves her people big and can be a little wild about it. She secured an AirTag in every pair of Wyn's and Jo's shoes after Wyn finally came back."

I don't know this guy, and I rarely find it in anyone's best interest to know details about my life or what I'm thinking, but I like Theo. Maybe it's the fact that he's the only other adult male who seems to be thriving around the Crowne women, or maybe just the simple fact that I haven't talked to anyone about my life in a long-ass time.

"How long since they've all been behind that bar together?" I ask as I watch them laugh as they move around each other.

"You know she hasn't stepped foot behind that bar since before she went to college," Theo adds.

"Why is that, you think?" I ask him.

"Wyn and her mother, Lu, fought a lot. But Lu said some stuff that she shouldn't have, and that was it for Wyn. She created boundaries, moved onto campus, went ahead and got her PhD in chemistry. Stevie would brag about her sister's research being published, but I don't think Wyn ever knew how proud they all were of her." He rests his head against the pillar, watching the Crowne sisters orbit each other.

"I'm sure you see it," he says. "Doesn't take long to feel the effects of the Crowne women. They're pretty spectacular separately, but all together…" He shakes his head. "They're a fucking force."

I've always been good at finding things. I had friends who were too. I knew what I was looking for when I showed up in

Montana. I'd always gotten what I needed by any means necessary, but the second I stepped foot out that back door and away from her, I fucking hated myself for it. And now, the part I never considered was that Hideaway was her home while her family believed she was dead. I want to know why. The truth doesn't matter; I just want her to trust me enough to tell me.

Theo tips his head to the side. "This town lives up to its name—and man, it's been brutal to those women. Wyn always hated that part. Then she comes walking back like her disappearing act wasn't going to stir up all kinds of gossip. Stevie just got into a fight with some asshole at the old Piggly Wiggly the other day when she overheard someone saying Wyn was in rehab and had a secret baby while she was there."

"Did Wyn tell anyone where she'd been?" I ask, trying not to seem too eager to know what she's shared and what she's held close.

"Nope." He glances at the stuffed cat I still have in my hand, and then back up to the bar as Jo yells into her mic.

"All of tonight's pussycat wranglers, I'm going to need you in front of the bar right the fuck now for your reward!"

Shit.

Three people hold up the same stuffed cats and shove through the crowd, settling against the bar. When the song changes, Jo stands taller on the balls of her feet above the crowd and searches around the sea of people. The second her eyes land on mine, I toss the stuffed animal I'd been holding to the floor.

"You'd better go up there before she makes a spectacle out of you," Theo says as Stevie skates over to the side of the bar we're closest to. The rowdy bar cheers for the few people who face the crowd, tilting their heads back and looking up at the vaulted ceiling, waiting for what's coming. Three of the cocktail waitresses who have been circulating the space hover above the two men and one woman who also caught the fucking stuffed cats. Stevie and two of the cocktail staff hover above them with a salted wrist, tequila shot in the other hand, and a slice of lime dangling between their front teeth.

Jo calls out, "Don't forget, if you want the happy ending, you've gotta tip for it."

Fucking hell.

I scan behind the bar, trying to find Wyn, but she's nowhere in sight. Tipping my head back, I look up to the balcony and see Birdie leaning on her elbows, hands draped over the railing, surveying the debauchery below.

The three people who caught the cats lick the salt off their server's wrists, then golden-tinted tequila gets poured from the shot glass into their waiting, open mouths, and then each person chases it with the offered lime wedges. The first duo makes it flirtatious. The two women play it up for the crowd with a little tongue to show for it, while the next couple keeps each other's lips for a few extra moments. Stevie and her person exchange the lime as tongues slip for people standing close enough to see. When he stands from leaning back on the bar, he turns around to face her and throws down a twenty with a slap on the bar.

I glance back at Theo, and he just sips his beer, watching on like this isn't anything new. Stevie grabs the tequila bottle, sits down on the bar, legs and skates dangling off. An air horn sounds off, and she takes a pull from the bottle. He waits with his mouth open as she spits it at him, barely any of it hitting his mouth. But she's not done. She reaches her open hand back, and with a windup, slaps him clean across the face. He fucking throws his hands above his head like he just won the lottery as his buddies whistle and shout that it's their turn next.

"Sorry, gentlemen, you didn't catch the pussycat," Jo croons over the mic, popping out her bottom lip to mock a pout. "And I saw who did. Ladies, we're missing one lucky kitty catcher..." She scans the crowd for show, and then lands her sights on me again.

Stevie crooks her pointer finger at me and yells, "Let's go, handsome. You caught the kitty, so it's time for your reward."

I shake my head—not happening. Maybe when I was in my early twenties, I'd consider it, but this isn't in my wheelhouse anymore—bullshit at bars. Out of the corner of my eye, I catch Wyn looking at me with a bottle of whiskey in one hand and an empty glass in the other.

I can't help but smirk at knowing that I have her attention now. If she's the one pouring, then I'll play. I drain what's left of my beer, ignore the people around me, and weave my way up to the bar.

I don't look up at Jo, who's standing right in front of me, yelling over the crowd as the band segues music from one anthem to the next—Benatar's "Heartbreaker" to Rhianna's "Rude Boy." I ignore her high heels that begin stomping with the music, and instead, keep my focus on the brunette who's looking at me like she's ready to settle a bet.

Oh, I bet I'm going to enjoy this.

Jo hovers a shot of tequila in front of me, but I slowly shake my head.

"He's not a tequila fan," Jo shares over the mic. "If you make the tip halfway decent, I'll let you pick your poison and your girl."

She knows exactly what she's doing when she looks over her shoulder at where I'm looking.

"Wyn Crowne, tonight's guest bartender, ladies and gentlemen," Jo croons out over the mic. And as if she's some kind of main attraction, the crowd starts hooting and hollering. "Time to show off those *fantastic* bartending skills you own and pour your fantasy something worth remembering."

CHAPTER 13

Wyn

My knee-jerk reaction *should* be to straight-up murder them, but my sisters read between the lines and have plucked out palpable chemistry like they're destined matchmakers.

Their motives have always been well-intentioned, but I never let them meddle in my social life. My version of a good time has never lined up with theirs—*I wonder if that's still the case*. Growing up with Lu as our shining example meant we accrued hard, unwavering shells but squishy, hopeful centers when it comes to love and relationships. And they're both acting on that hopefulness right now as they push me closer to Julian.

"Dealer's choice," he says with his eyes on mine. His attention on me is like a full-body experience. I feel it everywhere, like electricity lingering in the air just after a lightning storm.

The newest bartender with the long blond hair, who looks like she was born when I got my PhD, saunters up beside me. "I'll offer myself as tribute if nobody is going to take this one," she says, biting her lip as she mixes a cocktail in her shaker.

Suppressing the glare I'd like to aim her way, I look out

across the crowd, noticing everyone's focused either on Julian or my sister, and there's not a single face I recognize. The old me would've walked away and told the attractive man "thanks, but no thanks" to avoid whatever rumors this would start. Not to mention, if there was someone from the university, faculty or student, in this crowd…The cautious part of me knows that's still possible, but I'm not the kind of woman who runs anymore. The power of recognizing that winds its way through me.

I raise my leg, wedging my foot into the small step built into the bar, and hoist myself up next to Jo. The crowd cheers out when she smiles and says, "Consider this a very lucky evening, everyone. My big sister, Dr. Wyn Crowne, ladies and gentlemen."

Rubbing along the leather cuff on my right wrist, I don't dare look up along the balcony. Instead, I gaze down into the crowd, eyes locked on the man who has a teasing look in his eyes and his arms crossed as he waits.

"Dealer's choice," Jo explains on the mic, as if the drunk crowd are her eager students, "simply means, the bartender can pour whatever they want, however they want, and the recipient has to take it." Stevie cups her hands in front of her mouth and shouts, "Make it count, Wynnie!"

I spot one of Julian's tattoos peeking out from the neckline of his dark shirt and decide immediately what concoction to make for him.

Stevie jumps down from the bar top, snagging a couple of orders, skating behind me. "Call out what you need, Wynnie, and I'll grab it for you."

"The unmarked bottle with the dried orange wheel and rhubarb," I say, pointing to Birdie's homemade Aperol-style liquor, then call out the remaining bottles.

I settle my ass on the bar in front of him, trying not to mirror the smile he's giving me.

"Crowne," he says, stepping between my legs, and I can immediately feel the warmth of him. His broad body forces them wider, and the cutoff shorts I decided on ride up high on my thighs. "You heard the woman, make it count."

Trying to ignore how my stomach flutters, I lean back, reaching for the silver cocktail shaker. Before I tilt too far and lose my balance, Julian's hands grip the sides of my thighs, bracing and holding me in place.

"Looks like your sisters talked you into bartending after all," he says. And I don't know why that observation—which is very true, I might add—pisses me off.

"I'm surprised to see you…still in Rumor…in this bar," I challenge. Leaning closer, allowing my cheek to brush along his, the scratch of his beard and the warmth of his body nearly make my pulse careen off its cliff. "I would imagine it's frowned upon in your line of work to return to the scene of a crime."

He chuckles, and it's way too sexy. "They all keep telling me you're the smart one," he answers sarcastically as he looks down, just north of where he's holding me. The way that I moved caused my cropped shirt to rise a little too high. I flinch, trying to right the hem before anyone can see the marred skin along my left side. *Dammit.* It's not the fact that I have imperfections that makes me overtly aware of what's there, it's knowing that having a scar like mine will cause questions that need an explanation.

Julian's attention stays locked on where the shirt lifted for an extra moment—he doesn't look away or give me a sympathetic smile. Instead, when his eyes lift to mine, his curiosity feels as if it's laced with something more aggressive, maybe even angry at what and who caused it.

His grip on me pulses tighter, and when he leans in, it somehow silences the noise around us. He doesn't say a word, his lips brushing against my skin, ghosting the racing pulse point below my ear. The lightness of it sends a rolling thrill from the tips of my fingers to the very center of me. It billows out, making it crystal clear that my body craves to be touched and teased by him again. "Stop asking questions that you already know the answer to, Crowne."

I hate that he has no issue calling me out. He made it pretty clear already that he wasn't leaving just yet. The truth is, I want to hear him say it, and I want to know his reasoning.

"Spell it out for me," rushes past my lips. But a bottle thuds down on the bar to my right, and another immediately follows, cutting off whatever Julian was about to say.

Stevie rolls up behind me. "Let's go, Wynnie. Let's show Julian how we do things in Rumor."

Nerves swirl in my stomach, but I ignore them as Julian pulls back, creating just enough space between us. His words still linger the same way as his hands that remain on the sides of my thighs. Thumbs moving slowly back and forth against my skin, they sooth and tease just beneath the hem of my already hiked-up shorts. When I meet his gaze again, he mouths, *You okay?*

It doesn't make sense, the way that simple question and his touch eases me and makes me feel like he's got me. I tilt my chin up and give him a quick nod. With a newfound focus, I tip the bottle of Amarino into the shaker first, followed by the bitter orange liquor. Stevie glides behind me with a half of a lemon already stuffed into a juicer. She knows what I'm making just based on the ingredients and gives an assist by squeezing it into the shaker.

With a side-eye glance and a smirk across her lips, she asks, "Which whiskey?"

"Any whiskey preference?" I ask him, my attention stopping on his lips. I can almost feel mine tingle when I think about the last time I felt them kiss mine. I swallow roughly, remembering the details, the things he said to me, and the way they made me completely unravel.

"You're in charge," he interrupts my wayward thoughts. Slowly, and so smooth that it sounds as if this drink has already dripped down his throat, he says, "I'll take *whatever* you give me."

Well, fuck me.

I clear my throat. "Grab a bottle of ours," I call out over the music to Stevie.

Seconds later, a bottle from my distillery is placed in my hand. I give it a long pour into the shaker, making a little show of it, and then slam the heel of my palm against it to lock the silver tumbler over the top. My sisters are the ones with the bar tricks, so I look up at Jo and tip up my chin. She reads what I'm asking just as I toss it into the air. Without missing a beat, she catches the silver-frosted shaker.

Instead of watching her and paying attention to the show that both she and Stevie are putting on, I shift forward, closer to the man between my legs.

"What did you make me?" he asks.

"It doesn't matter, right?" I smirk. "You'll take what I give you."

He hums, and then says, "See? Sounds better when you say it."

I take a quick breath, not allowing myself to linger on how good it feels to say what I want, play with it, and get rewarded.

He surprises me when he yanks my ass forward, closer to the edge of the bar, and into him. "Who was the guy?" he asks, catching me off guard. "The one you were with at Moonie's."

I look at my sister with a smirk pulling at my lips. *He's jealous.*

Jo clears her throat loudly over the mic, drowning out the band. With the shaker in one hand and a strainer in the other, she stands there, watching and waiting for her next cue from me.

Julian guides my chin with the curve of his pointer and thumb, back to look at him. "Who. Was. The. Guy?" he asks, low and slow.

"Just a friend," I rush out on a breathy whisper. Tipping my chin down, I move my lips closer to his. "And you're sounding a little jealous."

He doesn't hesitate when he says, "More than a little, Crowne."

Why does that level of confidence and honesty hit me so hard? I can't help but smirk at his words and shift my legs wider to get just a little closer. I pick up the empty coupe glass perched next to my leg and hold it out. It's Jo's cue, and she strains the drink into it with precision.

With my free hand, I swipe my thumb along his lower lip and then move my fingers along his jaw and down the side of his neck. I stop at the small tattoo that peeks out and tap the dark triangle.

"Made you a paper airplane," I say, referring both to his tattoo and the drink. "Would you like a taste?"

He doesn't answer. He doesn't need to, not with the way he watches what I'm doing as I press the edge of the cooled glass against my lips and drink.

"Yes, I want a taste. But the thing that I want most," he breathes out. "Should be tasted without this kind of audience."

He didn't just say that. I can't avoid the gasp that pulls from me, my thighs tensing like they want to clench—except they can't because he's standing between them.

Fueled with a boost of confidence, I grab at the front of his shirt, making a fist to pull him closer. I hold the glass up, but just as he moves in, ready for the drink, I tilt it toward my mouth and finish what's left. "Dealer's choice means what I want and how I want it." I smile, looking into those hazel eyes of his. "Thank you for the drink and the lovely tip."

He watches my mouth for a moment as a smile dances at the corner of his lips. "You're playing dirty, Crowne."

The sounds around us creep in—people calling out shots, a saxophone mingling with the bass from the band. And what was only a few minutes has put me on edge, now feeling needy and turned on. Even as the echoes and whistles die down, and my sisters move on to the next spectacle, Julian's hands haven't moved.

"Julian," I tsk, leaning in closer. "You have no idea."

His eyes glance down to my lips as a smirk plays out along his. He doesn't move away from between my legs, instead his hands flex as they still grip along the curve of my ass. He leans in, the scruff along his cheek grazes mine, just before he says, "Show me."

A loud commotion at the front door pulls my attention away. I sit taller, trying to peer above the crowd and catch sight of two police officers spilling into the room. Jameson's speaking to my mother, coaxing her outside, while Sheriff Fury's scanning the space. I look behind me at Jo, whose focus is on all of it, and then up to the balcony at Birdie, who leans over, resting on her elbows, seeming not the least bit concerned. Instead, she's staring down at me.

"I need to see what's going on," I say to Julian, shifting to try to get down, and his hands move to my waist, lifting me up off the bar, helping my feet find the floor. My knees feel weak as my eyes stay locked on his for a moment. Damn, it feels good to be looked at and handled like this.

"What the hell did we do this time?" Stevie says, interrupting as she leans on the bar. "If it's another drunk asshole getting handsy outside, I swear to everything decent in this universe, I will just dick-punch first and ask questions second."

I shake my head as I move away. "Not the smartest solution. Let me go see what's going on before you start swinging."

I shift a glance at Julian again before I work my way through the crowd. Just as I shove through a small group, a finger hooks onto mine and Julian follows behind me.

The second I make my way through the front doors, I overhear Sheriff Fury talking to my mother. "The last person to see him said it was here, Lu." I release my hold on Julian's finger.

"Well, he wasn't here," my mother says, tapping her head. "I remember every goddamn face that walks into my bar, and Deputy Dumbfuck Billings was not one of them."

"Watch it." Fury points to her, then crosses his arms over his chest. "I'm just asking questions, no need to get fired up at me about it."

My mother's pissed off and ready to dole out a roster of insults. The funny thing is, nobody's ever prepared for the way she fights. It's dirty and she rarely loses. "So you thought the best way to ask me questions about whether I'd seen a missing deputy is to come here during a busy Saturday night?" She gives Jameson the side-eye. "You couldn't have said something and talked this yahoo out of traipsing down here and making a scene?"

Jameson looks annoyed that he even needs to be here when he says, "Lu, you and I both know he and Cora live less than a mile away. It wouldn't be unheard of for him to grab a drink down here."

"Except the part where he's not welcome here, and you've witnessed Cora talking shit about me for years," she says.

"Nobody is accusing you of any—" But he cuts himself off when he sees me. He looks up and over my head at Julian, and then back down to me. "Wyn, you mind having a word?" he asks and starts to turn away.

My chest hollows, and I try sucking a deep breath. My mind instantly wanders into a place that isn't logical. *"He's dead. You're safe. You can come home."*

"She ain't got nothin' to say to anyone here. She's filling in tonight," my mother interjects.

"Tell me what's going on?" I ask, ignoring her and focusing on Jameson. The reality is that he's homicide, and less than three nights ago, a person was very dead in the bar behind me. I run my fingers along the leather cuff on my right wrist.

The sheriff answers instead, "Deputy Stan Billings," he pauses to look at my mother, and then back at me. "He's been missing for more than seventy-two hours, and we're trying to retrace where he might have gone. Cora reported him missing and said she had no clue where he could have gone. So, we're asking around and trying to figure out his last whereabouts."

My mother looks at Jameson when she says, "You knew him. Not the most upstanding in law enforcement. I have no business with Stan fucking Billings. We don't mess around with pieces of shit who like to take advantage of their authority."

That has Jameson's brow furrowing and then looking to the sheriff. "That common knowledge?"

The sheriff holds his hand up to my mother. "Lu, that's enough." Then he tilts his head at Jameson, like that's a yes.

"I know that's just boys being boys to you, Fury. Might want to consider that your *boy* might have pissed off the wrong people, finally."

"Lu, knock it off," he says, getting fed up with my mother.

"I'm just askin' when the last time you've seen him was and if any of your girls might have." She does a double take at the doors and starts barking orders at Gina and Gail about not letting people linger. "They either go inside and have a drink or they get the fuck home."

Jameson ignores all of it, stepping closer to me, and more quietly says, "Wyn, I actually do need you for a moment." Holding his hand up to stop Julian from following, he adds, "Alone."

I glance down at the way Julian's fingers lightly hold on to the hem of my shirt, like he's ready to pull me away if I just ask. I take a steadying breath. Putting on my best fake smile, I tell Julian, "I'll be fine."

He looks at the way my fingers play with that leather cuff and then brings his gaze back up to me with a nod. "I'll be right here," he says without anything other than protection lacing his words. There are plenty of alarm bells ringing that kick my heart rate higher, but it's the first time I've ever believed someone when they've said, "I'm here if you need me."

As soon as I follow Jameson and turn the corner of the building, he asks, "When did your friend arrive in town again?"

That question is tinged with suspicion that I'm not prepared to digest. "Jameson, he's been here a couple of days, and most of the time when he wasn't with me, he was at either Birdie's or Tommy's."

Detective Jameson Bishop knows exactly where I was before coming home. He ended up being the person to tell me that it was safe to return. Jameson has always been a good guy. He has plenty of baggage in his past—Stevie's talked about Theo's dad over the years, about how he'd go undercover and leave for long periods of time, even after he came into Theo's life. Which is why, when he looks at me pointedly, waiting for more info, I tell him, "I met Julian when I was in witness protection, in Hideaway. I was working at a bar. He found me here again by coincidence."

"I'm not the biggest fan of coincidences, so do me a favor and just be cautious," he says, pulling out his phone. He puffs out his cheeks, blowing out a breath. "The sheriff wants all hands on deck with this one. I never liked the guy, but if a deputy of the law isn't showing up for shifts, there's something off." As we start walking back toward the noise that my mother's still making, he stops. "I haven't asked, but how are you doing?"

I know it isn't meant to be a loaded question, but it feels like it. I survived being kidnapped and tortured. And my case files were entirely redacted—the effects of departments messing up and allowing a serial killer to slip through the system. But Jameson knew all of that—he knew about the monster and his death, and he knew about the time I spent in Hideaway. I feel like I've lived two lives already, three if you count whatever the hell the past seven months have been since I've been back in Rumor, and I'm only thirty-five. But he doesn't need to hear any of that. He's not the person to unleash all of that on, so instead, I nod and tell him, "I've been trying to settle back in."

My life feels shaken up all over again. It took me nearly two and a half years to feel settled in Montana. For a year of that time, I was in regular therapy and figuring out what type of medicine would allow me to close my eyes and not wake up drenched in panic and sweat. The second year, I figured out a routine that calmed my nerves, food tasted good again, and I found an appreciation for talking without struggling to remain present.

I had moved on from questions I'd never get answers to like: *Why me? Why was it so easy to just take me?* I had been at a symposium in Nashville with plenty of colleagues and tourists, but it was me who he decided to take. There was no real reason other than he liked how I looked. He saw my face on a poster as the keynote speaker and watched. He never told me why, but I stopped speaking and never asked. I blocked out so much of those early days that I'm too nervous to even try recalling any of it. *Don't go there, Wyn. Focus on what's in front of you.*

"You know how to reach me if you need anything," Jameson says as he moves toward his car. Sheriff Fury is talking with two other officers just as they each break off.

This feels like a much bigger problem now.

As I brush past my mother, she's flipping off the sheriff as he gets back into his squad car. "Wynona," she calls out after me.

I look at Julian, who just stands there waiting. He feels like the kind of guard I wouldn't have minded being there for me when I was younger, ready to rescue me from my mother and her bullshit when it presented itself. He tilts his chin up, and it feels like a wordless confirmation that he's there now if I need him.

When I turn, Lu is holding up her phone. She shows me the screen—a picture of me and my sisters when we were kids, and the time—before looking over my shoulder to Julian. "That can wait," she says walking past me. "We're making after-midnight margaritas. Birdie and I need to have a chat with you at home."

"Lu, I'm not in the mood for—"

She stops and turns back toward me, cutting off what I was going to say. "I'm not asking, Wynona."

When I look up and see Birdie leaning in the doorway, I instantly know what needs to be discussed. My stomach bottoms out at the thought of what I might hear.

CHAPTER 14

Wyn

"You're going to have to talk to me eventually, Professor," he seethes.

Twelve weeks, and I haven't said a single word. My skin feels like it's crawling with tiny bugs, but it's simply the feeling of sweat dripping and slowly evaporating with the extreme changes in temperature—a sweltering humidity to the crisp cold. A train car came first, but I was in and out of consciousness for the ride. Then I was kept in a dark, smaller space, bound and gagged, brakes jerking me around enough to feel sick to my stomach. And now, I'm here.

Time doesn't feel like it's moving, but as I study the hairs that've grown from my legs and the length of my nails, time isn't slowing down. Maybe death is just taking its time deciding if I'm worthy of it. I'm almost certain if anyone had started looking, they would have stopped by now. I know I'll die here. The sharp sawing of a serrated knife cuts through skin with a burning sensation at first, and then sheer pressure and pain rattles my nerve endings as it seesaws through muscle up my side. I swallow a scream and plead with any kind of higher power that the depths of this will stop. Fear lingers like an old habit. Defeat doesn't feel like losing. Bravery never arrives.

The sound of cabinets closing and glass bottles clanging on the counter pulls me from the memory. I blink away emotion that threatens to drench me—*not here, not now, not in front of them.*

After a few moments, I finally focus on Birdie and my mother laughing at something I missed. The fact that I'm trying to pause a panic attack so my mother and grandmother can tell me how they've likely killed a man is so troubling that maybe I should just start laughing too.

The only relief is that I know these women—they raised me. And watching the easy way they are with one another has me feeling more jealous of not having that ease with them than scared at hearing about what they've done.

"I think Mr. Colton might have been right, Wyn," Birdie says, holding up the bottle of limoncello I brought over. She glances at me, her eyebrow quirked. "You looked like you were more than comfortable behind the bar tonight…" She trails off.

"Maybe so," I answer, smiling. "Felt good to be back there with Stevie and Jo."

My grandmother reads the undercurrent of things. She's always been good at that. An empath who could effortlessly read between the lines of what wasn't being said. There's too much more to my story that she doesn't push me to know.

"Birdie's right; interesting display at the bar, Wynona…" Lu gives me a pointed look. Opening the fridge, she fills her arms with limes and drops them onto the counter so that they almost roll off and fall everywhere. "There's a jam cake in here with your name on it," she says, tipping her head toward the refrigerator, like making an entire cake for a single person is a completely acceptable practice. And even though her tone sounds annoyed, like it was something she *had* to do, cakes are her olive branch. Tallulah Crowne is good at a lot of things, but she's exceptional at holding grudges, running a bar, and making the most delicious desserts—specifically, cakes. Until about seven months ago, the last cake she made for me was when I was still living at home. Sweets are the only language my mother and I speak flawlessly. We didn't have massive heartfelt moments or paint each other's nails to bond over bullshit. I know she missed me because she's been leaving me cakes ever since I've been back—a thief who breaks into my house simply to leave me a baked good, even after being a dick to my face.

"I'm rationing the last one you left me. It came out too good," I tell her honestly, and I catch her lips twitch with a smile as she turns back toward the margarita assembly line she and Birdie have going.

I watch the two of them behind the counter. They've always operated more like sisters than mother and daughter. When my sisters and I were young, we moved into Birdie's place. Our father up and left my mother without so much as a note. Disappeared, moved on, left his family behind for something or someone else.

People have always had a funny way of disappearing in Rumor. And now, watching Birdie cut limes as my mother scoots around, looking for tequila, there's a nagging feeling that my mother and grandmother know a bit more about that than they've let on.

And I can't help but wonder if Stan Billings isn't the first.

Birdie always said, "There's always a dab of truth in every rumor; it's up to us to decide what to believe." But what she's gearing up to tell me—a truth I've already mostly figured out on my own—I haven't considered what that could mean.

"You can't use whiskey for margaritas, Lu," Birdie says in her low and slow drawl.

But it's the echo of both me and my mother saying, "Yes, you can," that has her eating her words. I smile to myself. *At least we can agree on some things.*

"After midnight, margaritas should only be made with whiskey," Lu says, tossing in the entirety of the quartered limes. Next comes a can of coconut milk into the blender and a hefty pinch of salt. She pops the top back on and flips the blender on for another thirty seconds.

I rub at my wrist, feeling the smooth leather of the cuff beneath my fingers. I work to focus on its texture instead of the sound and my creeping nerves. *Stay present. Take a breath.*

When the blender stops, the room is quiet as Lu pours out three large glasses of the thick, slushy drinks.

Birdie circles around the counter, plucking two glasses. She passes one to me, glancing up at my mother as she grabs hers, and they exchange a brief look. Birdie moves toward the archway on the opposite side of the room, tipping her head for me to follow her. The house has always been referred to as Birdie's place, but my mother lives here too—this room is evident of that. She likely read everything in this place twice. The alcove-like sitting area is covered in wall-to-wall shelves stacked with thrillers and romances, well-worn favorites, how-to guides, and farmers' almanacs from nearly five decades ago, and everything in between. Peppered around the stories are glass jars filled with dried herbs and other tinctures.

Birdie holds up her glass and says, "To my darling girls."

My mother clinks Birdie's glass, and then mine, before they both take a sip. The moment feels heavy, like what comes after this drink can't be undone.

I lick along the rim of the glass, getting a mouthful of coarse salt. I let it rest on my tongue for a moment before my sip, bracing myself for what's coming. Paying attention to textures and tastes keeps me focused on the moment and prevents me from simply reacting.

Settling into my chair, my drink coats my throat just after the whiskey burns across my tongue. I watch my mother give a nod and then perch herself on the built-in bench below the window as Birdie sits in the chair across from me, sets her margarita down next to her, and then leans forward with her elbows perched on her knees. "This was never meant to be your burden, Wyn." She looks at my mother and gives her a tight-lipped smile before adding, "It was never meant to be your mother's either, but life has a real nasty way of reminding me that I only have so much control over how it goes.

"You're smart, Wyn. Always have been, maybe even more than we ever gave you credit for." She blows out a breath, her cheeks puffing on the exhale. "What do you know about Stan Billings?"

I glance at my mother first, who's watching me as she leans against the wall. "I know he was probably the situation that was being cleaned up inside The Whispering Fool the night I walked in on Julian."

"Anything else?" Birdie prompts before she looks at my mother.

"You've already started. Keep going," my mother says, wordlessly answering what Birdie's look was asking.

Birdie takes a drink, and then gives me a smile before she says, "I asked what you knew about Deputy Stan Billings, not his demise." Her eyebrow raises in challenge.

"I don't know much about him, but Cora, on the other

hand," I say, rifling through my memories of a woman who just loved leaning into the nastiest of the rumors when it came to my mother. She's been calling Lu all sorts of colorful things for as long as I can remember. I didn't even know why, other than she seems to be the opposite of what my mom represents. I tilt my head and look at my mom. "Cora loves her conservative values. I can't remember if she's Southern Baptist or Catholic, maybe something else entirely, but whatever it is that she believes, she looks at you as the antithesis of it."

"Don't get me wrong, Cora is an asshole. Don't let her pearls fool you," my mom chimes in. "But she didn't deserve the shit Stan dealt. And I'm not talking about the drugs he was dealing."

I raise my eyebrow and look at Birdie.

"He beat—" Birdie's eyes water as she cuts her words and looks up. When she swipes them away, she takes a sip of her drink, draining it halfway. "It didn't matter that he was a cop, or that he swore to protect, because what I've learned, my darling, is that monsters aren't only found in the dark. Sometimes it's the ones we're meant to trust in the light of day who turn out to be the scariest."

I know some things about monsters. The way they don't ask for permission, how they take whatever they want, and how some don't need submission. Screaming, crying, begging doesn't matter or change the outcome. Mine held me against my will, stole parts of me—physically, mentally, emotionally, and despite being ready to die, I survived it. I'm not as brave as some; I don't know how to kill monsters, but I *can* keep secrets.

Birdie stands, opening the slim double doors that lead to her garden. The smells of rosemary and damp earth waft inside as she lights a long skinny cigarette. She leans against the frame, half inside and half out, giving herself an extra moment to decide what detail comes next or to stop sharing altogether. She perches the filtered end between her lips, hollowing out her cheeks and taking a long drag. On her second pull, she finally looks at me. The herb-smelling smoke lingers on her exhale as she says, "There's a certain way we go about things like this—"

"Stan got messy," my mother cuts in.

Birdie huffs for being interrupted. But my mother finishes her margarita, and then claps her hands in front of her, doing it again. "I love the drama, but sometimes we need to cut to the chase, Ma." My mother shifts her attention back to me. "This will make you an accessory, Wynona."

I already knew that.

"You won't be able to unhear it. I know how you already think of me, but Birdie's flawless charm will seem a little less sparkly—"

"For fuck's sake," I breathe out, exasperated as I tip my head back. This isn't about her passive-aggressive tendencies shining through.

"Lu," Birdie says, pinching between her eyebrows. When she looks at me, she says, "Wyn, Stan Billings isn't missing. He is very much dead."

Hearing it and the details surrounding it have me feeling lighter, almost relieved. The reality of what it means settles like a heavy weight on my shoulders. I shake my head, knowing I need to hear more. "There needs to be..." I look over to Lu and more quietly say, "Tell me that there's a good reason why." I need *them* to not be monsters.

Birdie nods as she hops up onto the counter. She knocks over the saltshaker when she says, "Deputy Billings has been dealing drugs for nearly a decade, which, normally, I say, enjoy however you choose to get fucked up." Crumbling up a piece of paper, she plops it into her empty glass and nudges her chin to Birdie. "We'll call that fodder for now. His verbal abuse started by putting Cora down privately, then it turned public. It happened more and more often. I witnessed it a few times over the years. I'm sure plenty have, but then it escalated. Hurtful words and shitty names turned into shakes then shoves, slaps then punches, kicks then props."

My chest tightens, knowing what props had been used with me.

"Cora endured it for years." Birdie tosses my mom a gold lighter. She flips it, pulls, lights the wadded paper in her glass on fire. Gathering some of the spilled salt, she sprinkles a pinch of it into the flame. "It was easy to spot—the bruises and over-explained stories about how they happened." My mom takes a breath, runs her fingers along her palm and up her wrist. Her pause makes me wonder how well she knows the progression of abuse.

My eyes blur from the tears welling.

"You know people talk, but it's not our place to step in," she says as the small flame snuffs out. It leaves a stream of rising smoke that she wafts away. "Usually when the authorities aren't helpful, or if there's enough anger simmering beneath a woman's hurt, then those women find themselves flipping tarot cards and asking for help in a different way."

I swipe away the couple of tears that fall and sit taller in my chair. There were a lot of people in and out of The Whispering Fool, this house even, my mind swirls with thinking about how that could have been so much more than what I ever paid attention to.

All of the rumors that had been circulated about my mother

my entire life... *The Black Widow of Rumor. The most dangerous Crowne. A death trap.*

I look over to my mother. "People have been saying things for years about you," I say, biting back emotions as I look at my mom.

"You can thank your grandmother for that. Garden club and having an in with the church's prayer tree has its benefits, I guess," she says. "Sometimes rumors can mask the things we don't want people talking about, or noticing."

I look between the both of them, unsure how to organize any of this. All of those horrible things were there to take the focus away from what had been actually happening. I blow out a rush of air. Being responsible for one man's death is ridiculous enough, but this, what they're saying... "I have more questions," I tell them.

Birdie crosses her arms. "Thought you might. Just know we can't answer all of them."

"Then why tell me at all?" I push out a frustrated and almost angry huff at that response. "Why sit me down like some sort of intervention—"

"Because you walked into a storyline that you have no business being a part of," my mom shouts. Her brow pinches and lips turn down like she's mad, but her eyes shimmer with tears threatening to escape. "If I could erase it. If I could make sure you didn't need to know this about me and your grandmother, I would," she says, holding her fist to the center of her chest. "But you're a big girl, Wynona." She sniffs a laugh that isn't laced with any lick of humor. "I have a feeling you know exactly why we keep things from the people we love. Call it selfish, call it lying, but we've done it all these years to protect the people most important." A tear finally escapes, and she bats it away, lifting her chin. "And now the best I can hope for is that this is something you can live with."

Do I really have a choice?

"Is it just men?" I glance at Birdie, and then back to my mother.

They both tilt their heads to the side. "As it turns out," Birdie says.

I lean forward, elbows on my knees, and drop my head. Getting oxygen into my lungs feels like it's taking more effort than usual. I've been pretty exceptional at keeping my panicked moments away from them. Closing my eyes tightly, I press my tongue against the roof of my mouth. I run through all the tarot readings Birdie has done over the years. There have been thousands. *How many of those resulted in this same way?*

"What about my dad?" If there's a story behind anyone disappearing, there has to be one about him.

She laughs and mumbles, "I wish." But it's Birdie who interjects and changes the topic. "You have questions about Julian, too, I'd imagine."

I have plenty. They expand far beyond what my mind's able to process tonight.

A plume of smoke lingers around her words when she asks, "Would you rather ask him for those answers?"

"I'd rather not have any of this be an actual topic I need to consider," I bite back.

Birdie looks down at her palm with a tight-lipped smile.

"Yes," I say softly, knowing that what they've just shared is more than any one of us wanted. "I have questions for him. But can you tell me, how did you find him?"

"Family business," my mother chimes in. Looking down at her phone, she types away and adds, "Three, maybe four generations. Doesn't matter, because if he was doing his job like he's supposed to, then Julian should have already left. Him still being here attracts unwanted attention, as I'm sure you've noticed tonight. Don't think Jameson and Fury aren't keeping tabs on the comings and goings of people right now."

"Who are you texting?" I ask in an annoyed tone.

"None of your business," she says on an exhale. She looks up, and over to Birdie first, and then to me. "The Jeweler would only stay if something was keeping him here. Or someone."

"Are you planning to share about where you met him?" Birdie asks.

Mom points at me with a smirk, before I even try to answer. She hops down from the counter. "Looks like you're a Crowne deep down, after all, Wynona. Listenin' to tales about killin' bad guys and pining after morally gray men." She raises her eyebrows and lets out a raspy laugh. "You looked good behind that bar tonight too."

I bite down, grinding my back molars. She knows how to piss me off quicker than anyone else.

Moving toward the kitchen again, she says, "It would be smarter now if he stays. Maybe entertain the idea of fucking around with him for a little bit longer. He has a thing for you. Though I don't understand how a person learns how to erase a crime scene..."

I squint at her because she can't be serious with that line of thinking after telling me she and Birdie are out here killing people.

"His dad was always in and out. Never had to worry about police asking him any questions," she says, glancing at Birdie, who looks uncomfortable for the briefest moment. "I feel like I have to say it, but this is *not* something to talk about. You're not going to your therapist with a new level of detail contributing to all the ways your mother fucked you up."

I want to throw this glass at her right now.

"Your sisters do not know any of this either. This is after-midnight-margarita chatter only, Wynona."

I raise my eyebrow, and with a sarcastic laugh, say, "You actually feel like you need to say that to me?"

"Yes. Yes, I do," she says back with a snark.

I need to get out of here.

"I'm still trying to figure out who came back here seven months ago. I think this woman," she says, looking at me from the tips of my boots to the top of my head, "the one who's looking at me like she's not sure if she wants to deck me or hug me is the kind of woman I consider unpredictable. Before..." She shakes her head, cutting her words. "Before you were gone, I knew what to expect. But now, I have no clue."

I stand and walk toward the still-open doors that lead to the garden, just as my mother rushes out to the kitchen, full of added drama, as usual.

The one person I didn't expect to see me so clearly just read me like a book. I'm still not sure who I am here, and I'm not sure if it's more comforting or frustrating that she knows that about me. It feels like it knocks the wind out of me. I need to get out of here. I shake out my fisted hands.

"She wanted to keep this away from you girls. It's the one thing she's always stuck to her guns about," Birdie says as she watches me linger in the doorway. "You know your mother, she's a wild card in every way, except when it comes to you and your sisters. There isn't much she wouldn't do to make sure you all feel safe."

The problem is, it doesn't matter what either of them wants. There was a time when I wasn't safe, not even close.

"I have to go," I say, looking back at Birdie.

She fixes her caftan and nods just as I move through the doors. Instead of the path up to her garden, I bank a left and move toward the bar. My shoulders start aching from how they've been bunched, my jaw sore from clenching as I walk across the footbridge to my place, my feet moving forward on autopilot.

I exhale, feeling lightheaded as I type in the code and enter. I brace my hands on my thighs, bending forward. *In through your nose and count, dammit!*

It's not panic, but I need to calm down. I feel my pulse racing as I find the edge of my bed and stare out my window. My skin feels tight and my muscles tense as I play the conversation over in my mind, trying to make sense of it. Trying to berate myself for not knowing any of it before tonight. They gave me some answers, but I don't know if I'm better or worse for having them. If it was only Stan, then maybe I could justify it—the knowledge that he was a shit human and hurt people in various ways. But knowing that this wasn't the first, and there's no mention of it being the last, I'm reeling.

I think about the people who have disappeared, left town, or have gone missing, and I can't help but wonder if it was Birdie or Lu behind it. I'm equal parts horrified and mystified.

They've outsmarted everyone.

And as much as I want to feel good about knowing this truth, like I can wrap my head around their moral code and scream at the top of my lungs that they're unhinged but I love them, what I really want right now is a distraction.

CHAPTER 15

Wyn

I JAB THE FORK INTO the center of the cake. Blackberry jam mingles with the chopped pecans and caramel drizzle, and I can't help but hum at how good it is. On the third monster bite, my body slouches, even the muscles along my spine that I hadn't realized were tense and tight, ease.

Perched on my counter with an entire cake balancing in my lap, I take another bite and release another breath.

I laugh out loud, looking down, resting my head back against the cabinets as I finish chewing. *Now what? How the hell am I supposed to manage any of this?*

The sound of my phone vibrating is muffled. I look around me to find it, not even realizing I never took it out of my bag. I hop down from the counter and find it at the bottom of my bag. There's a wall of messages waiting for me. *Julian.*

UNKNOWN:

Do you need rescuing from your required margarita meeting?...

UNKNOWN:

Tell me you're alright, Crowne.

UNKNOWN:

Had an interesting chat with your brother-in-law tonight. He's chatty.

UNKNOWN:

And according to Theo, your sister put AirTags in all of your shoes when you came back.

"Dammit!" I yell, yanking off my boot and throwing it across the room. Tugging off the other, I turn it over in my hand. When I reach inside and pull up the sole insert, I spy the round AirTag. Eyes burning with emotion, I bark out a laugh. I don't know whether to scream at Stevie or hug her for doing it. I wipe away the tears that escape down my cheeks and tip my head back, eyes closed as I breathe for a solid ten-count. There isn't a formula or syllabus outlining what to do in this exact scenario. With a harsh exhale, I respond to his messages.

WYN:

I don't need rescuing.

I'm alright.

Theo loves a good story

I'm going to violently hug my sister

When I look up, I catch a reflection of myself in the window. I tug the elastic out of my hair. It falls just past my shoulders now. The light brown highlights look even better when it's wavy like this, maybe a bit disheveled. My cheeks feel flushed as a smile lingers from responding to his messages. The old me would be appalled, thinking I looked unkempt, borderline trashy. I look like the version of myself I was when I met Julian in Hideaway. I run my fingertips across my bottom lip. I'm more of a Crowne right now than maybe at any other time in my life.

I need to get out of my head. Tossing my phone on my bed, I flip open the record player and scan the stack of albums I found at the church's flea market. Nina Simone and her rendition of "Sinnerman" has played out in my house plenty of times. Jo watched *The Thomas Crowne Affair* like it was her bible, but it's the double time of the bass and the pulsing drumbeat now that vibrate around my space that mimics exactly how I'm feeling. A spectrum of emotions, slightly drunk on whiskey margaritas, and layered with complication.

It's not about right and wrong but the blatant reality that I've missed things, important things about my family, for my entire life. And now, there's a man, who's quite dangerous and who I'm undeniably attracted to, somehow folded into all of it. I want control over the karmic disaster that has become my life.

My phone screen lights up on my bed.

UNKNOWN:

Your sister said to pour "your fantasy" something worth remembering tonight. Am I your fantasy, Crowne?

WYN:

What do you think?

When my phone buzzes in my hand this time, the message that's waiting is a picture of a bottle of whiskey being held in one masculine hand that's tastefully decorated with two rings and a wrist wrapped in brown leather. I look down at the same one that I borrowed from him.

A shiver runs down my body, thinking about what those hands have done to me. And what I want them to do again…

UNKNOWN:

I think you should let me pour you a drink and you can let me convince you that I am.

I didn't need much convincing. Julian Colton is a fucking fantasy. I swallow the flood of moisture in my mouth and toss the phone back onto my bed. Overheated, I shed my shirt, and turn down the temperature.

I pour myself two fingers worth of whiskey and take a sip as I sway to the music that still plays throughout. I walk toward the mirror on my wardrobe. I feel confident. Shimmying my pants off, I turn in the mirror to really look at myself. My eyes water thinking about what it took to get me here. Years of comparing my size and shape to the women around me, and then losing body mass because of the torture I'd been put through. I finally have curves again—hips fuller and stomach softer. I feel the most comfortable about how I look, maybe more than I ever have. *Even here,* I think as I run my fingertips along the puckered skin that's raised along my side. It feels like a coat of arms—a reminder of what it felt like to live instead of die. Others hadn't survived like I had.

Looking over my shoulder, I can't help but smile at the tattoos that now run up my spine and across my skin in bright and bold colors. My favorite flowers from Birdie's garden are woven together so beautifully that it looks like a real bouquet of wildflowers placed along the length of my back. Therapy can come in many forms. WITSEC had a therapist I still meet with virtually, keeping our monthly sessions. But at the beginning, every week wasn't enough and too much all at once. My skin felt like it was scarring everywhere. It crawled with memories only of a monster and nothing else from before. I started erasing that feeling with pretty ink.

I glance back down at my phone and decide how I want to respond to the picture message, realizing he's holding one of my bottles of whiskey.

Holding up my glass, I snap a selfie.

WYN:

Already have a drink. Should we discuss how you plan on convincing me?

My phone vibrates repeatedly in my hand, and when I answer, it's Julian's voice on the other end as he growls out my name. "You sent a picture with no shirt on…"

Maybe this is what control and a little whiskey-induced confidence looks like.

He laughs quietly, and I can picture him smiling to himself, the way his lips tend to tilt up on one side, how his eyes crinkle in the corners like it's something he's done so many times and those lines are there to prove it.

"I'm not interested in reading between the lines with you."

I scoff. "Then let's start with you being honest with me, Julian," I demand as I drain the last sip of my whiskey.

His laugh rumbles across the phone line and, hell, do I feel it everywhere. "Alright," he says on an exhale. The admission makes me pause. "I'll expect the same from you then."

Moving toward my bed, I drop back, staring up at the worn wooden beams. I listen to the movement on the other end of the line.

Calmly, he says, "There are truths about what I do, who I am to certain people, what brought me to Hideaway and here." He takes a measured pause. "Then there are truths when it comes to you, Naomi, Wyn, Professor Crowne, whoever you choose to be."

I try to slow my breathing. Not all of those were choices. The way he calls out my names, and the way he says each the same, as if they're all the same person, when I've worked so hard to keep them separate. It makes me feel seen. And intensely naked—even more so than lying on my bed in my bra and panties.

In a low and deep tone, he cuts the bullshit. "The only one I care about right now is that I want you. I never plan to keep anything or anyone. I never walked into that Montana bar expecting to walk out and not being able to stop thinking about the woman I just met."

I want that to be true, but that's not what brought him there. Or here.

"I call bullshit," I hum.

He laughs out. "Bullshit?"

"Yes, bullshit. You went into that bar and needed information. I was your mark—"

He laughs out for real this time. "My mark? What do you think, I'm a spy?"

"I think you're charming and sexy. Mysterious and and dangerous. I think you know exactly how to get what you want and you got it out of me."

"Maybe that's how it started."

I hate the truth of it. I close my eyes letting the silence linger. Thinking about what I want if it's going to end.

"I went to Hideaway needing to confirm that it existed. I was looking for a friend. My job, the same kind I was here to do for your family, isn't paid for in cash and checks. Currency is paid out in favors. I owed a favor. That's what brought me to Hideaway."

I close my eyes and ask the one question I'm afraid to hear the answer to. "Tell me your friend didn't go there to hurt anyone."

"Just the opposite, Crowne," he says softly. "I promise you that when I found out what Hideaway was, who would be in a place like that, I wouldn't let anyone I didn't trust know about it."

I let his words linger and swipe away the tear that tracks down the side of my face. I think I needed to hear that.

"Those types of jobs are done. This one, in Rumor, was my last." He exhales loudly before he says, "I should've been gone the minute I got out of those fucking zip ties." I hear him moving around, a car door closing.

"If it's done, then why are you still—" I start to ask, but he quickly cuts me off, out of breath.

"You. I'm still here because, before you walked back into my life, I had every intention of finding you. It didn't matter that you lied. After I knew what Hideaway was, I understood why you did. And that you were there for a reason. And that none of it mattered because I still wanted you." He lets out a frustrated breath. "I didn't suddenly grow a conscience, Wyn. I'm not a good guy. But I sure as fuck met someone who knocked me sideways. Someone worth finding again and seeing if she felt, even a little of what I felt."

My pulse races, words instantly failing me. *Maybe I've wildly misjudged Julian Colton.*

"Say something," he says softly, vulnerability dripping from his tone and inflection.

My eyes shoot to his. "I've thought about you too," I rush out before I lose my nerve. And instantly, my body starts relaxing when I hear his quiet hum. It's enough encouragement to keep going. "I thought about how you looked at me." I smile, closing my eyes when I add, "You smelled so good. I felt so good being touched by someone after so long."

I want to tell him about what came before, why I'll always feel slightly broken, and why this pull between us could never work. I cover my eyes, shake my head. To be interesting to a stranger who doesn't know anything about who I was before, what I became, or who I'm trying to be now feels too good and has me buzzing from more than just whiskey.

Intimacy and sex should go together. If this had the makings of a healthy relationship, it probably would. But if intimacy is about sharing secrets that might make me crumble, then sex is the only part I can entertain. And oh, how I want to entertain. I uncover my eyes, a smirk still playing across my lips as I make a choice. And it's as if making this decision flips some kind of switch inside of me. There's no reason why I shouldn't enjoy every moment with him while I can.

"I thought about your lips," I tell him, the pad of my finger lightly swiping across my bottom lip. "The way they tasted and how they felt all along my throat." I run my fingers down the center of my throat, ending at my breastbone, brushing over the satin center of my bra. "When I'm alone, I think about all the ways your mouth could be put to use, Julian."

A breath of air whooshes through the line, as if he's been holding it and waiting. "And what would my lips be doing to you, if I were where you are right now?"

"Nothing. They don't get to taste." My hand glides across my chest, brushing my warm skin, the fullness of my breasts that so eagerly want attention. "But I would let you watch."

"Tease," he drags out in a deep, husky tone.

"And I'd want to see what watching me would do to you." I ghost my fingers down my bare stomach and across my lower belly. "If you're man enough to follow my direction or too turned on and already touching yourself."

I wait for a response. I get lost in the low lights and mood I've set before I realize he's not responding at all this time. Lifting the phone from my ear, I look to see if he's still there. "Did I render you speechless?"

Three rapid knocks come from my front door.

I sit up quickly. My stomach swoops at the possibility of him being on the other side of that door. Maybe a part of me wanted to see if he would read between the lines when I basically suggested it. I move toward the door, waiting to see if they'll knock again, pulling a caftan from the rack that's only ever been there as decoration. The thin material drapes around my shoulders, the jewel tones of the floral pattern reaching the floor as I hold it closed at the center of my chest.

"Who is it?" I call out.

Knock. Silence. *Knock*. Silence. *Knock*. "I thought you wanted to see what watching would do to me," Julian says, his voice muffled from the other side of the door.

I try to work through how I might survive this—if I open this door, I need to be sure I can trust myself and him. My mouth waters, renewed nerves creeping along my body and mingling with pent-up sexual attraction.

Flipping the lock, I lift the latch and let the door swing open. The warm summer air dances just beyond the threshold as Julian stands there like some kind of offering from the universe. Maybe this is my reward. The karma I'm due. Or simply what I need.

He doesn't say anything, standing there in his dark jeans and boots. A worn black T-shirt with the sleeves torn off and armholes stretched, wrists and fingers naked from any jewelry as he opens his hands and squeezes them into fists at his sides.

"Deciding how brave you want to be?" he asks.

A loaded question, and the same one he asked that night in Montana all those months ago. I look down his body, appreciating the sheer size of the man in my doorway—tall and thick, strong and unapologetic in every single way. Bravery doesn't have a place here with the way he's looking at me, and with the way I'm feeling, there's only one possible answer.

"How about I show you?"

CHAPTER 16

Julian

She turns on the balls of her bare feet, the nearly sheer robe she's wearing not leaving much to my imagination. It's belted at the waist, but the two sides of it don't meet until just above her navel. Bold colors of tattooed flowers trail up the length of her back, showing through the material. *Beautiful.* I run my palm across my mouth and swallow as I watch her peachy ass proceed down the small entry hall leading into her place.

There's no mistaking the push and pull we've had and the way the tension between us tonight is a hair's breadth away from fucking snapping. I knew it was a gamble coming over here, but I don't overthink when I want something. And, fuck, do I want her.

I sat in my Bronco parked across the street and watched as she walked across the bridge to her place. I wasn't going to let her leave my sight, not after telling her I was there if she needed me. I want to understand exactly what she's wrapped up in. I'm beyond the point of curiosity. I need to know that she's safe and what I can do to make sure she stays that way. That was my intent, but now? I blow out a breath as I close the door behind me, following her inside.

The low rumble of thunder sounds off in the distance as I take in the silhouette of her curves that show through the long, thin robe she's wearing as she turns to me. She looks down at the bottle of whiskey I'm still holding and then reaches out her hand for me to pass it over to her.

She smiles. "At least you have good taste."

"There was an incredibly insightful bartender I met once who really talked up Tennessee whiskey," I say as I look around the loft-style space. Oversize canvases hang along the largest span of walls. Books fill her shelves, and more are stacked and used as side tables in the living space. With her back to me as she pours, I walk through the studio-style room. The kitchen carries the same bohemian vibe as the rest of the place. Gold and brass fixtures, a mint-green fridge, and pots with herbs and tiny flowers line the counters and bar separating the kitchen.

"What would happen if you were in that bar again, with Naomi?" she asks as she turns.

Whatever it is her mother and grandmother shared, I'm sure she's feeling a lot of things right now. And playing along, taking her lead, is something I'm more than happy to do.

Looking at me with a glass in her hand, she adds, "Before she threatened you with a taser, before you saw things you weren't supposed to see in that office? What if we were back there right now?"

I swallow, knowing there are layers here to what's happening. That she doesn't want to be who we are right now. Maybe that's too difficult after hearing what her family had to say before I got here. Maybe she wants to hold on to some semblance of control. Maybe she wants to just pretend like the incredible coincidence of finding her again would only happen there and only as who we were while we were in Hideaway. My mouth waters, taking in the way she looks right now—messy and confident, determined and turned on. "I would say, if that's the game you'd like to play, then tell me the rules."

Her lips part just as they tip up along one side.

"Sit," she says, passing me a rocks glass. The room is charged with tension. The way she's taken command has my dick flexing. When she presses her pouty lower lip to her glass, my body tenses, fully aware of her every movement from her first sip to the path she makes to the record player.

There are many things that turn me on. I've enjoyed myself with plenty of people throughout my life, but the woman less than twenty feet from me has a hold on me in ways that I can't begin to understand. I feel protective and unraveled near her, aroused and pissed off, and I'm overwhelmed with longing that I've never experienced for someone before, so I sit.

The only sound that cuts the silence is of my pulse throbbing as she chooses a record to play. I watch her wordlessly, pressing my lips to the glass and taking a sip, tracing the shape of her body beneath the sheer robe. The bite and burn of the drink turns warm and familiar as I drain my glass. Rubbing my fingers and palm of my free hand along the plush velvet of the chair, I want to take whatever part of her she's willing to share with me. I'm internally praising her for letting me in.

A low vibration of bass guitar starts moments after the needle hits the record and an electric guitar chord cuts in just before a low and slow rendition of "Tennessee Whiskey" plays through.

I shift back, getting more comfortable as she walks from the record player to where I'm sitting. Two chairs make up the living space with a direct line of sight to her bed. And she stands at the foot of her bed, facing me, she drains what's left in her glass.

"I feel sexy when you look at me," she says, pulling the longest ribbon to the bow that's holding the front of her robe together. "Like you savor every glance, and that each time, it's as good as you're expecting."

I smirk, lifting an eyebrow. "You are. I do. And it does."

"Would you like to watch me now?" she asks in a purr, looking like a fucking goddess.

I rub my palm across my mouth. *Fucking hell, I'm going to come in my pants, aren't I?* "Yeah, Crowne. I want to fucking watch."

"So do I," she says as her robe drifts open and billows to the floor.

I've been around enough stylists to know that what Wyn is wearing wouldn't be considered by any of them as lingerie—my mouth waters—but there's not a single man on this planet, attracted to women, who wouldn't have tented pants seeing her in her simple bra and panties.

I shift in my seat, trying to ease the way my dick punches at the zipper of my jeans.

She looks down at my lap. "I said that I'd like to watch too."

"Fuck," I breathe out. Unbuckling my belt, I keep my eyes locked with hers. "What do you want me to do? You're going to have to be specific."

Her throat bobs as she swallows. "I can do that," she says quietly, lips parting as my fingers work to unbutton, unzip, and fold open the front of my pants.

My dick strains against the material of my navy boxer briefs, a wet spot expanding where the tip of my dick rubs lightly. "Tell me, Crowne, because I'm more than eager to know," I start to ask, dragging my palm over my lap, "how would you put my mouth to use right now?"

She gives me the most tantalizing tilt of her mouth, just before she turns, showing off the beautiful curve of her ass. *Fuck, I want to bite it.*

My dick twitches again at the thought. I squeeze my hand over it as she crawls up to the headboard of her bed. The brief pressure of my grip has me grinding out a sound that comes from somewhere deep in my chest.

Keeping me on edge, she perches herself against the ornate wooden headboard. It would only take a few steps to reach her. I'd drag her down the length of the bed and eat every drop of arousal her pussy is making for me. Pretty puckered nipples peek through the satin of her bra, and the illusion of light mixed with the color being so close to the tone of her skin, I can almost imagine what they look like naked. The fullness of her tits moves in time with her labored breathing as she finally answers me.

"I'd very much like you to suck on these," she says, drawing fingers in circles around the tips of her nips. "Paying attention to the way I react as you change from licking…to sucking…to dragging them between your teeth, just enough…"

I groan. "Tell me to touch myself, Doc." I sound out of breath, barely holding my shit together from just a few words. My fingers dig into the plush leather arms of my chair, trying to keep myself in check.

A slow smile pulls at her lips as she reaches behind her back and unclasps the bra so that her tits spill out with a bounce.

Fucking hell.

"Touch yourself, Julian," she demands smoothly. "I want to see."

The head of my dick rubs at the waistband as I push the

material down. I wrap my palm around the shaft and give my balls a good tug before I rock my wrist and pulse my grip. "Fuuuck," leaves me on an exhale as I tip my head back.

When I bring my gaze back to her, she licks at her bottom lip before biting into it. "I didn't think I could get so turned on by watching you work yourself like that."

Another groan leaves my throat before I make my demand. "Show me."

Her cheeks flush, and I notice the music looping in the background. The same song, like time doesn't matter, only the reality that she hasn't even touched me, and this might be one of the most intimate, sexy moments of my entire life.

She opens her knees, feet pressed to the mattress below her as she drags the material of her panties to the side, gifting me with a beautiful sight. Pink and puffy, warmed up, and if I had permission, I know my tongue would swipe along that perfect slit and she'd taste so fucking good.

One finger finds her clit immediately, then two. She drags them between her pussy lips, dipping ever-so-sweetly into her cunt so she can glide her wetness around where she wants.

My fingers pulse tighter, and I shift, slouching lower in the chair. My wrist drags up slowly, mimicking her moves and squeezing the tip where pre-cum beads and leaks along my knuckles.

"That's it, spread your juice around for me. Get everything nice and wet." I exhale and relax deeper into the chair. "I want to see what makes you feel good."

"Oh god." A shaky breath leaves her, cheeks tinging a deeper pink as she drags her fingers up and down, from clit to slit and repeats it until her middle finger is coated and dipping inside her, all the way to her knuckle and back out again.

I exhale loudly, not realizing I've been holding my breath as I watch, transfixed.

"Don't forget to breathe," she says teasingly.

"Can't help it," I rasp as I work my grip up and down at a measured pace. "Not sure I've caught my breath since the fucking moment I saw you." Her eyes meet mine as my arousal drips across my fisted fingers. "I've thought about this—you touching yourself like this—on your knees for me, me on mine for you..." I admit in a low, quiet voice.

She shifts her body up, fingers working her clit while the other hand moves up to her tits, playing with her nipples. "On my knees? Doing what?"

My wrist moves faster as her breathing picks up, a smile dancing on my lips. "Swallowing my cock, riding my face, fucking in my lap, slipping it into your ass—Fuck." I already feel like I could blow as I watch her two fingers stretch her cunt, working their way in and out. The sound of it, wet and sloppy, makes my dick harder.

Her legs butterfly out, dropping to the mattress as she says, "I've already enjoyed your fingers. Your cock, however..." She moans, looking at my dick as if she's never wanted anything more. "I know it'll fit so tight."

The thought of it has my skin slicked, my tongue numbing as I watch and listen to her work herself. I try slowing, loosening my grip—*fuuuuck*.

"Don't stop," she rushes out. "Don't you fucking stop." Arching her back, her chest expands and collapses with each breath as her fingers dip and glide. Sweat slicks between her breasts and the deviant sounds of our arousals mixed with the escaping moans pushes me further. I squeeze my cock tighter. The tendons in my forearms flex as I swipe my thumb along the slit, slicking from rim to crown, and back down, easing the friction of my palm. I stretch my legs wide and fight every instinct I have not to get up and go to her.

Her thighs quiver, and my breathing stutters. "Julian," she says in a breathy plea. "I want to see you come."

That's all it takes. Seeing her ready and telling me what she wants is enough to let my orgasm take over. My body jerks as my hand grips and chokes my dick. *Fuck*. Everything quiets, the faint sound of her moaning is the only thing keeping my eyes open as the first pulse of cum hits my chest. I hold on tight for the next pulse as another wave pulls me up, and I come on myself again. With my knuckles soaked, I loosen my grip and slow my strokes.

Only a moment later, and she sucks in a deep breath, mouth open, chin tilted up. Her chest bows as every muscle flexes, from her neck to her fingers. She barely makes a sound as her lips part and eyes close. The moment her orgasm lets her go, she's gasping for air. Her panties are stretched out, but still on, and a dazed smile works its way across her lips. A breathy laugh leaves her as she meets my gaze and blinks slowly.

"You were very good at listening to my rules." Her eyes close briefly when she adds, "But I still think you're right."

"About what?" I ask as she stretches and settles her body.

She hums, "We're nowhere near being done here."

CHAPTER 17

Wyn

"AM I MISREADING THINGS?"

I cough, waking myself up. *What was that?* I keep repeating that question, but I don't understand why or who said it.

As I turn over, paper crinkles beneath my cheek. I wonder for the briefest moment where I'll be when I open my eyes. *Breathe*. Listen. Feel. The hum of the air-conditioning, warm cotton sheets, and a folded piece of paper sticking to my face.

Remembering the last thing I did, I sit up quickly. *He's not still here.* I stare at the chair Julian sat in last night as he watched me, covering my smile with my hand at the audacity of my behavior. I felt so sexy, longed for, wanted, and in control. Looking down, sheets pool at my waist. I'm naked and almost entirely stripped of the armor I still feel necessary to wear. The scar along my side is exposed and my pulse ticks higher—I didn't think about it. And he didn't ask questions or flinch. Instead, he took complete pleasure in what I did to myself, working out every last drop of cum from his cock.

I pull the covers up over my face, dropping back onto my

mattress. *Oh god, I did that.* Embarrassment peeks out before I'm turned on all over again. *I wish he'd stayed.* I was so comfortable and felt so good that I must have dozed off. I felt his lips on my forehead, his fingertips in my hair, and then nothing after that until right now.

Shifting the covers, I sit back up again and reach for the folded white paper airplane. Its pointed tip and crisply folded wings are only slightly bent from being laid on. When I unfold it, there's a note waiting for me.

Borrowed back my cuff. Don't worry, I'll return it. Xo, Julian

P.S. You make the most beautiful sounds when you come

I smile and cover my face, and since he's not here, I punch the air in front of me repeatedly and squeal. "Holy shit!" I start laughing. When I finally calm my morning post-mutual-masturbation celebration, I stare at the door to my pathetic garden patio and see The Whispering Fool in the distance. The rest of last night pummels into me. The reality of what my mother and grandmother have done, or rather, do. Even though the details about how aren't clear, the reasons why are. I suck in a deep breath. *Don't spiral.*

I try taking my time counting down from ten. Exhaling all of the air from my lungs, I shake out the nervous energy from my limbs. It takes a dozen more times until I start rolling through logic. Pain can come in many forms. Helping Cora Billings meant hurting someone else. It feels justified. *If I think that, what does that make me?* I've been in the presence of death—what that looks like when it's for sport and when it has no purpose. That isn't what my family does, I know that without a doubt.

Glancing at the time, I'm relieved that it's still this early.

Sunday mornings are my time to focus and center myself. A tactic I've learned to help me feel in control when I start to get lost in bad thoughts and memories. When I shower and wash my hair, I let the steam fill the room. I play the latest episode of *The Distilled Truth* and listen to my sister talk about the nuances of bourbon being strained through charcoal to create Tennessee whiskey. As I sip my coffee, I shove aside everything else. It makes me want to skip breakfast and spend as much time as I can inside the distillery today.

It was a lazy morning before I found my way up the walkway to the distillery. Parked out front when I finally get to the top of the hill is my uncle's truck. While Tommy runs the only bed-and-breakfast in Rumor, he keeps things running around here, too. He always has and stepped in with my father being out of the picture. He might get on my mother's last nerve, but Birdie loves him as if he's family and not an extension of it. Truthfully, I don't know how he's survived all our bullshit over the years.

From here at the top of the hill, to the other side of the river and just beyond that, belongs to the Crowne women. On this side, there's the distillery and my place. I love this little plot of land. I smile and can picture a grandiose garden in the back, one to rival, or at least match, the one Birdie has. The river flows in a horseshoe, wrapping around the sides and back of The Whispering Fool—my mother's pride and joy. And on the other side, beyond the line of birch trees, is where we grew up in Birdie's house.

The minute I slide open the barn door, something feels off. The last time something felt off, I walked in on a crime scene. I listen and hear a transistor radio playing an old country station somewhere in the center of the big room, echoing off the walls and high ceilings.

I slowly walk past the pile of wood staves that's been

deconstructed from used barrels and through the entryway to the small office that was once used as storage. The second I walk past, I stop dead in my tracks, slamming my eyes closed, and then walk backwards to make sure I'm not hallucinating about what I think I just saw.

"Mom?" leaves my mouth before I can stop it.

"Oh, fuck me!" She flails her arms, nearly falling out of the chair. The same chair that Tommy is sitting in beneath her.

When the hell did this start?

"For fuck's sake, Wyn," she shouts, scurrying off Tommy's lap with such dramatic flair that I'm almost unable to process what's happening. Leave it up to Lu Crowne to get caught doing something, and then she's the one who gets out sorts about it.

"Are you shitting me?" I say to the both of them, pointing between them. "How long has this been going on?"

Eyes wide, I stare at the two of them, waiting for some kind of answer or excuse that I'm reading the situation all wrong, despite the fact that my mother is shoving her skirt back down over her hips and my Uncle Tommy is manspreading on the chair, trying to cover the smile playing out across his mouth.

"I don't know what you think is so funny right now," Lu says to him as she stuffs her foot into her heeled boot. "Dammit, where's my phone." Her eyes flick around as she squats to the floor.

"Are you wearing the same clothes you worked in last night?" I ask with a squint. Looking down, I close my eyes when I catch sight of something that definitely confirms any remaining doubt of what was going on here, and tip my head back to look at the ceiling. "Your underwear are on the coffee table."

"Lu," Tommy interjects, but she ignores him.

"Before you start getting all out of sort about this, do me a favor and don't," Lu says to me.

My eyes widen at her. "Getting out of sorts?!" *Is she for fucking real right now?* This isn't some random guy I found her giving a lap dance to, which I might add, has happened before. This is Tommy. He's been in my life for my entire life. I am all kinds of out of sorts about it.

"Lu," Tommy says again, but she flicks her wrist at him as she rummages through the desk on the other side of the small room.

"This is—" I blow out a breath. *How do I navigate this?*

But she finishes the sentence with, "None of your goddamn business, Wynona."

I shake my head and scoff.

"Tallulah," Tommy says louder this time.

"You just made it my business," I bark back to her.

Ignoring me, she turns toward him, visibly annoyed. "What?" Her arms fly out to her sides. "Thomas, what?" she yells. "I'm lookin for my—"

"Phone," he says with it held between two fingers.

She tries yanking it from him, but he holds tight.

I tilt my head, observing this wordless exchange between the two of them, and start to wonder how much more I've missed. Not when I was gone either, but how much I didn't see or wouldn't see when I was here.

When Lu finally pulls the phone away, she barely glances at me when she says, "I'm not interested in your judgment right now."

"I'm not judging you, Lu," I huff out. But she's well on her way through the sliding door and down the path to the house, stomping away like a pissed-off child.

"Could have fooled me, kiddo," Tommy says, buttoning the second button on his flannel shirt.

"What the hell does that mean?" I rush out. Propping my hands on my hips, I watch as he scoots forward on the worn chair.

With his elbows on his knees and forearm hanging in front of him, he exhales heavily. "It means, what you're saying isn't the same as how you're actin'. I'm sure you think you just walked in on your mother and I fucking around." He sniffs out a laugh. "Not happening. But she had a hard night. Those don't happen too often, but even the great pain in the ass that is Tallulah Crowne needs someone to melt into, lean on, and lose time with sometimes."

"And last night, that was you?" I say, lifting my eyebrows, trying not to smile at how I wouldn't have guessed it. My father's brother…

"I've always been that for her. Long before you were ever in this picture, Wyn. And she's been that for me," he says as he stands and moves past me, through the center of the room.

Have her bad nights been after murdering men in the name of revenge, or has it been the norm of shitty customers and the typical stresses that come with being a woman owning a business and navigating being a single parent?

"Whatever you're working really hard at in that big, beautiful brain of yours, I'll just ask that maybe you should give her a break." He tosses the long copper whiskey thief onto the bench in front of me. "You want to be pissed off at her, I get it, she's frustrating as shit. Your mother is complicated. Doesn't mean you have to absorb it or even understand it."

I wonder how much he really knows. Tommy has been around my entire life and long before it too. "She's shared some of what that complication looks like," I say leadingly. But he just listens and waits for me to say more. "I still don't know how I feel about some of the things she's told me."

"Here," he says, passing me the mallet and stopper. The drill in his hand lets out a loud zipping noise as he tests its battery. This is our routine. A lazy morning, followed by a weekend afternoon in the distillery for a few hours. When he finished the renovations on my place, he had more time and spent it here with me. Walking toward the barrels in the far side of the room, he adds, "Sometimes, sharing things with people makes you feel closer to them. Trusting them with details about the ways that life can be difficult is how we connect."

How do I ask, *Hey, any chance she told you about her passion project of "offing" men?* Or, *Is it possible that she killed my dad and your brother?* But I don't ask either of those things; instead, I sit with the fact that there's more here. Layers of life that I've been so unaware of and closed off to long before I ever disappeared. I settle on asking, "Did she tell you why she had a rough night?"

He gives his head a quick shake. "Didn't have to. We don't work that way. Your mother doesn't need to justify much to me. I'm not built like that. You want to tell me shit to feel better? I'll listen. But it's not necessary." He works the drill through the top side of the barrel, and once that's cut, I push the long end of the whiskey thief inside. It works as a long tube to siphon out just enough of the whiskey in the barrel to taste. "Explanations, details, excuses, whatever you want to call it—I made the choice a long time ago that when one of the Crowne girls needs something, I'll be there. No need for any currency."

The fact that he looked at that as a simple decision says enough about the kind of man he is, and I've been lucky enough to have him in my life. My dad wasn't anything worth remembering, but his brother, my uncle, has always made me feel seen and loved, despite the craziness that swirls around us.

Mint coats my mouth, and on the tail end, I can taste the

lime zest—tart and bitter, but it balances out the bite of whiskey that's been sitting in this barrel. It isn't long enough for what I like, but it still qualifies being called a whiskey, and I want to play around with it. I move toward the center bench to see if my idea might work.

"Not bad," Tommy says, holding up the glass in the light. "I like the bite, but it's intense."

Setting aside the rest of the shot, thinking he's right, I pull out the glass bottle of mineral water I stored in the mini fridge out here. Shaking it and pressing the spout turned it into carbonated water. It's an old-school way to make Italian soda. Something I watched Mickey Moonie do hundreds of times as a kid. It isn't anything original, but with the right flavors, it could be something new. I pour equal parts of the carbonated water into the shot glass and pass it to Tommy. "Now what do you think?"

He takes a sip and smiles after he swallows. "Wouldn't mind sipping on that at picnics."

I nod proudly.

"How long have you been thinking about this one?"

I shrug, not wanting to answer him. Probably too long for something that's a Sunday hobby. I knew that on its own, these flavor profiles might not work, but the mint and citrus mixed with carbonated water turned it into a spritz. *I could see people drinking this. Or even businesses buying it as concentrate and making their own.*

"It's a creative take. I haven't had anything like it," he says honestly.

And the sense of pride that fills me as I hear it feels so much more meaningful than being commended for grants and research by colleagues.

"Alright, I need to head back to the B&B," he says, kissing the top of my head. "You might want to take a look at those barrels over in the far corner. Your mom spent some time out here with that batch."

My heart stutters, and I whip my head to look at where he nodded. "Why would she…"

But Tommy's already halfway to the door. He shouts over his shoulder, "Like I said, kiddo. I don't ask too many questions, but that doesn't mean you shouldn't."

Looking up and outside, I lock my elbows straight and lean over my workspace. A sense of calm washes over me as I take inventory of each part of this view—tall oaks and stout maples, plenty of river birch that lean along the riverbed. In the ending dip of summer, only a few wildflowers still hold on, the pale yellows and creamy whites peppering the tall grass. All of it is land that hasn't been touched by anyone other than Crownes, simply because Birdie doesn't allow it.

There's a strategy to the way these buildings have been updated and laid out. My father's family owned what was on this side of the river, and my mother's family owned, lived, and thrived on the other. She used to say that they were the original Hatfield and McCoys, except most of my father's family died, leaving Tommy to handle what was left, plus the bed-and-breakfast.

There's been so much lore about my family over the years, it's hard to determine what stems from truth and what's wrapped in total bullshit, including the one about my mother being a black widow. There have been plenty of rumors about what had really happened to my father. I don't miss him. My mother hated him and had plenty of bad things to say over the years, and I understood it. One day, he was gone for good, and Birdie bought the whiskey distillery, allowing Tommy to stay and keep it up until she decided what she wanted to do with it.

The southwestern winds shake the three oversize garage doors, making them clang loudly, and I glance at my phone, noticing messages waiting for me.

JULIAN:

Do you know how hard it was not to touch you, fuck you, fall asleep next to you?

My lips part as I read the message more than once, suddenly feeling hot all over. He didn't gloss over anything, and I hate how much I like that about him.

WYN:

I had a very nice view of how hard it was, yes.

JULIAN:

Comments like that make things hard all over again.

WYN:

Sounds like you might have a problem on your hands.

JULIAN:

Tell me I can see you later.

CHAPTER 18

Julian

I READ OUR TEXT EXCHANGE again, smiling at the way she had no problem telling me exactly like it is. And yeah, she's right; we're nowhere near done.

Running my hand through my hair, I lean forward, elbows on my knees, trying to figure out how I went from being so adamant about this being my last job and to focus my attention on the work that is more palatable, to obsessing over this woman. I've never been this guy, the one who's head turns easily, getting caught up with a pretty face and a great body.

I shake my head. She's more than that.

"Fucking hell," I breathe out to myself. What the hell do I want to do next?

It was barely sunrise when I woke up with my dick still in my hand, in that same chair I got to watch her from. She was sprawled out on her bed, looking like a fucking fantasy. It took everything I had not to get into bed with her, but she had boundaries the night before, and I wasn't going to push them. I decided to take a beat, go back to the B&B, and have a shower.

I have no plans of leaving Rumor, but the stakes keep rising. Between the family who hired me, the homicide detective who's conveniently staying at the same bed-and-breakfast as I am, and now knowing that the dead guy in the bar, Stan Billings, was law enforcement, I need to navigate this carefully. Then there's the connection that my dad had to this place that seems to have been far more than just too-frequent cleanups.

I've been sitting out here, on the porch, making assumptions and plans for most of the morning. That is, before I decided to pull out my phone and make a call. And while the asshole on the other end of the line grated on me sometimes, I still appreciated the quietness of where I am. I always thought I'd end up in a city, owning a gallery. I'd keep my beachside spot in Oregon, but my plans were more conducive to city living. Now that I'm here, I realize I would hate that.

"Rhodes, this is a simple request. You owe me, not the other way around. I have no plans on making any pieces for your installation or collection. I'm merely asking if you have the tanzanite and emerald from the last auction in Antwerp."

He huffs out a laugh. "Julian, I outbid you specifically because I didn't want you to have them. Why would I sell them? The whole point is to make sure you can't do anything with those stones unless it's for me."

"You're in the diamond capital of the world and you dropped more money on other stones that weren't diamonds, just to outbid me," I say, putting him on speaker so I can swipe to my texts.

"Fine. Favor for a favor," he says, trying to negotiate.

"You already owe me. That's not how payment works. I've got something going on here, and I want those stones."

"I don't get what I want, you don't get what you want.

Seems fair in my book," he says as car horns ring out in the background behind him.

"Such a dick," I breathe out with a laugh.

"Foxx tells me you're in my neck of the woods," he says, shifting topic. Rhodes is exceptional at sniffing out details and twisting them to suit whatever's keeping him entertained. "I'm going to head up to him. Maybe you can convince me over something expensive in his bourbon vault."

I stretch out my legs, crossing my boots at the ankle, and look out at the overgrown field at the front of The Rackhouse B&B. While Tommy could do with some landscaping, the long grass and wildflowers give this place an untouched feel. My friend on the other line would be anxious at the thought of a spot like this one.

"I'm in a small town about an hour or so south of where you are. Thinking about sticking around here, opening up a workspace, see if it'll be the change I've been needing."

"Who is she?" he asks almost rhetorically, and then mumbles, "Better yet, how long?"

"None of your business," I clip back. "And fuck off." Humor lingers in my response.

Letting out a long sigh first, he says, "You know what? Let's plan on that drink up in Fiasco when you get bored, and I'll consider what it is I want for the stones."

"The cleaning business is wrapped, Rhodes, so your payment comes in cash or other jewelry."

He lets out a defeated grunt. "You're a man of many talents, Julian. I'm sure we can figure something out."

But before I can respond, he hangs up on me just as Tommy comes through the front porch door. "Your last name is Colton, right?"

"It is," I answer as I watch him walk down the stairs and toward the big barn about a hundred feet from here.

"Any chance you're related to a Sam Colton?" he asks.

My stomach bottoms out at hearing my father's name. I clear my throat as I nod. "My dad's name is," I correct, "*was* Sam."

He stops walking and nods with a tight-lipped smile. "Had a feeling." Tilting his head toward the large barn, he says, "C'mon, got something you might want to see."

For a man who's supposed to be nameless and faceless on these jobs, there are quite a few people in this town who knew him. I walk along the cement walkway lined with river rock on each side, connecting the barn to the driveway. The barn's exterior is white, just like the main house. And whiskey barrels flank the sliding main door. When I follow Tommy inside, it's sectioned off into workspaces instead of stalls for animals.

Most of it is Tommy's tools and equipment—a variety of carpentry and things I recognize as part of the distilling process. Some larger pieces of furniture that are in the middle of being fixed or refinished are spread out, but farther down, there are canvases and paints, drop cloths and brushes. The massive fans above move slowly but whirl cooler air around the space, negating the fact that it's still hot as hell in the late afternoon.

"I didn't put it together until Jo started moving things out of her workspace." He glances up at the stacks of canvases. "She made such a big deal about you being an artist at dinner the other night, but I didn't connect it at first." Rummaging through a junk drawer, he pulls out a pouch filled with keys. He moves past me after finding what he was looking for and back toward the counter that lines the entirety of the wall. "I have a feeling some of this might belong to him," he says as he unlocks a black-and-silver tool cabinet.

I stop mid-step and swallow roughly. *That can't be right.* Between hearing about my father at Moonie's and now this? I've got more questions than I know what to do with. It feels like I'm unearthing an entire life he had that I never knew existed.

When he opens the bottom drawer, there's a few large items—jeweler's saws, a small tank of oxygen, and a lathe.

I sniff out a clipped laugh, not expecting to see any of that. For anyone just looking through, they might see randomness or junk, but the lathe would typically be used for watchmaking—a hobby my father said he was never good at but tried anyway. I tilt my head below the bench and see a propane tank. If it's combined with the oxygen, they'll power torches and control the high temperatures for shaping metals.

Tommy pulls open the drawers above, and they're stacked with files and hammers. Pliers are meticulously lined in the top drawer, but it's when he opens the lid that I know exactly who all of this belongs to.

"Stayed here when he came into town," Tommy says with a thoughtful expression. "He kept to himself, mostly, but I liked him. Salt of the earth kind of guy." Tommy claps his hand on my shoulder as he walks away. "Take what you'd like from here, use it, whatever you'd like to do. I'm sure he'd want you to have everything."

"Appreciate it," I say as I start to pick through the discarded pieces of metal and soldering, pulling out a few unfinished pendants and rings. Beneath it is a folded-up piece of paper in a familiar shape—a pointed front and a symmetrical fold of wings that I know when I pull out will be a basic dart fold. "I didn't—" I clear my throat, shoving down every single feeling that's threatening to surface. "I didn't know he had spent time here."

Tommy turns back and says, "I'm not as loud or pretty as the Crowne girls, but I know how it feels to love them, and to want to be near them, even when it's not an option. I don't know why he came so often. I have some theories, but then again, I have some of those about you too." He smiles to himself.

I wonder exactly how much he knows about all of it.

"I'd really like to not be wrong about you, Julian. So do me a favor; if you're here for anything other than the right reasons, leave. Stop by the bar, hedge your goodbyes, and let Wyn move on from wherever it is you followed her from."

That isn't going to happen. I lift my chin and sit taller. The last thing I normally do is care what someone thinks about me, but Tommy seems like the closest thing to a dad in Wyn's life, so I'll treat him that way. "I'm staying for the right reasons," I tell him. "Whatever your theories might be, just know I'd never hurt your niece. And I'll make sure no one else does either."

Clapping his hand on my shoulder, he smiles, shaking his head like I missed the punchline. "I'm glad to hear that. And it's not Wyn who I'd be worried about getting hurt," he says as he turns and moves toward the doors.

I crack a smile, because it's not lost on me the threat that lingered in his words. As I look around at the bench and the few cases filled with tools, I'm more caught up in understanding the semi-permanence of what my dad had built here.

"Dad, why keep this from me?" I say quietly as I catalog the different sizes of metal files and pliers. I start thinking about all the parts that I still don't have clear answers about, and it makes me uneasy. I want to close out this part of my life, wrap a legacy that doesn't feel right anymore without him, and now I'm here and feeling like I'm sinking in information that I won't ever fully understand, not without being able to ask him.

"An accident," was what the deputy had told me. And his cause of death was a heart attack. The injuries to the body had been postmortem, as his car collided with a building on the north side of Queens. It all sounded like some kind of fucking mistake. He was supposed to have been in Tennessee for a job, not up in one of the burrows of New York City. It still feels wrong to this day.

I drag my fingers into my hair, thinking about what he'd say to me about listening to my gut.

"Met a woman once who told me it isn't your gut that tells you when something isn't right. That the world is far more complicated than that. You have to look for all kinds of signs. And listen."

I remember how he folded the blue paper down its center and the top left corner next. I'd already made three and he was still on his first.

Sunday morning coffee with my dad often turned into lunch on days we'd talk about the jewelry business. He'd always ask me, *"Find a woman worth mentioning yet?"* I'd always shake my head and tell him no. I never asked him.

I can't help but smile thinking about what I'd say if he asked that question again now.

With a deep breath, I pull open the last drawer and most of it is just saved pieces of metal, steel nuts that have been filed down, and a pouch of small gemstones that are an interesting mix. But there's a polaroid beneath it that I don't recognize. It's not me or an old one of my mother, but my dad smiling at the camera, holding up his glass with a much younger Birdie Crowne nuzzled into his neck.

"What are you doing out here?" Jo Crowne asks from behind the red pickup.

I shut the door to my Bronco and walk around as she stands to her full height, hauling a sack of something heavy from her shoulder and making the truck bounce as she drops it into the bed.

"Is Birdie inside?" I ask in response.

Stevie comes out from the old building, popping a pink bubble in her mouth. "Thought you'd still be here."

My heart picks up pace at that idea. Wyn is complicated and the situation that keeps unfolding between us gets more and more messy. I'd be fucking lying if I said she doesn't make me feel things, but I'm a bit distracted after what I just found. I don't say anything about that, though. Instead, I smile at the insinuation and say, "Sorry, just came looking for Birdie."

Jo raises her eyebrows and smiles, wide-eyed at me first, and then Stevie.

Ignoring me, Stevie says, "We all watched that little spectacle last night at the bar, Julian," Stevie says, hand propping on her hip. "You guys bang it out yet?" She wiggles her eyebrows.

"Stevie," Jo warns with a roll of her eyes. "Ignore her. She watched too many soap operas growing up, turned her into a hopeful romantic. But Birdie's not here." She points to the wood and rolled-up canvas next to the truck. "Mind getting that?" she asks.

I move around to the back of the truck and grab what she's asking for. "Any idea when she'll be back?"

"She's helping out some of her garden club girls prep barbecue for the Bluegrass Full Moon Fest this weekend. I think she said she had to pop up to Nashville and see a man about some meat."

Stevie snorts out a laugh. "How long have you been wanting to say that?"

Looking at the decent-sized pile they had in front of them to load, I haul some of the wood into my arms and shove it along the far side of the truck bed. "This a music thing?"

"It's a Tennessee thing," Stevie says. She doesn't elaborate any further as she heads into the garage and comes out with two gallons of paint in each hand a beat later.

"What is all of this?" I ask, looking at the truck being stacked with hardware. It's loaded with art supplies, raw materials, and a rolled-up rug, while the front seat is already filled with greenery, with even more green leaves pressing against the back window and draping out the side.

Jo hops down from the truck, closing the foldable bed, and claps dirt off her hands. "I finally leased an art studio. Want to come see it?"

I'm nothing more than a stranger to these women—a dangerous one, if they know why I was brought here to begin with—but they talk to me like I'm a welcome friend. I know their mother and grandmother shared the real purpose for my sudden arrival.

"Don't overthink it, Jules," Stevie says, slapping my back as Jo starts the engine. "Follow us over. We could use the help." The loud muffler almost drowns out what she says next.

"You might know my sister and my grandmother, but we don't know you," she says, pointing her finger between her and the truck where Jo's sitting. "We can be exceptional allies or your worst fucking nightmare." Popping another bubble, she hops into the truck bed before shouting, "You decide!"

I'm not good with threats. They usually make me want to push and do exactly the opposite of what's being asked of me, but this is Wyn's family. And like it or not, they hold far too many cards that I can't see.

"Wouldn't mind your opinion on a few of the pieces I've been working on. Some rich asshole commissioned a series of paintings." She leans out, arm propped on the open window of her truck. "Anyway, he gave me a word and asked that I deliver three paintings of my interpretation. He sent the first set back and told me I lacked originality." She grins to herself. "Kind of need another creative person to take a look."

"Alright," I say as I move back toward my truck. "I'll follow you."

Rumor, on the outside, looks like every other small town I've been to before. Brick buildings housing small businesses, old Victorian homes operating as a combination of doctors offices, a dentist, or attorneys offices, but something about this one feels like there's still room for growing. It doesn't feel like it's peaked yet, despite the empty storefronts. Maybe it's because I like turning basic materials into shiny and pretty things, this place has possibilities. Nosy neighbors and busybodies also linger outside in the late summer afternoon. Some even stop what they're in mid-motion of doing to watch the Crowne sisters in a red pickup truck park out front of the long, empty building.

When I shut my door and I look down the block, it's more of the same. The police station is at the beginning of the long stretch that makes up Rumor's downtown, and here, there's a lot of rundown buildings and only a few local businesses peppered throughout.

"Nosy assholes," Jo breathes out as she looks down the street. A woman with a broom stares at where we're parked, and a few cars slow down as they drive past.

In the back of the truck, Stevie shouts, "Mind ya business, Mary Jo! Keep drivin.'"

The woman, whom I'm assuming is Mary Jo, opens her mouth wide and does the sign of the cross as she picks up to the twenty-five miles per hour that's stenciled in paint across the road.

About an hour later, after unloading all the supplies, I'm staring at a painting that looks like it was stolen from the very secure walls of the Art Institute of Chicago, and wondering, again, who the hell these women are. "You painted that?" I ask, crossing my arms over my chest.

"Fuck yes, she did," Stevie croons from the kitchenette on the far side of the loft space. I glance around and see the corresponding oils on plates, rags smeared with dark greens and deep reds, brushes soaking in turpentine, and the smell of it all still lingers in the air.

I hum out thoughtfully. "Impressive," I say, looking closer. Because while my expertise lies in metals and gems, fine art is easily appreciated by most creatives. It isn't as cliché as Van Gogh's *Starry Night* or *Sunrise* by Monet, but the late-night diner scene of Edward Hopper's *Nighthawks* oil on canvas would be recognized by anyone having taken an art history class in the last forty years. There's a story in it. The creative part of my brain used to live for the story surrounding any piece of jewelry I made. *Where would it be worn? Who would look close enough to see it? Or what would its owner do while wearing it?*

I feel along my wrist at the leather cuff. This one has a new story, and the matching one that's folded in my pocket had a different owner for a while. Seeing it on her lit something in me—pride, or maybe possessiveness at seeing her with something I'd made, I don't know, exactly. It made me want to adjust it for her—to tweak the size so it fit her better and fix along the edges that had been worn away. It's simple, but I haven't felt a desire to make a damn thing for so long that up until now, I don't think I realized how uninspired I had been.

Clearing my throat, I ask Jo, "What was the word?"

She moves to stand next to me, taking in the same painting.

"The one your benefactor gave?" I study along the painting's edges. There's always a detail an artist could be known for. Sometimes, it's the metals and tools used, or the method of creating. For painters, it's about the edges.

"Pith," she says with a smirk.

It was an interesting choice. Pith could be as simple as the white lining the rind of an orange. It's bitter and often avoided. But as I glance around the warm colors of the 1920s diner painted on a large canvas, I think about where this painting originated. "You know this was inspired by Ernest Hemingway's *The Killers*?" I ask.

"I'm aware," she says as she moves behind me, folding up a tarp.

This family is anything but boring, that's for fucking sure. If I had to guess, Pith, in Jo's interpretation, means something entirely different to her.

"I have a feeling you're a fire sign," Stevie says, tossing an orange at me. I catch it and start to peel it.

"Did I say I was hungry out loud or did you have a sixth sense about that too?"

She smiles at what I've said and chucks one to Jo. "I'm a mom. I have snacks all the time, even when I'm kid-free for the day."

I peel away the rind and glance around the room. I've talked about myself more with these women and this family than maybe anyone. It wasn't hard to do, which I'm not sure if that says more about them or about where I am in my life right now. I look up at Jo first, who's working her way around the peel, and then to Stevie. "Sagittarius," is my delayed answer.

Slamming her hand down on the countertop, she points at Jo. "I called it!"

Jo moves toward her, slamming down a twenty-dollar bill, and says, "I was almost positive you were an Aries."

Popping a quarter of the orange into her mouth, Stevie adds, "Wyn is a Gemini, so that would make sense. Smart, and you saw the chemistry." They talk about all this as if star signs and pairings are common knowledge and a forgone conclusion. Like everyone should know their own astrology details and its nuanced interpretations.

"Not sure I believe in any of that," I say to them, letting my mask fall for the briefest moment.

They both gasp loudly, making a show of it.

I can't help the laugh that it pulls out of me, and it feels good to loosen up and let them in a little. "Fine, fine. Tell me why I'm wrong."

"Not wrong, just not as aware as we may have assumed," Stevie says at the end of a hearty laugh. "Everyone thinks that astrology and palm reading, hell, even tarot for that matter, are these woo-woo witchy practices, but the core of each, are rooted in the stars and planets. Details like where the Earth was in its rotation when you were born. The astronomy that existed in the place you were brought to life. It's like any other practice rooted in truth; it's about interpretation and how much belief versus common sense you're willing to put behind it. Flipping a card that gives you permission to look at yourself and your choices from a different lens. It's as subjective as art—what's beautiful to one person could be totally absurd to another—but that doesn't mean it isn't real or doesn't exist. It's okay if you don't believe in it, just don't knock it."

I can see the differences between them, each Crowne sister, but they each look the same when they talk about something passionately.

Jo folds her arms over her chest and tilts her head to the side. "If you find yourself here longer than expected, Julian, I wouldn't mind sharing some of this creative space. There's plenty of room down that way for another artist."

This could easily be transformed into a gallery space—display and offices. There's great lighting, and it's framed by the windows overlooking a town that could use something new.

"If you can handle the little quirks of a small town, that is," she says, peering out the front window. The tinny sound of harmonicas travels from the far side of the street as we step outside toward the truck.

"That's Skip practicing for this week," Jo says as she moves around quart-sized paint cans.

"Whispering Fool performer?" I ask with a smirk. He doesn't seem like the kind of guy to be in a band on stage at the rowdy bar. I've spent plenty of time in small-town Kentucky. Fiasco always has festivals and live music. I know a harmonica in the summertime could very well mean a performance and a party.

"No," Stevie laughs out, furrowing her brow. Like I should already know this information. "Starting in May, all the way through November, there's live bluegrass," she explains as she finishes her orange. "Near the town line, every full moon, there's a spot on the other side of town called The Lucky Hole. They have bluegrass on Sundays, but in the summertime, it's a bigger deal. More people. Tons of barbecue. Dancing and singing under a full moon…" She audibly sighs. "It's one of the few charming things we have left around here."

Jo widens her eyes. "You think Wyn will go?" She looks at Stevie, as if she'll know the answer to that.

"Might be worth asking her," Stevie says, shrugging her shoulders and looking at me, even though I didn't ask.

If it wasn't already obvious at their family dinner or in the way the Crowne sisters orbit around one another, these two women love their older sister, and it isn't lost on me that they like the idea of me spending time with Wyn.

Glancing at Jo first, Stevie adds, "Wynnie survived things that most people…" She shakes her head, trailing off. "She's trying to be less careful, ignoring the noise this place likes to make, and just enjoy life." She pauses, lost in her thoughts for a brief moment before she looks up and smirks at me. Wyn makes a similar face when she's about ready to tell me like it is. "My sister will be fine, no matter what; I'm going to just put that out there. We're Crowne women, we survive at all costs. But you're still here. And I'm guessing it's because you want to be more than to be just a good story." She glances at Jo, and then down at her phone. "She's in classes today until at least four o'clock."

She still hasn't answered my last text, but I wouldn't mind seeing what Dr. Wynona Crowne looks like in front of a lecture hall filled with students.

"Where?" I ask. I need to talk to Birdie about my dad, but it'll have to wait.

Jo smirks at Stevie, like they're reading each other's minds. "The university. Chemistry building."

CHAPTER 19

Julian

I EXPECTED TO SEE IVY lining the brick walkway, or at the very least, draped along the Gothic arched windows. But the university where Wyn taught and researched organic chemistry was anything but predictable. The buildings are busy with students making their way to classes and others leaving for the day, but none of them gives me a passing glance as I walk by. It's a stark contrast to the small town of Rumor, where people casually pay too close attention and are ready to offer a quick bite of gossip, even to a stranger like me. This place feels much bigger and far less personal.

I shoulder past a student coming out of the first open office door inside of the chemistry building.

"I swear, if I hear one more of our students getting bulldozed," a woman behind a row of desks says quietly as she hangs up her phone. "The sheriff has already been here, and I don't think it was about any of those things that've been swirling about you know who."

"I don't like any of it," the woman wearing pink glasses beside her says on an exhale. "Thanks goodness Dr. Crowne came back, I mean, I'm all for hiring young professors like Dr. Andrews, but—"

"You've heard the rumors 'bout that…"

Maybe I was wrong about the gossip piece.

"The one about his TA? Sure did," pink glasses says, shaking her head. "Not sure what to think."

"And then that cop down in Rumor? Been hearing all sorts of things about how he was supplying drugs to our student population."

I lean against the doorway, wondering if they'll take a breath and look up.

"That whole town is a cesspool of unfortunate events," she continues.

"Excuse me, may we help you?" pink glasses rasps with a Southern twang, finally interrupting her colleague when she glances my way.

I smile at both of them. "I'm looking for Dr. Crowne," I say, stepping into the main office.

"Let's see," she says as she looks at her computer. "She has a lecture right now, but it should be finishing up any minute. Did you have an appointment?"

Shaking my head, I give them both a tight-lipped smile. "I'll wait for her by her office," I say, pointing toward the hall I just came in from. "If you point me in the right direction."

"Take a right out of here. Her office is at the end of the hall past the lecture rooms," pink glasses says as she stands. "Are you a friend, or—"

"Or," I answer her over my shoulder as I move down the hall, not elaborating any more. I'm not interested in trying to define who Wyn is to me. I'm still trying to figure that out myself. But she's more than a friend, that's for fucking sure.

The smooth rasp of her voice has me stopping in my tracks. When I step back and peek inside, the stadium-style hall is nearly full. Students with open laptops and others with notebooks abandoned listen to the beautiful professor with rapt attention.

"Let's talk about whiskey," she says as I quietly step inside. I take a seat in the last row, getting a death glare for distracting the guy three seats down. When I look down and toward the podium at the base of the room, there she is, looking like a fucking wet dream. In this librarian-meets-1920s-archaeologist attire, with glasses perched on her nose and her hair pulled back halfway as wavy pieces escape, there isn't a single revealing thing about it. But it's a sexy look—smart and put together. Not perfect, and I like that even more.

I run my thumb along my lower lip, remembering the woman who laid naked and needy in front of me just a few nights ago. I'm feeling enamored all over again, seeing her command a room filled with people.

"There are numerous ways to make it, but the incredible parts happen when we don't touch it. When it's left to its own devices. Let's look at the fermentation of glucose—who can tell me what it turns into?"

While a few students answer, she nods and stands behind the podium, listing out the formulas of the reaction. All of it looks like chaotic combinations of shapes connected with letters and numbers.

"I want to see the chemical equation including the Lewis structures in your exams, so please make sure you're understanding the reactant as well as the conditions."

It doesn't take any of that to be impressed. Watching someone own a room like this is impressive, and I'm taken back by how beautifully complicated she is. How I don't know so much about her and who she was before I met her, but I want to know every detail she'd share with me. Outside of finding her intensely beautiful, she's intelligent and articulate. Talking with her makes it feel like something's clicked for me, something that never has before, not with anyone else.

There isn't a bell, but a buzzer next to her goes off, like her time is up. She glances at the clock behind her, and in tandem, every single person peppered throughout the room stands and collects their things, some already rushing up the stairs and past me.

"Please check your syllabus for the deliverables for next class," she calls out.

Two students linger and talk with her about something that has her smiling and nodding. She hands them each a piece of paper, and then stares at the steps after them as they hustle up toward the door. When the sound of it closes, Wyn blows out a breath. She hasn't noticed me back here yet, and I'm not sure why I haven't made her aware that I'm here.

Bracing her hands on the podium, she looks down at it for a beat. She pulls the pen out of her hair, and with it, her hair falls forward draping around her face. She doesn't look happy. If anything, it's like whatever mask she wore while in front of her students has fallen away, and now, she looks stressed. A huffed laugh leaves her, and with a defeated tone, she says to herself, "That was absolutely awful."

"I don't know," I call out from my seat.

She jumps slightly, her hand splayed on her chest. "Julian," she exhales.

"I thought it made perfect sense to me." I stand and walk down the first couple of steps.

Shaking her head, she asks, "What are you doing here?"

Walking down a few more until I'm across from her, I look

at the equation projected behind her. "Apparently, learning about the chemistry of whiskey."

She glances around to check if anyone else is in the room. "You realize you need to pay to take classes here?"

"What's the currency, Dr. Crowne?"

Her eyes meet mine, and she tries to stifle the smile that question pulls from her.

"Wanted to see you," I tell her honestly. "I spent some time with your sisters today—"

Her brow furrows. "What? Why?" she asks, crossing and then uncrossing her arms.

"I was looking for Birdie, and they ended up convincing me to help move Jo into her new studio space."

She rubs along her forehead and closes her eyes. "I'm not sure how I feel about that."

I take two more steps down, trying to erase the space between us. I know this is complicated; everything about this woman and her family is the biggest red flag, but I like color. My life has felt too black and white for far too long.

"You went quiet on me when I asked to see you later." I rub at the back of my neck. "I don't really care how that sounds. When I want something, I ask for it. And the only games I want to play with you, Crowne, are the ones that'll have you coming like you did the other night."

Her eyes widen as they instantly meet mine.

"You and I started out with more secrets than I think we knew how to handle. I'd like for that to only be our origin story. Not the rest of it."

"So you're here now," she says, watching me move closer. I take another step so that the two of us are at the center of this space.

"I'm here now." I swallow, knowing this is coming on strong, but I'm too old and too caught up in this with her to play casual. "What we did the other night, even if you ignore how much I wanted it, I know that whatever your grandmother and mother spoke with you about, you needed to react, to be in control of something afterwards..." I take one more step until I'm right in front of her, and her gaze follows to look up at me. "I'm glad I was the one there to be of service."

"Who knew you were so selfless?" she teases, finally letting a smirk play out along her pretty lips.

I take a moment to appreciate how fucking beautiful she looks in this skirt and blouse. "This is a good look on you." My eyes make their way down her body.

"I'm assuming you're referring to my clothes and not the whole 'flustered when you're around me' vibe I'm putting off?" she says, laughing at herself.

"I was referring to both, actually, now that you mention it." My eyes roam down her body again, and I can't help but step closer when I see her touch along her wrist in the same place she had been wearing my leather cuff.

"Your sisters seem to know you pretty well, and they had some interesting things to share," I say to her. "I learned that Geminis and Sagittariuses are great matches."

She sniffs out a laugh as she starts packing things into her bag, holding on to a small notebook with one hand, and with the other, she holds her open laptop by the screen with two fingers. Starting to move toward the stairs, she stops and turns toward me. "What else did my sisters say to you?"

"Just a little bit about you, talked about Jo's art, ate some oranges, a few veiled threats, nothing too concerning to worry about," I tease.

She pauses on the step in front of me, working through what I've just said. When she leans closer, her concern breaks away and in exchange she sounds amused as she says, "Careful, Julian. If they end up liking you too much, they'll make it their mission to make sure you never end up leaving."

That didn't scare me, if anything, every warning I hear from the Crowne family has the opposite effect on me. It makes me want it more—her more.

Walking ahead of me and up the stairs, she heads toward her office. Her perfectly shaped ass clings to the skirt that flows just below her knees, the deep burgundy color matching the heels of her shoes. She stays quiet as we reach the hall, a few students lingering and looking at posting on the bulletin boards, but none of them are waiting to speak with her.

"What made you want to be a professor?" I ask, looking at the laptop and then around to the few things displayed along the walls that lead to the suite of offices at the end of the hall.

Unlocking her office door, she flips the lights on.

I follow, unaffected by the silence as I wait for her to answer. She drops her notebook on the oak desk, squaring off her stance. With her hands on her hips, she looks at me, and I take a step closer, placing her laptop and bag down around her. When I perch my ass on the corner edge of the desk, she doesn't budge.

"It was the polar opposite of what my family did," she admits. "But then I got passionate about it, dug in, worked really fucking hard to get here." She shakes her head with a sarcastic smile when she looks around her office space. "I never thought I'd be here right now. But..."

"But?" I dip my head to find those green eyes of hers.

She lets out a long exhale. "It's what I'm supposed to do," she says, staring at me like she's trying to work something out.

"But so much has happened since the last time I taught a science lab or gave a lecture." She glances around the room, where boxes are still packed with framed certificates not hung up. White boards behind her display scribbled shapes with letters and numbers that were on the screen in her class. "And I thought maybe it's just having a routine or feeling a bit rusty working through a syllabus I haven't seen in ages." More quietly, she adds, "It feels all wrong now."

"I know a little something about that." I sniff a laugh to myself. "And now that you know things you didn't before, your life looks completely different somehow, but you're supposed to be the same, do the same that you've always done."

She smiles at me, softening slightly. "So you've been there then?"

"Been there and in it now," I say on a sigh. I realize that this is partly why I wanted to come and see her. I wanted to talk to her. *Shit.* I tilt my head back for a moment, realizing this is already more for me. I'm not the kind of person to overshare, not the man that'll tell anyone much about anything. But this woman has a way of making it okay to do it. Like she'll allow the weight of what I'm navigating to land easy.

"My dad," I share, clearing my throat, "left for a job." I shake my head. "He hadn't been making jewelry for a long while—he relied on me to do most of it," I say with a smile. "Always told me I was more talented, but he was really fucking good. I think he just lost some inspiration." I look up at her, eyes already on me, waiting. "Sometimes he'd stop after a job and buy materials for me for upcoming pieces—precious gems that could be bought directly from mines or collectors." Running my hand behind my neck, I pinch at the base to relieve some of the tension that thinking about this brings. "I just assumed he was traveling to a few spots, but then a couple weeks went by without hearing from him. I didn't talk to him every day, but a couple times a week was normal for us."

I swallow the bitter taste of knowing now that my father had been dead, and I wasn't even looking for him. "He always came back, and he'd tell me about where he'd been. Until very recently, I thought I knew everything there was to know about him." I hurriedly blink back the blur of my eyes watering.

Her eyebrows pinch as she lets the quiet linger, listening without interjecting.

"It took my father dying for me to realize that the family legacies that had become my entire existence look different without him in my life, so much so, that it made me question why I would want to do something that couldn't be talked about or shared, with almost everyone," I say cautiously, as if I'm disappointing him for even thinking about it.

When I finally look up from toying with the leather cuff on my wrist, she's looking at where my fingers run along the worn edges, and I realize I'm doing the same thing she does. Nervous energy working its way out, maybe.

She lets out a laugh, tilting her head, fingers grazing along her wrist, where she had been wearing my other leather cuff. "You said that my family's job was your last. Seems like you're already making changes for what you want."

I don't tell her that I don't know if that choice feels right either, or if I've just lived so long doing what I was told I should do that I don't know how it's supposed to feel when I'm doing something my own way.

She smooths her hands down the sides of her skirt, trying to harden herself for what she's about to say. "Now what? You finished your last job... We've had a few private moments—"

I smile at that, almost laughing, but move my palm across my mouth to cover it. "And that's good enough for you? A few private moments?" I ask, rubbing my hands down the tops of my thighs. I need her closer.

She tips her chin up. "That's not what I'm saying."

Relief washes over me with those five words. I can work with that.

"'Cause that's not fucking good enough for me." I reach for her, my hands gently wrapping behind her thighs and pulling her closer. I need to make sure she really hears me when I say this. I pinch the ends of the black silk tie hanging in a looped bow at the center of her blouse—the material soft and smooth. Tugging on it, I urge her closer as I widen my legs and make space for her to stand between. "I told you already, I'm here, because I choose to be." I search her eyes to make sure she's hearing me now. "I have no problem taking my time, Crowne. I can be a patient man," I say honestly.

"I find that hard to believe," she teases. Her bite back makes my lips and dick twitch.

"The things I've learned to do take an incredible amount of focus, attention to detail, time, patience…" I drift off, getting lost in the way she's looking at me, hearing me. "If you knew the willpower it took to let you lead the other night." I hum as I gently pull at the tied bow and watch the knot come undone. "Or the way I held back."

She inches a fraction closer, her hips brushing against my inner thighs, on the cusp of either shoving me away or putting me out of my misery and kissing me.

"You may not have been the reason I came here, but you're why I still am." I swallow, knowing I've just laid all my cards out on the table for her again. "I know what I want, Crowne."

Before she can say anything in response, there's a double tap on the door.

She pulls back, just out of reach as she looks over my shoulder. I don't turn around until I hear a man's voice. "Everything okay here, Wyn?"

I recognize the country drawl. "Reed, hi." Clearing her throat, she adds, "Of course, everything is fine. What did you need?"

This fucking guy.

I stand to my full height and turn around.

"Julian, right?" he asks, pointing at me. "Good to see you, again."

I don't answer. Instead, I stare back at him. Navy suit pants and white dress shirt. Loafers and glasses. He isn't a bad-looking guy, and I'm not sure he's a bad guy at all, but I don't fucking like him. And she might have called him a friend, but I know what it looks like when someone wants more.

Wyn glances at me, looking surprised at the fact that I'm not going to say shit to him in response. If I blinked, I would have missed the way her lips twitch in amusement.

"Alright," Reed says slowly, turning his attention back to Wyn. "We were going to discuss the lecture series I have planned for the incoming freshman. You said you wouldn't mind giving me feedback and then perhaps we could swap?"

She stays quiet, looking at me again and keeping her attention there for a few beats as if she's trying to work something out. "I—um— Actually, Reed. I can't do that today."

"I'm sorry, what?" he says with a disbelieving laugh. He looks at me, and I stare right back.

Asshole.

Out of my periphery, I watch her reach down, grabbing her oversize bag and moving around her desk to pluck things from it and then stop next to me. "I just can't today. Something came up, and I need… I just need—"

"To get out of here," I finish for her. Her eyes meet mine in surprise, searching for how I would know that's what she needs right now.I lean closer to her, taking the heavy bag from her hand, and say, "Ready, baby?"

I know calling her that threw her for a loop by how her mouth parts slightly, but she doesn't seem to mind when she says, "Ready."

Wyn walks past Reed, giving him a tight-lipped nod, who still looks like he's missing what just happened.

I don't smile or rub it in his face that she wants to get the hell out of here, and with me. But I'm happy to usher her away from whatever or whomever is making her feel stifled and anxious right now.

Once we make it to the parking lot, she pauses, looking at her car and then toward my truck. "I'll worry about mine tomorrow. Mind driving?"

I shake my head, my lips tilting up into a smile when I ask, "Where are we going, Crowne?"

She exhales, "Just drive."

CHAPTER 20

Wyn

"TURN DOWN THERE," I SAY, sitting taller. When I caught a glimpse of his tattoo and then saw the airplane overhead, and realized where we were about to pass, I knew it was too perfect not to stop.

Julian pulls off the main road and down an unmarked gravel and dirt road.

It took me most of the drive to work out just leaving the way I had. I'd gotten into the habit of never leaving without office hours and prepping for the next day of class, but it feels good to be swept away for a bit. And I'm relieved that the ride here wasn't filled with anything more than a few stolen glances and the sound of cars rushing by once I put the windows down.

There are plenty of spots like this in Rumor, forgotten roads and overgrown trails. At the end of this one, I know what we'll find. The wall of vines and branches that look like they've taken over what was once a chain-link fence are the cover or guards to a spot that I haven't been back to see in far too long.

Hopping down from his Bronco and rounding the front of it, Julian pauses and looks at me like I've done something wrong.

"What?" I laugh out nervously. But he just shakes his head quickly, so I ask, "Any chance you have something in here that we can sit on? There's a nice view behind that thing." I nod at the long wall of weeds and woods.

"Leading me into the woods feels like this could go one of two ways," he says, rounding the back of the truck and opening the trunk.

"The two ways being?" I ask, already amused with where I think he's going with this.

He grabs a small duffel bag and says, "A beautiful woman leading me into a wooded area, who just so happens to have an interesting family with questionable habits, sounds like the beginning of a slasher film."

I bark out another laugh. "And yet you're still coming with me willingly. You're the prepared one," I tell him, looking down at the bag he's holding.

He shakes his head. "I'm in the habit of always having an emergency bag. A blanket, change of clothes, snacks, whatever might be useful when I'm on a job."

I have about a dozen questions about what else is in that bag. We walk about twenty feet down the length of the wall, and I find the cutout I was expecting. When I duck under the low branches and through the parted section of the chain-link fence, I stop and take in the view. It's as beautiful as I remember. The screeching sound of a small plane landing on the farthest strip of concrete and the whirring sounds of its turbines echoing out across the open landscape have me feeling relaxed and like I can breathe. "I bet the other way you were thinking it could go wasn't taking you to see planes fly in and out of a private airfield."

"No," he says, shaking his head with an impressed tone. He looks out and around at the open space that wasn't visible from the road. "I was going to say that maybe you had an unexplored kink for primal play, wanted me to chase you, find you, then..."

I swallow as my cheeks heat. "Then what?"

With a smirk, he lays out the blanket from his bag where I've stopped. "Use your imagination, Crowne."

That's the problem, though, I don't allow my imagination to run wild like that. Julian behind me, finding me—*Calm down, slow your breathing.* The idea should make me feel panicked or triggered, but I don't. The way Julian says it makes it feel like foreplay.

I yank the sides of my skirt to keep it from riding up as I take a seat on the small plaid blanket. When I look out toward the open airfield on the edge of this hillside, it's the lightest I've felt.

Julian sits down next to me, bending his long legs and draping his arms over them. His leather cuff fastened to his wrist and brushed silver rings adorning a few of his fingers hang casually as he looks at the concrete and painted lines below.

"I've been here," he says quietly. "Flew in down there," he adds, tipping his head toward the airfield and hangars. "I hadn't planned on sticking around for long enough to see it from a different angle."

Everything in my life feels like a different angle now.

It gets quiet enough to listen to the breaks between chirping crickets and the buzzing cicadas. It feels so good—to sit and feel for a minute. To be still and unmoving in a spot that I thought held unimportant memories, realizing now that maybe that's how most seem at the time, but later, they become an anchor.

I lean back, crossing my feet at my ankles and slipping off my heels. This place has parts of who I was at different times baked into my visits. I look out at the horizon line when I share, "I ran away once when I was just about fifteen. I didn't know where the hell to go." I smile. "Stevie found me after about an hour. We sat here for most of the night, sipping on those tiny bottles of alcohol—nips—Birdie stocks them in her curio cabinet."

He reaches around me to drag his bag closer. Rummaging through it for a moment, he pulls out a small round flask. "No clue what's in it, but I'm guessing it'll be reminiscent of those little bottles you chugged."

I twist open the tarnished silver cap and take a swig. The immediately familiar bite of whiskey hits the tip of my tongue, but it's the burst of cinnamon that has me instantly coughing. "I had no idea you were a Fireball guy." I pass him the flask.

The smile on his face when he swallows a sip makes him seem a decade younger. "That would be my dad," he says with an exhale. "He loved it. Always had a bottle in the freezer."

He looks out in front of where we're sitting as the sunset paints the sky varying hues of pinks to oranges. So beautiful. For as much as I wanted space from Rumor, Tennessee, there's no arguing that it has its moments. This is one of them.

"What are we doing out here?" he asks as he reaches up to brush a piece of hair from my face. The gesture is so innocent and intimate, it makes me shift closer to him.

"It's just a place," I say quietly. "One that I forgot all about, but then sometimes I would think about it. When I needed to disconnect from what I was going through, I would think about this spot and . . . escape to for a little bit." I smile nervously. "I don't understand what you do to make me feel like I can just let go." I shake my head, thinking about how passive I've been since I've been back.

He pushes a piece of hair away from my cheek. "I don't know either, but—" His attention shifts so his eyes meet mine when he says, "I've got you."

I look around his face, cataloging the way his scruff comes to just below his cheeks, and the way his lips have the most perfect bow, the warmth of green and brown in his hazel eyes, and the way his dark hair frames all of it, even pulled back. I don't understand why I believe him now, even with the history we've had, but I do.

"Today, I stood in that lecture hall, and I hated it so much that I almost couldn't breathe. I was in the same room, the same place in life physically that I had been, but I've seen and been through too much to still be there. And then you walked in, and all of a sudden…it was the same feeling as the other night. I could do whatever I wanted, like I finally had permission to take and lead."

He looks away and back toward the airfield. "Careful, Crowne," he says, smiling, bringing his gaze back to me. "You might just make me fall in love with you over stuff like this."

The second I hear him say it, my pulse picks up, nerves taking off like a shotgun at the start of a race, and I ask myself, would that be such a bad thing? *A man like him falling in love with a woman like me.* A smile spreads across my face when I say, "You're the only person who calls me that—Crowne."

He hums, like he's agreeing with what I've said. "You wear it well."

I laugh first and then sigh as my stomach flutters, thinking about all of the different ways I can interpret that. "I never used to feel that way."

When I take another sip from the flask, this time, it's less jilting. "Once you can get over the proof of the alcohol"—I raise my eyebrow—"the cinnamon is strong, but I wonder if it was toned back slightly and then offset with something like dried apple and hibiscus, it might taste like a dessert."

Julian leans back, bracing his weight on his hands when he says, "You like to pair flavors. You did that in Montana with your tasting flights."

I shrug my shoulder, even though I love that he recognizes that about me. "Result of a hobby that became my whole personality."

He looks over at me after a few quiet minutes. "In case you weren't aware, I'm fairly drawn to this whole personality of yours."

"I've noticed," I whisper. He keeps his attention on me as I watch the movement down the hill below. I don't mind being watched and observed. It makes me wonder what he sees. If he could see the broken parts, or if it's the professor or the woman he left back in Montana. I don't see any broken parts of him. He has a twinge of arrogance beneath his surface, a questionable hobby and family legacy, but then again, so do I.

I turn to look at him and ask, "What did you mean when you said you thought you knew everything about your father?"

"You might be the only person who really listens," he says, running his fingers along his opposite palm. "Haven't had anyone like that in my life since my dad—listening and just being there."

I lean over and draw along the same line he was mindlessly roaming over. "I couldn't see it there," I say, tapping his palm and along the edge of his heart line. "Figured it couldn't hurt to ask."

That gets a laugh out of him, but it also has him opening his palm wider, allowing me to lightly touch and draw along the places I had once read.

"My father had been doing cleanup jobs for your family for at least two decades, maybe more. But then your Uncle Tommy showed me a workspace inside of his barn that had some of my dad's stuff, things that he purposely left to work on whenever he was here, and I have questions, ones that I won't get answers to from him."

"But maybe you can get some from Birdie? She would be the most levelheaded of the two people you could ask," I suggest. It takes him a moment, but when he turns back to me, he masks a bit of his feelings with a reassuring smile, his hazel eyes glassy. His fingers close, pressing my palm to his, holding my hand.

"Did Birdie ever mention anyone? Or did you happen to see her spend time with—"

I'm already shaking my head slowly before he finishes. "For as many men as I've seen my mother cycle through over the years, there's never been anyone with Birdie. My grandfather died long before my mother ever had me, but Birdie has always been Birdie. A big, bold personality that my sisters and I always thought had been beyond finding someone for herself like that."

He nods, working something around in his head. "Mickey at Moonie's said he knew my dad too." He runs his hand behind his neck, beneath the long hair that covers it. "Which isn't something he would've allowed to happen on jobs." He shakes his head. "Regardless of whether he came to the same place repeatedly, it wouldn't be smart."

Being smart sometimes doesn't have anything to do with why we did things; he and I are the case and point. I run my fingers along his leather cuff, feeling the smooth edge of it, and thinking about all of the things he's done that he might catalog as "not smart."

"And here you are, pulling up a chair at my family's dinner table, ordering dealer's choice at The Whispering Fool, and making friends with Mickey at Moonie's."

He turns his body slightly toward me, close enough that I watch as his eyes focus on my mouth just as his tongue wets his bottom lip. "I know why I'm doing it."

It's really hard to think about anything else when Julian is looking at me like this. My cheeks feel flushed again, and I'm lost on any logical reason why we shouldn't be sharing this moment together.

"You play dirty, Crowne. Brought me to an airfield, got me to tell you more in the last few hours than I probably have told anyone in my entire life," he says with a smile dancing on his lips. "Pretty sure you're the one doing the romancing now."

I laugh, and he reaches up, pushing a piece of hair that fell, his fingers twirling the strand as I really look at him. The things I didn't notice until now, like the small dimple to the right of his mouth that only pulls when his smile seems devious. I like that he talks to me.

"You call it playing dirty, I call it learning," I say playfully as I shift a bit closer to him.

"I'm trying to figure out what you want," he says softly, lifting my palm to his mouth and kissing the center. This is what I've never had before—feeling important enough to someone that they wanted to divulge the hard things.

"So am I," I answer quietly and honestly.

"Can I ask you something?" he says, looking at my palm and then back up to me. "With your colleague, Reed, at Moonies, it wasn't a date. But does he know that?" Julian asks with a smirk.

I have no reason not to share this with him. "Reed was a

mistake," I answer, pulling back enough so that I can look him in the eyes and tell him all about my poor decision-making. "I'm not going to make excuses. He was an assistant professor when he started at the university, and we became friends."

"Doctor Crowne," he says in a teasing tone, knowing where I'm likely heading with this.

I shrug a shoulder and stifle my smile. I'm not proud of it, but I'm also human and need to remember that sometimes. I watch as his fingertips draw along the lines of my palm. "We had worked late, and he told me he had a crush on me, and I was..." I release a heavy breath, knowing how this is going to sound. I haven't told anyone about what happened with him. My sisters knew I liked Reed back then, but I never mentioned what transpired. "It felt good, to have someone interested and bold enough to say it. I was in my early thirties, having only ever been with one guy, and I was thinking maybe this is it. Maybe this is my love story, the one I didn't let myself believe I was going to ever have."

That feeling with Reed was so different than what I'm feeling with Julian now.

"Why did you think you wouldn't have that?" he asks curiously, his eyebrows slightly pinched and his hand closing around mine.

"I was never the one who got the guy. My sisters smiled, and men fell all over themselves. My mother would call someone an asshole, and that asshole would be walking out of her room the next morning. But I'm just not built that way."

He quirks an eyebrow. "Easy?"

When I give him a leveling look, he chuckles. "I just mean that most men see someone smart and complex, a beautiful woman who intimidates them, and they decide they're not man enough to put in the effort."

"Maybe." I smile at the way he so easily made me see it as a them problem and not my own.

"I didn't feel very good about what we did. I had a moral crisis thinking about how I was in a position of authority. And I mistook friendship and the attention of a guy as something I should act on. I wanted to take it back. But he said he was fine with being friends." Pausing, I recall the days after. "The semester was ending, and I didn't see him again until he showed up in Nashville at the symposium..." I clear my throat. I don't want to think about the dark stuff. I want to shove it back into its box and feel normal just for a little while longer.

The sound of propellers breaks the moment, pulling our attention to the airfield below. A small, double propeller plane moves forward down the landing strip, readying for takeoff. I always held my breath watching this part as I quietly cheered on its pilot as the distance between its wheels and the ground grew wider. This spot on the hill has two extremes—complete silence, as if the air is settled and waiting for the next plane. Or it's so loud that the ground vibrates and the sound of the propellers or turbines erase whatever you were thinking about.

I smile as the plane on the strip picks up speed and moves toward the blinking red lights that line the concrete. The sound grows louder and the breeze swirls up just as its wheels lift. My hair whips at my face, my heart rate skyrockets, and the rush of watching it take off has me leaning back and laughing, turning my body to look behind me as it sets off to wherever it's headed. The science of aerodynamics is fascinating, but watching it without the logic behind it feels like witnessing magic. I shake my head at the way that would sound if a scientist said that out loud.

When I push my hair away and steal a glance at Julian,

he's still looking at me. I wonder if he'd been looking at me the whole time.

A smile or maybe curiosity plays out on his lips like he just heard what I was thinking. His gaze flicks down to my mouth again, making the smile I had and the question of whether he saw it or not, completely falter. It's a fleeting moment between us, both knowing what we want and the spike of courage to give in to it.

"That might be one of my favorite things to watch," I say with a shy smile.

His fingers glide along my neck and into my hair, when he says, "Mine too."

I sway closer, unsure if he means the planes, or me. The warmth of his palm pulls me to his lips with measured urgency. As our mouths meet and lips taste, our tongues collide effortlessly. It's carelessly wet and driven simply by the need for more of each other. Climbing into his lap, I pull my skirt higher so I can straddle my legs around his. Julian's fingers move from my hair, down my back, helping my skirt higher so I can sit where he wants me. I loop my arms around his neck and tease my fingers into the hairline at the back of his head. His arms wrap around me so tightly that I rock forward.

A small breath escapes my lips as a groan rumbles from his chest. I want to feel it and hear that again. I roll my hips.

"Crowne," he growls my last name, like he's warning me.

I smile against his lips and nip at them in response.

"It's too easy to get lost with you," he says, moving his mouth to my neck, finding a spot just below my ear and dragging his teeth against it. It makes me shiver, pulling a needy and pleading moan from my throat, and my hips grind harder. I know exactly what he means.

He shifts his weight, holding me close as he lifts us up and changes our positions. My back meets the blanketed ground as he moves his body off to the side of me. He ignores the piece of his hair falling forward as he says, "I've been trying to remember the taste of you." Nipping at my lips, he kisses me so passionately I feel fucking dizzy. My fingers delve into the hair at his nape as he leans forward and bites along my still-covered breast. He practically growls as he pulls away, shifting his weight back to kneel in front of me. With his eyes on mine, hair disheveled, his fingers toy with the hem of my skirt that's already ridden up to my hips.

"Keep going," I breathe out as my thighs rub together.

His gaze never leaves my face as he slowly shoves it higher up one side, then the other, repeating until it's bunched up around my waist. The moment he catches a view of my panties, he licks his lips. His thumbs trace along the seam and then dip inward along the creases of my skin.

"That wet spot, right here…" he says, brushing his thumb over my clit. I whine at the sensation, which has a smirk tugging at his lips. "It makes me want to rip these right off of you. Clean up your pussy with my tongue and make a mess of it all over again."

Holy shit. His words roll through me like a prequel to the orgasm I know he'll make follow. "I should probably let you do that then," I rush out, as if I'm out of breath.

Humming, he nods in a way that shouldn't be so sexy, looping his thumb around the front of my panties and pushing them to the side. Shifting forward, he drags his tongue along my pussy's lips the same as I remember, with enough pressure that they part as he licks up my slit achingly slow until he reaches my clit, closing his mouth around it and sucking. The sounds he makes meet the whoosh of air that expels from my chest and out my mouth with a groan. His other thumb moves lower as his grip on the material tightens, and with a twist, he rips my underwear clean off.

Gasping, my hand reaches into his hair, gripping it with the same force that his tongue and lips work me. He pushes my left thigh up, holding me open as he teases me. I tilt my head to look at him between my legs, wanting to see my arousal all over his mouth. Pulling on his hair, I urge him to lift his face, and when he does, I'm met with his intense eyes and then a playful smile surrounded by glistening wet lips as he says, "Fucking delicious."

He bites at my inner thigh, forcing a laugh to bubble out of me as I ease up on his hair. With a groan against me, he shoves my ass up higher, moving his head left and right as the flat of his tongue rubs exactly how I need. The pressure and warmth that keeps building along my body from the backs of my knees to the tips of my fingers is going to have me crashing, I know it. But still I want more.

"Tell me, Crowne. Go ahead, ask for it," he says between breaths and licks. "You can demand my fingers," he adds, just before his teeth graze my clit and then suck it between his lips. He moans at the way I grip into his hair, my other hand moving between buttons and over the cups of my bra to play with my breast and nipple. I want to come so badly and to make it last all at the same time.

"Give me your fingers," I nearly whimper.

And immediately, two fingers glide up and down my pussy, once, twice and then he twists his wrist so that the same two fingers slide inside me, curling forward as his mouth descends back to my to where I want it. His tongue teases me, warm and wet with the perfect pressure that has my thighs shaking.

It's barely enough time to realize he's too fucking good at this, and my neck is arching back, a cry escaping as my pussy pulses around his fingers. He draws it out somehow, my body writhing and tensing beneath him.

"That's it, just like that," he says softly, resting his chin along my thigh as I catch my breath. His scruff is drenched with me, and I love how messy he looks. I love that I've affected him like that. He shifts, looking down at where he just played with me, his fingers slowly pulling out to their tips.

I want him. I don't want to overthink. I don't want to forget how this feels.

"I want one more," he demands in a low gravel. My eyes shift to his just as he bites along my thigh and stretches me again with his fingers. Moaning, I watch as he makes a show of extending his tongue out flat and licking along the base of his fingers. He drags it up to my clit again as if he doesn't want to miss a single drop of the arousal he's wrung from me. It's so fucking good that I move my fingers into his hair again and pull. When he looks up at me, I shift and grab at his shirt. I want the weight of him, want to feel more of him.

"It's not enough," I rush out just as his lips find mine. The taste of me on his tongue pulls another raspy moan from me. "Please, let me feel you," I beg, pulling at the back of his shirt.

He sits back on his heels, grips at the neckline of his shirt, and pulls it over his head. Every inch of him is mouthwatering to look at, from the broadness of his sculpted shoulders to the thickness of his arms and chest. It's not chiseled muscle or overtly cut lines, but the deep-set curve of strength that spans from chest, down his stomach, and to his thighs. Just as he's lowering himself over me, my hands smoothing up his chest, buzzing drowns out the sound of our heavy breathing.

My phone lights up from more than an arm's length away. It's vibrating without stopping, meaning someone's calling, and I'm almost exclusively a texter. *Shit. Something is wrong.*

"I need to see who—" I say as I move to reach for it.

He leans over to grab it for me. Before I answer, I see it's a picture of Stevie and Nash smiling on the screen. I slide to answer right away. "Hey—"

"Fury is detaining me," Stevie rushes out, sounding pissed and maybe on the cusp of tears.

"What?" I suck in a breath as I turn to look at Julian, who's brow furrows at my concern.

"Sheriff Fury is trying to helicopter his tiny prick around," she yells out, so I'm sure he or whomever is close by can hear what she's saying. Emotions with her always come out more like anger—and she's the loudest of us.

I hear someone in the background say to her, "Watch it, Stevie…"

"The sheriff marched up to my recording space and demanded that I drop the conversations around Billings being a piece-of-shit cop and how plenty of rumors are circling about his side hustle in narcotics and opioids. That," she pauses to groan in frustration, "and I quote, 'Rumors are not facts and shouldn't be reported as such.'" She barks an unamused laugh. "Do you believe that shit? As if we don't understand the damage rumors can have." She gets louder when she says, "And it's a podcast you asshat, not hard-hitting journalism!"

"Okay, ease up and tell me what happened after that," I ask, trying to get a full picture here. I know *The Distilled Truth* ruffles plenty of authority feathers, but being detained seems a little extreme, if not infringing on an amendment. "He couldn't have arrested you over that."

She huffs, and then takes a deep breath. With that pause alone, I know there's more. "I told him that he was a paper-pushing manbaby who takes handouts from sociopaths and blatantly ignores criminals within his own precinct."

Julian kisses my shoulder and slowly sits back on his heels as I sit up taller.

"Stevie," I say, trying to get a word in.

I start to fumble with the buttons that came undone on my blouse as I glance at Julian, who's already reading the situation right as he puts his shirt back on and moves to help me up.

"And that he's no better than a cult leader with the way he brainwashes everyone into believing everything is fine around here. He didn't like that one."

I don't need to know why she's asking for my help. And I would *never* call her an idiot—my sister is smart. She just likes to play it off as a flaw most of the time.

She exhales. "You can tell me I'm an idiot and lace into me later. I just need you to come and get me—I didn't know who else—"

I stop her right there. "Stevie, I'm on my way."

CHAPTER 21

Julian

"You can't tell me that this isn't all somehow related, Fury," I hear Stevie shout from a chair in the far side of the station's bullpen. "There are missing persons, more overdoses in the past handful of years than ever before in this county, I've seen now two college aged-girls coming out of here looking worse than when they came in, screaming sexual assault being mishandled, and then you, and you," she says, pointing at Jameson, who must have just come in, surveying what's going on in front of us. "The sheriff, the county's lead homicide detective, and your paper pushers come into *my* family's bar to throw around your weight, looking for a man who we all know knocked his wife around like a goddamn pinball machine. And again, you did *nothing*."

Wyn lets go of my hand and rushes up to the main desk. I overhear her say, "Being detained? For what reason?" Wyn asks. And without letting the deputy answer, she adds, "And she's not a minor. It isn't required for her to have someone come and get her. Does she need to appear in court after this?"

I smile at hearing her tear the deputy behind the desk a new one. I run my fingers beneath my nose as if I'm scratching an itch, but really, I just want to remind myself of the smell of her. She smells as good as she tastes, and I swallow roughly, trying to focus on where I am and what we're walking into.

"If you're not arresting her, I'd like to take my sister home now, please," Wyn adds as the deputy gets up and moves towards a still fairly loud Stevie Crowne.

When I glance at Detective Jameson Bishop, my unofficial neighbor at The Rackhouse this past week, he looks more pissed off than usual. He stands back with his arms crossed, observing the commotion. Sheriff Fury seems more distressed than I would expect in his own station, but I'm sure the Crowne sister spouting off facts and making him look like an idiot wasn't on his bingo card tonight.

I watch closely as Jameson steps up next to the deputy sitting at the desk she's cuffed to. He doesn't look down; instead, his eyes stay locked on the sheriff when he says, "Those cuffs better be off her wrists within the next minute, Deputy, or I will not hold back on writing up every last person inside of this place for abusing their authority."

"Oh, how scary. Threatening paperwork and a written warning," Stevie seethes with sarcasm. "Such a fucking hero."

His usual stoic and impenetrable exterior cracks just a little as he turns away, his hand running along his mouth, wiping away whatever he wanted to say back to her. I recognize that frustration. I've felt it myself from the beautiful woman a few feet away, giving her sister wide eyes and a wordless look of what I assume is *Shut the fuck up and let's go*.

When I look back at the officers and sheriff, I find Fury's attention on me now. *Fucking hell, I shouldn't be inside this damn station.* He glances toward Jameson, who still seems pissed off, at the very least. The entire station, regardless of the fact that there aren't many bodies inside, feels thick with tension that I don't belong anywhere near.

Stevie rubs along her wrist where she'd been cuffed, before she hugs Wyn, and Sheriff Fury meanders closer. "Wyn, please make sure she gets home. I'd really like to forget this all happened."

Wyn gives him a tight-lipped smile while Stevie says, "I'm sure that would be very convenient for you." She gives him a double thumbs up as she adds, "Superior job, spending taxpayer money on ignoring my rights and getting your panties in a wad about a podcast. I'm sure a judge would agree."

I don't miss the exchange of looks between Jameson and the sheriff. I can't figure out the context.

"Julian, fancy seeing you here," Stevie says as she struts up next to me. Her eyes go wide, like she just realized something.

"Are you alright?" I ask as I look up and around. A lot of cops are paying attention to all of this and not a single one except for Jameson did anything about it. That pisses me off.

"Oh fuck, you came here together." Covering her mouth, Stevie mumbles, "Was this a date?"

My eyes connect with Wyn's before I answer. Her lips twitch, knowing I was just knuckles deep inside of her and licking up every drop of it. "Not a date," I answer. "She let me rescue her and take her for a drive." I flash Stevie a smile and sarcastically add, "We were being very respectable."

"You call me, anytime," Wyn cuts in. "You know that." She widens her eyes at me, trying to stop from smiling.

"Okay, well, thank you for coming to get me. The good news is, I finished recording before the whole Fury incident," she says, waving it off like it was a minor inconvenience. "Nash is already having a sleepover tonight at Mom's anyway, so I will be self-soothing with the apple stack cake she brought over, and you two can go back to whatever it is I interrupted." She glances at the desk, smirking. "This'll catch fire quickly."

Wyn looks at her quizzically. "Should we tone it down? I mean, you're not even out the doors yet, and I know that look. You're stirring shit."

"You know that the second I tell Birdie about this, she'll get on the horn with the garden club biddies, and then someone will start gossiping on the prayer tree. I'm so tired of the bullshit we're just supposed to swallow. Fury is tightly wound about something, I know it." She looks over her shoulder, glaring at him.

Jesus Christ, that one has no fear.

"The fucking county sheriff doesn't throw his weight around like he just did if I didn't strike a chord somewhere," she says as she throws the doors to the station open.

Wyn turns to look at me, just as we start to walk out. She doesn't need to say anything. I know she wants, or maybe even needs, to spend time with her sister right now.

Seeing the way she interacts with her sisters, witnessing how important they are to one another, and listening to Jo and Stevie talk about and be protective over Wyn, it dulls their initial intimidation. Instead, it makes me want to be around them and a part of it. I wrap my hand around her wrist, pulling her closer, and she comes to me so easily. I kiss the palm of her hand at the top of the stairs of the sheriff's station.

She tilts her head back to look up at me as she says, "Tomorrow night, there's this bluegrass thing, and I was thinking that maybe—"

"Are you asking me on a date?" I ask as I pull her closer. The tone of who we are to one another feels like it's changed. I've never felt so eager to spend time with anyone like I do with her. There's something about her that's grounding, and fuck do I want to be that for her too. She raises up onto the balls of her feet as I lean down, and she brushes her lips teasingly against mine.

"I don't think that's our style. Maybe we'll both be there, and I'll run into you. We can listen to some music or dance and then you can whisk me away somewhere and get lost all over again." She pulls back and starts down the steps. "Thanks for the *rescue*."

"Any and every time, Crowne," I say, watching her walk away.

She tosses me a smile over her shoulder before she goes to catch up with her sister. "Stevie," she calls out. "Did you say stack cake?"

I don't make it more than a few feet from the front doors before I hear my name.

"Colton," Sheriff Fury calls out.

"Have a nice night, Sheriff." I wave over my head as I keep walking to my Bronco. *I need to get the hell out of here.*

He catches up, calling out once more. "Colton, while you're here, now might be a good time for us to have a word." He huffs and puffs his cheeks out like he just finished a marathon, as he stands in front of me. I can't figure out what it is about him that I don't like. Maybe it's just that he's a cop.

I smile, like someone totally unfazed. "About what, exactly?" I ask, shifting my arms over my chest.

"I need to clear up some timing coincidences between your arrival and my deputy' disappearance. Should only take a few minutes."

Fuck.

"Colton," Detective Jameson Bishop says from the top of the stairs. The Rackhouse Bed-and-Breakfast is big enough that I should've been able to miss seeing yet another fucking cop in my path.

"No *fucking* way," I mumble to myself as I open the porch screen door and head outside. I'm jogging down the steps and toward my truck when I hear him hustle up behind me.

"Colton, will you fucking—" I hear him rush out.

I haven't figured out the homicide detective yet. Fury is an asshole and seems like he's got plenty of shit to cover up, but Jameson isn't that. My gut has always said to steer away from getting too friendly with anyone who has the power to put you in handcuffs, but he cut into the almost two hour "chat" Sheriff Fury requested as I was leaving last night.

"Sir, there are two homicides that I'd like to wrap up and need your signature on my reports. I'd really like to get the hell out of here." He glanced at me and then back at Fury. Quietly he leaned into the Sheriff and said, "This isn't progress, it's going to be a problem." It was enough for the sheriff to thank me for my cooperation and politely suggest I do not leave town.

I'm not fucking planning on it. And there isn't a damn thing I cooperated on. He asked questions and I danced around the answers.

Did I know Deputy Billings? No.

Had I ever met him or crossed paths? Technically, no. He wasn't crossing anything when I saw him.

Do you know what might have happened to him?

All I had to say to that was, "Never met the guy. If I was to guess what had happened, I doubt I'd be right."

I look over my shoulder at Jameson hustling toward me. *What the fuck is it with cops following me lately? I'm usually better at evading this shit.* "Unless you're going to tell me I look pretty, Detective, I've got somewhere to be," I call out.

Inside that station last night exercised the very last of my patience. I got home late, spent the day finally working through commission requests and voicemails from my agent. And now, I want to see the woman I haven't been able to stop thinking about.

"I'll take a ride if you're heading out for Full Moon Fest," he says, now standing next to the passenger door. When I raise my narrowed eyes to his, he holds up his hand. "Tommy mentioned you were going. I didn't peg you for a bluegrass guy."

I look over at his truck, but he's already got the back door of my Bronco open, sliding his guitar across the back seat before I can ask why he won't drive himself.

"Not so much a bluegrass guy as I am a Wyn Crowne guy," I tell him honestly.

He shuts the door and looks at me with a shit-eating grin.

With the exception of Nash, not much seems to crack the detective's deliberately stoic exterior. I understand it. Career aside, I know the effectiveness of taking emotions out of situations—I've been doing it most of my life. Until recently.

"We haven't known each other very long, but you smiling like that is throwing me off," I say to him jokingly.

He shakes his head. "You're throwing a lot of people off around here. But I'm not going to pretend I'm not glad to hear that, about Wyn. I mean, the bluegrass part's a shame. You might change your mind on that one once you see this thing we're heading to."

I flip on the radio and glance in the back seat. "A musician and a cop? Wouldn't have guessed that one, either, Detective."

He sniffs out a laugh. "Haven't been one in a long time. Tommy dug that thing out of his workspace and casually left it for me outside my bedroom door this morning."

That seems to be a bit of a pattern for Tommy, digging things up. The pieces I found that connected my dad to this place seem like an anchor to a life I don't know anything about.

"I used to live here, I'd play at this festival once a month every summer, and then left for a while," he says, pausing. "I'm a couple towns over now. I'm in and out of Rumor for cases. Thought I'd miss this month's full moon, but this bullshit with Deputy Billings has kept me here for way longer than necessary. Tonight is a silver lining."

I wanted to know a little more about the body I'd erased. "Heard some interesting things at Moonie's about him," I offer.

"Billings?" he asks.

I nod, and he adds, "Yeah, I'm sure you did. Everyone in this town really makes sure it earns its namesake, but the more I hear about the shit Billings was involved in—" He cuts himself off. "I doubt he ran off with someone. I'm almost positive it'll end up in my caseload soon enough."

A few minutes go by of listening to the sound of Stevie's voice play over the speakers, talking about the stupidity of local law enforcement. "I'm assuming this is the episode Fury detained her for?" I ask him.

He's trying to keep from laughing when he says, "If I had to guess. I mean, she's not wrong. Although, the visual of Sheriff Fury fucking himself on a pogo stick, as she so eloquently put it, is one I didn't need.

"Turn down that way." He points to the unmarked road up to the left. "There's a small bar in the next town that hosts bluegrass sessions every Sunday," he says, looking out ahead at the park beyond the dirt and gravel lot. "*This* is something entirely different." Leaning forward, he points to the row of cars parked off to the side up ahead. "Pull up on the end there. We're not going to find a spot any closer right now."

"This happens once a month?" I ask, hopping out once I've parked.

He nods, meeting my stride around the front of the truck. "Every full moon, every summer, for almost as long as I can remember, just about every musician who's ever heard a chord and tried to play, comes out here." He lets out a clipped laugh. "Helluva time and maybe one of the few charming things left of small-town living."

Food trucks and grills with spit roast barbecue line the perimeter of the park while the sounds of bluegrass, from guitars and mandolins to harmonicas and accordions fill the air. There isn't a single moment in my life that I thought I'd be walking through a festival in Tennessee with a homicide detective, much less enjoying his company while doing it. The music drowns out the collision of it all.

"Want a beer?" the detective asks as we walk up past a makeshift beer garden.

I nod as I scan the crowd. The ever-growing band seems to take up the farthest part of the vast lawn. It's the biggest small-town gathering I've ever seen. Black strings of round bulbed lights drape across the wide field from tree to tree. There aren't any stages or any kind of production other than what's needed for people to hear the music being played. There have to be at least twenty, maybe more, musicians all keeping time. Speakers are peppered along the long rows of wooden tables and benches. Every seat looks taken as people drink beer from pitchers or sip from brightly colored cans with the name stamped Yazoo. Popcorn overflows from plastic picnic baskets and flimsy paper plates hold dark, slathered barbecue and bright-yellow cornbread.

Couples move around the dance floor, some line dancing in unison, but most twirling like they've danced with their partners for so long they don't even think about the steps.

It's when the crowd breaks off and the singer at the center hits their chorus that I see her. It's like a collision of relief and adrenaline inside of me the second she turns. She laughs at something her sister says, and I find myself smiling along with her, regardless of being at least a hundred feet away. She's swapped her tailored trousers and satin blouse for a short skirt and cowgirl boots. Between the tight jean vest and her hair pulled up off her neck, I can't help but stare. *Damn.*

"I like Wyn. Smart and always the most levelheaded of that family. I'm glad she's found her footing since she's been back," he says, taking a sip of his beer. I can see him looking at me out of my periphery.

I nod, listening, because while I like him, I'm not about to trust him.

He furrows his brow, turning toward me. "But I'm curious if she's told you what she was doing out there? Where you met."

I unclench my jaw and tip my beer to take a sip. I've been waiting for the rest of what he wanted, because he sure as shit didn't need a ride.

"I know enough," I say, trying to keep my emotions in check. "Is this the part where you play protector and say something that'll end in me getting arrested?" I turn to him and flash a smile.

He nods and huffs out a laugh in response.

We both watch on as Wyn steps over to where Birdie has her setup. An ornate rug with a table at its center. Birdie's perched behind it, with another person sitting across. Lit lanterns aren't giving off much in the way of lighting, but it sets the mood of what I would assume is either palm or the tarot readings that she's so known for doing.

"That wasn't what I planned, but I will say this, and take it exactly as I mean it." I turn to look at him once again. "That woman has been through enough. The entire family, really, but Wyn has lived through things that most wouldn't. So if you're bringing more trouble her way, I'm not asking nicely, Colton." He clears his throat. "Tommy won't say it, so I will. I'm telling you to get the fuck out of here now if you're going to make more of a mess for her."

A part of me respects and appreciates that she has someone to say it. The irony is that I typically clean up problems, not make new ones.

I drain what's left of my beer, giving myself a minute not to overplay this. It feels genuine and like he's coming from a good place. "I have a feeling you understand what it's like to be an outlier here." I shake my head, swallowing past a sudden lump in my throat. "The new guy, showing up at the wrong time… but I've been trying to find her since the moment I thought I wouldn't see her again."

He tips his chin up, listening intently to the honesty of what I'm sharing.

I look out at the crowd, taking inventory of the faces—very few that I recognize from my short time here. "I'm not planning on hurting anyone, but most definitely not her."

It must be enough for him, because he nods and pivots the conversation. "Theo mentioned you were on the invite for our next guys' night."

I glance at the detective, and then back to the crowd, trying to catch Wyn's eye. "Did he?" I ask, feeling like being included with these men might not be the worst idea. If I was going to be here, then carving out a place with the men woven between the Crownes seemed like it's exactly where I should be. I've been so used to coming and going, spending time with friends while I'm in and out of their towns, I don't think I've ever been included in a guys' night.

I watch as Stevie walks ahead of Wyn, holding Nash's hand on her way toward the horde of musicians, but Wyn stops to talk to someone, maybe two people. *Who is that?*

Jameson continues as I try to see through the crowd. "Listen, Nash heard him say the guys' night thing, too, which basically means you have no choice now." He's about to take another sip, but then stops his cup halfway to his mouth just as someone new starts singing over the mic.

I look out at the center of the semicircle, and crooning away on the microphone is Stevie Crowne, singing about *driving nails in my coffin*, shutting every damn person up with the way she's singing without a single instrument backing her up. A three-count from someone in the second row gets called out, and the full crew of instruments hops into it just as the crowd starts hootin' and hollerin'.

When I look back towards Wyn, there's more of a gap in the crowd now, and I can see her talking with Sheriff Fury. And next to her is her colleague from yesterday, Reed. *I fucking hate that guy a little more now.* That's when Wyn finally looks my way. She smiles instantly, looking down at her palm, and then back up, locking eyes with me. There's a smirk on her face as she tries to keep her attention on whatever they're talking about.

"The fuck is he doing?" Jameson mumbles next to me, looking at the same group and conversation I am.

"That one has trouble written all over it," Cora says as she walks up in between me and the detective. It only takes a second to know she's a few cups in.

"Cora," Jameson says to her, and then glances up at me briefly. "Any word from Stan?"

She barks out a laugh, looking out at where we just were, at Wyn, Reed, and the sheriff. "Fury is real keen to find my husband, that's for damn sure," Cora says as she nods toward him. "That one." She hiccups. "Pardon me." A laugh bubbles from her lips and she covers her mouth. "He's a pompous asshole and serious trouble. Always thought so."

"Which one are we talking about?" I ask, leaning down next to her.

She smiles, turning her head to the side to look at me. "You're a good one, aren't you?"

I give her my best smile. "Been called a lot of things, Cora. Not sure that good has been one of them."

She pats my arm, and I look back up to see Wyn's smiling, but it's not the kind that plays out across her cheeks and crinkles the corner of her eyes. That's the smile she had after her lecture class, the one that made her sigh in relief when it was done. Cora raises her hand, wiggling her fingers. "It's my turn next," she loudly singsongs, and then rushes off, as if she didn't just barge her way in between us.

Just as I'm about to abandon the detective and weave my way through the crowd to Wyn, Jameson hums, "Strange."

I glance at him, wondering what he's talking about.

"It was the department that called Cora about Stan not

showing up for work. She didn't report him missing." Jameson tosses his empty cup into the trash and looks around. "I hope the person I choose to spend life with would notice if I went missing." It's a leading comment. I'm not going to weigh in on it, but I sure as hell heard him. I haven't had anyone in my life who would notice if I'd been missing. I catch Wyn smiling again as her eyes meet mine through the crowd. It hits me square in the chest. *I want her, but I also want to matter to her.*

"You going to play tonight?" I ask, glancing at his guitar perched next to him.

"Just waiting for Stevie to finish doing her thing." He tips his head toward the center where Stevie's still singing. "I'll jump in afterwards. This crowd gets too rowdy when we're up there together."

Before I can step away, Tommy waltzes up with Nash in tow. "Gentlemen," he says, passing us each a bottle of beer as Nash catapults himself at Jameson.

"Sonny, did you hear Mama?" he asks, hanging on the guy. "Hi, Julian."

"Hey, Nash," I say, looking at the hair tie pulling a cluster of hair together on the top of his head.

"Your hair is still looking cool. I tried to do mine like that, but I think it needs to grow more."

I smile, feeling caught off guard by a six-year-old.

Tommy adds, "Stevie tried to help him, but he said he could do it so—" He holds up his hands.

I look back down at Nash. "I think if you want to grow your hair out, it would look really good on you." I glance at the two men watching on before I add, "I'm around if you want me to show you how I do mine."

"Yes, definitely, yes," he says.

Tommy looks at me, and then nods to Jameson. "This guy working up the nerve to pick up that guitar and play?"

Instead, he points at Tommy. "Don't push it, old man," Jameson says before he takes a pull of his beer.

"Sonny, you have to play," Nash interjects. "Please?"

He smiles at him. "Just waiting for your mama to finish up first."

"Old man?" Tommy says, holding a hand over his heart, smiling. "You're not all that far behind me."

"Says the guy whose bedtime is in about thirty minutes," Jameson throws back as Nash plucks the five-dollar bill from Tommy's hand.

"First of all," Tommy says, "I'm flattered that you pay attention to my bedtime. And second, I'm a morning person, so you can go ahead and fuck right off."

It's hard not to laugh at the way they go back and forth.

Tommy looks back at the stage as Stevie hits a high note. "I watched Rhonda Vincent sing this song once, in that very spot, and I'll be honest, Stevie puts her to shame."

Nash chimes in, "My mama sings better than anyone I've ever heard."

Almost the entire semicircle of musicians, at least four rows deep, playing every string instrument, from banjo to violin and even an upright bass, joins in on this song. It's the strangest thing to be in a crowd of strangers, all listening to this music, yet somehow it makes you feel like you're a part of something. I've been to plenty of concerts and shows, but this is something altogether different.

Nash hangs onto Tommy's forearm, like he's trying to do pull-ups on it. "Hey Nash, want to snag some cotton candy?"

"The blue kind. It freaks mama out when my tongue is a different color," he says as they start walking away. "Sonny, you want some?"

"Grab me some, Nash," he answers.

When they start to walk off, I look back to where Wyn has been and find her already looking at me. But something's off. She's not smiling, and there's something else. She's looking at me the same way she did when I first showed up—leery, nervous, and absolutely angry.

CHAPTER 22

Wyn

"I'M GOING TO JUST SAY this, Wyn," Sheriff Fury says. He holds up his hands like he doesn't want to offend me, which is the tell that he's about to do just that. "I know you've been through it—"

I cut him off right there. Glaring at him, I hold up my hand. "Fury, not for nothing, but you have no idea what I've been through. So please don't try to get on my good side here when you're about to tell me something that you already know I'm not going to like."

Reed can't help but snort out a laugh, knowing I've just shut up our county sheriff with a few words.

I glance at Reed, almost annoyed that he's listening to any of this. He barnacled himself to me as soon as I showed up here.

"Fine. Fine. You should know then that I spent a couple of hours last night talking with Julian Colton."

I furrow my brow. "Wait, what?" I ask, coming back to what Fury is saying to me.

"Julian was real honest about some things, mostly about being here."

My stomach sinks at his words. There's no way he could really be honest with him, not about what brought him here. And there isn't a single part of me that could see Julian cooperating with Fury.

Fury loops his thumbs into his belt loops and adds, "I'm not convinced that he's not hiding something. The timing of your friend's arrival in town keeps gnawing at me."

What the hell would have taken a couple of hours to talk about at the sheriff's station? The reality that knocks the wind out of me isn't the fact that Julian knows the whereabouts of Deputy Stan Billings, but that he could easily negotiate saving his own ass. If he cooperated and shared what he knows, my family would be the target. I swallow and try to remain unaffected at what their conversation could've resulted in.

When I look out to the crowd, and past Birdie doing her reading, Julian's having a beer and laughing with Jameson. *When the hell did they get friendly?* Jameson doesn't like very many people.

I tune out the rest of what Sheriff Fury's saying. I'm embarrassed for allowing other people's opinions of my family to play such a huge part in my choices when I was younger. I wish I'd paid attention instead of shoving the distance between us. I hate that they kept secrets from me the same way I'm lucky that they had. But at the core of the choices they made, they protected who and what they could.

"Sheriff, are you assuming Deputy Billings is dead, or still missing?" Reed asks next to me, but my focus is on my grandmother now. I watch as Birdie fans out her cards, asking the woman sitting across from her to choose. It isn't often that a reading takes all that long, but sometimes, when there's more to be discussed, she has her company pull out more cards to help explain a situation more clearly. *Or maybe it isn't a reading at all.*

I replay every word she and my mother said in that kitchen, trying to think about what I could have missed over the years, but I come up with nothing every time. Nothing has stood out to me, but now…

Birdie isn't looking at the cards being pulled; in fact, she isn't saying much at all. When I see who's sitting across from her, it makes me pause. Blond braided hair and dark-rimmed glasses—Andi. I haven't taken all that much time getting to know this semester's assistants yet, but she's been paying Birdie quite a few visits lately—her visit at the house during dinner seemed like that wasn't the first time she'd met with my grandmother, and now, tonight.

Andi swats away at her cheek like she's batting a tear, talking quickly and looking upset. Normally, it isn't my business, but after knowing more, it feels like it is. Like she can feel curious eyes on her, Birdie glances up and stares right back at me.

"Ah, shit, there's Cora looking a little more drunk than I expected," Sheriff Fury says as he moves around us. "If you'll excuse me."

"When was the last time she did one of those for you?" Reed asks, but it's Andi who's walking past that steals my attention.

"Andi, are you alright?" I ask, stopping her in her tracks. Her eyes are rimmed red as she offers a barely believable smile when she realizes who I am.

"Dr. Crowne. So sorry. I didn't see you there." She clears her throat. "I'm just really stressed with my class load, and—" She waves it off, seemingly more jumpy than overwhelmed, but I know the requirements of the graduate program and what was expected of teaching assistants. She keeps her focus on me until she pulls her phone from her back pocket. "I have to run. So nice seeing you," she says, all of a sudden seeming like she has to rush off.

"I'm going to grab something to eat. Want to get a plate?" Reed asks, seemingly just as eager to get away from me now too.

"Oh, no, thank you." I have no plans to spend time with him. I'm here for someone else tonight. Someone I need to talk to, immediately. "I'm actually meeting someone. Thanks anyway, Reed," I shout in his direction, and just as I do, I see Julian walking right toward me.

I can't figure out how I should be feeling or which emotion is the right one for this situation. One moment, I want to flirt and play, and the next, I'm trying to navigate authorities, and now, I'm anxious at the idea that someone I want to trust might have just spent hours building a case against the two women who raised me.

"Crowne," Julian says as he reaches me, his deep voice like a caress.

I shake my head, ignoring how he affects me. "Don't Crowne me. And definitely don't look at me like that," I say, trying to skirt around him. I need to move. If I don't move, I'm going to pick the wrong fucking emotion, I know it.

"Okay got it." He nods. "Do not *Crowne* you and don't look at you," he says with a lilt of humor in his voice. "I am going to follow you, though, because clearly I've done something you're not thrilled about."

"I'm not thrilled about a lot of things," I mumble to myself as I weave through the mass of people. I keep having to stop and pivot around them.

"Wyn," he calls out, louder than the music.

I stop and take a breath. Standing at the edge of the make-shift dance floor, just as another chord starts, I can feel Julian step up right behind me. The smell of oak and mint lingers in the air with him so close. His hand grips my shoulder, steadying me. I see his brown leather cuff out of the corner of my eye for the briefest moment, and I find myself exhaling. *Hold it together.* Moving from my shoulder, down my arm slowly, his hand reaches my wrist, and then he's intertwining our fingers until our palms meet. He holds my hand without saying anything more. This simple touch, the warmth of his palm against mine, feels like my undoing. It softens me, almost too easily.

I'll ask the question I need to ask, but with just this simple gesture, I already know the answer.

He steps closer, brushing against my back, and I instantly feel safe. The music lingers around us, along with people standing and watching others dance a few feet away.

Lowering his head next to mine, his mouth hovers next to my ear as he says, "Want to tell me what's going on now?"

This is the part of him that I didn't expect—the calm and patient. On his exterior, he comes across as intense and confident, arrogant even, with the way you have to earn it to get him talking with you. But when he starts talking, the charming parts of him bleed out, and having his full attention feels like an achievement. But this, right here, with my hand held and a simple question asked, it's like he knows I need this before anything else.

I take a step forward to turn and face him, which forces our hands apart. "I'd like to dance," I say, lifting my chin.

He doesn't answer, just holds my eye contact, knowing there's more.

So I clear my throat. "On one condition," I say, trying to steal my reserve.

At that, he smiles, looking down as he takes a step closer to me. "Okay, but only because I'd like to dance."

I try to suppress my smile, so I glance to my left, making

sure this interaction doesn't have an audience. A few glances, but not enough to keep me from saying what I need to say. "You tell me what the hell you talked about with the sheriff for *two* hours after I left with my sister last night."

"That's her," I hear someone loudly whisper, stealing my attention. "The one who apparently died?"

"Are you surprised? I mean, look at that family…" The insult drifts off, and what would have made me self-conscious in the past now has me ready to fight.

My posture changes, my back straightening and the muscles in my shoulders tensing.

Julian watches me, because I know he heard it too.

I shake my head, trying to laugh at how damn stereotypical this is right now. "If you ever forget where you are, the people around here will quickly remind you how this town earned its name," I say, feeling angry and defeated by the callousness of their words.

"I didn't hear anything worth remembering," he says, refusing to look away from me. "And I know exactly where I am, and where I want to be."

Another woman in the same small group asks, "But, who is that…with *her*?"

I know they're talking about Julian.

Someone in the small huddle snorts a laugh. "A tad out of that league, if you ask me."

But just as I turn to tell them where they can shove it, Julian wraps his hand around my hip and pulls me closer to him. His other hand wraps along the back of my neck, his thumb grazing my jaw. The move shakes me and has me forgetting all about them. Everything tunes out—the snarky comments, the low hum of the crowd, the instruments gearing up for another song.

"I'm going to say this once, Crowne. It's your call whether you choose to believe me. There's nothing for you to be worried about when it comes to me talking with the sheriff or any other person who has the power to do damage to you, to me, or to your family."

I glance down to the collar of his shirt. I have no reason not to believe him. He could have shared everything he knew, taken a deal, and left town, but he's still here, dancing with me.

"Tell me you understand," he says, holding me close. His grip on my hip pulses tighter as his thumb grazes back and forth from my cheek to my chin.

On a breathy exhale, I nod once. "I understand." I melt into the way he's touching me.

"Good, now, I'm going to shut those women up over there and kiss you like I've been thinking about since the last time you let me."

I don't get to tell him please before his lips take mine like he's been starving for them. It's the kind of kiss that tells anyone who's watching that this man *knows* what he's doing. Within a few seconds, his tongue finds entry as he tilts my head just where he wants me. It's intense and deep, and just as quickly as it happened, he pulls back. Breath stolen. With his forehead touching mine and lips hovering inches from where they just made their fucking point, I can't help the way my face feels flushed and my body sways as if we're dancing. I smile at the small horde of assholes who were just talking too loudly to not be shut up.

"You just gave people plenty of fuel for the next week with a kiss like that." I lick my lower lip as I stare at his, wanting to feel that all over again.

He kisses my temple. "You're looking at me like you're ready to leave with me. But I need to dance with you first," he says as he moves around me, grabbing my hand again and weaving us through the dance floor crowd. The bright bulbed lights that are strung above the floor keep the entire area well lit despite the sky being dark and already peppered with stars.

I run my fingers down his forearm and over his leather cuff as his fingers hook with mine and we find a spot on the crowded floor.

"You don't need to romance me, Julian. I don't mind leaving right now," I say boldly as his arm bands around my back.

"Crowne," he growls, pulling me closer.

"Or maybe we don't leave," I say to him, lifting onto the balls of my feet so I can keep what I'm about to say for his ears only. "Imagine what they'll say if you play with me in those woods over there, or in the parking lot."

With a deep hum, he adds, "I'd want you to be nice and loud about it too."

My whole body reacts to the way he plays along, a full tingle and swoop running up my center and settling right in my pussy. "I imagine they'd be appalled. Pearls would be clutched. Rumors would go wild."

Smirking, he holds me against him, and we get lost in the music for a few moments. I'm so aware of every place his body touches mine. *This is what it feels like.*

Looking out at the semicircle of musicians, he asks, "How do they all know what to play and when to play it? There must be at least two dozen people with guitars. I think I counted five banjos, a couple of violins—"

"Fiddles," I correct with a smile, looking at where he is now. "There's a good handful of these folks who play together often at bars and on nights like tonight." So many of the faces are ones I recognize—the shirts and slacks that tended to be worn to "nights out" like tonight or skirts and boots that operated as their bluegrass-best. "Those are the people who are usually in that inner circle," I say, nodding to the players who keep rotating to the front. "Most of the time, there's a leader or two"—I point to the left side—"like Cliff with the white hair and ZZ-Top beard"—I point a little farther to the left—"and Skip with the harmonica contraption on his neck, holding the mandolin." I smile, watching how the crowd starts singing along with the song they're playing. "Those two will always take the lead here. Cliff or Skip will call the key, and it seems like sometimes they're having a conversation with the music. It's not a language I totally understand, but it's beautiful to experience."

He kisses my forehead, and it has me leaning in closer, wanting more. I watch as the second row moves their instruments ready to adjust and join.

"And then one of them will call on someone to take the lead on solo. Oftentimes, it'll be someone confident in that inner circle. Everyone along the outside is there to join in."

"Stevie jumped in on that solo," he says.

The musician playing the upright bass starts the tonic, and the mandolin joins in, giving the beat just as the accordion player starts up.

Nodding, I look over at my sister, who's shaking a tambourine and starting to sing backup for whoever's on the mic now. "When she was about seven or eight years old, she was determined to learn the Nashville number system."

At his confused look, I explain, "Chord structures that just about every local musician learns over time. Someone calls out a key, and the Nashville number gives the structure." I laugh. "It's a whole world that I only understand because my sisters have a knack for making their passions into everyone else's business."

"Does that mean you know a lot about art too, from Jo?" he asks.

"I know enough about what she likes," I say, peering up at him. "But I'd guess you probably know more. I'm sure you could teach me a thing or two."

He looks down at my lips and licks his.

It makes me smile—half turned on and slightly embarrassed by how quickly he can make me feel like the most wanted thing. Staring at the shoulder of Julian's dark shirt, quiet words slip past my lips. "You're right, this feels so easy with you." I shake my head slightly and add, "I mean, there are plenty of complicated pieces between us, but this"—I move closer—"being like this with you feels easy."

He hums, like he agrees. The music is still loud, even as it changes to something slower and more drawn out. There are still plenty of people paying attention and ready to eavesdrop whenever possible. I have a feeling Julian's finally beginning to understand the dynamics of how things work around here.

I move from holding one of his hands to draping both arms around his neck and tangling my fingers into his hair—thick and soft. The move feels familiar, like I've done it thousands of times.

"I can tell you one really important thing that I'm not sure you're aware of yet."

He leans in close, and the tight scruff that's groomed along his cheek brushes against my neck. His lips find the spot just beneath my ear, kissing it ever-so-lightly before he moves his mouth up and quietly says, "When you play with my hair like that, it's an instant turn-on. I get hard just thinking about it.

And right now," he adds as he briefly kisses my lips, "I'd very much like to leave with you."

"I think I'd like that," I say back as my cheeks heat and the rest of my body follows. Around him, I'm a simple slut for dirty words. And holy hell, do I want more. I swallow, shoving down what's left of my nervous energy and ignoring what I may have thought or felt before this moment, before him, or just *before*.

He leans closer, his lips close to my ear when he says, "I think we're all finished with dancing."

CHAPTER 23

Wyn

"Slow down," I say over the crowd's whistles and hollers.

I never thought I'd enjoy a light jog in a pair of cowgirl boots, but being ushered out of this park, weaving through parked cars has its perks.

"I definitely don't hate the view, though," I laugh out, and he glances back at me with a quirked eyebrow.

Julian is a very well built man, but I don't think I've truly appreciated his ass in a pair of well-fitted jeans until now.

"My stride is, like, half of yours. You're going to have to—"

He stops as soon as we hit the edge of the grass and turns to face me. Bending at the waist, he hoists me up and over his shoulder.

"Julian!" I yell out, laughing breathlessly as I smack his ass. "I have a skirt on."

"This is faster." He bites at my upper thigh and then holds down my skirt. "Nobody's out here right now anyway. Were you serious about the woods? They're right over there…"

It's almost obscene how sexy I find it to be manhandled like this.

Slowly moving me down the front of him, he makes sure my feet are on the ground before removing his hands from my body. As he reaches for the door handle, I realize I'm not interested in going anywhere right now. I don't want to get into that car, so I slide under his arm and between him and the door, closing it and mustering the courage to ask for what I want.

"You just threw me over your shoulder to get me here," I say, smiling up at him coyly. "Now, that we're here..." I trail off, leaning against the door as I run my fingertips along the front of my vest. I've had a day, but in the quiet parts, the ones when I could escape and think about him, my mind kept replaying what would've happened if we hadn't been interrupted looking out over the airfield. He's so wildly handsome that it's almost laughable.

His lips tilt up as he glances out at the rows of parked cars across the street, then turns slightly to glance over toward the park. Before he turns to look the other way, his fingers find the front of my waist, and he guides me so that my back hits the side of his truck.

"Unbuckle it," he says in a deep gravel, like the version of him I'm about to experience is something far more animalistic and demanding. My pussy is already eager, adrenaline coursing through me, wanting every fucking word and inch he wants to give me. The bluegrass music still echoes loudly from the park, but here, it's just background noise. His belt buckle jangles as my fingers work quickly to do as he's asked—intent on touching him, feeling him, tasting him.

Julian's hands move at the same pace as mine. He shifts one hand to the back of my neck, threading his fingers into my hair, while the other moves up and under my shirt. My heart races as his warm, calloused fingers find their way over the cup of my bra as his thumb rubs back and forth over my hardening nipple. He keeps his eyes on mine while I unbutton his jeans and then lower the zipper.

"I need your hands on me," he says, almost pleading. I bite my bottom lip at his words. With his hand around the nape of my neck, he uses his thumb to pull my lip free before he kisses me hungrily. Coaxing my tongue with his, he hums the moment my hand moves beneath the waist of his boxer briefs and down the length of his cock.

He breaks his lips away to look down at my hand that moves beneath his waistband. I drag my thumb across the tip that's already wet. Watching his jaw slack and feeling how hard he is for me makes me want to taste him and make him feel as good as he made me feel.

"You want me in your mouth then, don't you?" he says, looking at me already as I glance up.

I smile and nod. Because I fucking do.

"You can show me how well your throat can take me later. But right now"—he tilts his head back, trying to focus while my hand works him up and down at a measured pace, his arousal leaking as I grip him tightly—"I want to watch my cock slide into that very…pretty…pussy."

Thighs clenching, my body feels flush and eager to watch the same. I grip him tighter and run my thumb just beneath the head of his dick.

"Fuck, Wyn. Let me feel how wet you are right now."

There's something powerful in it, a brimming confidence that surfaces again like it had the night we watched each other come. Leaning forward, I lick and nip at his bottom lip.

I swipe my thumb along the slit of his dick as I move my hand out. With my eyes on his, I drag his arousal across my lower lip and then run my tongue across it. "Yeah, I think I'd like that."

"Fuck," he breathes out.

It's the last quiet and soft moment. He moves his hand from behind my neck and down to my thigh, his fingers digging into my skin, and my skirt hikes up. With my weight leaning against the truck, I loop my arms around his neck, and with his free hand, he finds my pussy, yanks my panties to the side like he promised, and swipes his thumb through my already drenched lips.

My fingers thread through his hair, pulling him closer. When our lips meet this time, it's urgent and needy, tongue and lips, teeth and nips.

"So fucking wet for me," he growls as his mouth moves to my neck, and I tingle all over. He licks along my pulse point, teeth grazing as I roll my hips for some kind of friction. His thumb drags up over my clit and back down through me, never giving me more or filling anything other than the need for more.

"I should take you home, spend time…" His thumb moves away, his other arm holding my leg slightly higher, and he pulls back, looking down as he drags the head of his cock in the same slicked path, making me shiver. "I want you to make me nice and messy."

I grab at his shirt, looking for purchase as he taps my clit like it's his good fucking pet, forcing another audible breath to rush out from my lungs.

"I'm going to need you to be quiet, just for a minute," he says as he looks over my shoulder. Suddenly, I can hear people talking from not that far away, and the reality of where we are, out in the open, doing this without any thought other than wanting to finally feel the other, sinks in. We should stop, but the part of me that's always been careful and cautious has changed into someone far more daring.

"Julian," I whisper, leaning forward and doing exactly what I've wanted and dragging my flattened tongue up the side of his neck, feeling the scratch of his scruff all the way to his jaw. A moan leaves me at the feel of him, the way he grips me tighter.

"Crowne," he grits out, and then smiles at me, moving his thumb from my pussy and shifting it to my throat. I trust him to touch me however he'd like right now. It feels like letting go and gaining a new kind of power all at once. "I think we're going to need to get out of here." Leaning forward, he nips at my bottom lip.

"I haven't finished yet," I say as my lips caress his.

But it's the sound of my name from the other side of the truck that has the both of us freezing any and all movement. "Wyn?"

"I'm telling you, she left," my sister huffs out.

Julian pinches my clit.

My mouth opens as I suck in a breath, my wide eyes locking onto his amused expression.

"I'll make sure you finish," he says, and then does it again. *Oh god.* "Just not here." With a quick kiss, he pulls away from me just as people come closer.

But the gut punch is hearing Nash call out, "Auntie Wyn?"

I look at Julian, eyes widening even more as he looks the same back at me.

"She wouldn't leave without saying goodbye, right, Mom?" Nash asks sweetly.

"I'm telling you, that's Julian's Bronco up there," Tommy

chimes in. *No, no, no.* "If he didn't leave, then I promise you, Wyn is still—" My uncle's voice cuts out as Julian lets go of my leg and helps me to shove my skirt back down over my hips.

Before I turn and move toward the hood of the Bronco, he pulls me close. His eyes search mine, and then look around my face. "This doesn't mean we're done, baby," he whispers as he pulls his pants back around his waist.

"I know," I say with a smirk, remembering what he just said to me. "Just a little while longer..." I lean in, kiss him on the lips, and then look down, brushing my palms along my skirt. Taking only a few steps toward the front of the truck, that's when I see them—less than fifty or so feet away and walking closer. "Here," I call out, raising my hand as I hear his buckle clang as he puts himself back together. "Still here."

Stevie stops and then snorts out a laugh the second she gets a full look at me.

"See," Nash says from Tommy's shoulders, with Jameson right beside them. "Told ya she wouldn't have left without saying bye."

"You're totally right, Nash baby," Stevie says with a big-ass, knowing smile on her face. "I've never been prouder of my big sister."

"Nash," I say like I'm out of breath. "That, um, cotton candy looks really good."

"Want some?" he asks.

I shake my head. "I'm good, thank you, though. Pretty full."

"She's good alright," Stevie says. "Probably full of somethin' back there."

I widen my eyes at her, and then watch as Jameson looks down, trying to keep the knowing smirk off his face too.

"Looks like we're going to need that ride, after all, Uncle Tommy," Stevie says, smiling big and wide, with at least a thousand questions running like a ticker tape in her brain. I know it's taking unimaginable willpower not to start asking them all right now.

"Sure thing. I'm parked just a few down," he says, and all I can think is if he'd been alone, or just a minute later, the man who practically raised me wouldn't have been able to unhear or unsee what we were about to do. "Get home safe, you two. Try not to get arrested for messin' around in public, will ya."

I snort out a laugh almost as loudly as Stevie does. Jameson follows behind them as she loops her arm with our uncle's, and Nash feeds her a piece of his cotton candy while still perched up high.

"I love them and hate them so much right now," I say as I watch them walk away.

He laughs quietly from behind me, leaning in to speak against my ear. "Get in the car, Crowne."

It's less than ten minutes to my place from here, but I rub my thighs together, very aware of how stretched out and wet my panties are. Once I'm seated in his passenger seat, Julian rounds the front of the truck and hops in. There's a podcast queued up when it turns on, and as much as I love listening to them, I'd much rather hear the noises I can get him to make.

It's reckless, but I unbuckle and twist my body toward him. He glances at me, doing a double take as I reach for him. "Crowne."

"You drive," I say, unbuckling his belt. "And I'll play." As I open the button to his pants, he lifts his hips just enough so I can run my palm along his length.

"Fuck, the way you want me," he says on an exhale. It's not lost on me that I feel that same way—lust-filled and awestruck at how this man makes me feel so incredibly wanted.

I swipe my thumb along the slit and drag his arousal down the smooth underside of his hard cock. He hums his approval. It's not enough to touch, and yes, I want to make him feel good, but selfishly, I want to taste. And I want him to moan for me again.

The moment I run my tongue along the tip of him, he lets out a gruff moan, and my pussy throbs. It spurs me on, so I wrap my lips around him and use my tongue to tease and explore. The angle is all wrong, but it's impossible to stop when I feel his fingers glide into my hair.

"Your mouth," he whispers. The car brakes jerk us slightly as I take him deeper and swallow. "Sorry." He sucks in a fast breath. "Oh, fuck. That's it," he grits out.

I drag my tongue back up and swirl, gripping at his thigh for leverage with one hand, and with the other, I reach down and play with myself.

"Tease me just like that." He must look at what I'm doing because he groans and says, "You're so fucking sexy. That's it, play with that pussy. Get her nice and ready for me, baby."

The dashboard light is dim, but it's enough to see how impossibly hard he's gotten in just a few minutes. I flatten my tongue, gliding it up and down as I move and grip him at the base. He tastes like the both of us, and that alone makes me hum around him. My fingers tease my clit and drag through my pussy with every sound he makes.

A small laugh escapes him, having heard me. "My mouth is watering thinking about how wet you are doing this right now. Does sucking my cock turn you on, Crowne?"

I smile the moment my lips pull away and breathily answer, "Apparently."

He groans in response, his cock flexing in my palm like that answer was heard all over his body. I like how that pleased him and my pussy tingles in response.

Wrapping my lips around him, I circle and flick my tongue where he's most sensitive, gripping his base and slowly pumping my wrist. So focused on him, and the way my other hand is teasing myself, I don't pay attention to where we are, only that when we turn, one arm holds me, keeping me steady from too much. I realize he must have turned down my street because he floors it.

Oral sex has never been on my must-have list, but with him, it's almost as much fun to give as it is to receive.

When he shifts the truck to park, I work my way down once more before my lips pop off of him. He shoves his seat all the way back and tells me, "That might have been the hardest drive of my fucking life."

"Definitely the hardest thing I've ever had in my mouth on a drive," I say in a sarcastic tone that has him smiling.

"Did you just make a dirty joke?" he asks as he reaches behind me and grips the back of my skirt, palming my ass cheek and squeezing. I don't have a chance to respond to the question before his hand wraps possessively around the front of my neck, moving me up and to his waiting lips. His tongue meets mine in a clash of lips and teeth. My hands grip along the front of his shirt, trying to pull closer. *I want more.* I want to finish what we've started in that parking lot, right now. And while it would take less than twenty feet from the front seat to my door, I can't wait. The windows are already fogged, despite the truck still running with the AC on. The only thing out here close enough to see what's going on here, is my place, everything else is fields and a river, but nobody here to see.

When I pull back from his mouth, it's as if he heard me. He nips at my lips and says, "Glove compartment."

I turn back and open it, an eager smile tugging at my lips as I pull out a condom. "You always this prepared?"

He plucks it from my fingers, and I pull off my cowgirl boots.

"This truck was waiting for me in the airplane hangar when I got here—there's safety features in every compartment of this thing."

Lifting his ass up, he shoves his pants and boxer briefs down enough for his cock to spring free. As he rips open the condom and rolls it on, I shimmy my skirt back up around my hips and rise to my knees on the long seat, lifting a leg over and then the other to straddle his lap.

"Let me see you," he says, wrapping his hand around the back of my neck and pulling my mouth to his again. His other hand roams to my pussy as two fingers glide through my stretched-out panties. A whimper crawls up my throat as he shoves them aside and runs the pads of his fingers along my cunt and up to my clit. My breathing is already heavy, but the way his fingers drag through my mess has me rushing out every bit of oxygen I've got. He hums in satisfaction before lifting the same two fingers to my bottom lip and then pulling me in to kiss them. It's urgent and carnal as he nips and licks off my arousal, and I grip onto his shoulders, grinding my pussy forward. Needing him inside me, I lean back slightly, barely breaking away from his kiss to look down and watch as he drags his cock through my wetness. Once. Twice. I tremble at the third swipe when he circles my clit.

"Show me. I want to see my cock stretch you nice and tight," he says, still gripping it. "How's that sound?"

It's a needy whimper that comes from my throat, one I have no control over, because I *want* that.

Shifting my body over him, I move my hands to his shoulders, as he drags himself between my lips, but this time the teasing is rewarded as I watch myself sink down slowly. And he was right—the way his cock fills me, it's a tight stretch that I feel all over my body.

"So fucking tight," he grits out, his hands gripping at my hips helping guide me. He holds my hips down when I'm fully seated on him.

"Julian," I breathe out, tipping my head back. He flicks open the top button of my jean vest, then the one below that, and then the next.

My chest rises and falls quickly as his fingers trace the lace of my bra. His thumb lingers back and forth over my nipple, making it harder and more sensitive with every teasing swipe. It's what has me rolling my hips, desperate for more friction, for more of him, just *more*.

"Not yet, baby. Stay like that for me," he says, just before he yanks the front of my bra down so that my breasts spill out. "So beautiful." Leaning forward, he runs his tongue across each breast, and a loud moan flees me. He wraps his lips and tongue around my already aching nipple—I never realized how much I liked attention on my breasts.

Dragging his teeth, he flattens his tongue, teasing me before sucking again. I moan on my exhale, shoving my fingers into his hair as I watch as he plays.

It takes everything in me not to roll my hips and chase the friction I'm so badly craving. I feel so impossibly full and my pussy pulses. I know he feels it, because when I start to tip my hips back, he holds me tighter, not allowing me an inch.

"Stay." He inhales sharply, wrapping both arms around my body now as he sits taller. "I want to feel you just like this," he says a breath away from my lips.

He lifts his head away from my wet and swollen nipples, tilts his head back to the headrest of his seat, and says, "Go ahead, ride me. Take everything you want, Wyn."

Without wasting a second, I'm rolling my hips, feeling how deep he hits, and I feel like I can't breathe. The angle of him massages a spot so perfectly that my pussy throbs. I want to feel it again, so I roll my hips and keep the same pace over and over, making myself moan as he plays with my breasts. Sweat slicks my skin and his as he leans forward again, licking a path up the valley of my breasts and then holding my shoulder down and fucking me deeper. My gasp turns into a whimper when he does it again, then guides my hips in another grinding motion to give my clit some attention. I chase this feeling, how I'm clenching around his length on every thrust, the pleasure he's giving me spreading throughout my body.

"That's it. So *fucking* good," he coaxes, encouraging me to keep going. "Don't hold back," he rushes out.

The way our bodies move together feels too good, and I know I could come within moments. The full length of him is buried as I find purchase, one hand gripping at the nape of his neck, fingers fist into his hair as the other holds myself up as I brace my palm on his chest. My fingers fist his shirt as I roll my hips again, only this time, it's like it unleashes something he's been holding back. He thrusts up, fucking into me deeper, no more taking his time.

"I'm so close," I whisper, wanting to come and also not

wanting it to end. The intensity of how he's looking at me, the fullness of him inside me, the build-up to this point, and the need we both share are nearly as good as I know the payoff will be.

"Come on, let me feel it," he says, and something inside me releases. My eyes lock on his as my orgasm slowly starts like it's crawled along my skin quietly, until this very moment at his command, when he pulls his hips back and then thrusts them at the same time as I roll mine. Body tensing, my mouth falls open, but not a single sound leaves me as I completely unravel around him. But I don't stop moving, wanting more as Julian fucks me from below.

One—*oh god*. Two—*right there*. Three—I feel him tense completely, holding my body tight to his until he comes just as hard, his mouth open and buried in my chest as he moans, wet lips brushing the curve of my breast. I keep moving, readying to chase another orgasm that feels like it's built up again.

With my fingers tangled in his hair, I hold around his shoulders, forehead pressing along his as we try catching our breath, enjoying every last pulse of an orgasm that's left me panting all over again, and him nearly shaking.

Minutes tick by before he loosens his hold around me. He leans back, seemingly dazed and content. Hair messy from the way my fingers toyed with it, lips smirking, hopefully replaying every little detail of what we just did. My body is still keyed up and wanting, my pulse racing against his chest. I feel undone and vulnerable, my clothes bunched and stretched out. The smell of sex, of us, lingers around us. A smile takes over my face as he grins up at me, dragging his fingers up between my breasts and up my neck, gripping my nape and pulling me to him. "Still nowhere near done," he says before punctuating it with a deliciously slow kiss.

"Come inside," I say, pulling back. "I need to be fed, then fucked. And if you can make me come like that again, I might ask you to stay this time." I nip at his lower lip.

One hand frames along the side of my face, keeping my lips close to his when he responds, "I love a good challenge."

CHAPTER 24

Julian

"THERE'S A PLACE IN MAINE that Birdie is always talking about," Wyn says as a piece of hair falls from the way she's tucked it behind her shoulders.

Without thinking, I push it away from her face, tucking it behind her ear as she keeps talking. She looks so damn beautiful like this—hair messy and cheeks pinked. Her vest is only buttoned in one place, and her feet are bare as she sits on the counter in front of me. I did that to her, made her wild and come undone. Of all the things I've done in my life, watching her talk to me so comfortably, and the way she makes me feel just by being close to her, might be at the top.

"She went when she was younger," she carries on. "Found a lighthouse attached to a beautiful bed-and-breakfast and said it was the most incredible winter solstice of her life. I've always wanted to see it," Wyn says as she drizzles honey over the almost-stale bread.

"You never went?" I ask as she holds up the bite of sticky bread and cheese to my mouth.

She shakes her head. "I haven't."

I take a bite, and then she licks her finger before assembling another one. "We should go," I say mid-chew. *Fuck, that's good.*

"To Maine?" she asks with a little laugh.

I lean forward and bite the piece she's just put together. "Sure. Anywhere." I look at her staring back at me, surprised I would suggest it. "I'd go anywhere you want, Crowne." Leaning in closer, I nip at her lip. "Thought that was clear by now."

She looks down at my lips and runs her thumb along my chin and the scruff of my beard. "It sure is starting to be."

"Can I have a bite of that?" I ask, glancing at the cake she pulled from the fridge.

She nods, smiling, and digs the fork next to her into the side of the layered cake and then holds it up for me to bite.

When the frosting hits my tongue, I almost hum. "Why is that so good?" I mumble.

"All my mom. She can make just about any dessert the most delicious thing you've ever tasted. Her superpower."

"I can't cook. Or bake, but I can make a decent cup of coffee and order one helluva pizza," I say, wiping up the honey that dripped on my shirt.

"You should probably just lose the shirt," she whispers, scrunching up her nose.

I grab the bottom of it and lift it up and over my head, tossing it off to the side.

When I look back at her, she's paused licking along the side of her thumb. "That was rather easy."

I keep my eyes on hers when I take a step back and yank my belt out of the loops of my jeans. Smirking, I toss it to the floor and then unbutton my pants. "I wildly misjudged how much you would enjoy me doing this," I say teasingly.

She smiles. "You're very nice to watch. Might be one of my favorite things."

I unbutton and then lower the zipper, taking my pants off. Kicking them to the side, I pull off my socks and then fix my dick so it's tucked up and into the waistband of my boxer briefs. "That's better," I tell her as I move back to where she's perched, nudging myself between her legs so I can be close to her again.

She hums, "Hmm, for now." And then wiggles her eyebrows. She holds up a piece of apple dipped in honey like it's a religious offering. I open my mouth and accept it, chewing it as she does the same.

"I like these," she says, touching along the base of my neck and down between my shoulder blades. "I thought this was beautiful when I saw the reflection of it in the bathroom." She bites her lip, I imagine, recalling those moments in that bathroom in Montana.

"I would sit in my dad's design studio and watch him draft out designs from stones he wanted to repurpose. I was maybe seven or eight, and I didn't know it then, but that was how he and my grandfather were paid for their cleaning *expertise*—with jewelry."

"So then your origin story wasn't jewelry, it was the cleaning business?" she asks.

"Their origin story. Mine started with jewelry," I say, watching her closely as she continues drawing her fingers over the dark triangular shapes.

"Turn, let me see the rest of these," she says as her fingertips glide across my skin. I can't remember a time in my entire life when I've been touched like this, studied, and appreciated. It feels fucking good.

As I turn my back to her and lean my ass against the counter, she traces along the pattern of paper airplane shapes between my shoulder blades.

"Keep talking," she says softly, and I don't know if I'll ever understand what it is about her that makes it easy, but I want to tell her all of it.

My eyes close as she keeps moving her fingers, tracing each paper plane. "Jewelry made for less curious transactions. It was easy to transfer, pawn, and resell. I didn't know any of that growing up, but the cleaning business was the first business. Making jewelry was the cover, and for my dad, the hobby." Looking down, I drag my finger across my palm the same way she's moving hers across my back. "He would draft out tons of rings and pendant designs on tracing paper. I remember thinking it was really basic stuff, but my dad liked to think through things before just starting. He always had a plan. The Pacific Northwest during the summers, in a beach town, turned busy quickly, but he wanted me to enjoy time off and not be in camps. I think he just liked spending time with me when he could, so I hung out around his workspace. Spending time with him was never a bad thing to me." I pause, thinking about him like that, so young and alone raising a kid on his own. "I started making airplanes with his discarded designs. And he'd take breaks and make them with me. We got pretty good at all the different folds there were." I laugh to myself, before adding, "Of all the things we'd done together over the years, something as small and basic as making airplanes on the floor with him ended up being a core memory for me."

She leans forward and presses her lips along my upper back, likely kissing one of the paper airplanes. "It's always those moments that stick with you for the long haul," she says quietly, almost as if she's lost in her thoughts. As she wraps her arms around me, legs too, I cover her hands with mine while she holds me from behind. "For me, it's cakes with my mom. My sisters and I would sit in the kitchen and watch her stress-bake. She's not the stand-still-and-reflect-on-her-feelings kind of woman." She smiles against me; I can feel her lips pull as she keeps a hold on me.

"I can relate a bit to that," I say, turning slowly to face her.

She looks at me, weighing what else she might want to say.

"My mom is"—she breathes out—"complicated, a bit selfish, maybe even an asshole at the core of it." She threads her fingers into the hair at my nape as she says, "She would repeat shit that famous people said, or quote songs like they were snippets of wisdom that she'd come up with on her own. Out of all the ones she's droned on about over the years, it's the one that Dolly Parton said that lingered loudest for me."

"Which one is that?" I ask.

"Find out who you are. And then do it on purpose," she says with more of a twangy accent than what she typically has. "She would say prolific things like that and then look disappointed when I was twenty-three and starting a thesis on the chemical composition and complexity of whiskey. We didn't have the kind of relationship that you and your dad had." She lets out an exhale. "I don't think she knew how to connect with me."

I turn around as she drapes her arms around me. I run my hands along her bare thighs. The Whispering Fool T-shirt she's wearing has the arms cut off and barely reaches past her ass, and it's the sexiest thing I've seen her in. Freshly fucked and not giving a shit looks good on her.

"I didn't want the things she was always stressed out about. When I was young, the goal was never to snag a husband and kids. Or run a loud-ass bar. I wanted the things that made me feel good—a really incredible garden like Birdie's." She looks up like she's thinking through a list. She smiles when she adds, "Maybe a dog, and to try making something I could be proud of, something as complicated as whiskey, like my dad's side of the family."

"Is it any better now?" I ask, cuffing a piece of hair away from her face. "Now that you know a little more about her and your grandmother?"

She swallows, her demeanor changing to something more rooted and darker.

"I was..." she pauses, "embarrassed by all the rumors that circulated about Lu Crowne. Embarrassed of her, for her. And I was her daughter." She puffs out her cheeks and blows out a breath. "God, I spent almost my entire graduate program with the single motivation to show everyone how much I *wasn't* like her and the rest of my family."

"And now?" I ask as she plays with the ends of my hair.

"I thought I might never see them again, *her* again, and all I could think was that she never knew how wrong I was. That when it mattered, how much I wish I was more like her. How she would have never allowed—" She cuts herself off and smiles, like she just realized something. "All of the rumors that swirled about her, turned out to be more true than not, and I don't know what to do with that."

A heavy breath leaves her as I trace along her cheek. When her eyes finally shift to look at mine she says, "My dad wasn't a good man. A part of me is too nervous to know if that's where it all started. If he was the reason—" She stares at the center of my chest. "If he hurt her enough to make it okay and ignore her moral code."

I tip her chin up to look at me. "How can I help?" I ask,

leaning forward and kissing across the base of her neck. The truth is, there's no sage advice or role that I need to have in how she comes to terms with what her mother and grandmother have done. If she wants me to leave, knowing what I've done and how I've helped them, I would hate every day hereafter, but I would go. I think I'd do anything she asked of me.

"You already are," she whispers.

"Moral codes are subjective," I tell her softly, running my fingers along the edges of her shoulders and then down her arms. "Right and wrong depends on the side of the situation."

"Is that why you said this was your last job?" she asks, taking my fingers that hovered over her side and pressing them there. She holds my palm against a place that I know hurt her, and it makes it impossible to be anything but honest now.

"I lost sight of the reason why we did it. And then without him, I didn't have an anchor."

She hums in understanding, without asking what I mean. She understands what it's like suddenly finding yourself alone. "Tell me more about him," she prompts. "About your dad."

"My dad was..." I shake my head and smile, even as my chest tightens with emotion. "He was funny. Stoic around the people he didn't know—a little like me in that way, but he made me laugh. And he was smart. He turned the jewelry business into something. My grandfather had gotten the nickname of 'The Jeweler.'" I let out a grounding breath. Fuck, it feels good to have someone who wants to listen to this—someone I don't have to hide from. "But really, that was my dad. He was a goldsmith—so damn talented too. He learned and then made the most intricate details with the most basic handcrafting tools. He wasn't designing pieces; he would just make what he wanted and sell them." My fingers roam around her waist, making me want to hold on for as long as I can. "I didn't think twice about the fact that my dad was my best friend. Not even when I was a kid. When my friends were embarrassed of their parents, I thought they just weren't lucky enough to have one as great as mine."

She smiles at hearing that. "And he taught you, all of it?"

"The basics of goldsmithing, a little about gemology, but most of that I learned later in school and apprenticeships. But the cleaning business?" I nod. "Every detail in situations where details are the most important thing."

I shift my weight forward and lean closer, drawing my fingers up and down the center of her back. "My mom wasn't in the picture for long. I barely remember her, but knowing now the kind of life my father led, having to be two different people and carry this legacy, this secret…" I sigh and look at where my palm rests, wanting to know more of her story too. "Who would want that? Cleaning horrific scenes where death lingered was why there would always be a part of him a partner would never really know."

"I think some people are more understanding than others." Her fingers roam along my shoulders, tracing a path to the paper airplane shapes that start there. "And I also think we share things with people when we know they can handle bearing the weight of it," she says, and then takes a deep breath.

What she's saying somehow helps make sense of this pull between us. My mouth tips up along the side when I say, "I met a woman. Beautiful, smart, she said something to me, and it clicked. I wanted her more than favors and secrets and a legacy." I clear my throat and shake my head. The conflicted feeling that I've been stifling finally surfaces. "But then I came here, thinking this is it, I'm done. And she's here, you're here, and you see what I do, who I am."

She moves her hands to frame my face, all of it registering with her that it wasn't just a connection and hot hookup in Montana. She shifted something within me—and maybe it was a long time coming, or maybe she was my *someone worth mentioning*.

"And then come to find out, there's a whole part of my dad's life that I didn't know about."

"How he used to stay in at the Rackhouse when he would come to Rumor?" she asks.

"There was a picture of my dad and Birdie together, and I had wanted to ask her before I made any assumptions about it." I shake my head, knowing what I saw in an old photo between the two of them. "They looked young, maybe around our age even."

I get lost in her green eyes, knowing now what that look between them was. I was wrong. "It was never about the job or having to keep this secret. It was being able to share it with someone who could handle knowing and wanting him anyway. It's why I need to talk to Birdie. I need to know that I was wrong. That he didn't die alone, not having had someone who cared for him like that."

She hears me as she says, "Okay," taking in all that I'm saying, what I've confessed to her, and the truth that I've been feeling. "Then I think we need to have a chat with Birdie," she says, moving her fingers along my hairline.

I close my eyes at her touch, leaning into it as I say, "Even if I hadn't decided to stop, it would've eventually ended with me. I wouldn't force my kid, if I ever had one, to take on this burden." I don't know why saying that out loud sits differently right now.

"Is that what it was for you? Did you *not* have a choice?" she asks, a pout pulling at her lips.

The question hits me square in the chest. "I had a choice," I tell her. "I wanted to do all of it, be like him, make him proud, but then I liked it. Being a creative has always felt good. But I didn't mind the meticulous details of it, and I believed in the morals my father lived by, so I went along with his clients and partners—some of them even became friends."

"You still have a choice. You can always change your mind," she says, leaning back on her hands.

"I do," I say, working through if I want that. "And I can."

She tilts her head and gives me a smile that somehow calms my thoughts even more. "What was it that beautiful woman said?" she asks playfully, knowing that the woman I was referring to was her.

"The devil is in the details," I say, leaning forward and kissing the center of her chest. "It wasn't a phrase I hadn't heard before, but this stranger said it, and for some reason, it made me want all of it—every last detail about what she was doing there, why she was in a place that couldn't be found on any map or GPS search. I wanted to know every detail and share mine."

"Julian," she whispers, and I have to kiss her. My lips press against hers, and she opens for me, guiding my tongue and taking my fucking breath away. Her legs wrap around my waist, and we get lost in each other. When we both need a breath, I pull back, letting my forehead rest against hers.

I flatten my hands on the inside of her thighs and push her legs wider. There isn't a need for any more words or clarity and truths. The intimacy of everything said between us needs action and payout, and *fuck,* am I willing to pay.

CHAPTER 25

Wyn

THE SMELL OF SUGAR AND yeast wafting inside my home might be the best way to wake up. It helps that I just had the best sleep after nearly three and a half years. I fell asleep somewhere between the haze of a middle-of-the-night orgasm and before sunrise. If I'm smelling the latest mash, that means it's easily close to noon—the distillery barely has a schedule, but it's usually midday when Tommy fires up a mash that's been waiting.

I stretch out in my cool sheets, wearing only an oversize Whispering Fool T-shirt and nothing else. My phone buzzes on the kitchen counter all the way across the room, but I take my time enjoying the feeling of being tired and sore. I smile to myself, draping my arm over my eyes. *I had so much sex last night.*

"Julian?" I call out and turn my head toward the bathroom. The door is open, no light on. Sitting up, I look around the room, noting his boots are still here. His T-shirt is a ball on the floor near my clothes. My phone buzzes again.

When I finally drag my body off the bed and reach my

phone, there's a wall of text messages from my sisters. I swipe to make sure I'm reading them in order.

STEVIE:

I'm just going to say it—you two were fucking behind the truck last night, weren't you?!?

JO:

WHAT! What the hell? I miss one lame festival, and apparently, our older sister is an exhibitionist now?! Wait, what did you see?

STEVIE:

Just the fumbling of trying to look like they didn't get caught doing something. Wyn, can you PLEASE share? I need more details. I'm withering in celibacy-land

JO:

Fucking around in public is not a new concept for you...

STEVIE:

JO:

You're also married, so obviously you're not celibate.

STEVIE:

Do I need to explain my relationship with Theo to you again?

The wall of texts continues into this morning.

JO:

Good morning, my beautiful old hags. Why have we still not heard from Wyn?

STEVIE:

Wynnie, are you getting railed right now?

STEVIE:

I swear to every goddess in the universe that if she answers yes, mid-pump, suck or thrust, I will be the happ-happ-happiest.

JO:

It's really you that we should be most concerned about. Happ-Happ-Happiest!??

STEVIE:

Yes, fuck you very much. I'm excited that my big sister is having a taste upgrade in men. Still not sure where he came from, but yum, Wyn. Yum.

JO:

Nom nom nom, Wyn.

STEVIE:

I'm eating breakfast and still no response...

STEVIE:

Should we be concerned? I'm going to do a drive-by.

STEVIE:

We can paperboy more condoms at her door, just in case.

Oh shit.

I rush into the bathroom, quickly typing a response.

WYN:

Do not do a drive-by. I'm fine. Just tired. I'll give you all the details later.

I load my toothbrush with toothpaste and brush, then wash my face and run my fingers through my hair enough so that I can pull it into a messy bun. When I come out of the bathroom, that's when I hear the muffled yelling.

Peering out onto my back patio, I find Julian, facing in the other direction toward the river.

Something thumps against my front door, making me stop and spin towards it. I wait a few seconds, and then there's knocking. The knocks hit double-time, and I know instantly that both of my sisters ignored my last text. There's a little part of me that warms at the idea they wanted to be sure I was okay, even if it's fueled by nosiness.

When I open it, they both stop talking and give me a once-over, and the widest, most-knowing Cheshire cat smiles spread across their faces. "You've finally hit your hoe-phase," Stevie says, double-fisting boxes of condoms. "Didn't know the size, so hoped for the best," she says, opening her arms wide.

"Nope, no. You're not coming in—" I say, getting cut off as Jo chews a potato chip from the bag she's holding and then ducks under my arm.

Goddamnit.

"Is he still naked in your bed?" Stevie asks, covering her mouth, like that's exactly what she's hoping for.

I whisper-shout, "No!" and shut the door as they walk in. "See, I'm fine. I love that you were concerned. And I'll share all the details if you want them later, but please, I would *love* to not explain why my sisters are here..."

They both stand at the window, facing the patio, and stare out, disregarding the fact that I want them out of here. I cross my arms. They do well with threats. "I will not swap or share another pair of shoes with either one of you if you don't get—"

"What in the jackpot of man did you get yourself under, Dr. Wynona Crowne..." Stevie mumbles out.

Jo keeps staring out, holds her hand up, and waits for my high five.

When I slap it, she turns and winks at me. "I won't tell you to be smart. Have fun instead." Moving to the fridge, she pulls out the last slice of cake we'd left and a fork. She takes it with her and yells out to Stevie, "Alright, let's go, you horny little nymph, we're leaving."

"That's my cake, Jo!" I yell after her.

"There are so many inches, aren't there?" Stevie says in a low voice as Jo tries boxing her out. "Gah, if anyone gets to get the guy, it's you, Wynnie."

I just shake my head, biting back a smile, because they might have just been the comic relief I needed this morning.

"Don't get knocked up!" Stevie shouts as Jo shoves her outside. "Use the condoms!"

I can hear Jo quietly reprimanding her as they walk back toward the car. "Seriously, you're a wet blanket when you say shit like that. Nash is the best thing..."

When I open the patio doors, the heat hits almost as hard as the sight in front of me. *Almost.* Full back on display, a compass and birds that shift into paper airplanes running from the center of his back out to his shoulders. Shiny and sweaty, his jeans hang low as his garden-gloved hands lean on the handle of a rake propped next to him.

"We need to have a conversation about my dad, Birdie," he shouts across the river to my grandmother, who's got her basket of day-old bread so she can feed the ducks and birds that sometimes wander down here.

"Yes, that sounds lovely," she says in a too-chipper, almost placating tone. "Is that my beautiful granddaughter over there?" she calls out to me. "Well, good morning, Wyn. Did I just hear Stevie's car?"

I wave at her, giving her a tight-lipped smile, just as Julian turns around. He's dirty and sweaty and delicious. *Did he just weed my pathetic excuse of a garden?* The once mess of weeds and my slightly functional irrigation system looks like it's been cleared out and reconfigured.

He smiles at me, looking from my face and down the front of me. "Good morning."

I bite my lip, stifling my smile. "Good morning."

I look up and over at my grandmother, who's wearing the world's largest black sun hat and tossing food into the river.

"Why are you feeding the ducks?" I call out to Birdie.

"Well, your sister wanted me to see if you were home, which obviously you are. And the gators haven't had a meal in a while, so figured I should fatten these up for 'em."

Julian's head whips back to me. "Is she serious?"

With a wince, I nod and give her a thumbs-up, because really, how am I supposed to respond to that? "The negative of living a stone's throw from family," I say to him with a shrug. I leave out my least favorite circulating town rumor—the Crowne women feed people they don't like to the alligators that live in the river next to the bar. It's ridiculous, but that one followed me throughout middle school. Kids called me Gator-aid for the entirety of seventh grade.

Stepping closer, I glance around the cleaned-out space. He can't be serious. "You did all of this?" I say, almost in shock. "How long have you been out here, Julian?"

"You were out cold and this"—he walks closer to me, moving his finger to point around the weeds—"would make a really nice garden, but you needed to clear it out before you started planting anything. Your irrigation system needs to be spread out, but it makes sense to see what kind of space you're working with first."

He rests the rake against the small bistro table and grabs the hose.

"And you just know this?" I say, amused, crossing my arms over my chest.

Twisting the head, it turns on without leaking everywhere, and he hoses off his hands and up his arms. He drags his fingers into his hair, wetting the strands more than they already were.

"Anything I design, I have to have a plan for." His lips tip up as he looks at me. "And in case you forgot, I'm actually *really* fucking good at cleaning things up."

Ignoring the fact that I'm pants-less, he's wet, and my grandmother is very likely watching all of this, I wrap my arms around his shoulders and lift onto my toes to kiss him. His lips claim mine like they've done it millions of times.

He hums as his arms wrap around my back and hands roam to the hem of my shirt. "You have no pants on," he whispers against my lips.

"You have no shirt on," I say against his lips as I smile.

Lifting me up so that my feet dangle just above the ground, he walks us back inside. "I think I need to shower again. Mind helping me, Crowne?"

"I like to think that if it had to be determined, whiskey is a woman," Stevie says and follows it with a dramatic gasp. "I know, I know, if I have any male listeners who still have a skewed perspective of gender roles, this is probably the episode I'll lose you. Ciao, fuckers!" She laughs. "I think about all the kinds of whiskey in the world too—bourbon whiskey, Scottish whisky, Japanese, all of them different in the way they're filtered and finished, but holy shit, doesn't that feel feminine? Whiskey has been postured as a man's drink for a long-ass time. I know plenty of men who claim women the exact same way. Whiskey is a fucking lady, and I have a flight that'll twist your panties on the podcast's website listed. I'm going to sip on one that my

gorgeous sister doesn't know I stole from the latest batch she bottled. I promise you, it's not just because she's my sister; this woman makes elite-level tasting profiles of Tennessee whiskey."

I smile as I listen to her latest podcast, and a part of me misses Thursday nights in Montana when the bar packed in and I could do a tasting flight to complement the episode. *Maybe it's something I could do again?*

Spotting my nephew on the footbridge that connects the bar to this side of the property, where my house and the distillery are spread out, I pluck out an earbud.

"Nash, what are you up to over there?" I call out.

His head whips around, binoculars pressed against his eyes. He's wearing a fishing hat and vest, but as I walk closer, instead of lures and lines on the pockets and loops, there are dinosaurs and a magnifying glass. He holds his finger up to his lips to signal to me to be quiet, and I can't help but sniff a laugh in response.

As I approach and step foot over the weathered wood, I ask, "What are we looking for?"

"Ralph's family. Did you know that alligators are actually prehistoric? I wonder if Ralph knew dinosaurs when he was a kid," he says, lifting the plastic blue-and-yellow binoculars up to his eyes again.

"I think it would be pretty cool if he did," I say looking out across the river. The water seems quieter lately. In the spring, it's always higher from the rain, rushing by faster, but this time of year, I forgot how much it dries up.

"Birdie says Ralph's family roams up and down this river looking for him, but this is the time of year that we'll likely see them." Peering through his binoculars, he adds, "Don't worry, Auntie Wyn. I know better than to get too close." He holds up his air horn. "I also know to sound this. Mama says gator or stranger, I can use it when I need it." He hits the top of it, and a loud, blaring sound comes from the horned end.

Less than ten seconds later, we both whip our heads toward the Whispering Fool when Stevie comes running out, yelling, "Nash!" When she sees that he's fine, and I'm with him, she shouts, "Emergencies only, I said—that's gators or strangers! Not Auntie Wyn."

I hold my hand up. "My fault, I told him to test it for me."

He gives me a side-glance and a knowing smirk.

"Are you okay out here if I go over to the distillery?" I ask him, crouching down and kissing his cheek.

"Of course," he says. "Oh." He reaches into his vest, along one of the many pockets, and plucks out a brown-and-orange rock. "I found this for Julian. Can you give it to him?"

Caught off guard, I ask, "Sure. What is it?"

"Just thought he'd like it. He wears jewelry, and Auntie Jo said he's an artist and makes things people wear for lots of money." He shrugs his shoulder. "It's nice having more boys around here."

I smile at the gesture and how damn sweet this kid is. I try not to think about how I wouldn't have had a chance to know him if I never came back. I would've only been a story of a person in his mom's life and not someone who he would feel love from. "Sure is nice to have you around here, that's all I know," I say, giving him a hug before heading toward the large black building on my side of the river. "Love you big, Nash."

Every time I've walked up this path toward the distillery, I'm in a good headspace. The man I've been wrapped around helps too. I smile, thinking about all the ways I feel more myself than I have in a long time... Maybe ever. And I want this feeling to last.

The sliding door of the distillery is wide open as I get closer. My breath catches, and I stop in my tracks as my mother hoists up a case of whiskey. "Mom? Where are you going with those?"

"I made it, I'll do what I want with it," she says flippantly, moving toward the sidecar of her motorcycle. I glance at the back of the rickhouse where Tommy wipes his hands, leaning against the doorway, watching the exchange. He told me what she'd been doing when I was gone, but I want to hear it from her.

"What do you mean, you made it?" I ask, following her.

"I mean, I made it." She rests her fists on her hips and looks back at Tommy. They don't say anything, but he nods and gets into his truck and drives off.

I want to hear why. All the time I spent out here, she never joined me. She was jaded, opinionated, practically a vampire anyway, or a witch. I thought pretty hard about how that could've been true when I was in my late teens. But for some reason, right now, despite being in my mid-thirties, I just want to talk to my mom, want to understand her. I've spent too long thinking I might not get a chance to again. For all the complex molecules I've studied and theories I applied throughout, the equation between me and my mother has always been the most complicated.

"Lu," I breathe out, frustrated at how this entire relationship with her seems to constantly feel like I'm wading through mud.

"Don't 'Lu' me, like I'm an errant child, Wynona. Fine, you need to hate someone, at least call me Mom and then go on hating me," she says, like that was something I declared. It twists my stomach.

I jerk back. "I don't hate you, Lu."

She scoffs. "*Lu*," she mumbles, shaking her head.

I started calling her by her first name when I decided I wanted to study organic chemistry. She told me I'd never find what I really wanted if I kept doing what I was doing. I resented her for that comment, but it seems she may have been right.

I stare at her dark hair, the angular cut of it, and how it somehow makes her seem tougher, harsher. I had colored it the same shade, chopped it too when I was relocated. I didn't even realize I had done it. I wanted to be like the toughest person I had ever met at a time in my life when I had been so severely broken.

She waves at the air in front of her. "You know what? Let's not do this right now. Birdie's got a bunch of garden club bitches showing up later, and I need to get my ass outta there before they do."

"Mom," I say more intently. "I don't hate you."

"You sure about that? Wynona, you leaned into all those rumors about our family—about me. Didn't once think about sticking around or standing by. You wanted distance. I embarrassed you, and I'm allowed to be upset about that."

She's right. I didn't like people saying things about my family, but I didn't stand up for them. I chose to step aside instead. And I never realized how much that hurt her until right now.

I have my chance to fix things here, and I keep pushing her away.

"You know what I really want? A whiskey neat and to kick my legs up on the sticky bar and listen to my mom bad-mouth whatever asshole mansplained how she should run her business."

She looks over at me, surprised or maybe pleased with what I'm saying.

I laugh, thinking about how often this happened. "Or a

really juicy story about how she talked the latest bachelorette into canceling her own wedding."

She smiles, looking down and toying with the hem of her shirt. I glance around the space, taking inventory of the barrels that need to be turned and the cases of old glass bottles that need to be washed out and sanitized.

"I'm sorry that you had to find out at all, but especially in the way that you did," she finally says. "I didn't want you girls to see the darkness of it." She shakes her head. "Maybe if you knew what we did or who we were sooner, it would've made sense that we *wanted* people talking. That all those rumors you hated so much were a good thing."

I furrow my brow, not having thought of it that way at all.

"When people say crazy things about others around this town, it's always easier to pass off as a rumor and not suspicious behavior.

"I never wanted you to hate me." Her eyes brim and spill over with tears. "I never wanted you to look at me like you are right now. Like I'm some kind of monster for the things me and your grandmother have done."

I close my eyes and shake my head slowly. That wasn't what I thought. I haven't allowed myself to really settle on how I feel about the things they've been doing. The shock of my family being capable of murder hit me square in the face, but I'm not disgusted or ashamed. Hearing her talk about it, knowing at their core, who my mother and grandmother are, I understand it. I'd had a front-row seat to death and torture. There hasn't been a single moment when I thought the person who killed the monster who had hurt me deserved anything more than my complete and utter adoration.

When I finally focus on her again, trying to stay out of

my head and in this moment with her, she takes a step closer. I notice her hands fidgeting and looking more nervous than I ever remember seeing her. "When you disappeared, or left, or whatever it is that happened to you that you refuse to tell me—" she starts to say, but I cut her off.

I can't avoid this any longer, not now. Not after what I know and listening to her open up like this with me.

"I didn't leave willingly," I rush out. "And as much as I wanted to, as much as I disappointed you, I didn't just leave." I look up at the vaulted beams above, trying to take a deep breath. I've always felt safe here—the distillery was a safe space for me, even as a kid. I've only held back because I didn't think she could handle it, Birdie either. But they're stronger than I've ever given them credit for.

Lifting the side of my shirt and holding it up high, I display the scar that runs the length of my torso.

"He started with a fillet knife. It was so sharp, it almost didn't hurt. Then he switched to a serrated. It felt like teeth gnawing at me each time he dragged it back and forth. He told me if I screamed, if I shared with him what it felt like to be so smart, then he would stop." I shake my head as tears cloud my eyes. "I didn't scream. I didn't tell him what it felt like knowing I was smarter than him, but that he outplayed me." I swallow down the truths that linger, the pieces that she doesn't need to know. "I passed out three times before he got so frustrated that he left and came back with someone else who he…" I suck in a breath, trying to keep myself from picturing it all over again. Reliving it in therapy had been enough. "The infection it caused probably should've killed me, but after that, he was very adamant about keeping me alive."

Her hands cover her mouth, and her tears keep falling even

when I let go of my shirt. I didn't show her to upset her. I wanted her to see that I didn't choose any part of leaving. "Who?" she asks, the question muffled behind her hands.

"There are all different kinds of men," I say, finally allowing what she and Birdie shared to settle. "But only a monster is capable of the things I witnessed."

"Who, Wyn?" she says, more loudly now. "I will kill—"

I shake my head, as pent-up tears escape, even knowing he's already gone. "The only reason I can tell you any of this is because someone else was brave enough to kill him." I was able to come back home because the woman who had pulled me out of that storage unit ended up being the person who killed him in the end. She was the brave one—I just survived.

My mom picks up one of the empty bottles and chucks it across the space. It hits the wall and shatters everywhere. The sound of it makes me jump, but it's when she screams at the floor, fisting her hands that makes me understand how difficult that must have been to hear. Grabbing another bottle, she holds it out to me. When I meet her green eyes, they're as tear-filled as mine.

I take another deep breath, and on the exhale, I grab the empty bottle by its neck. With a shout, I throw it as hard as I can against the farthest wall. It makes a popping noise as it hits and shatters. I look back to her again, needing my mom to tell me that it's okay. That all of this is okay.

"Breaking shit helps," she says, batting another tear away.

I can't help but bark out a teary laugh. Nodding, I say, "Breaking shit helps."

Picking up another one, I heave it across the room. This isn't going to lead to a big, warm embrace—hugging isn't really our thing. Maybe breaking shit could be.

She pulls two of the workbench stools over and sits on one as I grab one of the recently corked bottles of whiskey—it was being steeped with Earl Gray tea and vanilla bean—and bring it over with two rocks glasses. She tosses another bottle against the wall. Once I've poured each of us a hefty amount, I sit on the other stool and chuck another one, each time exhaling and trying to let all of this settle more softly than it's felt to carry. Between us is a case of empty bottles that were meant to be used to bottle up whatever whiskey had been ready, but I think there are other plans for these bottles now.

She's quiet for a moment after taking her glass of whiskey and clanking it with mine. Taking a sip, she says, "You never disappointed me, Wyn. Dammit, I was just a kid when I had you. I was barely surviving with you and your sisters after your father—" A breath whooshes out of her, and she takes a moment to collect herself. When she does, she picks up another empty bottle from the case and hauls it across the room. The sound of it breaking feels relieving. She doesn't finish her thought. Instead, she says, "Then you grew up to be someone who intimidated the hell out of me."

My eyes widen. "I intimidated you?" I point to her, laughing. "Have you met yourself?"

"Oh, yes, I work very hard at that. But for you, it's natural. There's something different about it when someone isn't trying."

"Mom," I say, not knowing how else to respond. I never imagined her looking at me that way, just the opposite, really.

She shakes her head when she looks at me. There are some things that changed while I was away, but she barely ages. She and Birdie both look nothing like the respective years they have under their belts, but something about her is softer now. Maybe it's this moment, maybe it's seeing her with Tommy, or just knowing more, but this is the kind of different that I've always wanted.

"I don't understand how I can have the one thing back that I begged for, and here I am, still messing it all up." She practically smacks away a tear that had the nerve to fall down her cheek.

"Let's both stop messing it up," I offer, holding up the bottle of whiskey to pour her out another.

Holding up her glass, she says, "Then let's stop messing it up." She takes a sip and holds it back up to the light again. "Why does this taste like dessert?"

I chuckle at that. "It's tea. And vanilla. It'll probably pair well with the cake you made with the blackberries."

"That one was good, wasn't it," she says, smiling into her glass. "You're good at this, Wynona. Far better than your father or any of us were at trying to do something with this place." Swallowing roughly, she pauses for a moment. "I started coming out here when you left. Asked Tommy to help at first." She lifts her chin, more emotion lingering on the surface as she finally shares this with me. "This was always your thing, Wynona. Figured I would miss you less if I could do something you enjoyed doing."

"Mom," I whisper, looking up, trying to keep the tears from spilling over. "Thank you,"

She's trying to keep it together as she nods, swiping under her eyes, and then blowing out a slow breath.

We let silence linger around us. She chucks another bottle at the wall, and both of us laugh.

"Who's cleaning that up?" I ask, looking at the pile of shattered glass.

She shrugs. "Tommy always likes a task," she says, polishing off her glass.

"You going to tell me what's going on with you two?" I toss back to her with a quirked eyebrow.

She takes a deep breath, tilting her face up at the bit of sun that breaks through the windows. "Nope," she says, popping the *p*.

I laugh. "Oh, come on, am I supposed to pretend like I didn't see that?"

Standing, she holds up another empty bottle and turns it in her hand. "If we're talking chemistry, me and your Uncle Tommy have always had it." She launches this one hard over her head, and it slams against the wall, some pieces reaching all the way back to us. "Can you do me a favor and keep it between us?"

I smile at her, but can't help but ask curiously, "Can I ask why? Stevie and Jo would probably be thrilled."

She takes a step away, back toward the sliding doors. "Like most stories, there's more to that one." Smiling softly, she leans against the entryway in the afternoon sun, making her look like some kind of goddess. "Stories are harder to tell if they're not over yet."

Then she's turning on her heel.

It felt good. This moment with her, putting all of it on the table. "Mom," I call out, and she glances over her shoulder. "What happens now?"

"I've got a cake cooling. A bar to run. And everything else, we'll just see what comes of it. Maybe we just need to enjoy a few new rumors and whiskey."

CHAPTER 26

Julian

I STOP SHORT AT THE edge of the pebble-stone walkway and get a full picture of what I'm about to walk into. My shoulders are tense, and I have a knot in my stomach about what Birdie Crowne knows about my father. A part of me has been fighting off jealousy even more than curiosity that someone, other than me, would have known more about a man I considered my best friend. I swallow down all the emotions—if I was good at anything, it was stifling those down and focusing on the present.

I've never in my entire life thought about attending a garden club. Up until this afternoon, I hadn't even realized it was actually a thing that people did. When Birdie suggested to Wyn that I come tonight, I had expected something more along the lines of a barbecue in the garden. I was terribly mistaken.

JULIAN:

Where are you, Crowne?

WYN:

All the way back. I'm talking tea leaves with Birdie and one of her girls

Through the pergola archway that's wrapped in green vines and small twinkling lights is one very long table, low to the ground, and peppered around it are at least a dozen women perched on oversize floor pillows. Taking in all of them at once is intimidating, but individually, they're all engrossed in conversation, eating from the ornate display of food that runs the length of the table, and laughing together.

Dark green arborvitaes serve as a barrier between whatever happens outside and the things that happen inside. Warm yellow string lights are for vibes rather than efficiency as the sun still takes its time setting this time of year. The lights continue from the edges of the space to being tightly wrapped around the trunks of willow trees, swooping across and over the long table, gathering where a chandelier hangs from a thick branch of the massive oak in the farthest corner. But it's the plush array of roses and oversize pots of thick herbs that make the outdoor space feel cozy. Wildflowers sprinkled between have muted blooms like they're holding out a bit longer, regardless of it being the end of summer. The colors and shapes remind me of the flowers that are tattooed along the center of Wyn's back.

The garden itself is as much the host as the matriarch of the Crowne family as she sits behind sheer, billowing curtains surrounding the small pergola archway in a chair that looks more like a dais than a well-cushioned patio lounger. And to her right is the woman whom I am so easily and intensely falling for.

She sees me approach and gets up, moving through the curtain and coming out as I get closer.

Fuck, she's beautiful.

My body responds to her simply knowing I'd see her, never mind once I do. All the different smiles I've clocked have made me realize that this one is one of my favorites—I didn't know how powerful it would feel to be seen by another person and for their reaction to feel the way hers does.

As I pass by the table of women, I hear someone say, "That's the one Wyn brought back from wherever she was."

Another whispers loud enough for me to hear, "I wouldn't mind dying and coming back with a souvenir like that."

I look right at them, letting them know I heard every word. Not a single one can keep eye contact when I do. *I'm not surprised.*

Cora Billings sits at the end of the table, smiling into her glass of wine as she wiggles her fingers at me. Next to her is the owner of Moonie's, who's deep in conversation with two other women dressed in barely-there attire that drapes along their arms and chests. It doesn't feel like a small town that gossips about the Crownes like Wyn painted. It feels like friendship over a meal, or at the very least, a pause on responsibility for some camaraderie.

When I reach the end of the table, Wyn stands up, wrapping her arms around my neck and kissing me. Her tongue slides against mine with not an ounce of hesitation or care of who's watching. Kissing her is the easy part; it's stopping that seems to be the piece we both struggle with. Her fingers glide into the hair at the nape of my neck as I wrap my arms around her waist and lift her up off the ground. Whistles and hoots from the table pull our attention.

We both smile against each other's lips and look down toward the crowd. It's not my idea of a good time, being the center of attention anywhere, but there's something about claiming Wyn in front of a crowd that feels really fucking good. She pulls me down the length of the garden and back to where she had been sitting, where, on the other side, Birdie sits, sipping on something bright green while smoking.

"It's about time you found yourself here, Mr. Colton," Birdie says. The way that could be taken in so many ways isn't lost on me. I want to know what she does about my father.

"Birdie, I think you can call him Julian by now," Wyn says as she sits on the bottom half of the lounger with her grandmother.

I take the velvet red chair opposite them, which clearly was set up for her tarot readings. A deck is placed in the center of the table with a satin pink cloth draped over it.

"I've been wanting to talk with you," I say, glancing at Wyn before I add, "I found something of my father's." I shake my head. "I need to understand who he was to you." Swallowing past a lump in my throat, I look down at the rocks and crystals spread out around the table at the center between us. "I've spent the last three years trying to come to terms with the fact that my best friend isn't alive any longer. And then I come here and find out there was a whole part of him I didn't know about."

"I'll stop you right there." Birdie holds up her hand. She looks regal in her chair, as if she's wiser and stronger than the rest of those around her. She's dressed like the seventies were her favorite decade, wearing her usual flowing dress with a sheer blue shawl over her shoulders. Apart, each Crowne woman is beautiful, but when you start to put them in the same space and pick out the features that are the same, they each become more breathtaking. With Birdie and Wyn, it's their eyes. Both deep and bright shades of green, with thick lashes and the same cheekbones. "You knew him better than anyone, even I know that."

The only thing I know for certain is that I've been missing something.

I glance at Wyn first, who gives me a reassuring smile and a tiny nod, and then back at Birdie. "Were you and my father ever more than just business acquaintances?" The picture of them together, him staying here for longer than what would've been usual, makes it seem like that was the case.

Birdie unfolds the cloth at the center of the table. "Cut the deck, Mr. Colton."

I stare at her, waiting for her to answer my question first. I can see Wyn out of the corner of my eye, observing but not interjecting.

"Fine." Birdie exhales. "You're stubborn like him." Grabbing the deck, she starts to shuffle it as she says, "Yes, we were… more."

"Birdie," Wyn says quietly. *She didn't know either.*

I already assumed, but hearing it out loud has me bracing for more. I bite down on my molars, trying to keep my emotions in check for this. *Dad, why wouldn't you have told me any of this?*

She puts the deck down in front of me and looks at it, waiting for me to do as she asked and cut it. The chatter behind us around the table kept pace—plenty of their own conversations happening to focus too hard on what we're discussing.

I glance at Wyn, whose attention is on me already. There isn't anything I'll ask or likely hear that I wouldn't end up telling her, so I cut the deck and ask my next question. "How long had that been going on?" The reality is that Birdie might be Wyn's grandmother, but she's close to my father's age, give or take a few years.

"Almost as long as you've been alive, Julian," she says, draping the silk cloth over the cards, and then holding out her hands, palms up.

The detail feels like a gut punch. Like I've been too selfish for never knowing this. I feel guilty for not asking him the question he'd always ask me: *Is there someone worth mentioning?*

"Let me see your hands, please. You're too closed off for cards tonight, and I need some assistance here," she rushes out.

What else could I do other than what she asks. I wanted the truth, so I put my hands on the table, palms up. It doesn't matter if I believe in any of this—she does, and I want to hear what she has to say.

"Wyn always enjoyed reading palms," she says, glancing at Wyn. "I taught each of the girls a little part of all this. You can call them gifts, beliefs, rituals. You can believe or not believe in it." She runs her pointer along the deepest and longest line of my left palm. "But for me, they allow a sense of grounding. A better presentation of a choice I can make." Her eyes meet mine for a moment, moving her fingers along the lines of my right hand next.

She exhales, and then gets up, moving to the bar cart that holds jugs of water with lemon slices and herbs floating inside, along with bottles of liquor and plenty of crystal glasses. Wyn pops off a stopper on a round glass bottle and pours out what looks like two whiskeys neat.

"Seems like you're at a bit of a crossroads right here. I wonder if you even realize the impact your decisions might have if you choose one way versus another," Birdie says. "I know there's something that will shake you." She looks to Wyn, and then back to me. "And how you choose to handle it is the crossroads."

When Wyn brings me one of the two glasses she's poured, and moves to sit back on the chaise, I stop her. Wrapping my arm around her hips, I tilt my head up and smile at her, coaxing her to sit on my lap. I need her close to me for this conversation.

She loops one arm around my neck, sitting across my thighs. I like that she didn't hesitate to sit with me like this in front of her grandmother and the rest of the people here.

"Don't ask me what it is; I don't know that much. I am not clairvoyant," Birdie says as she takes a pull of what she's smoking.

I sip the whiskey. "This was the last place my father had been before he—" Clearing my throat, I shove down the emotion that naturally comes every time I think about him. "Rumor was on our books as the last job he'd been on. I don't care what the hell he cleaned up here, or if he cleaned anything at all, but he didn't come home after it. He took a detour up to New York, a place he'd never just go and visit on his own." I swallow before I say, "He went there and never came back."

I can feel Wyn's body tense as she looks at Birdie.

Birdie sits motionless for a beat as her eyes water. But instead of answering me right away, she looks down at the table and at her deck again. Moving the satin cloth first, she flips over a card. *Queen of Cups.* It means nothing to me as it faces me upside down. She studies the picture for a moment before looking back up at me.

"I fell in love with your father over the course of three decades," she says softly. "It's not what most people would consider a love story, but I like to think that every story needs to be a little different, simply based on who people are."

She gives her granddaughter a placating, tight-lipped smile. "Imagine having a secret that makes you a morally gray person, and then finding another who can understand it, embrace it… live with it." Glancing between the both of us, she adds, "I feel like you *can* imagine." She bats away a tear that starts to fall down her cheek. "There wasn't going to be a happily ever after.

He had his life, and I had mine. We didn't ever talk about a future, and when we saw one another, it was always business. Until, one day, it wasn't."

She takes a sip of her whiskey and flips another card over. *Strength*. The Roman numeral eight is at the top, and below it, an upside-down image of a woman and a lion.

"The last time I saw him, I wasn't okay." She looks at Wyn first, and then lifts her chin a little higher before she says, "Wyn had been missing for more than two months, and I knew in my heart that she wasn't gone." Birdie looks down at her hands and then at the deck of cards on the table before she lets out a steadying breath.

I grip my hands along Wyn's hip tighter, knowing whatever comes next is something that I'm not sure I'm prepared to hear.

"I begged your father to help me find her. Somehow. And I thought he would, at the very least, just hold me for a little while, let me feel the loss of someone who's so important to me. We talked about all the dead ends and last people who had seen her, and then the next morning, he was gone. Left me a note on a piece of paper that said, 'I'll do everything I can.'"

From my back pocket, I pull out the picture of the two of them I found in the workspace at Tommy's place. I slide it across the table toward her, but not before Wyn sucks in an audible breath when she sees it. She stands up abruptly, pulling away from me. Holding her chest, visibly upset, she nods like she's trying to work out what Birdie just shared.

"Wyn?" I ask, concerned, wanting her to say something, but instead, she stumbles back and takes long strides back toward the vined archway. I don't understand what has her spooked.

"Wyn," Birdie calls out, but she doesn't turn around or add anything more. When I stand to follow Wyn, she adds, "Before you go chasing after my granddaughter, you need to hear this, Julian." Something about her tone halts my steps. "She hasn't told me much about where she was. I shouldn't have told you this with her here. We did everything we possibly could while looking for her. I didn't mean for him to get involved." Her face squints, not able to hold back how much she's feeling all of this. "I'm so sorry your father didn't go home right away. Maybe if he had..."

"I don't understand any of this, or why my father never told me about..." I shake my head and stand. "Is it strange to say that I'm relieved that he had someone. And that there was more to his life than just me or making jewelry or our fucked-up legacy?"

"It doesn't sound strange at all," she says.

I look down the length of the table at the group of women who have now stopped their individual conversations. I don't care about anyone else or what people might overhear. I need to make sure Wyn is alright. "I need to—"

"Julian," Birdie says, her eyes watering as she covers her mouth, "When you told me he was gone, I had this feeling." She shakes her head. "He made me a promise, and then I didn't hear from him again."

I furrow my brow. "What do you mean? When?"

"I didn't want to think that something had happened to him; it had been so long. And then Wyn came home...." She smiles as she bats another tear away.

My gut sinks at what I think she's telling me, knowing what kind of man my father was, and now just hearing about all of this between them.

"I expected him to show up when I texted this time. And he didn't. The man I loved for most of my life told me he would try to find my granddaughter." Taking a pause, she searches my eyes. "She came home. And then, you showed up in his place."

CHAPTER 27

Wyn

I'M NOT EVEN SURE WHERE I'm going. I just know I need air. *Oxygen. Symbol is 'O' number eight on the periodic table.* I need to breathe.

In through my nose, out through— *Not so fast.* In through my nose— *Oh god, I feel dizzy. Do not pass out.* Sixteen steps down the side of the house. Keep counting.

I recognized that man.

There are seventy-eight steps from here to the front of the bar. Someone's shoulder knocks mine. Oh, fuck.

"Hey!"

Too many people are in line out front of the bar. Thirty-one to the edge of the parking lot.

"Isn't that Professor Crowne? Dr. Crowne!"

Breathe. Someone shouts from behind me, but I tune it out. *I know him. I knew him.* Fifty-six to the other side of the footbridge. *Breathe.* You're almost there.

I shove past Gail and Gina, and one of them calls after me. One foot in front of the other—the sound of water rushing, muffled voices. When I cross the threshold, I expect relief, but when I try sucking in a deeper breath, my chest won't let me.

"Isn't our new friend absolutely the most clever one yet, Professor? Aside from you, of course."

No.

"Wyn," Julian's voice calls from behind me. It sounds different, like *his* voice. *I knew him.* Please don't let all of this have been a dream. My palms scrape along splintered wood.

I know why Julian seemed familiar. I know because he reminded me of his father. I can still hear his voice: *Wyn, run!*

"Look at me," Julian says as he approaches, nearly out of breath from running after me. He doesn't sound angry, if anything, the softness and concern in his tone makes me feel even more horrible.

"Julian," I rush out. *How am I supposed to tell him any of this?*

His hands frame my face, moving me so I'll look at him. "Look at me, baby. Come on, breathe for me." He blows out a breath for me to mimic. I look at him for a second, but I close my eyes. This is too much.

I can't slow it down. I can only take in small puffs. My lungs won't allow it. It's too much. *I knew him.*

"You gotta slow it down for me, c'mon," he coaxes. Leaning into me, up against my ear, he says, "You're going to need to slow down. I'm right here. I'm not going anywhere. If you pass out, I'll be right here. Take your time. Breathe for me." His arms wrap around me, and I let him. "Jesus, you're shaking."

He runs his hands up and down my back. Up and down the tattoos I've gotten, the pretty to offset the ugliness. "I've got you. Just breathe for me," he says softly just as he lifts me in his arms.

Breathe.

"I haven't told you about my favorite piece of jewelry, have

I? Well, maybe my second favorite now," he says, his voice measured and calm as we move.

I suck in another breath and can hear the familiar sound of moving water from the river across from my house. This time, it feels like I can get more in. I blow out, pursing my lips and trying to close them to inhale through my nose. My hair is stuck to my neck from sweat, but my whole body trembles from the inside out. The tighter he holds me, the better it feels.

"It was this pendant necklace I had designed for a client, a dainty gold chain and a pendant that had the most beautiful emerald. It had an eight-prong setting. The piece was very art deco. Think Gatsby, roaring twenties, distinct," he says, out of breath.

My face is wet, my chest hurts, but I know he's carried me across the footbridge and to my house. Without asking for keys or the code to my front door, he brings us around to the side and through the back. "I ended up finding it at an auction almost ten years after I designed and sold it. It was from an art installation I'd done in Los Angeles. Anyway, I knew I'd figure out a way to get my hands on that stone again. Maybe for another piece, or keep it. I don't know. I didn't have a plan for it, just that I wanted it back. I couldn't forget that thing, and for a long time I thought, that's just what art is—a piece of yourself you leave for someone else. I always looked at it that way, but this was different. I'd made so many pieces after that one, and I couldn't tell you a single special thing about them."

I smile, letting out a small cough when I ask, "So did you find it? Keep it?"

"There you are." Smiling, he kisses my forehead and wipes the streaks of tears from beneath my eyes. "Keep what?"

"The emerald. The necklace," I say as I sit on his lap on the stairs of my patio.

He shakes his head. "Auctioned it off. I couldn't keep it. The emerald had been payment for one of our cleaning jobs. I'd probably buy it back if it ever was put up for sale. I didn't have a reason to keep it indefinitely, but I like the idea of being able to see something so beautiful again."

He looks at me with so much emotion that I almost choke out another sob. I don't know if anyone has ever looked at me the way he is right now—softly, reverently. The way he's holding me, not like I'm fragile or broken, but intensely cared for. Like he knows what I'm thinking, he holds me tighter as he tucks a damp piece of hair behind my ear.

I take a deep breath, and on the exhale, my breath stutters, but my chest feels less heavy. I do it over and over. In his arms, I finally breathe. Looking around my face and pushing away the pieces of hair that have fallen, he kisses my forehead like I'm something precious to him, like I'm something more to him than to anyone else. And he is something more to me.

"Tell me," he says, his eyes searching. "Whatever it is, baby, I'm right here." He tucks a piece of my hair behind my ear, and his thumb brushes away the wetness on my cheek.

I take one more deep breath and know that there's no other way, that what happened has happened, and he deserves to hear it.

"I woke up in a train car. At first, I wasn't sure what it was, but the sounds of it moving along the tracks clicked, as did the way it moved." I swallow, my mouth flooding, trying to keep the nauseous feeling down as I play back my living nightmare.

"Professor." He claps his long fingers together, like he's so pleased I'm finally awake. My head feels heavy, and so do my limbs, like I'm moving in slow motion, but hearing everything in real time.

"Professor," he says as I suck in a breath and cough. My heart

thumps so quickly, I know I must have been given something to jolt awake like this.

"I screamed when I realized I couldn't move my hands. I kept screaming when I realized nobody was close enough to hear me. When I begged him to let me go, I watched his pants tent and his head tilt to one side, like he didn't expect it. He wanted me to be impressed by him. He had two other women in that train car, and he would..." My stomach churns at the memory of what he did to them.

"You don't have to," Julian says, holding my hand.

"The person who took me is dead now," I say abruptly. "I wasn't the only person, but the only one who survived it." A shaky breath leaves me. "The only reason it was safe for me to come back to Rumor is because he was gone." More tears track down my cheeks.

You're safe.

"I had a student who started as an undergrad and was a person with selective mutism. I remember seeing her with her parents at graduation, and she was speaking with them. I was aware of her diagnosis, but to witness it..." I shake my head. "She was an entirely different person than I remembered. That's always been something that stuck with me, how the mind works and copes in various ways when we feel varying levels of anxiety or even threatened." I take a grounding breath. "I didn't speak for one hundred and twenty-two days." My nose scrunches, and I shut my eyes, thinking about all the ways he tried to get me to speak after that. An unpleasant shiver ripples through me, remembering what it felt like to watch him slice my side and the willpower it took not to scream when his two fingers moved skin and muscle and dug around. I bat away another tear and sit up in Julian's lap, shifting next to him to sit on the step.

"That was a choice, unlike my student. But it was the only sense of control I had left. It was intentional, and he hated it. The only thing I had in my favor was that I was a professor of organic chemistry—he told me how he had watched me deliver a keynote speech in front of a packed auditorium of brilliant minds. A monster that wanted to impress the smartest person in the room. When he realized that was me, he took what he wanted, thought we'd become colleagues or something."

With his hand open and pressed to my back, it's the only connection I can handle as I try to work through the rest. The piece that I didn't see coming.

"He would take souvenirs of people, ingest parts of others—"

Julian covers his mouth, rubbing his palm across it. "Jesus Christ," he whispers on an exhale. I knew there would be a chance he wouldn't be able to handle this, or the details that I still haven't shared. *Please let him be strong enough to hear this, to survive it with me, to stay.*

"After the train, I had been drugged. I woke up inside of a small room that was soundproofed. I didn't scream or make much noise, but the others he brought inside did. And he was prepared. I expected to die inside that room. It was a storage facility. I didn't know that at first, but eventually, I saw the outside of it." I clear my throat. "It was in a quieter section of Queens. Just off of I-95 in New York."

"There's something so pretty about decolletage, don't you think, Professor?"

I don't answer. I don't look. The last "guest" he brought in here, he had slowly sliced the skin that rested along her collarbone. He said, "It's just like peeling an apple, Professor." When I didn't answer and tried to keep my eyes from watering, he asked, "Did none of your students ever bring you an apple?" As if that was why I struggled to keep tears from falling and not the meticulous violence playing out in front of me.

He tsks, like I've given him a response. "I hadn't planned for it, but when the world decides to deliver," he pauses, "you take."

A grunting sound echoes, deeper in cadence than what I've become accustomed to hearing. It instantly registers that his newest guest is not another woman.

"He wasn't a large man. Tall and thin, strong enough to overpower a woman my size, but a man your size…" I shake my head. "Not unless they wanted him to."

"I've always admired men who grew too quickly. That's all that makes up an Adam's apple—rushing to grow bigger than the body is ready. But it's lovely when it protrudes like this."

"I focused on the sliver of light that came from under the garage-type door. It pulled up to open, and that time, he didn't lock the latch. Like he'd been distracted. He wasn't careless. The same way there was never another man in there. The space was no more than fifty square feet, at most, so when there were grunts and yells, and the sound of two large bodies hitting the cement floor, I stood up. I hadn't been tied up—he had given me leeway with no longer being bound."

"Go!" he yells as he pins the monster.

I stand, my legs barely holding me upright, heart pounding so fast it makes me dizzy.

There's another grunt and the sound of flesh being ripped.

I shuffle forward, bend over, and grip the latch. Pulling up the door, bright white light blinds me. I squeeze my eyes shut just as a deep voice bellows, "Go! Wyn. Runnnnn!"

"He knew my name," I say, thinking back. "Of all the things I've replayed in my mind and all the things that haunt me, running into the woman at the end of the hall screaming, the way the monster chased us both. Pulling the fire alarm, the lights from the trucks when we made it outside." I shake my head, my chest heavy again. "I forgot that the man *knew* my name."

Julian leans his elbows on his knees, looking at his palms and running his fingers along the lines that I once read playfully at a bar. *How could this ever work between us?* I'm the reason his father isn't just dead, but what happened to him was undoubtedly ugly.

"The things you survived," Julian says, sounding in disbelief. "I don't know if I'll ever understand the strength you have."

I look up, feeling his attention on me. His eyes are glassy from all of it until he looks down, his attention on his palm, silence settling heavily around the two of us.

Wiping away the tears that keep falling, I try to tame the way my hands shake.

"I'm so sorry." My stomach is tense and my heart races, knowing that this is so much, too much. I sit up taller, waiting for him to stand and walk away. I'm bracing myself for the things that could be swirling in his mind to come out unfiltered. *I am brave.* If I survived all of that, I can survive this.

He swipes at his cheek, brushing away the tears that managed to escape, and finally looks up at me again. Then he reaches out his hand, palm facing up.

I look down and then up at him, not sure what he's asking me.

"I'm not asking for a palm reading, Crowne," he says with a small, watery laugh. "Hold my hand, baby. If you're okay with me touching you now, I'd like to hold your hand."

I slide my palm against his—large and warm.

"I've been running through every possibility as to why my

father was in a place he wasn't meant to be. The authorities told me he had a heart attack, but with minimal details around when and who had found him. None of it felt right." He clears his throat, brushing his fingers along the top of my hand he's holding.

I move closer, standing up slightly so I can shift and wrap my arms around him. I need to be close to him, even if it's only for a little while longer. I breathe him in as his arms wrap around me, the way his hair feels between my fingers, and the warmth of his skin at the nape of his neck has me feeling like I can breathe.

He pulls back slightly, tipping my chin up, and kisses my forehead. "Thank you for telling me all of this. For trusting me with what happened to you." He pauses, his face squinting as he tries to hold in his emotions. "I'm grateful that my father was smart enough to find you, to get into that storage unit, and help you. He had always been a hero to me; I just didn't know how big until now." His arms wrap tighter, both of us moving as if there's music playing. His heavy breath is laced with the pain of what he lost. I feel helpless, knowing that he's forced to feel it all over again.

When he pulls back, he presses his forehead to mine and whispers, "You are so fucking brave." I want to believe that, but there's a part of me that can't feel it, knowing other people did more, sacrificed more. His hands move up my back and up my neck, into my hair, guiding me to look at him. I close my eyes. That isn't what I was.

"I gave up," I say, hating that it's the truth. "I didn't fight. Other people—other victims, your father, the woman who found me in that storage unit, they did." My chest heaves at the admission as a sob rushes from me. "That doesn't feel brave, Julian." I shake my head and quietly confess, "That's barely surviving."

"Crowne," he whispers, like that's an impossible thought.

But I shake my head again, trying to get this out. "I spent every day experiencing a fucking monster trying new ways to gain my admiration and then trying to break me like it was for sport." I wipe away the steady stream of tears that track down my cheeks and chin. "I didn't break, not for him, not for the others either." I breathe in slowly, out slowly, as his hands slide along my skin, never wavering. "But hearing who it cost *you*." My body trembles all over again, my words stumbling over each other. "I've never felt more broken."

He kisses my head again, holds me, arms wrapped tightly, breathing slowly, and drawing lines and circles around my back.

"At some point, you'll feel and know with certainty how brave you were. That it was a choice. That you didn't need someone to tell you that you could be brave, Wyn. You simply chose it." He drops a kiss on my shoulder. "I always thought there wouldn't be anything I wouldn't do to have him back." His breath stutters, as if he's trying hard to hold himself together. "I miss him every day. I'll keep missing him every day. He would be so happy if he saw the incredible woman I'm with right now," he says, moving his hands from my back up to frame my face. "There are plenty of pieces of this that I would change if I could, but you and I both know that isn't possible. And I wouldn't change this, what this is between us, to feel this, with you," he whispers as his thumbs brush the tears falling down my cheeks. "*That* would be the thing I wouldn't undo." He wraps his arms around me again, and the only thing I'm capable of doing is letting him. My body slumps into his, all of my weight and everything I never wanted to surface. Grief and loss, anger and pain, and through all of it, his arms simply wrap tighter.

It's the last thing I ever would've expected. And maybe that's why I cry so hard that my body feels limp and exhausted.

I wait for him to pull away, for him to stand up and realize all of this is too much. The trauma that exists below my surface that'll never go away. How it's been intertwined with his family and the destruction of it. But he doesn't. He doesn't let go. And he doesn't leave. Not even when we finally move inside. He doesn't leave after he runs a bath for me. And he doesn't leave after he peels off my clothes and helps me into the water. He stays, quietly and purposefully.

"Stop looking at me like you're waiting for me to change my mind and leave," he says, almost as if he can read my thoughts.

The damp air in the bathroom is warm enough that the mirrors and windows are fogged. It smells like the rosemary in a pot perched on the window and him. A warm oak that lingers on his skin and clothes. I feel relaxed, relieved, like layers are slowly being peeled back now that all of me and the ugliness I've endured is out in the open.

He combs his fingers through my hair, lifting the ends that had dipped into the water. I tilt my neck back to look at him when he asks, "Want me to wash it or pull it up?"

"Up, please," I answer. He reaches for a tie on the sink, and because this man has insanely great hair and pulls it up regularly, he does the same with mine. Gathering it into his hands, he twists it up high and into a bun. "I was going to stay there," I say, feeling like he should know he was a part of the reason I came back here. "Being alive was enough," I correct, "is enough." I sit up in the still-hot bathwater and rest my arms against the tub's curved sides to face him fully. "I finally stopped thinking about the days I lost and found enjoyment in the small things again. It should've been enough." I move back and rest my back against the tub.

He watches, listens, keeping his eyes trained on mine.

"And then, I met you." I run my wet fingers along my lip. "I left Hideaway because I knew it would never be enough for me. I missed my family. God, I missed them." I close my eyes and take another grounding breath. But if I had gone back when it was safe, when my captor had been killed, I wouldn't have been okay. I needed time.

"And you feel guilty about that?" he asks, leaning forward, elbows on his knees.

I nod.

"The things you went through, Wyn," he shakes his head. "There isn't a single person who would question the amount of time you needed to start feeling good again."

I swipe a tear away. I knew that, but it feels good to hear it.

"I thought I was going to be asked to leave, after you had left out that back door. I messed up the one rule they had there—make sure Hideaway is kept secret. But they didn't ask me to leave, and I still chose to come back."

"You were ready then," he says, trying to work out what I'm sharing.

"If I stayed, I could never tell someone I cared for the whole truth without putting others in danger. I had never felt what I did with you in those moments, in that bar. I thought if I got even the slightest taste of that again, it would be worth it."

"Come in here with me?" I ask, looking up at him. "I'm not ready to get out, but I want you closer." I smile a little, dazed by the warmth.

His eyes never leave mine as he toes off his boots, then socks. Lifting his shirt at the hem, he pulls it over his head. He takes out the elastic that held back his hair, and his dark-brown hair falls to his shoulders.

He shoves his pants to the floor. Stepping out of his boxer briefs next, I get a full glimpse at his broad back and the way his sculpted ass flexes with every move. Even now, I can't help but smirk at how much I like looking at his body.

He's beautiful, more so than any other man I've ever seen, but the parts of him that are the most breathtaking come with the things he says and the actions he takes. It doesn't feel like taking or settling with him. It's uncontrollable, as if I'm falling for this man in a way that'll alter everything all over again. Or maybe I already have. Maybe this is just the proof.

Pulling another towel from the rack, he smiles at me when he notices my attention on his cock.

"I have minimal control over how my body reacts when I'm close to you, Crowne," he says as he lowers himself into the warm water.

I shift around, moving my legs so that there's space for him to fit. "Believe me, I understand," I say on a breathy exhale. The water rises and splashes over the edge as every inch of him lowers into the bath.

"Then add in the fact that you're naked in a tub," he says with the slightest smile on his lips. "My dick didn't get the memo that I'm only here to be close to you, take care of you, and make sure you're okay."

Leaning forward, he smooths his hands down my legs and lifts my feet so they rest on top of his thighs. He runs his fingers over my skin soothingly, and it feels so damn good, my body relaxes muscle by muscle. This is what safe feels like—a warm bath, understanding that doesn't feel earned, but given freely, soothing touches. The details that were just shared, what he's just learned about his father, none of it can be easy to hear and accept, and yet he's letting himself relax the same way I am. The back of his neck rests on the tub's edge, and his eyes drift closed.

"Come here. You're too far away," he says without opening his eyes.

I sit up and shift closer to him. Julian lifts his head to watch me as I lean forward and kiss the center of his chest. Turning around, I settle myself against his body. I glide my fingers up and down his forearm, draped along the edge. Lost in this moment—the quiet and warmth—my entire body relaxes.

"Tell me you're okay," I whisper. "Or tell me you're not." I tilt my head slightly against his chest so I can see his face. "You're taking care of me, but this isn't just about me, Julian."

He moves his hand into the water, and his fingers brush along my scar. He runs his touch up and then down before he holds his palm tightly against my side. My face squints up, but I shove away the anger and embarrassment. Instead, I take a deep breath and exhale through it. Even when he should be thinking of himself, what all of this took from him, he's still holding me in the most tender place. *I've never felt braver.*

"I'm okay, baby," he says as he kisses my head. "We're going to be more than okay."

And for the first time in a long time, I believe it.

CHAPTER 28

Julian

SHE FELL ASLEEP SOMETIME AFTER midnight, wrapped up in my arms, right where she belongs. I held on to her long after she drifted off, and long after I finally had as well. I wanted to tell her I'll never leave her side, that she's the easiest choice I've ever made, but that will have its time. There's a part of me that knew as soon as I saw her here in Rumor. As I was strapped to a fucking chair, I knew that even if I wasn't bound to it, I wasn't going anywhere.

If anything had gone differently, if a single one of the tragic things that crossed our paths had been different, I wouldn't be here.

Staring out the side windows, I catch movement in the river across the way. I woke up this morning and watched the room turn from gray to gold, and it felt like I was exactly where I'm meant to be. The sun still has some time to rise fully, but it's light enough, and the river is low enough that I can see more slow movement along the banks. Two, maybe three, alligators, like the ones Birdie was talking about, are right there, minding their own business and enjoying the same morning I am.

Rumor is a long way from the Pacific Northwest, but this view feels right and more like home than the beach views from my place in Oregon. A home, not just a home base.

My phone buzzes on the counter as Wyn stirs in her bed.

I fire off a text message, confirming the plans I started to put into motion. I meant every word I said to her last night, and while I know that I'll never stop missing my father, I woke up today feeling content about knowing what happened. I feel proud that he was exactly who I thought. That it wasn't about the pieces of him I didn't know, but that when it mattered, he was exactly the man who raised me.

"You're going to file that thing down too thin. It'll snap, I'm telling you," he says, laughing.

"This entire series is supposed to show off the stones, not the metals," I tell him as I turn on the polishing burr.

"Agree to disagree." He studies the sapphire that he got from his collector. "Donovan might be a son of a bitch, but this is a beaut. Come take a look."

I walk to his bench as he holds it up with tweezers, the magnifier and light showing off insanely intricate cuts that pick up the light in such a way that it looks more vibrantly green.

"I met a woman, a long time ago, with the prettiest green eyes… Reminds me of her," he says, longing in his tone I'm not used to hearing.

"Does this woman have a name?" I ask curiously.

He doesn't answer, just starts whistling and gets lost back in his work.

"Are you making me coffee?" Wyn mumbles from across the wide space.

I smile, looking down at both the mug I've already drained and since refilled, and the ice-filled glass next to it. "I am." I pour the cooled coffee over it and add a splash of milk. Her sister said she liked it sweet and with a crunch, so I give it three heaping spoonfuls of sugar. "Breakfast?" I ask, holding up a slice of the cake.

She sits up fast, the sheets moving to her waist, giving me a helluva view of her full and pretty tits. Her mouth opens, but nothing comes out right away as she looks at the cup and then back up to me. "You, and this moment, feels like perfection," she says, her voice raspy and groggy from sleep. I had no idea coffee would get this kind of reaction. I smile, draining what's left of my second cup.

"Perfection is a better word for you in that bed right now, Crowne," I say, looking at her beautiful tits again. Her eyes are still puffy from crying, but her hair is a wild mess of waves, and her lips look like I need to take my time and kiss the fuck out of them.

"Birdie texted me asking if you were alright and that your mother dropped off this blueberry butter cake." I turn and hold up a plate with a slice on it. "How do you feel about eating this?" I nod to the plate I hand her. "Drinking that," I say, putting her iced coffee down on her side table, before I sit and lie across the center of her bed. "And then coming with me so I can show you something?"

She smiles wide after taking a bite, humming lightly at the taste.

"I feel great about that." She looks at my chest and down at my jeans. With a smile, she uses the fork and cuts another piece, holding it out for me. I sit up and eat it as she takes a sip of her coffee and crunches the sugar that made it up through the straw. "It was nice waking up with you this morning," she says.

Last night was *a lot*. But right now, in the morning light, it feels less like a weight and more like just another part of our story. I take in this exact moment with her. It isn't that she's beautiful and half naked in bed—though that doesn't hurt—or the fact that she leans forward and kisses me before sharing her bite of cake again. It's having someone to ask the question. Someone who's been through more than I have any desire to imagine.

Reaching up, I brush a piece of her hair out of her face. My fingers graze down her cheek and to her jaw. I lean forward and kiss her lips lightly, deciding this is how I'll wake up for the rest of my days, if she'll let me.

"It was more than nice, baby." I kiss her, this time taking the plate out of her hands while I do. She reaches up and drapes her arms around my shoulders as she kisses me back, her lips parting for my tongue to glide against hers. I pull her onto my lap as her fingers run up and into my hair. It feels so fucking good every time. "Before I end up not wanting to leave this bed, there's something I want to show you."

She smiles against my lips and moves back in for more. "Do I need to put pants on?" she asks playfully, moving her lips along my jaw.

I smile, looking up at the high ceiling as I glide my fingers up and down her back. "This might be the last time you hear this from me, but yes, Crowne. You need to put pants on, or shorts, or a skirt, whatever won't get you arrested in public."

I feel it in the center of my chest as she laughs right now. Last night, I wanted to erase every awful thing that happened to her. And she still asked me if I was okay. I breathe her in, coffee and the cake we've just shared. Hearing her happy right now feels fucking good. The things Wyn told me about my father, hearing what he did for her—there must have been plenty of favors he cashed in to locate a person who everyone else couldn't find. But for someone he loved, which is how I'm guessing he felt about Birdie, he wouldn't have stopped looking until he found her. The only reason the cleaning business stayed intact the way that it had wasn't because of my grandfather. It was my dad—the details and focus it took to make people and messes disappear is equal parts strategy and tenacity. Thinking on our feet when cleaning agents weren't cutting it and there needed to be a complete reconstruction of an area, he never flinched. It doesn't surprise me that he could have found her, that he was brave enough to help her. The part that I don't know if I'll ever fully comprehend is how she ended up in my arms after all of it. Loving my father was never the issue, it was finding out why he never came back… and now I have—and I have her.

There are plenty of vacant spaces along Rumor's downtown. Maybe it was once a bustling spot, but with the exception of Moonie's train car at the end of the street, there aren't too many places worth seeing. The brick building has plenty of boarded-up windows and runs the expanse of this side of the street, but it's an open floor plan loft with the potential to be a helluva gallery and workspace that called to me.

"This is Jo's new studio," Wyn says, hopping out of the Bronco.

I smile, knowing that while she's right, it's also mine.

"I thought before I signed any papers, I should get your approval on it," I tell her as I walk past Jo's entrance and toward the one next store. When I key in the code from the realtor and open it, Wyn blinks, wide-eyed. With a smile tugging at her lips, she asks, "This is what you wanted to show me?"

"It's the legacy I'm most proud of, the one that I can show off to the world," I say, walking through. At the center of the dusty space is an old desk and chair that look like they've been long since forgotten. Along the room's edges are exposed brick and a spiral metal staircase that leads to a second level overlooking where we stand. "I helped your sisters the other day and ended up coming back to take a look." Holding her hand, I move toward the desk I had dragged to the center of the space. "Jo mentioned the building was vacant, and I thought this could be a studio and a gallery. And it could be *my* new beginning."

I watch to wait for her reaction, but she simply says, "I always thought these buildings were so pretty—the brick and big windows. I kind of love that there would be art and jewelry and all the things you creative people are capable of doing in here."

I smile to myself as I brush off the thick dust and remove the drop cloth, pulling out a few tools that I've been using to work on the leather cuff she had been wearing. Sitting down in the chair, I take in the view from here—a view of a quiet street in a small town, but it has potential. She circles the desk and sits on top of it, turning over the metal file in her hand first and then feeling the smooth strips of leather. Opening the black pouch, she empties the small chips of gemstones that have been left over, likely from larger pieces. An orange and brown rock comes out too.

She smiles, holding it up. "This one is from Nash."

I hold it between my fingers. "It is. Started working on it when you gave it to me. I drilled a small hole here." I point to the 3mm-size hole at its center. "I just need to find a chain or maybe a piece of leather rope for it."

When I look up, she's staring at the stone, then shakes her head before looking back at me. "He's going to freak out about this. You're going to end up with a bestie for life."

I turn the rock in my hand, liking how that sounds and feels much more than I ever thought I would. Staying here with her also meant I'd have her family in my life too. Nash and her sisters, Theo and Tommy, even Lu and Birdie. The Crowne family is as intimidating as families come, but I like being around them. I've gone so long without having any family, and then even when my dad was alive, it was only the two of us.

I push a long, rectangular bracelet box from the top drawer, across the top of the desk toward her. A sense of pride rushes through me as she lifts the top and takes a moment to look at the newly shaped leather. I reach forward and take it out. "This will fit your wrist better now."

"I wasn't sure you were actually going to give it back to me," she says as she holds out her hand. The fingers on her other hand brush along its edge, the same way I had noticed her doing before, as I fit it around her wrist.

I made the leather thinner and sized it so it would fit tighter. The piece still takes up space along her wrist, a reminder that it was once mine, but small changes make it more like hers now.

Smiling, she watches as I fasten it.

I run my fingers along the textured leather edges, the place I noticed she touches often, and I kiss her palm.

"I don't think you realize what it did to me to see you still wearing it," I tell her as she runs a finger over the gold stitching details.

Her eyes flit to mine as she smirks at my words.

"What do you think? This space and me here permanently?"

I look around and can picture it. The windows cleared, and a rotation of artists' pieces on display in addition to my own. The upstairs loft would be ideal to work in, and if I need more space, the building is big. I'm ready to purchase the entire thing.

"I want to see you make all sorts of beautiful things here"—she looks around at the open and empty space—"in this space." With an exhale, she runs her fingers along the bracelet's edge, admiring it like she's missed the feeling. "I think a new beginning sounds scary," she says, looking up and around. "I've done it a few times." She leans forward, tucking her hands beneath her thighs.

I pull my chair closer, wrapping my arms around her ass and resting my head on her legs.

Her fingers glide into my hair and it forces my eyes closed. Every time she does it, I stop holding my breath without realizing I had.

"So, considering I'm what you would call a professional at it, my advice?" she asks playfully. "Find someone, preferably a badass scientist who has a penchant for cake and your cock," she laughs out. "Fuck around, maybe even fall in love—" Her fingers pause along my hairline, as if she wasn't prepared to say that. But *fuck* am I ready to hear it.

"Personal recommendation? From experience, is to fuck around and fall in love?" I ask, lifting my head and sitting up so that we're eye level.

"In my experience," she says softly and with a nod, "it makes starting over so much more fun." Her eyes stay locked with mine when she whispers, "I like this bubble we're in right now."

"So do I, baby," I say, standing. I tilt her chin up so I can bring my lips to hers and kiss her. Her hands cup my face as my arms wrap around her, pulling her closer. When her phone chimes, she pulls her lips back, resting her forehead against mine.

"Reality reminders," she exhales. "I have so many papers that I need to review before my end-of-the-week classes. I never loved this part of teaching, but the idea of getting back into my lab and standing up in front of students used to be such a high for me. And I've been waiting to get that feeling again—to want to do this job I worked so hard for…" she says as the rest of her words drift off.

I don't want to read between the lines. She's a smart woman, probably the smartest person I've ever met, but I'm starting to learn what she looks like when she's happy. Returning to the university doesn't seem to make her all that happy.

I look across the table at the solder and buffering tools. It's nowhere near all of the equipment I use, but it's some of the basics, and as much as I haven't felt inspired, I still love doing it.

"Want to ditch responsibilities for a little while? Go somewhere with me for a night or two?"

There's somewhere I know she might feel inspired. And I have a friend who I plan to collect a favor from.

She takes a moment to think. Maybe she won't want to, maybe she'd rather stay close to home and gain her footing after the last day. But when she looks up at me again, her green eyes crinkle at the sides as she smiles wide.

"When do we leave?"

The beauty of having friends in plenty of places with endless means is that getting what you need when you need it is as simple as asking. Atticus Foxx is the head of Foxx Bourbon in Fiasco, Kentucky. Anyone who knows anything about the bourbon business knows Ace, if not personally, then from his reputation for impeccable taste and the ability to build a brand and somewhat of an empire.

JULIAN:

I'm heading up your way tonight. Any chance you're free to show someone around the distillery and have a drink?

ACE:

I stopped giving tours decades ago.

JULIAN:

You're really aging yourself with that comment.

ACE:

My wife likes to remind me daily.

JULIAN:

Is Lincoln free? She might want to talk shop.

ACE:

She?

JULIAN:

Long story. I'll tell you over some whiskey.

ACE:

You mean bourbon.

JULIAN:

I prefer whiskey now.

ACE:

Not everyone has good taste.

ACE:

If you need a place to stay, the Midnight Proof apartment is yours. Rhodes is in town. I'll see if he wants to join us.

I knew Rhodes would be there. He makes frequent trips between Nashville and Louisville, stopping in Fiasco when he can to purchase whatever rare cases Ace is willing to part with. I've been friends with Rhodes Donovan for decades. He's an asshole who likes to throw his money around and has a helluva time at auction houses, bidding on things other people want just to be a dick. He also happens to have something I want.

Wyn decided to take a few days away. She meant what she said about wanting to be in our bubble for a little longer, so she went into her office and spent a few hours wrapping up whatever it is that she needed to do to make sure her teaching assistant was prepped for end-of-week classes.

"There wasn't anything specific, she said, but when I told Andi I was heading out of town, she looked anxious, like she wanted to tell me something." Wyn shakes her head.

"Andi is the woman who came to Birdie's house during dinner?" I ask.

She nods, "And one of the teaching assistants in the chemistry department."

I pull into the private road and down toward the parking lot for the airfield.

When she hops out of the Bronco and stares toward the

east side of the private airfield, I can't help but think, *This feels like our airfield now.*

"You sat up there with me," she says, pointing to the hill, "and you didn't mention that you actually know how to fly a plane? I feel like that would have been information worth sharing."

I smile as I check in with air traffic control. When I've gotten the approval to take off, I tell her, "You already know about my paper airplane attachment, so I grew up a bit, had some money to spend, and I learned to fly the real ones."

She nods and sarcastically adds, "Yup, totally. People just do that—learn to fly planes and make gorgeous things."

Laughing, I load our things into the small plane and then open her door. "Crowne, you can do whatever the hell you want, you know that, right? Just make up your mind and do it."

CHAPTER 29

Wyn

THE IN-FLIGHT TIME WAS QUICK, and the minute we step foot outside, my mouth tics up at the side as I close my eyes and inhale.

"Where did you say we are again?" I ask, looking around at the flat landscape.

"I didn't," he says, grabbing my hand and kissing the back of it. "I wanted to surprise you. Friends of mine and of my family's for generations."

"You brought me to a distillery." I smile as I look out the window toward the Foxx Bourbon Distillery.

"I brought you to a distillery," he echoes back, watching me as I take it all in.

I've never been, but I've read plenty of articles that spoke of Fiasco always smelling sweet—the sugars that are cooked and settle into the air when the corn, rye, and barley mix together for their bourbon's mash. Today, it smells a little too sweet. I prefer the savory twinge that lingers in the air around Rumor.

The property is expansive, with the main distillery at the center and multiple rickhouses peppered throughout the property in the distance. The very recognizable brand logo sits prominently above the door to the distillery—a black, wrought-iron letter *F* with a fox head wrapped around it.

"This is what you wanted to show me?" I ask as we walk inside. "I thought you were going to romance me or something, but this?" My eyes water slightly; this was more than just impressing a girl or a weekend to meet friends.

"Just trying to get you to fall in love with me," he says, pulling my hand to his mouth, turning it over, and kissing my palm.

"It's working," I say quietly, as I look at him. He keeps surprising me in ways I don't anticipate.

He smiles at me as he looks up and towards the crowd gathered around a tour guide.

"Thought you might want a tour." He waves at a tall, broad man wearing glasses, who's already walking toward us. "And to talk a little bit about distilling with their master distiller, trade some secrets or equations, whatever it is you do."

He squeezes my hand as the man stops in front of us in his Foxx Bourbon polo and a pair of dark slacks. With his hand out for Julian to shake, he says, "Julian, my brother said I should make myself available to show you and your friend around." He gives me a warm smile.

"Lincoln Foxx, I'd like you to meet Dr. Wynona Crowne," Julian says. "Her family has a small whiskey distillery down in Rumor, Tennessee. She talks about making whiskey the same way you do about bourbon. Thought it would be convenient to put you two in the same room for a little while to talk shop while I tie some things up with Ace."

"I looked you up, Dr. Crowne," he says to me. Most of the articles that come up with my name are around my work, but a few are peppered in about when I was missing. "Organic chemistry and a pretty damn impressive resume," he says, relieving my worry instantly. "Please tell me you have something wickedly brilliant to tell me that you've discovered about a new distilling process."

I shift my hands into the pockets of my long skirt. The cropped T-shirt I'm wearing hits just at the waist, only showing a slip of skin when I move to shake his hand. It's an almost perfect blend of what feels comfortable and makes me feel confident. My shirt reads *The Whispering Fool* across the front, and my chartreuse Louboutin pumps are the perfect pop of color to offset the basic black skirt and white shirt. I had no idea where we were going, so I curled my hair at the ends, twisted and pinned it in the front to keep it out of my face. Standing in this place, dressed like this, with Julian at my side, I feel damn good.

"I'm not operating at any real scale compared to here. It's mostly been a hobby for me. I'm in Tennessee, which means to make true Tennessee whiskey, my waiting time is just as strict as yours. I've been having fun merging different types of finishing barrels for the whiskey I'm too impatient to wait for."

"I can understand that," he says, slinging his hands in his pockets. "Anything worth sharing notes about?"

I nod. "There's a small spot in town that brings in classic cola for a lot of our particular old-timers," I say, smiling, thinking about the way people love the cola at Moonie's. "Anyway, not important, but the cola syrup arrives in small barrels before it's cut with soda water."

"My mouth is watering thinking about it. How'd it come out?" Lincoln asks, looking like he's about to box Julian out and steal me away.

"It just went in a few weeks ago, so I haven't tried it yet," I say, glancing at Julian.

Lincoln nods toward the way he originally came. "You're going to need to send me a bottle. I feel like it'll be a great sipper," he adds as I follow him.

"I've started infusing dried herbs into one of our oldest aged barrels. It's got great color, but I've had it in my mind that something a little more savory might be enjoyable."

"Like a gin," Lincoln adds.

"Exactly. Like a gin," I say, pointing at him. "Flavor profiles hold better when they're dried or cooked down into a syrup, I've found." I laugh nervously, shaking my head. "Sorry, all I wanted to say was that, it's just a hobby, barely a side hustle, at that, so—"

"Do you want it to be more?" Lincoln asks point-blank as he fixes his glasses.

I look around, taking in the small groups mingling near the tasting bar, and the larger crowd that's starting off the formal tour. "I have no idea what that could look like," I say. But I'm starting to really imagine the possibilities. "I want it to be more."

Lincoln claps his hands in front of him. "I'll happily talk about our processes and the mashbill combination we've been using lately. My oldest brother, Ace, who I'm sure Julian has mentioned, can discuss most of the business elements, and if you wanted to talk about cooperage and barrels, my younger brother Grant is somewhere around here," he says, looking around.

We shift toward the tasting bar and dive into talking. Julian leans up against the bar and pays attention to something on his phone as we start talking. The oak finishes and masculine metals that accent the distillery are so ornately designed that I know I won't forget the vibes that it puts off. I like it, and it has my mind swirling, thinking about how Jo would be able to put her own spin on a place that felt like a merging of masculine and feminine.

Lincoln discusses all of the details that have made his recent releases exceptional blends. I share some of my thoughts regarding finishing barrels and the endless possibilities for infusing flavors. Every so often, I check in on Julian, who hasn't left my side. He enjoys a few drinks from the tasting bar and listens to Lincoln, and I shift from one conversation to the next.

"Julian," a man with salt-and-pepper hair says in a deep voice as he walks up. I know who he is right away.

"Atticus Foxx," he says, holding out his hand for me to shake.

"Wyn Crowne," I say, meeting his extended hand.

He glances at Julian and asks, "So this is her?"

"Yeah. This is her." He stands a bit closer to the stool I've been perched on for going on two hours now.

I don't know how to label what we are together. Girlfriend feels too young, partner seems too soon.

"She and Lincoln have been talking about things way above my head, while I waited for you to take your sweet-ass time."

"Ah, yes, my younger brother. Here he comes now," Lincoln says. "I'll introduce you to Grant, too." But as I look to where he's gesturing, a woman laughs next to him, loud enough that it has me trying to figure out why it has my eyes filling with tears.

I recognize it. There isn't an accent to it, and I couldn't describe it if someone asked me, but I know it. *I know her.*

My stomach lurches.

"Wyn? Everything okay?" Julian asks, his hand coming to my back.

But I ignore his question and instead ask Lincoln, "Who is that? The woman with the red hair, talking to your brother."

"That's my sister-in-law, Laney," he says. "She runs most of the organized events around here, tackles anything around public relations, really."

"Wyn?" Julian asks again as I take another step away and in the direction of her.

"How?" I whisper to myself as I think about the last time I saw her.

I run. He told me to run. I don't know where I'm going, but I need to get away. It's the only chance I'll have. I know at least that much. I haven't spoken, I haven't had any liquids in nearly three days, my throat is so dry that the first time I open it to scream, nothing comes out. I trip over my feet, not having moved them much in so long, but I keep going. I turn down the brightly lit hall—it's a storage facility. This time, I scream. I scream as I run down the hallway, barefoot. I can feel the latest stitches along my side tear. Fuck, that stings.

"Help me!" I scream. And that's when I see her, a blond woman around my size pulling down the door of her unit and rushing toward me.

"You're okay," she says, trying to hold me up as I finally reach her. "What happened?"

But that's when I hear him. "We need to run, please. We need to run!"

Her hair is different—red now as opposed to the blond that I remembered. When she turns to the side, her belly is swollen and pregnant, and she looks happy. That makes my chest feel tight. She didn't get hurt. She didn't stop living. I knew that; the U.S. Marshal who worked my case told me as much, but she's right there now. The person who got me out of that storage unit, killed the monster months later, and now she's right there.

"Wyn," Julian calls out behind me. Loud enough this time that a few people turn to look, including her. I stop and cover my mouth with my hand. If she doesn't recognize me, then I can pull myself together, and at the very least, go talk to her afterward, but I don't think I'll have time for that. She smiles, finishing a laugh that she was sharing with the man to her left. He stands close to her as I stop and stare.

Her brow furrows, and a nervous smile pulls at her lips before she says, "Oh my go—" Breath catching, she takes a step toward me. I take two more toward her and nod, wordlessly answering what I'm sure she's trying to work out. Tears fall as she takes me in, finally putting the pieces together of who I am and why I might be familiar. "You're here."

"Laney, what's going on?" the man behind her asks as he stands protectively next to her.

"It's her...the woman from the storage facility in New York. The survivor," she tells him, wiping her tears. "I didn't know what had happened to you afterwards, only that you were safe—" She braces her hand over her chest. "Can I hug you?"

I swat away the tears, nodding. "I'd really like that," I say, wrapping my arms around her.

"I can't believe you're here," I say again.

"Same," she says quietly as both of us cry. She pulls back to look at me again. I look very different from the last time she saw me. I was half-naked, covered in filth and blood, screaming as I ran toward her. She holds tightly, and I do the same right back, as if we're old friends who haven't seen each other in a long time and not strangers who met in the most terrible of situations.

Quietly, she says just for me, "He's gone, you know." She pulls back, her eyes meeting mine, and in a reassuring tone says,

"I watched a rickhouse on the back property here burn so hot that they couldn't put the fire out for days."

I nod. "I hope it hurt." I blink away another tear.

"I can almost guarantee it did," she says with a firm squeeze of my hand.

"Wyn?" Julian says, breaking into the moment.

Stepping back, she holds on to my hand. I sniff and wipe away what's left of the tears before I say, "Julian, this is—"

"Laney. I know. We've met before. But how do you know her?" He glances at the man with the mustache behind her—Grant Foxx, according to his brother.

"Grant?" Julian asks him like he's the last to know what's going on here.

Grant looks between Laney and me before he says, "I think my wife is talking to the reason why she ended up in Fiasco." His lip twitches in something that looks like a smile.

"Laney," I say on a sigh. I close my eyes for a moment, not caring about coincidences or fateful meetings, and simply say, "Thank you for saving my life."

Before Grant and Laney left, having promised their nieces a sleepover, we spent another hour together talking about what her life was like right after the night she pulled the fire alarm inside that storage facility. How she ended up in Fiasco and why she wouldn't have wanted it any other way. I shared with her what I did for a living, and we didn't talk about the darkness or the details of what I survived, but she held my hand the entire time.

"Are you okay?" Julian finally asks, dragging his hands through his hair and resting his palms along the back of his neck. "That was not a part of my plan."

Julian held my hand tightly as we walked quietly from the distillery to Fiasco's downtown. He would kiss the back of it every so often, but he didn't push any more than that, giving me a chance to digest everything that had just unfolded. I worked through the details she shared, how she's built a life here, and how she wouldn't have changed any of it. Fresh air and time to reflect on what just happened felt necessary. When we stop at the Crescent de Lune, the French bakery building, I lean against the brick and take a deep breath—that sweet smell in the air is something special. It followed us all the way from the distillery to here, permeating the gentle breeze through this small town. Closing my eyes, I take a grounding breath and tell him the simplest truth. "There couldn't be a more complete feeling than the one I've just experienced."

He pushes a piece of my hair that's fallen behind my ear. He keeps his eyes on mine as his thumb brushes against my cheek.

"That woman saved me. She didn't try, she didn't know who I was or what was happening, but she stepped in, and because of that, I didn't die in that room like I thought I was going to. Your father's selflessness in finding me and helping get me out of that space wasn't all for nothing. And that's because of her." I laugh lightly, eyes burning with more emotion. "I'm grateful." I look at him when I open my eyes and whisper, "I'm so grateful."

"We don't have to go out. I can tell my friends that I'll take a rain check and—"

I shake my head, cutting off that idea. "You don't need to do that. I don't want you to. I feel good, just maybe need a little bit of time to shower and pull myself together."

He leans in and kisses my forehead as he pulls me into a hug.

My arms wrap around him, and I say, "I want to have a good time tonight and get to know these Foxx brothers a bit, drink some good bourbon." I lean back to look at him and smile, thankful for the way our lives keep weaving together in ways I don't know if I'll ever understand. "And I want to enjoy every moment of being here with you."

I think about what this could be like in Rumor—a distillery that produces Tennessee whiskey in a way that hasn't been done yet. Experimenting with flavors and finishing barrels, a whiskey brand that would be women-owned and run. It isn't a novelty, but an asset, one that my family had been working in our favor for a long time.

Taking a sip of Foxx Bourbon, I sway to the low music filtering around the studio apartment that's ours for the night. It's modern luxury with hints of opulence and old money, from the brass and gold fixtures to the crystal chandeliers that seem like the preferred lighting here. I love it. The building is beautiful, with a speakeasy called Midnight Proof hidden below the ground floor beneath a bakery and the apartment nestled in the well-hidden top floor.

The convenience of it allowed me to shower, freshen up, and take some time alone to reflect on the emotional swan dive of seeing Laney. I turn and look at the door, and from where I stand, in front of the long windows overlooking Main Street, I don't know how many steps are from here to there, but I realize I haven't paid all that much attention to escaping anything lately. I'm not sure if that's a good thing or careless of me, but right now, I feel...content.

Fiasco, even outside of the beauty and bourbon, is already nothing short of spectacular.

I run my hands along the tight black material—thick leather straps and a balconette-style top that once it hits my ribs, turns to a smoother, softer black fabric, cinching in at my waist and hugging my hips and down just past my knees. The shoes I picked are vintage Christian Louboutin platform peep-toe booties. I bought this pair when I got my first decent paycheck from the university and never let my sisters borrow them. My bank account never really recovered after that, but then it didn't matter. Now, I turn my ankle in the mirror and marvel at how they look. Perfect.

I don't count the steps down from the apartment on the top floor to the bakery. I only thought about seeing Julian. The corridor that hugs the side of the bakery is beautifully decorated as if I'm walking through a small Parisian pâtisserie. Julian said that while the bakery is quite popular and fully functional, it serves as the "front" for the well-known speakeasy, Midnight Proof. The secret bar is more than what I expect, but that's apparently par for today's course. Chandeliers that hang throughout the space put off just enough light and shadow that they make every person in here seem more sultry and mysterious than I'm sure they would be in the light of day. The music is moody and slow, despite the way the bartenders move behind the bar as I approach. I know Ace Foxx's wife runs this spot, along with another club that's on the distillery's property, but invite-only.

"What can I get you, doll?" a beautiful brunette asks as she slides the check to a few people next to me.

"What's your favorite right now?" I say with a smile.

"Oh, I like you. Alright, what do you usually like?" Plunging the shaker into the cleaner, she leans forward on the bar as she puts the seasonal drinks in front of me.

"I'm usually whiskey forward, but tonight, I can be talked into something else if it's delicious." For some reason, it feels like flirtation. She's incredibly good at leaning into the vibes of this place.

"You're speaking my language, gorgeous. I got you." She moves around the bar with ease and pulls out a few familiar bottles: a Foxx bourbon—the words The Sugared Daddy drawn in cursive letters across the label, a bottle of Chartreuse, amaro, and then a squeeze of a half lemon. She shakes it up and asks, "Are you here with someone, or just enjoying a solo night out?"

Smiling, I tell her, "My person is somewhere around here. I just need to find him. But a drink sounded like a good idea. This place is beautiful."

"Thank you," she says, cracking the two frosted shakers apart. "This is my place."

"You're Hadley Foxx then? Ace's other half?" I ask as she pours the drink into a beautiful crystal coupe glass, topping it with a curled orange peel.

She chuckles. "I am very much more than half, but yes, that is my husband," she says, a little sparkle in her eyes as she looks up behind me.

"Holy shit, you're Julian's?" she says in a surprised whisper.

I turn to see where she looked and find both Ace and Julian lounging in chairs lofted on the second level. I love how that sounds—*Julian's.* It's almost like he heard it and glances down from where he's sitting. His hair pulled tightly back and wearing all black, he watches me with a smirk playing across his lips as he sips something from a glass. I don't need to hear what he's thinking right now, not with the way he's watching me. And I feel it buzzing across my skin and rolling through my body. He looks downright dangerous.

I smile at her and hold up the drink. "Here's hoping." When I take a sip, so many different notes dance across my tongue, from the sweetness from the blend of bourbon, to the bitterness of the herbs from the amaro, and the tang from the Chartreuse that I watched her pour. It feels a little like kismet, considering the liquor in my drink and the color of my heels are the same. "This is—Wow."

"I know. It's a little adjustment to the classic Final Word cocktail. I like to call this one the Next Chapter," she says with a wink. "I think we can all use more of things that are next versus final, don't you think?"

I smile widely at the way she just summed up every thought that's been swirling since we arrived here. "I like that, a lot."

"Me too," she says as she taps the bar in front of me. "You can head up there any time you'd like. I'm sure they're waiting for you." She shifts down the bar to help the people at the other end.

I call out, "Thanks, Hadley. It was nice meeting you."

"Pleasure was all mine, Dr. Wynona Crowne," she says with a smirk.

With a returned smile, my brow furrows, wondering how she knows my full name.

"Oh yeah, if anyone is going to annoy details out of him, it's going to be me." She mouths, *He's obsessed.*

I bite my lip, trying to hide my pleased smile, and turn in my chair, sipping on my drink.

Making my way up the spiral stairs to the second floor, Julian and the three other men he's been with stand as I approach.

"Gentleman." I nod with a smile.

Julian wraps his arm around my waist and leans into me, kissing close to my ear and whispering, "You look so fucking good, Crowne."

My cheeks heat at the compliment and the way he holds me close. He offers me his seat, a low leather club chair that I take. Crossing my legs and focusing on the person who I haven't met yet, he tips his head and says, "We haven't had the pleasure."

Julian snickers beside me, perched on the arm of the chair, and mumbling, “Fucking typical.”

The man, who’s meticulously dressed, the only one here in a white dress shirt—the rest wearing black or blue, introduces himself. “Rhodes Donovan.”

Smiling, I say, “Dr. Wyn Crowne.”

Julian pipes in, “Rhodes and I have known one another for a long time.”

“You’re the collector, then?” I ask, sipping on my drink.

He tuts. “Of many things, yes. But regarding Julian, I can usually acquire the types of gemstones he wants when he can’t acquire them on his own.”

“Or steal them from me,” Julian mumbles.

“Gems and diamonds are two things I don’t steal,” he bites back with a sly smile. When he glances at Julian and then back to me, he adds, “All of the stones he’s whining about, he lost during an auction. Couldn’t ante up.”

“Oh, I’ve heard,” I say, smiling as I glance at Julian.

“I’m flattered that I’ve made it to your pillow talk time, Julian,” Rhodes says with raised eyebrows.

Julian runs his middle finger across his lips, trying to mask his smirk.

“Rhodes has an impressive art collection. Something I bet Jo would be interested in seeing, come to think of it. Owns galleries all over the world. Quite a few other businesses as well,” Julian says as I lean closer to him, my shoulder grazing the side of his leg as he sits along the arm of my chair.

“See now? Flattery will get you everywhere, my friend. You should have started with that,” Rhodes says. I don’t doubt for one minute that Rhodes might be the most dangerous at this table. And in this company, that was saying something.

"Wyn," Ace Foxx cuts in. "Lincoln was telling me about the blends you've been working on in your spare time." He glances up at Julian first, and then his brother, and back to me before he adds, "Might be an opportunity for us to collaborate. Even make a little noise about it. It'll help get your name out there a bit when you're ready for it."

We talk about what that might look like as I watch the bar below as two women pour flights along the bar—a far more tame sight than the ones people witness at the Whispering Fool, but it also makes me think of podcast nights in Montana, and of my sisters. I know they have their own lives, career paths, and even hobbies, but I wonder if they'd consider opening the whiskey distillery with me.

This lifestyle and the way the Foxx family has made it work for each of them in unique ways is impressive, but even more so, it's inspiring.

Lincoln speaks with me about the business side of bourbon, how events have brought on an entirely new revenue stream, and, not to mention, the way they're experimenting with new blends. The more I spend time thinking about it, the more it seems like I always should've come to this conclusion. I want this—my version of it, at least. Making whiskey, folding it into my family's bar business, all of us included in different ways, that we're passionate about.

A business instead of academics. A career that's an entirely different approach to the life I thought I was coming back to. Maybe he's right, I've just made up my mind. *I'm doing this.*

CHAPTER 30

Julian

"He just offered." She snaps her fingers as we move into the apartment above Midnight Proof. "They run the bourbon industry, and you're friends with him...*them*. What if I do this?" She spins around, excited and smiling, maybe even a little tipsy. "Can I do this?"

"Crowne, I'm pretty certain you can do anything you want," I tell her, running my hand along my mouth, taking in this beautiful woman in front of me—happy and confident, looking like fucking dream, and I can't help but clock this moment. I snap a mental picture, realizing how goddamn obsessed I am with her. She's the first person I've ever brought somewhere that wasn't a client or for photographs, but just for me, to meet people that I consider friends. The way she looks in that dress right now, all curves and confidence, turns me on and melts away everything else. *Fuck, look at her.*

She rubs her fingers between the little rosemary plant that's perched on the counter and then the lavender next to it. "I can see us doing pairings and tastings at the distillery at home.

Matching up flights with episodes of *The Distilled Truth*. Maybe even cake and whiskey flights—my mother would jump all over that." She sighs.

"If you want to do this, then do it. I don't think it's a matter of can—only want," I say, moving closer to her as she leans against the kitchen counter. She became a respected organic chemist in a leading academic program out of proving a point and a twinge of spite, so I wonder what the hell she'll be capable of doing with something out of her own desire?

She looks at the bar cart in the corner of the room. "Will you pour me something from there?" she asks in a lower, more sultry tone.

I glance over and do as she asks. Unbuttoning my shirt sleeves, I roll up the left side and then the right as I make my way to the far corner of the dimly lit room.

"Maybe bring me the entire bottle instead," she says as she lifts her skirt higher, just enough to hoist herself onto the counter.

I can't help but look down the curve of her thighs and at those sexy black heels. "I'll do whatever you want, Crowne, especially looking like that," I say, tipping my head toward her.

"And how exactly do I look?" she asks with a smirk dancing on her lips.

I nearly groan. The straps that hold her stockings are peeking out as she settles herself on the counter. *How can the tease of a strap make my mouth water?* "Like mine," I tell her.

She must like that because she sits taller and slips off her red-bottomed heels. "How do I look like yours?" she asks.

Licking my bottom lip and feeling my cock harden at the sight of her, I take slow steps back to her. "You're the most beautiful woman I've ever seen. And I plan on worshipping every fucking inch of you tonight. Tell me you'll let me. Tell me you're mine," I say, stepping closer.

The confidence that's vibrating around her right now… It's impossible to look away from her.

She uncrosses her legs and widens them as I approach. *An invitation.*

"And yet, somehow, just hearing you talk about this thing you enjoy, the way you light up just by thinking about something you want…" I shake my head. "The wildest part, Crowne, is that you're not even trying, and I'm so fucking impressed." I pause as I move to stand between her legs. She makes more room for me, immediately running her hands up my chest as mine find her hips. Her touch feels too good.

"Say it…" I whisper.

With her free hand, she curls her fingers into my shirt, tugging me closer, as her deep green eyes stay locked with mine. "You're mine, baby?" she rasps, with a playful smirk, and my dick fucking flexes at hearing her call me that.

A low and deep hum rumbles from my throat. She knows it isn't what I wanted her to say, but fuck, that sounds good too. "I'm yours," I smirk. "And really fucking obsessed with you calling me baby," I admit as I smooth my hands along the tops of her thighs and play with those straps.

She wets her bottom lip. "I believe it's been said that men should kneel before their goddesses," she says, taking the bottle I brought over and pouring it into the empty rocks glass next to her.

I'm happy to kneel before her, let her play, reward her, praise her in whatever way she might need. This is the woman who's been peeking out behind the heaviness of what she's gone through and where she came from, and I want her to embrace it.

Eyes widening slightly, she smiles into her glass as my knees lower to the floor. My hands drag up and down the sides of her thighs, toying with those straps some more, and my mouth waters being this close to her pussy.

Her fingers glide along my hairline softly as I look up at her. "Keep your hands on my thighs," she says softly as she pulls the hem of her dress higher, spreading her legs wider.

When I look down, she flashes me her bare pussy. "No panties, Crowne?"

She bites her lip, shaking her head slowly.

"Fuck," I breathe out, moving my nose and mouth closer to where I want, but her fingers glide farther into my hair, stopping me.

"Would you like some?" she asks me, holding up the glass.

"There are plenty of things I want right now, baby," I groan. My lips tip up in a knowing smile as I try moving closer to her pussy, but she tightens her grip on my hair and slowly tilts my head back. "Yeah, I want some."

"Open," she says, in a low, sexy voice.

With my eyes locked on hers, fingertips pressed into her thighs, and so fucking turned on, it's hard to stay still, I open my mouth.

She could've pressed the glass to my lips or forgone all of it and simply demanded that I lick her pussy, but instead, she holds the glass above my waiting mouth and pours. The whiskey splashes and drips down my chin, but enough of it hits my tongue, and I swallow that familiar bite of smoke and caramel. I barely register the way it burns at first and then eases down my throat, but it still warms my chest, heating me even more than I already am. I roll my hips, trying to ease the ache.

"Maybe this is the kind of whiskey tasting we should do more of—you down there ready and waiting for me," she says slowly, her chest rising and falling in a way that lets me know she's just as aroused as I am. "How badly do you want to touch me, Julian? To touch yourself?"

"So badly," I growl, turning my head slightly to graze my teeth along the inside of her thigh as goosebumps rise up along her skin. She eases her grip in my hair to allow it. My hips roll on their own again, looking for the slightest bit of relief as my dick rubs against the suit pants and grinds along the cabinets in front of where I'm kneeling. I tilt my head and do the same to her other thigh, relishing her shaky exhale. "You smell so fucking good," I mumble against her skin as I drag my mouth along the other thigh.

"Is your cock dripping for me, Julian?" she asks as she puts the glass down. She releases her grip on my hair and then pulls out the stopper on the bottle. "Because I am for you." She smirks, liking how the filthy words feel. "Can you see how wet I am from there?"

"Jesus Christ," I breathe out. I look down, and yeah, I can fucking see her pussy glistening like it's more than ready to take me. "Give me more, Crowne," I demand, sounding almost needy. And I fucking am. I'm so eager for whatever she wants to give to me.

I move my hands from her thighs around to her ass, rising a little higher on my knees to get even closer to her. The sound of music, quiet and low in the background, barely registers as I sit waiting for her lead.

It takes every ounce of holding back not to stand up and fuck her right now. I rush out a breath, so turned on and teetering on the edge of snapping.

She wraps her lips around the rim and takes a pull straight from the bottle.

I press my fingertips into her skin and squeeze her ass as I open my mouth, stick out my tongue, and wait for her to share.

There's no hesitation or even a second thought. Tipping the bottle back to her mouth, she takes another pull while wrapping her free hand into my hair. She spits her whiskey right into my mouth, and I savor every fucking drop of it. It's enough for my control to snap. I'm on my feet in the next second, taking her lips in a hungry kiss. She moans as I devour her mouth and drag my tongue along hers, enjoying the sweet and charred flavor of the whiskey with the unmistakable flavor of her. My hands frame her face, fingers tangling into her hair as I pull her to the edge of the counter.

Her knees widen, and she wraps her legs around me tightly. Lifting her, I move us toward the bed along the far back wall. She holds on, arms wrapped around my shoulders, fingers thrusted into my hair as her tongue and lips play a languid and sensual game with mine. When I reach the mattress, she loosens her legs, and I let her slide down my body just as she nips at my lower lip.

"I want a taste of you," she says when her feet hit the floor.

"Fuck," I exhale. "You can taste me, but that's all it's going to be. Just a taste."

I move my fingers to the buttons of my shirt and undo one at a time as she licks her lips. She doesn't let go of the bottle. Instead, she tips it back, taking another pull of it as she takes a step back to watch me peel off my clothes for her.

"Show me what's mine, Julian."

Fucking hell.

Her dress is still bunched around her hips, the deep cut of it showing off the fullness of her tits. Her hair is curled and slightly disheveled, lips swollen and pink from the whiskey and kissing me. I wasn't joking or feeding a line when I told her she looked like mine; I want all of her.

With her attention focused solely on me, I toss my shirt aside and move to unbuckle my belt. Her eyes draw up the height of me, stopping at my hands as they work my belt from the loops, up to my bare chest. "Yeah, all of that looks like mine," she says with a smile.

I can't help the laugh that pulls from me as my belt clanks to the floor. My pants are quick to follow.

Stepping up to me, she takes in a breath and then brushes her fingers along my skin, drawing across the waist of my boxer briefs and up until her palm flattens against my chest. She pushes just enough of her weight forward, making me move backwards, until the back of my calves hit the side of the bed. I sit and look up at her, drawing my hands up the back of her thighs, pushing her dress up higher so I can palm each ass cheek and see how wet she might be for me.

Before I have a chance to lean forward and lick her pretty wet cunt, she says, "A quick taste." She sinks to her knees in front of me, and it's a move that I'll replay over and over again. I tilt my head back, a breath rushing from my chest. I look back down, watching and feeling her hands drag up my thighs and toward the top of my boxer briefs, her fingers looping into the waistband she was just toying with. I brace my hands beside me and lift my ass as she pulls them down. I think about the way she's in control, how fucking sexy it is for a woman to be so comfortable with me to play.

My cock springs free, and she doesn't waste a single moment before her tongue hits the base of my dick and drags flat up the length of me. I moan, long and low, as her lips wrap around me, and she shifts up on her knees to take me all the way to the back of her throat. The wet warmth of her mouth and the way she hums as she takes me feels too damn good.

"Fuck, that's it," I breathe out. She works me so damn good, taking her time with every stroke of her tongue as she moves up and down my cock. She uses her hand to help, gripping the base of me and rocking her wrist to follow every time she takes me in and out of her velvety mouth. The way she sucks me off is a damn awakening. I brace myself with one hand, holding my body up as the other hand moves to her head, fingers gliding into her hair. Getting lost in her touch, I flex up, trying to chase the feeling, and she doesn't even gag, simply digs her nails into my thigh and ass with a muffled moan, as if she wants more.

"Baby, if you don't get up here," I say through a groan, just as she works her mouth so far down that she gags, pulling off and out of breath, saliva glossing her lips. I don't let her recover from it, pulling her up and into my lap, kissing her and tasting myself on her tongue. Working her dress up her waist and up over her head, I toss it to the floor.

She laughs as I lie back and pull her with me.

"Your mouth is too good," I tell her before I kiss her again.

"I like hearing what that does to you," she says, smiling against my lips.

I run my hands down the length of her body as she straddles me, my hands wrapping around the backs of her thighs. She's still wearing nothing but the sheer black thigh-highs strapped to the garter belt. "These are going to need to make another appearance," I say, running my fingers along the length of the straps. With one more kiss, I move my body lower, lifting her just enough so I can get what I want.

"What are you—" Her words are clipped with her laugh at my eagerness.

"You've earned a ride, Crowne," I say as I shift below her. "Sit on my mouth, baby, and let me hear you moan nice and loud for me."

She bites her lip just as she places her knees on either side of my head.

I pull her down exactly where I want her and hum at the arousal that's soaked between her thighs and along her slit. A breath escapes her lips just as she settles against me. She doesn't try to hover or even hold back. She grinds her pussy on my mouth, rolling her hips, and moans as she takes what she needs. I work my tongue so she can use it, the scruff of my beard running up and down her clit on every roll, making her shiver. She gasps when I wrap my arms around her thighs and hold her down, nearly suffocating myself. It would be the best fucking way to go. Looking up, I see her playing with her tits as they move with her body. *Fuck.*

I can tell she's about to come with the way her breath catches again, her moans turning quieter and her body going taut. I don't let up, moving my tongue, adding more pressure, swirling and sucking, and the second I do, she cries out. Her body jerks forward as her orgasm works its way through her, thighs trembling and hands smacking down onto my chest to steady herself. She soaks my tongue with her cum, the taste of it changing just slightly, sweeter, as it wets my beard and drips along my chin. *So fucking good.*

The moment her body slackens, I move from under her, and she sprawls on her side, smiling. I kiss her shoulder and kneel behind her, wrapping her in my arms, my front to her back as she catches her breath. She hums as she nudges her ass against my cock.

I hiss out through my teeth, nearly ready to come. "Is this okay? Bare. Without—" I rush out.

She nods. "It's okay," she whispers.

I don't want a condom. I don't want to stop, but I'm not going to do anything that she'll regret later. "Are you sure?"

On a breathy whisper, she says, "I want you to slide that cock right inside and—"

Her words are cut short as I pull her body against me, drape her leg over mine, and angle us so I can drag my cock through her slicked pussy from behind. My fingers find her clit as I nudge my dick against her slit and slide in fully. A whimper leaves her at the stretch, and she lifts her knee for a better angle as she gasps my name. I can't help but moan at how wet she is, the grip of her, and the slickness has my eyes rolling back.

"Like that," I grit out, my lips pressed against her neck, just below her ear. "Fuck, baby, just like that."

Working my fingers against her clit, it only takes a few minutes before she's pulsing around me, an audible gasp fleeing her chest, and then a moan that pushes me right to the edge. I drag my cock in and out, only twice more, unable to hold back the guttural sound that escapes me.

"On me," she says, tipping her head up.

"Fuck—" I grit out, biting along her shoulder. Sweat drips down the center of my chest, my forearm tight from holding her against me. "Wyn," I moan, sliding out of her and doing exactly as my dirty fucking girl asks.

My body shudders as my orgasm works me over, starting from every limb to the head of my dick, my spine curves, body jerking forward as I paint her pussy with my cum. I drag my dick through it, rubbing it along her skin and down the inside of her thigh as one last tremor works through me. Rocking my wrist slowly, I drag my palm up my shaft to the head of my dick, squeezing out every last fucking drop and spreading it on her skin. Both of us ride out what's left of each other's orgasms, messy and sweaty, and more satisfied than I can ever remember being in my life. Kissing up her neck, I come down from the high of it.

I'm still panting, my cock still semi-hard, as she says, "That was..." She sighs and takes a deep breath, melting back into me. I can hear her smile. "That was..." But instead of finishing that thought, she says, "You're the most fun I've ever had."

I smile against her, loving the way that makes me feel, and all I can think is that I want to be even more.

"Me too, baby."

Thunder rumbling has me stirring out of whatever deep sleep I fell into. The spot beside me isn't as warm as it was, and it forces my eyes open.

Across the room in the oversize leather chair, Wyn sits curled up, wearing my dress shirt and writing vigorously in a notebook. The light from the corner is just enough to bathe her in shadows, her wavy hair tossed to one side. She has a smile spread across her lips as she looks out the picturesque windows, thinking about something. Whatever she's focused on has her shifting back down to that notebook and writing more.

Sitting up, the thunder rumbles out again, and I decide to bring the comforter with me.

She finally notices me as I get up. "Did I wake you?"

I shake my head. "Just want to be near you," I tell her, and she smiles softly.

She stands, making room for me on the chair, and then sits back down in my lap, the comforter pulled over us both. I kiss along her exposed neck and look at what she's writing. Formulas to equations and then a doodle of two *W*s. On the page across from that is a list of things that were front and center at the Foxx distillery today—*water filtration system, UV filters, bottle shape and design…*

Looking out at the dark sky, she says, "I don't think I've ever been this excited about anything. And I know I can do this."

Pride swells in my chest at hearing it. "I know you can too, baby." Pressing another kiss to her shoulder, I reach for the notebook, looking at her scribbled pages.

"It feels right," she says as she flips the page and jots down another item for her list of to-dos. "And I'm just deciding that I want it. Have you ever done that? Just listened to your gut, because you simply knew it was right?"

My chest warms as I hum and play with the ends of her hair. "Only once," I say without any hesitation, and she turns her head to the side to look at me. "Falling in love with you," I admit as her eyes meet mine. "Easiest feeling and decision I've ever made."

"Julian," she whispers, not expecting that from me. I didn't expect to say it either.

Pulling her chin toward me, I kiss her lips lightly before I smile and add, "Since the minute you threatened me with those self-defense cat ears."

She barks out an adorable laugh and covers her mouth. "And I did it twice."

As she smiles, I run my fingers along the side of her cheek and feel like, of all the things I've chosen, this one, with her, is the most right of all of them.

The things she's shared with me, the parts of her I know more about than any other person, are bigger to me than what

I can put into words, but it's all the pieces that make up loving someone—understanding and truths, respect and encouragement, lust and trust.

Lightning in the distance flashes. It's too fast to see where it struck, but it was there. Like it's punctuating this moment in my life.

She sets the notebook aside and settles against me, nuzzling into my neck, legs curled up and over mine. Her fingers play along the leather cuff on my wrist as I hold her. It's a quiet calm, with only the sound of rain pattering against the window and her warmth in my arms, that has me content and nearly dozing off when she whispers, "I feel it too."

CHAPTER 31

Wyn

"I KNOW THEY'RE WORKING, BUT I'm—" I cut off my words as my fingers glide through the wind of the open window on our way to The Whispering Fool.

We spent another day in Fiasco so I could talk business with Lincoln and Ace. For the last twenty-four hours, including on the plane ride home, I've been putting together an actionable business plan that I can hit the ground running with as soon as the bank opens on Monday morning. I have some money put aside, but a loan from the bank will allow for flexibility instead of having to rely on any investors. I didn't want to wait to do this. I'll need to put my notice in at the university, but I didn't want to waste time, not after knowing exactly how time can be so messy.

The two other pieces of this puzzle are a gamble, but I want to try. I need to talk with Stevie and Jo. I know them better than almost everyone. My sisters wouldn't want a business plan or logic; they do well with the unexpected and spontaneous.

"Excited to talk to them?" Julian smiles, lifting the back

of my hand and bringing to his lips. I glance over and watch him kiss my hand as he listens and unknowingly makes me feel safe.

"Just a bit. I think they're going to really consider it too," I say, knee bouncing. "I mean, they'll at least be supportive even if they don't want to roll their sleeves up."

WYN:

I need to talk to both of you. Please tell me you can spare a few minutes. I promise it's all good.

STEVIE:

I love surprises. You married?

JO:

You're serious with that question?

STEVIE:

Is it really a huge stretch? I mean, you've seen the guy...

WYN:

My marital status has NOT changed

STEVIE:

Did you buy those MIU MIU platforms I sent you a picture of the other day?

JO:

I call dibs if that's the big news

STEVIE:

I hate you

I'm laughing at the texts when Julian pulls right up in front of the bar. The crowd spills out the front door and the noise filters in, laughter and shouting. Gina looks more pissed off manning the door than usual as she pulls one cosplay cowboy off another. The music from the band echoes into the truck and two Harleys rev their engines and roar past. I forgot how packed the bar would be for a long weekend.

"You head inside. I have to talk to Birdie about something," he says, glancing from his phone to me. "Going to remind her I'm still done. I meant what I said about this being the last for me."

So my grandmother was texting him about something new, another person who had crossed too many lines, someone she and my mom would need to deal with. The gray area that all of this lives within doesn't mean anything, not if someone who had been hurting people got a heavy dose of karma. Whether or not Julian was a part of that wasn't going to stop Birdie and my mom from doing what they believed they should.

"I support whatever you choose to do, but you told me you wanted to be done with that part of your life to find me," I say. "It was the last one because you wanted to live a different life than your father had…and to find me. But Julian, I'm right here." I squeeze his hand and pull it to my lips the same way he had done to mine. "You have me. You don't need to change your whole life just to get the girl."

He smiles, shaking his head as he mumbles, "Just to get the girl." I watch his Adam's apple move up and down, silently working through what I'm telling him. "And I've done that?"

I raise my eyebrows, surprised that he doesn't know.

He clears his throat. "I've got the girl? 'Cause I've heard some rumors about the oldest Crowne sister."

I smile at him as he lifts me off the seat and into his lap. "And which one are we repeating this time?" Wrapping my arms around his neck, my fingers draw along the nape of his neck and into his hair. I know he loves it just by his quiet hum every time I do it.

"The one where the prude professor fucks around her boyfriend in a field." He looks around and out the window. "Maybe the one where she goes down on him in a parking lot. Or the one where she rides him parked out front of her house inside his truck."

Chuckling, I smile, tilting my head to the side as he kisses along my neck. "I do really like that last one..."

The little bit of light from the parking lights help me find him when I grit my teeth and say, "Don't you fucking dare go anywhere." I smile realizing the choice I'm making—*him*. "My plans only work if you're here and in them with me."

There isn't anything soft about him on the outside, hard lines and the look of pure intimidation if he really wants to, but right now, in my arms, none of that is present. He feels like a version of home I've been trying to find, and then confirms it when he says, "I go where you go."

His hands roam around my back, one snaking up to the back of my neck, pulling me to him, and I go willing. Julian nips at my lips playfully before kissing me. His tongue rolls with mine as he groans in response to how I kiss him back just as sensually.

"We need to get out of this car, otherwise I'm going to have to have you..." I say as I move across the seat.

He opens the door, and we both get out. Turning my hand over, he kisses my palm first before he steps away, moving toward the path that connects The Whispering Fool to Birdie's house. "Hey, Crowne," he calls out.

When I turn and look over my shoulder, I smile as he shoves his hands into his pockets. But he doesn't say anything.

"What?" I say, laughing, moving closer to the front doors of the bar.

"I love you," he shouts as he keeps walking backwards, eyes still on me. "I won't be long." Then he turns the corner toward my grandmother's place.

It makes me pause, looking down for a moment. I've walked into this bar so many times throughout my life, but never this optimistic, feeling this good.

I smile at the security pillars who make up The Whispering Fool's security team.

"I know that look," Gina says, shoving her hands into the front of her mustard-yellow jacket. "Someone is gettin' it good."

She isn't wrong.

"Gina, the first rule of watching young people fall like idiots is not to call it out," Gail says, checking an ID and shoving it back at the girl in front of her.

"Gail, I wasn't talkin' 'bout love, but by the look on this one's face, I think you're right."

"I don't know what ya'll are talking about. I'm a Crowne, remember? Falling in love is never a good idea," I say, teasing. "For anyone." I stick my tongue out at them.

But it's Gina who adds, "I've never seen anyone love harder and care more than a Crowne, darlin'. Just happy to see it's your turn now."

I swallow, lingering in the doorway, but before I can thank

her for saying that, Gina is already telling two patched bikers, "If you don't get your intimidating asses in the back of that line over there, I will run hard and fast into your hogs and tip 'em over."

The moment I step over the threshold, I practically laugh at myself for thinking I'd be able to steal my sisters away for a minute. It's a swarm of people. The band is wrapping up a cover of Dolly's "Blue Smoke," and the crowd eats it up as both my sisters play a healthy game of tossing bottles to one another. Stevie's on roller skates, chiming in at the top of her lungs in the center of the bar, while Jo sits perched on the shot swing above. I know they both love the tips and having a good time out here, and a part of me worries they won't want to bite off something else. But I'll ask anyway—let them make their own choices.

"Wynonaaaaaaa!" Stevie sings out as I weave through and over to where she's perched. The band starts another set moments later as she sits on top of the bar. "Move the fuck over, let my sister in here." When I get closer, she smiles wide. "I'm on the edge of my seat here, what are you telling us?"

"I want you and Jo to hear me out about an idea I have," I say tapping my hands on the bar. Looking around and seeing the way this place is stacked tonight, I know this conversation will need to wait.

"Of course." She looks up around behind me. "You're looking all kinds of shiny, big sister. 'Bout time!"

I don't even try hiding my smile. "I don't know what you're talking about," I joke sarcastically. Putting my fingers to my lips, I blow her a kiss. "It's too nuts in here right now. I'll call you tomorrow," I shout up to her.

"Better!" she shouts and winks at me. "Alright, you savages," she shouts to the crowd. "I'm feeling like life's about to get all sorts of wild. Jo, you up for a dealer's choice?!"

As I turn away and pull my phone from my back pocket, a familiar voice, close to my ear, says, "You look rather pleased with yourself."

Turning quickly, knowing it's not Julian, I smile and say, "Reed, hi." The crowd pushes us too close together as he holds two shots of what looks like tequila, rimmed in salt with two tiny slices of lime floating in each. "You here causing trouble?" I ask jokingly.

But he looks at me as if he doesn't see the humor in it at first. "I asked you first," he answers, flashing me a smile back. It isn't strange for him to be out at the bar, I just didn't expect to see him in the packed crowd.

"I think I might be celebrating," I laugh out. "Cheers!" And boldly, I take the shot from his right hand.

As I toss it back, I catch the eye of a university student sitting at one of the high-top tables, looking our way. Andi. *Shit.* I just downed a shot in front of a student. But then she closes her eyes tightly and then opens them like she's trying to focus. That's not good. I look toward the front doors, where Gail and Gina are still carding and charging cover. I'm going to have to talk to them about that in a minute, or at the very least have a word with my sister about closing out her tab.

Looking back at Reed, I notice the shot in his hand. He shifts slightly, and I let out a nervous laugh and ask, "You're not going to have—" I cover my mouth with a wince, amused and a little mortified for assuming he was double-fisting two shots for no reason. "That was for someone else, wasn't it?"

He gives me a tight-lipped smile.

"Okay, quick, you take that shot, and I'll just snag you two more," I tell him, fanning my hands forward, encouraging him to take it quickly so I can fix what I just interrupted. But it's the way he looks at me that has me glancing at the shot glass again. I don't have a chance to question him, though. Out of the corner of my eye, Andi looks like she's about to fall over and onto the floor. Brushing past Reed, I move quickly to stand next to her, crouching slightly so she focuses on me.

"Andi, honey, are you alright?" I ask.

"Dr. Crowne?" she mumbles, almost slurring my name.

The band hits a louder chorus, the electric guitar riff is the cue everyone needs for the entire bar to join in. Stevie is on stage with the mic in hand, while Jo kicks her legs out, making the shot swing soar. I don't see my mother or Birdie, at least not in this crowd of people.

"Andi, I think you might have had too much," I try shouting over the noise. "Where are your friends?" And then she looks past me, eyes glassy and dazed with slow drawn-out blinks. I swallow roughly, knowing in my gut where she's looking. *What the fuck, Reed.* When I turn slightly, peeking over my shoulder, Reed's stepping up beside me.

He leans in close to me and says, "You remember what it's like to have some fun with the TAs, right, Professor?"

A stone-cold chill runs from my spine and out through my limbs. I instantly feel sick at his words.

"What did you just say to me?" I shoot to my full height, hands still bracing Andi's shoulders as I search Reed's face. But the man looking back at me doesn't seem like the one I thought I knew. The softness and kindness aren't there. Instead, he stares, his mouth tilting into a smile that instantly makes me want to punch him and run.

When I hear Stevie over the microphone calling out shots, it stirs up something she said on one of her podcasts—something that stuck with me, and I couldn't figure out why it hit me so hard when it did at the time. *"The easiest way for someone to take your control is to manipulate your power to say no."*

My mind scrolls through what I know of Andi that I somehow missed. Thinking about what I witnessed at Birdie's tarot table during the Full Moon Festival, even Andi showing up at family dinner… All of the behavior never would have pointed me to look at Reed the way I am right now.

Hands quivering with adrenaline, my mouth dries.

This isn't going to happen.

My stomach recoils the moment I wonder if it's happened before?

"That was not *tequila," I say to him, laughing out loud. "Or they poured the cheapest tequila I've ever tasted." My lips pucker from sucking on a quarter of lime.*

He smiles at me, a charming, warm smile that I've always liked. He's a good guy, but I don't want to settle. And I don't want to cross that line with him ever again. It was nice for him to be here, to support me during this keynote I'd been so nervous to deliver, but I wasn't expecting to see him tonight. "I don't think you'll ever understand how much your friendship means to me," I tell him, gesturing between us, trying to make it clear that while we're enjoying a laugh and a drink, that line won't be crossed again. But my fingers and arm suddenly feel heavier as I move them. Bitterness still lingering on my tongue, I swallow, blinking slowly.

Reed curls a piece of my hair behind my ear, and then stands from his stool. I didn't like that he did that, but I don't move fast enough to pull away. He leans into me and quietly says, "Friends? You don't mean that, Professor, right? Or am I misreading things?"

Am I misreading things…

I stare at him, eyes wide open, in the middle of my family's rowdy bar, paralyzed by the memory of the symposium night I've shoved down. It's all flooding back into focus now.

"I'm not sure how I feel about that," he continues, taking the empty glass from my fingers. "Why don't we finish this in my room."

I squeeze my eyes shut and then open, trying to focus on him.

"We're away from campus. No one will know."

I try thinking clearly, despite the haze. "You'll need to close the tab and give me your key," I say as I give him a placating, tight-lipped smile.

I don't wait around. Something isn't right, so I head right for the door.

At the time, I didn't comprehend it. I barely remember it. I didn't ever want to go back to that night and what came next.

I wander outside, more drunk than I should be, lightheaded, hazy. The brick wall feels cool on my back as I lean against the side of the building, trying to get my bearings.

"This is a beautiful turn of events," someone says to me, but I don't recognize their voice. "I saw your picture when I walked by and thought, 'Professor Crowne, I wonder how someone could be that intelligent and beautiful.'" As I try to focus on what he's saying, this tall and lanky man, and I don't like the way he walks closer. Too close. "You weren't who I planned for tonight, but how do I pass up an opportunity like this?" he asks.

It isn't fear that billows around me now, it's a vibrating anger that travels through my veins and has my hands shaking as I focus back on this moment.

"Andi, honey, let's go to the ladies' room, maybe splash a little water on your face." I need to get her away from the noise and crowd, away from him. She isn't drunk. She's been drugged. I know what it's like, what it looks like. And the culprit hovers behind me.

Instead of Andi standing and moving with me, it's Reed's hand that wraps around my elbow, gripping it tight as his body pulls me away.

"The fuck? Let go of me!" I try shouting, just as the band ticks higher. My mind races as I try to shove him away, but the grip he has on my arm moves, twisting it in a way that if I don't move with him, something will snap. I blink hard, trying to see through the pain, and can barely gain traction as he drags me toward the long hallway that leads to the back exit. "Ow, fuck, you're hurting me. Reed. Let go of me!" I yell, but he doesn't react at all.

He turns his body, his back toward the crowd, blocking anyone from seeing what he's doing. That's when he shifts me, and I feel a sharp object pressed at the base of my spine. I freeze, no longer trying to pull out of his grip. No. He leans in, his hot breath against my ear as his threat registers.

"Shut your fucking—" He sniffs out an exhale against my ear. Every part of me wants to recoil and shove away from him—thrash and scream, but if I move, I don't trust he won't hurt me. In a more collected tone, he says, "We need to clear up this misunderstanding."

Tears I didn't even know had swelled, fall down my cheek as I try to keep my focus locked on Andi for as long as I can. "Andi!" I try shouting. But it's too loud in here. She starts to slump forward as I'm pulled down the long hall that runs the length of the bar and toward the back.

How didn't I see this? Anger and terror fight and churn in my stomach. *Be smart. Do not panic now.*

I don't remember much of *that* night—the all-consuming terror that followed drowned out the origin of it. "It never should've been that easy," I say to myself, even more confused. It never should've been so easy to take me like the monster had.

If Reed hadn't drugged me, I might have had a fighting chance. I fell from the grasp of one monster and into another's. I try sucking in a breath as I frantically look around.

"We both know you're not a fighter," he grits out.

All I can think is, *Yes, I am.*

"You said we're friends, how much my friendship means to you," he says against my ear. "Were you lying, Professor?"

My body seizes at the way he says it, my skin crawling.

"Don't you remember how friendly we were? I didn't even need to coax you; you were so eager for it," he says, dragging me, jamming the tip of a sharp object into the skin at my back.

There's no alarm when he shoves the door open. *Goddamnit.*

I try yelling again, but nothing comes out. *No.* I open my mouth again, my breathing labored, willing myself not to shut down. *Stay present.* A hollowed-out feeling settles in the pit of my stomach. I promised myself this would never happen to me again. *Never again.*

I eye the fire extinguisher on the opposite wall and lean my body in its direction. The weight shift throws him off enough that I hit the wall. *You're a fighter.* But he rights me quickly, even more pissed off now. *Yell, goddamnit!* The grip he has on my arm shoots a blinding pain across my chest, making more tears fall. *Be brave.* I grit my teeth and try seeing through the pain. I won't go quietly, *never again.*

Open your mouth and scream!

CHAPTER 32

Julian

I PEER UP AND OVER the crowd gathered toward the stage and another horde of people wrapped around the bar inside. I don't see her. Damn, The Whispering Fool is packed tonight. *Maybe that was part of their plan.*

The minute Birdie said his name, I knew my gut had been right. It wasn't just jealousy I felt toward Reed *fucking* Andrews. My instinct is to protect Wyn, and that was what keyed in when he was around her. From what I've learned, he's the kind of dangerous that escalates. I need to find her and figure out a way to tell her what Birdie and Lu had asked of me, and why.

The text I received on our drive home needed to be addressed right away.

BIRDIE CROWNE:

I'm going to need a full set. Before you say no, come see me so I can lay it all out for you.

"Reed Andrews has become a problem. The kind of problem we can't just leave unattended," she says with a solemn look. "We've been watching him for a while, and I had a gut feeling. I knew I should have listened..."

"Ma, the hardest ones are the ones we don't see right away," Lu says, perched on the counter. She glances back at me when she adds, "He took advantage of at least two of his students, as far as we're aware. The sheriff's department is, in no surprising turn of events, fucking ignoring it. The university needs more proof and formal reports. They want these women to recollect every detail when they've already told them they couldn't remember anything, other than they had been out with friends, ran into their professor, and from there, only flashes of the night." She glances at Birdie, who sits in the large leather armchair across the room. "It's fucking a guidebook on how to handle sexual assault all wrong, those fuckers. That's the problem with having a good ol' boy in charge here. Fucking patriarchy."

"Lu, knock it off with that." Birdie waves her off.

"I'm not interested in seeing another woman get hurt and then told she should have watched how much she was drinking. It's almost poetic, flipping that on its head."

Birdie nods at her daughter, before looking back to me. "It's rare, but this time, I agree with her."

I know what these women are capable of. I've been around plenty of dangerous people throughout my life, but this is personal for them. It makes what they want to do feel justified.

"If you need something cleaned up, I'll make an exception," I say to Lu, then look at Birdie. "For you. And for this."

Birdie sighs, knowing what saying that means for me. Stan Billings was supposed to be my last. I was ending that part of my family's legacy—I told her as much. What she doesn't know is that the reason for that choice, at the core of it, is Wyn. I wanted to find her—I wanted to have a life that didn't include lies or secrets about who I really am. Even if I never found her, I was choosing something different for myself.

She tilts her head and watches me when she asks, "You love her, don't you?"

That's when I hear her—*Wyn*. The sharp, high-pitched scream isn't to cheer on or chant about shots. It's faint in comparison to the speakers pushing out music mixed with the crowd laughing and hollering.

Fear slices up my spine. I don't think, I just move. Turning on the ball of my foot, frantically searching for her, I shove inside, past Gail and Gina, who yell out behind me.

"Stevie! Have you seen Wyn?" I call out as I head right for the bar.

"She was just talking with Reed," she shouts back, looking toward the high-top tables. There's a commotion of people around a drunk girl, but no sign of Wyn.

I turn, head whipping around, looking back where I just came and down in the other direction. But it's the movement toward the back hallway past the bathrooms that makes me do a double take. The exit sign bathes everything in red. Except at the very end of the hall, the door is closing and the outside flood lights pour inside. That's when I see her. *And him.*

"Wyn!" I shout, but the bar is so rowdy, only a few people turn as I plow into them. I almost topple over as I race toward the far back side of the bar, my heart pounding in my ears. I right myself as I reach the short hall. But I don't stop, picking up speed and driving into the almost closed door. It knocks Reed down and shoves Wyn in the process, all of us hitting the ground hard. With a shout, I get up fast and shove him back down as he tries to stand.

"Get the fuck off," Reed seethes as I reach around his neck, tucking him into the crook of my elbow. I pull back as he tries moving forward. If I can lock my legs, I know I'll be able to cut off his air supply and make him pass out. I know who this man is, what he's done, the people he's lied to and fuck knows what else.

"Julian!" Wyn cries out.

"Wyn, you alright, baby?!" I yell out to her. But instead of a response, she screams just as Reed twists his body and elbows me right in the ribs, knocking the wind from me. Cursing, I kick his legs out from under him, coughing as I try to catch my breath.

I turn away at the wrong moment, because he's righted himself enough to gain the upper hand. His fist connects to my lower back, punching me in the kidney first, and then another quick blow across my chin. *This fucker.*

Out of the corner of my eye, I see Wyn scurry back on her ass as gravel and dust fly up around us. "Stop! Oh my god," she cries out. "Reed, stop!"

My mouth floods with liquid. I instantly recognize the coppery taste of blood. Spitting it out, I take a wide step back, looking at her over my shoulder. She never answered me, and I need to know he didn't hurt her. "You okay?"

Her eyes dart over my shoulder, and I know I've turned my attention for too long as Reed's hands shove at my back, and I shuffle forward, trying to gain my footing. I don't hit the ground; instead, I'm just closer to her now.

"Tell me you're okay and then get the hell out of here, Crowne." I look around her body, scouring for anything that looks like she's been injured. The side of her shirt is shoved up, her scar dirty with mud and dust. Her bottom lip has a streak of blood across it.

All of it is enough to flip a switch inside of me.

"Not fucking okay," I grit out.

"Julian!" she shouts in warning.

Reed's hand is moving at me, and in reflex, I throw my hand out, stopping the bullshit knife that he's trying to slash me with. It slices through my palm but stops at the leather cuff and gets knocked away as I move fast. Adrenaline spikes through my veins, and I barely feel the burn of ripped-open skin. It's like flint and fuels, it sparks and ignites the devil that simmers below my surface.

I smile at him, the warm taste of blood lingering along my teeth, an internal demand to show him how it'll never be okay that he put his hands on *my* girl.

This wasn't ever going to be a fair fight, but since he started it, I will happily finish and erase all traces of this man.

Rearing back, I throw a right hook, catching him clean across the jaw, and then launch my body forward to tackle him to the ground. Wyn runs toward the door, hopefully doing as I've asked and getting the hell away from this.

I get in two left bloody hooks across his face and a right jab along his side. Leaning forward, I shove my weight against my forearm that I've thrust against his windpipe, making him gasp and cough.

Reed takes advantage of my injury and punches at my bloody hand.

"Fuuuuckkkkk!" I grit out, more than feeling it that time. He flails beneath me, and it's enough that he rolls us over, the back of my head hitting the gravel hard.

Wyn screams my name gutturally, and moments later, she's running back in our direction. He wrestles on top of me as he tries to choke me, all while I attempt to hold him still, my hands digging into his, just as she swings her arm out and screams at the top of her lungs. It collides with Reed's side so fiercely that it forces him to lurch over, "Fuck! God fucking, gahhhh!" he shouts. With him. Distracted, he eases his grip on me, and I shove out from under him with a grunt, yanking him with me as we tumble closer to the edge of the embankment leading down to the river. Along the back side of the bar, it's a bit deeper of a drop-off. Mud and rock dig into my arms and legs as we fight for the controlling position again.

The loud echo of a shotgun fires off above us, one concussive boom that cracks the air open. Silence consumes the air as we topple over. The second shot jerks us apart from each other, my breath labored as I twist away and search for the source of it. On the edge of the embankment we just rolled down stands Birdie with a sawed-off shotgun cocked at her hip and a bottle of whiskey held between two fingers. The muffled sound of the band plays in the background and rumbling engines from motorcycles pull in closer. On one side is Lu with her arms crossed and on the other stands Wyn, chest heaving and half hunched over. My brave girl.

"You okay, baby?" I call out to Wyn, keeping my eyes on her before they quickly snap to Birdie.

Her voice is quiet at first, but then she calls out louder, "Yes. I'm okay."

"This isn't how we do things around here, Mr. Colton," Birdie says coldly to me.

My body coils even tighter, eyes narrowing on her. I must have fucking heard that wrong.

"Birdie," Wyn shouts in a reprimanding tone.

"That's enough, Wynona," she says, raising her eyebrow. *Birdie never calls her Wynona.* "Reed, are you alright?" she calls out to him.

What the fuck is going on?

The asshole shifts his weight to stand, but he favors one side. Glancing over, I see a familiar shiny black tool sticking out from his side. *The fucking cat ears.* That must have been what Wyn did when she swung at him, embedded it right in his side.

Walking closer, Birdie tilts her head and looks at the protruding object.

What the fuck is she doing? Wyn's eyes meet mine when I look back at her, and she's wearing the same pissed-off question plastered on her face.

My hand burns and pulses as blood drips down my forearm. *Shit.* Lifting my shirt over my head, I twist and wrap it around my hand that still bleeds steadily. Wyn notices and moves slowly from where she stood next to Lu, bypassing a locked and loaded Birdie, toward me. She glances at my hand and then back up to me, silently asking if I'm alright.

I give her a short nod while still trying to keep focus on the standoff playing out in front of me.

"Birdie, everything alright out here?" Tommy shouts from the back door, standing shoulder to shoulder with a big guy in leather cuts.

"I'm sorting it out, Thomas. No need to get the sheriff." She lifts her shotgun and rests it on her shoulder. "Unless you want to press charges, Reed."

Reed glances at me first, nostrils flared, and then Wyn, before he turns his head, and says, "That won't be necessary. I'm sure we can sort this out."

"Good." Birdie nods, holding out the bottle of whiskey to him. "Take a sip. We're going to need to pull that out to get a better look." She gestures to Wyn's handiwork.

Wyn grips onto me as he reaches for the bottle, pressing it to his lips while Lu pulls the cat ear weapon from his side. She's not gentle about it either, which has him hissing through his teeth. His dress shirt soaks red more quickly than I would have expected. But it's the way he starts coughing that has him looking up at the Crowne women with widening eyes.

I look down at Wyn again, and she raises her chin as she watches on, like she understands what's happening. And now, so do I.

"You're a smart one," Lu rasps to him. "I think that's why Wyn liked you so much at first. You were the opposite of every other man I had been around." Humming, she looks at Wyn, who's still at my side, holding on to me tightly. "She's smarter though. She knew you weren't ever going to cut it for her."

Reed coughs out again, holding his punctured side.

This is how they do it.

"The beauty of whiskey is found in what we like to call the heart. Not sure if you're familiar," she says under her breath. "That's the part that'll warm you up or fuck you up, just depends on your plans for it. But the head..." She trails off with a smirk, turning her head slowly, left and then right.

Birdie tips her chin up, a satisfied look in her eyes.

But it's Wyn who chimes in. Her shoulders shove down, chest out as she says, "The head is dangerous. The scientist in you should know that methanol evaporates at lower temps. It's the first thing to discard when distilling. It's either careless or intentional when it's not properly separated. A small sip will make a person go blind. Anything more and it'll race to poison the bloodstream." Tilting her head to the side, she deviously asks, "How big of a sip did you just take, Reed?"

The realization of it hits, blood draining from his face as he tries swallowing again and then spitting out.

Wyn carries on, "Do you think it was more than what you slipped into my drink the night I ended up being taken?"

Her words have my stomach bottoming out—that better not be fucking true.

"You may not be the same monster who took me, but you made it easier for him."

I glance at Lu and then Birdie, but the looks on their faces seem just as surprised by what she's saying. Wyn moves into my side, wrapping herself as close as she can. When she looks up at me, I know instantly.

The growl that escapes my throat has Lu and Birdie turning toward me.

Lu laughs out, "Oh, you have so many people lining up to punish you, Doctor Boring. You. Are. *Fucked*."

Visibly trembling, he looks around at each of us, realizing nobody here is in his corner. In fact, the one person who he maybe thought would've believed him, just poisoned him.

"He was buying drugs from Stan Billings," Lu continues, keeping her eyes trained on Reed.

He looks nervously to Wyn and then to Birdie as he coughs out again.

"Cora, Stan's wife, confirmed it when she was drunk as hell at the bluegrass festival. And he was the last person two young university students had been with before they woke up in their apartments. And while Andi was crushing real hard on you, she couldn't understand why the same thing had happened to her." Lu shakes her head, blowing out a breath that speaks for how disgusted she is. "And your stupid ass went ahead and tried it again tonight, under my goddamn roof."

Birdie's Southern drawl shifts our attention as she takes a

few steps closer. "It must have felt nice to fall through the cracks like that, to get away with such things just because your gender and status allowed for it. Did you think you wouldn't be held accountable?" It almost sounds sweet until he registers what she's saying.

Reed shakes his head as much as he can. The reality of what's happening must finally be kicking in as he raises his hands in front of him. "Birdie, please? I didn't—"

"Lu?" she says, looking at Wyn's mom and cutting him off.

It's their quick silent exchange that has Lu giving Reed a nice shove. The embankment isn't far enough to cause much of an injury, but the sound of him hitting the water with a thud has Wyn gasping and covering her mouth.

"That's how we do things around here," Birdie says as she walks closer to the edge. "Let's see if the gators are hungry tonight. If not, then it looks like that cleanup job is still on, Mr. Colton."

"Oh, they're hungry," Lu says as she looks over the embankment.

I'm usually the cleanup, not the killer. But tonight, that would have been different if these two hadn't stepped in. And I would be here in the morning if they needed me. There wouldn't be a sign of anything happening here, I'd make sure of it.

Wyn locks eyes with me and a thousand emotions run wordlessly between us.

Reed was bleeding pretty heavily, but the drink Birdie handed him is what made it fairly simple for Lu to catch him off guard and tip him over the edge. The sound of water splashing ferociously and a clipped yell, echoes out just as the door to the bar swings open.

"Wyn, my dear." Birdie tucks her shotgun into the crook of

her arm. "Why don't you go now. Get Julian cleaned up while we figure out how best to proceed here. I think maybe you've seen enough."

Wyn's teary eyes look to her mother and then back to Birdie. With her chin held high, she gives them both a nod and maybe even more with the way they look back at her. They've just put her in the middle of what they do and the summary of what they've done to those deserving in the past. It's a legacy I don't think she ever planned to witness, but I'm betting she's glad she did.

Tommy stands in the doorway with his arm out, encouraging us toward him. "Julian, let's take a look at that hand" he says, ignoring what just occurred behind us. A part of me knows that this isn't anything new for him—a supporting character in these women's lives when they needed him to be and even when they didn't.

"I've got him," Wyn calls out to him. She looks down at my wrapped hand. Her shaky hands move down around my forearm as she leads me forward.

"Wyn, I can back off, I just need to know if you're good," Tommy says with his hands out. "Look at me." Tilting his head down, he meets her attention as she stares back at him. "You need me, I'm here."

She lets go of me and shakes out her hands as she steps forward, giving him a curt nod.

I glance at him just as he gives me a tight-lipped smile, like he knows how to handle this or maybe just that he's been around long enough to know when to back off.

She walks ahead of me, picking up the pace as I hustle up next to her. I know what she just survived and witnessed, but something's shifted and I can't read her right now. "Talk to me,

Crowne."

She gives me a side glance, her cheeks flushed as she takes quick breaths like she can't get a deep one in. But she keeps going.

We hustle along the side of the bar, and she doesn't say a damn thing. My mind reels about how she's reacting and trying to process all of this—to go from the high she was on when I dropped her off, to being shoved around, having someone she trusted betray her, and then watching us fight. Add in the poisoning, the history, fuck, even witnessing the things her mother and grandmother are capable of… Even for someone without the trauma she's had to endure would be unraveling.

Fuck, my hand hurts. I look down at my blood-soaked shirt, feeling how the adrenaline is quickly dissipating. "Wyn, baby, I need to have my hand looked at."

She doesn't slow. She keeps walking, over the footbridge and along the path that leads to her house. Scanning the fingerprint lock on her front door, she shoves the door open, striding toward the bar cart in the corner. If there was ever a good time for a drink, it would be now. She pours out a splash in a rocks glass and tosses it back. Without even turning, she pours herself another as I reach her.

"Hey," I say quietly. "Talk to me." I wrap my fingers around the bottom of the glass just as it reaches her lips. I slowly pull it back, holding her glare. Moving the glass to my lips, I sip half of what she poured. If she needs a minute, the familiar taste, the burn to take the edge off, I won't be the one to stop her—I'll drink with her.

She holds the bottom of the glass with me, drinking what's left.

"More?" I ask, my heart racing.

She nods slowly and steps back. Taking another, she looks

down at the gash in my hand.

"Can that wait?" she asks, chest heaving as if she's trying to gauge what she can have right now. Taking a step closer, her fingers flex at her sides.

Without hesitation, I say, "It can wait."

CHAPTER 33

Wyn

I'm shaking, nearly vibrating with adrenaline coursing through my body. It's not from nerves or anxiety, from pain or distress, it's the intense need for release and for him to use my body. I want to feel good and to make him feel good after what just happened.

He doesn't have a chance to pour any more. Instead, he puts the glass down, watches as my chest heaves, and bites the end of the material that's wrapped around his hand to tighten it.

"Tell me what you need, Crowne," he grits out. "I don't want to read this wrong right now, so tell me what you need from me and I'll do it."

My eyes water, trying to stifle the possibility that something could have happened to him. He put himself in danger to protect me. And he did it without hesitation. I look up at the vaulted ceilings of my home and refuse to submit to fear anymore. If there's anything or anyone I want to submit to, it's him. His body. The way he loves me. The way I know I'm so fucking in love with him.

I lick my lips, tasting what's left of the whiskey we've just had. I feel out of breath. I don't want to think. I *want* to relinquish every bit of control I've had to hold on to for so long. I don't want to be coddled or cuddled, I don't want to be reminded about what I survived or who I was before. I want to be, in this moment, with him, used, fucked, loved and worshipped.

"Crowne," he growls, eyes on mine.

I tug the hem of my shirt, lifting it up and off.

"Don't be gentle," I tell him as I reach behind my back and unclasp my bra. My breasts spill as I toss it to the side.

"Fuck," he mumbles, dragging the palm of his good hand across his mouth before his fingers immediately fly to his belt buckle. "Get your pants off right fucking now."

I do as he says, eyes still locked with his as his belt hits the floor.

He looks around my body as I step out of them. The way he studies me, I know he's making sure I haven't been injured anywhere else.

"Tell me you're okay—that this is what you need right now, and I'll take over from there," he says, a pleading edge to his tone. *Fuck, I love this man.*

I need to get out of my head. I need to stay clear of the tiniest flicker of blame and self-loathing. I watched Julian bloody up another man to protect me and then get hurt in the process—history almost repeating itself. It's why I didn't think twice about jabbing that self-defense weapon into Reed's side. The one that I had hidden behind the fire extinguisher again, since the second day I came back to Rumor.

"I'm okay," I say on an exhale, and I mean it. "And I need you. Now."

It's all he needs. He flips open the button on his jeans

one-handed, shoves inside his boxer briefs and pulls out his hardened cock. "Make it wet," he demands.

Without thinking, I sink to my knees, open my mouth, and take his cock all the way to the back of my throat. I nearly gag, but I go back for more and do it again. I wrap my lips, let my tongue drag on the underside of his fat cock, all the way to his thick tip, and have to touch myself with how needy it makes me.

His cock flexes along my tongue, getting harder with every inch I lick.

"So fucking good," he grits out, his hips flexing forward, chasing more. I do it again, only this time, I hold it there and swallow. "This turns you on, baby?" He tilts his head down, his fingers gripping my hair to make me look up at him. There's blood on his lip and streaked down his neck, and it makes me rub along my clit faster as I hum around his length.

When I pull back, I smile up at him, knowing I've done exactly as he asked. He wraps his hand behind my head, fingers threading in my hair, and pulls me up toward his waiting mouth.

He kisses me urgently, wet and messy. I moan at the way he wants to devour me, how he's tasting himself. I nip at his lower lip, and he rewards me with an approving smile. "Face down, legs spread," he says against my lips, and then glances behind me.

The chair he sat in the night he watched me fuck my own fingers is where he wants me now. He toes off his shoes and shoves his pants off as I do exactly as he instructs. I bend forward, my breasts brushing against the plush velvet just before I feel his touch. His knuckles graze along the center of my ass as his fingers loop into the back of my panties. He tugs the material to the side, causing friction against my clit, making me shudder. A small, needy whimper escapes me as I push back into him.

Sometimes a woman just needs to be bent over a chair and fucked.

"Your pussy is so ready for me, isn't she?" he says. "Fuck, just look at how wet and swollen she is." He taps the head of his cock along my ass. "Keep playing with her for me, Crowne. I want her nice and juicy."

I smirk, loving the way he talks so damn dirty to me.

"Make me feel it, baby," I say as I glance back over my shoulder. "Fuck me, *hard.*"

He hums a low, approving laugh.

I want to feel him long after he's finished and still dripping out of me.

He drags his cock between my pussy lips, once, twice, and on the third, he pushes into me with one hard, fast thrust. Both of us groan with relief—the way he makes me feel so full isn't something I can describe, it's too *fucking* good for words.

Pulling back to the tip, he does it again. The angle of it reaches the spot that's going to make me see stars. The stretch of him is enough to make me moan, but the way his hips roll forward has me taking it deeper and gasping. I work my fingers against my clit and drive my hips back to meet his. The sensations are so overwhelming that I almost can't catch my breath.

His hand trails down my spine and his thumb runs along my ass as his hips roll, cock spreading me. I hear him spit, then feel wetness hit my skin and slide down my crack to my asshole. His thumb rubs his spit along my asshole gently as he drives his cock in and out of my pussy. "I want this one too."

My pussy pulses in response. That's a first for me, and it sends goose bumps along my skin, the sensation of it and the promise.

I reach one arm forward to grasp onto something as he fucks me harder. He doesn't rush or chase, he pulls back with purpose and makes sure to feel every part of my pussy. I know he's watching. He inhales sharply as he brings his cock to the tip just before he drives it back in to the hilt.

"Oh, god, Julian," I groan. "I love—" I rush out, cut off by a whimper as he seats himself deep inside of me.

"That's it, keep talking, Crowne." He leans forward, his cock buried as he kisses the center of my back. His lips draw along the petals of the flowers tattooed there. I can't see it, but I can feel the way he worships me. "What do you love, baby?" As he grinds in deeper, it steals my breath all over again. His arm snakes around me as his fingers meet mine and pinch my clit. I let out a raspy groan. But the roll of his hips slows, and he pulls my body up, turning me to face him and pulling out. I search his eyes, not wanting to be done yet. "Look at me," he says as I spread my legs wider for him. His thumb moves up and down my pussy, breath labored, teasing what I really want.

"Tell me," he says as he replaces his thumb with his cock, dragging it up and down from slit to clit.

"Julian," I whisper, my eyes brimming with tears. Emotion floods forward as his eyes stay locked with mine.

"I've got you, baby," he says, rolling his hips into me, spreading me all over again. He leans back, looking down at where my pussy stretches around him with every slowed thrust. A growl rattles his throat before he says, "Look at how you fit me, Crowne."

Something's shifted as he looks at me with tenderness instead of hunger, like he knew what I wanted and delivered, but somehow, this is what I need now. He pulls me closer, his arms wrapping around me, eyes never leaving mine as my fingers delve into his hair.

The intensity of the moment, the urgency of having him doesn't change, but what started as fucking has turned into something deeper and more reverant.

"Julian," I rush out as the exquisite pressure of him pushes me closer to tipping over with every pull and push. He buries his face into my neck, as if he needs to feel me, breathe me, hold me and never let go.

I feel weightless as he works my body with measured thrusts, the angle allowing him to grind against my clit, one arm braced around my lower back and the other cupping the side of my face, fingers tangled into my hair.

My legs tremor, and my core contracts—everything so full and so tight.

"You feel so fucking good," he says, voice rasped as he fucks me deeper. He pulls his cock out just to the tip and then fills me harder. "Wait, for me." My eyes roll back from the overwhelming pleasure as he kisses my lips and then slowly pulls out, before fucking into me again even deeper. "I've got you." It's exactly what I didn't know I needed—the pace of it, the fullness, the way he holds me, speaks to me, and looks at me. I can barely catch my breath.

"Julian," I whimper. The pressure builds so deep within me, my nerve endings tingling. I can barely hold out, my emotions teetering as I give myself over to him fully.

His mouth covers mine in a barely-there kiss, his eyes never wavering as they look over every feature of my face. With one more roll and grind of his hips, his cock massages the spot that has my release crashing over me. I hold him tightly as I cry out, nearly screaming as my body pulses from every tip down to my very center.

"Fuck, baby," he grits out, kissing up from my neck to my lips. He grinds into me again—once, twice, and moans my name on the third as his cock throbs inside of me, filling me, and somehow making me want him all over again.

"I love you," I say on a panted breath, my forehead pressed to his shoulder. My lips ghost against his skin, and I know he heard me, because his fingers flex and grip around me tighter.

"Say that again, baby," he says, pulling back slightly to look at me. His smile reaches his hazel eyes as they find mine.

I exhale the breath I had been holding and smile as I repeat how I feel. "I said I love you. I'm in love with you, Julian."

"Come here," he says, lifting me up with him as he stands. When he pulls out of me, I feel so empty that I let out a small whine. The sound makes him sniff out a laugh. "Tell me again, Crowne. I'm already getting hard again from hearing it the first time."

His mouth collides with mine, and he kisses me like it's the one thing he's been waiting to hear. "I said, tell me again," he says, smiling against my lips, both of us breathless all over again. With one hand framing my face and the other wrapping around me, I start to say it again but pause.

Because I feel his wrapped hand along my back. When I shift to look at it, a blood spot is visible along the center and red streaks down his forearm. He watches me as I run my fingers along the material. The things we just came from, the mess we left behind, all of it comes back into focus.

"I love you, but we need to get you to a hospital," I say, sniffing out an unbelieving laugh. "I just made you fuck me and—"

"Believe me, you didn't make me do anything I didn't want to do." He tips my chin up. "Look at me, Crowne."

I look up into his eyes as mine water, and I can't help but smile.

"I did exactly what you wanted, what I wanted, and what you needed. Now, we're going to get this stitched up, and then we're going to come back here and I'm going to fuck your mouth and this delicous pussy again, and then you're going to fall asleep in my arms after you tell me you love me over and over." He kisses my lips. "And we're going to keep doing that, because I'm here. I've got you, Crowne. No matter what."

I tilt back, running my fingers along his scruff and into his hair as I look up at the man who has been so much more than what I ever thought I would have. Julian Colton went from a charmingly beautiful stranger to my personal fantasy, my protector, and now this.

"And I've got you. No matter what."

CHAPTER 34

Wyn

Five days later, Sheriff Fury came looking for Dr. Reed Andrews who had been reported missing. A professor who didn't show up for classes had set off enough warning bells that eventually made it to the Rumor County Sheriff's Department. After all, this wasn't the first time a professor at the university had disappeared. It is the first time, however, that I know for a fact that a missing professor wouldn't be returning.

Fury asked that I come down to the sheriff's station for a statement about the last time I saw my colleague, and if I knew his whereabouts. My mother had told me to be as honest as I wanted, so that's what I did. Birdie reported the aggressive nature of some of the wildlife that had been residing in the river around The Whispering Fool to animal control, but all of the dust settled without much repercussion.

Without a body there isn't a crime. That was when the rumors started. My home is a town named after its ugly little super power—rumors that muddied the waters and caused a sense of confusion. It was rather brilliant when I finally saw it for what it was. Little lies and embellished truths that made people talk instead of look. I knew where the rumors started and how they caught fire. This time, they swirled around a young professor with a gambling addiction. There was another about the predatory teacher being arrested across state lines, making it the FBI's problem. My favorite one was the conspiracy story about how Reed had killed Stan Billings and then got away with it.

I'm not a liar. I told as much of the truth as I could. He drank some whiskey, said some shitty things, there was an altercation, accusations, and then we left. Whatever happened later, he would need to ask around somewhere else. I'm positive my mother and Birdie had answers, but they're Crownes, so nobody would ever know what happened unless they wanted that to be the case. When I walked out of Fury's office, Andi sat waiting, along with two other women, one wearing a sorority sweatshirt and the other with university sweatpants.

There were plenty of people to shoulder some of the damage in all of this—the university, the sheriff's department, and anyone else who knew and didn't make enough noise to stop it from happening. I left the sheriff's station feeling a sense of pride, knowing that something's finally been done to put a stop to it. Something that felt more like what was due instead of what was accepted. I don't know what kind of person that makes me, other than a Crowne.

A few days after I walked out of the sheriff's station, I submitted my formal letter of resignation to the head of my department, officially ending my time and tenure as professor of organic chemistry.

"Do I want to know?" Jo asks as she sketches in her notebook. I stop mid-pour and remember what my mom and Birdie's wishes were. If my sisters are ever going to find out the things our mother and grandmother have done, it would come from them.

"I find it incredibly convenient that a sexual predator just disappears the moment he's about to be found out," Stevie says, clapping her hands together after she runs it across the workbench.

My sisters are smart. They know something had happened with Reed. Stevie's been putting pieces together about his involvement with the sexual assault allegations that had been barely reported at the univeristy. But outside of Julian's stitched-up and bandaged hand, there isn't much of a trace of that night.

"Slipped with one of my files and really got myself good," he said to Jo.

Julian clued me in later that my mother and grandmother had plans for Reed. They had plenty of eyes on him while he'd been at The Whispering Fool. The pillars of security, Gina and Gail, clocked him in every time he walked through those doors. I don't think they thought he'd be ballsy enough to do anything in plain sight at my family's bar like that, but I suppose that's the fucked-up thing about sociopathic sexual predators—they have no rules. It made sense that his punishment hadn't either. I was the variable they didn't expect. After they learned the part he played in my kidnapping, it just confirmed that the role Birdie and Lu Crowne play in our small town isn't simply justified, it's necessary.

"You know you can always bribe me to come over when you're feeding me, but this," Stevie says when I don't respond to her suspicions, looking at the massive spread I nervously cooked early this morning. "It's hella early to be drinking, Wynnie. Do we need to have a talk about healthy consumption?"

Jo throws a crinkled-up paper at her. I think she knows I want to talk about the distillery, since I clued them in about that much, considering there hasn't been any time this past week to spend together. But I'm not sure she has any idea what I'm about to ask of them.

"What?" Stevie barks out a laugh. "We're inside of a very dirty distillery at ten-thirty in the morning on a weekday, it feels like it should be said."

"I quit," I tell them.

Jo sits up and puts the notepad down. Stevie glances at her with wide eyes, then back at me, waiting for me to elaborate.

"I wasn't happy with going back and doing what I had done before." I look down at the flight of glasses I've poured and the names that I've scribbled next to them. "And this place, making whiskey, running a distillery, it feels like what I should've been doing all along."

Taking a breath, I look at two of the most important people in my life, the women who make me remember what it's like not to be alone. "I have a business idea, and I wanted to run it past you two before I really dug into it. Or even mention it to Mom and Birdie."

They both glance at the other again. For once, my sisters are silent, and it almost makes me laugh.

"I'd like to know if you both would want to do it with me. You can be as involved as you'd like. Put to use your strengths or interests. You don't need to distill or work the whiskey product side of it."

I try to gauge their body language or their gut reactions, but they're not giving me all that much. I think I may have shocked them slightly.

"Jo, there's a logo, bottle designs, creative things that I

couldn't even start to wrap my head around that I would want you to lead and own." I take a seat around the round table at the center of the space. "Stevie, you make more noise about things than any other person on the planet. You don't have to give up your shifts at The Whispering Fool. But I could see you helping me run the business side of this—and the public relations. If anyone can hype and help schmooze people in town about it, it's you all the way."

"So you're saying you need us," she says, squinting her eyes at me.

That was wildly accurate and far more so in the grand scheme of my life. I smile and nod. "I'm saying I need you, always have." I tilt my head to the side. "I'm doing this, no matter what; I just want to know if you want a piece of it with me."

Jo claps off the sugar on her hands and shifts out of her stool to stand. "It's a fuck yes from me. I wouldn't mind scaling back at the bar and leaning into doing more creative things."

We both look at Stevie, who's smiling, looking between the two of us. "Mom is going to run The Whispering Fool until she loses her marbles, and even then, there's a part of me that knows she'll never want to give much of that place up."

She sits down and kicks her feet up, the chartreuse MIU MIU pumps front and center. "I'm keeping my podcast and nights at the bar—I still need to pay bills and feed Nashy. But I'm in." Then she gasps. "Oh my gosh, Theo is going to be so jealous. I bet he could get bottles circulating with all of the schmoozing he does too."

"When I was in Montana," I say, looking at my sister, "I listened. All the time." Pausing, I swallow the emotion that still holds. "It was how I felt like I didn't lose"—I look around—"all of this and all of you." I smile and wipe at the tear that escapes. "We did tasting flights of all your recommendations. I want to do that here."

Stevie looks up at the ceiling, trying to keep from letting her welled tears fall. "Well, fuck you for making me cry before noon, Wynnie."

"This feels right, Wyn," Jo says, breaking through the dramatics of our middle sister. "You've always been brilliant, but taking something and making it even better is your superpower."

"What are we going to call it?" Stevie asks. "The whiskey brand or the distillery, what should we call it?"

The firewood cracks loudly and sparks move up and into the air. Evenings in autumn are such a tease—they make us think that brisk nights and warm blankets are on the agenda until the next day, when summer teases her way back in. But tonight, after a big dinner with everyone I love in one room, I look up at the way the clouds move with purpose and feel content that maybe I've found mine as well.

I never thought I'd see this part of my life again, the one where my family had a late dinner together and then a drink around the firepit. I spent too much time thinking I didn't want to have anything to do with it, then craving nothing more than to see them all one more time, to this—standing here, I don't know if I feel like crying or laughing.

I smile right before I feel him. Large arms weave their way around my middle from behind, and the warmth and smell of him follow. "You look like you've had a good day, baby."

As I lean back into him, his chin rests on my shoulder, and

we look out at the same things—family, friends, the chaos of all of it when we come together. It isn't perfect by any stretch, but I don't want perfect, I just want them. And him.

"I did. Made plans with my sisters. We figured out a schedule to be at the distillery together and the things we can accomplish on our own. Oh, and I spoke with Lincoln Foxx for a while this afternoon. They want to host an event with us at Foxx Bourbon this spring." I run my fingers along his forearms that hold me to him. "Whiskey Women Distillery and Foxx Bourbon," I say with an unbelieving sigh.

He presses his lips to my neck and asks, "How are you feeling about all of it?"

I have a tattoo appointment set for next week and weekly therapy back on my calendar, but I know myself, or at least, I'm learning more about who I want to be. I have explanations, about my family, about the night I'd been taken, all of the pieces that had been left making me uneasy have now been accounted for. And after seeing Laney, thanking her for what she did, it was more than what I thought I'd ever be able to do. But big life things mean big feelings, and for me, that will always mean finding ways to manage them.

"I'm thinking I'm so fucking excited." I close my eyes and hum at his touch and the way it feels good to lean on him, talk to him, have him ask me the question in the first place. "How about you?"

"I'm feeling like I missed you today," he whispers quietly in my ear.

"Thomas," my mom calls out from inside, peering out the kitchen window. "I thought you were going to help me here?"

"Hold your damn horses, Tallulah," Tommy calls out. "Julian, am I going to see you for coffee tomorrow morning?"

he asks as he starts walking toward the house. Before he heads inside, he says, "There's this pour-over contraption that Jo brought over, said it's foolproof good coffee."

I think the only person who was sad about Julian checking out of the B&B is Tommy. Jameson was heading back out and Julian took the few things he brought with him on his travels and moved them into my place a few days ago.

"I'll be there," Julian says. "There's something I wanted to talk with you about that can wait until tomorrow. Mind if I come by a little earlier. Say seven a.m.?"

"Thomas, if I didn't mean right now, I wouldn't have said it!" Mom yells from the window.

Tommy glances at me, and then looks down, smiling. Giving Julian a nod, he keeps his path toward the house, calling out, "What crawled into your panties today? Christ, I'm coming."

Julian kisses the same spot on my neck again before I turn around. His hair is pulled half back, and the way the scruff along his cheeks barely hides his dimple beneath and frames his lips makes them look so damn kissable. I loop my arms around his neck, twirling a piece of his hair with my fingers as he lifts me up, just enough so that my feet hover off the ground. *Weightless, that's how I feel with him.*

"Made some progress with a few pieces I've been working on for a while," he tells me as he kisses me softly.

"Anything I can see?" I ask. I love watching him work and talking about the things he was passionate about.

He smiles against my lips. "I'll show you one I've been working on soon."

"Take it somewhere else, you two!" Jo shouts from her spot next to Nash.

"Is Julian eating her face?" Nash asks. "Julian, when you're done with loving on Auntie Wyn, can you come show me that airplane trick again?"

"Love on me one more time and go show my nephew your paper folding skills."

I squeal out laughing as he lifts me off the ground and kisses up my neck. My hands move into his hair as he kisses me.

"Disgusting," Nash yells out and it has both of my sisters laughing.

He puts me down just after he gives me one more peck on the lips, and he walks backward. "Alright, Nash, let's do this, buddy," he says, clapping his hands together and joining my nephew on the grass. Nash pulls out a stack of colorful paper from his backpack, and Julian starts showing him step-by-step how to fold the first one.

"I swore that he had something to do with it," a deep voice says from the other side of the patio. I turn and find Jameson finishing off the Lego set that he had built with Nash earlier. At the picnic table by himself, he takes a sip of his drink and adds, "Your disappearance," he adds.

I clear my throat. "Please tell me you're not referring to Julian?"

Jameson laughs quietly, shaking his head. "Not Julian. Reed," he says instead.

Playing off information I already know, I deflect, and he probably knows it, too. "I knew you worked my case, but I didn't think about the people you would have questioned."

He crosses his arms over his chest, planting his feet wide as he stands. "Wyn, you're Nash's aunt, you're family. Not to mention, that my job is to work homicides. And homicide was a real possibility when you had been missing beyond the seventy-two-hour mark. I've worked with the local FBI and their Behavioral Analysis Unit. Serial cases usually need bodies, and we didn't have one for you. The evidence that had been left in your wake didn't point to you being killed. But the night you disappeared." He shakes his head. "Reed was one of the last people to see you, and I had a gut feeling about that asshole. There hadn't been anything tangible for me to move on it, though," he says, looking toward his grandson.

"If that's true, your gut instinct, then I hope whatever has happened to him was deserving," I say with a shrug before moving toward the kitchen, pointing at the house. "I'm going to see if my mother is causing irreparable damage."

I want to see if Tommy needs rescuing from her, but mostly, I need to cut this conversation off. Jameson is smart, and I wouldn't doubt that if he wants he could figure all of this out—what happened to Reed, who made that happen, hell, even whatever sorry shitheads came before.

Just before my foot hits the step, Jameson calls out behind me. "Sheriff Fury is doing a fine job of effectively not closing cases, as your sister keeps pointing out."

"Is that a gut instinct I'm hearing about your boss?" I ask with a quirked eyebrow.

He takes a big breath before he says, "Yeah, maybe. We'll save that story for another day."

Nash starts laughing, pulling both of our attention his way.

"It's convenient..." Jameson adds a beat later. "Reed disappearing like that. Deputy Billings, too. Don't you think?"

I give him my best casual smile when I say, "Convenient? Maybe just good old-fashioned karma."

He pauses, his cup halfway to his mouth before he smiles into it, making me take note of the things left unsaid. "I don't know much about karma, Wyn, but I do know patterns. A few of them seem to point in places that I'd rather not be looking." He looks out at Stevie and Nash belly laughing about something. Swallowing, he looks back at me. "I like being at this family table and on your side."

I raise my chin and reach for the handle on the double doors. "It's a smart place to be, Detective," I say with an appreciative smile, and then move inside.

I'm not going to overthink any of it. If Jameson wants to, he'll ask questions and dig a little deeper, but I really hope he doesn't.

Passing through the solarium, I see Birdie on the chaise lounge. With a joint in one hand and her corded phone in another, she says, "You're an Aries rising, Luna, so that makes sense that you want Mickey to step aside a bit." She glances up at me and smiles, but continues talking. "That reminds me, have you heard about the billionaire who's apparently buying up a bunch of real estate here? Heard he was one of those old money men."

I shake my head, knowing that the source of rumors aren't just a single person, but rather a handful of women, a garden club perhaps, who look out for each other in ways that are bigger than most could ever understand.

As I turn the corner, the smell of sage burning hits me. Not as hard, however, as that sage burning on a dish next to the sink, where my mother's hands are submerged in water, and pressed up behind her is my Uncle Tommy. I watch for a few seconds at the way they sway back and forth together—no music—just the sound of each other and whatever they're quietly exchanging. In another life, I would have never paid attention to it, the way they regarded the other. The years they've spent arguing, but always being around. I wonder if it's an entire love story that I was just too closed off to seeing until now. I've experienced enough to know that it's none of my business unless they want it to be, so I take a few steps back the way I had come and call out, "Mom? You need any help?"

When I turn the corner again, Tommy is leaning against the counter with a beer in hand as my mother says, "I wouldn't mind it. Thomas thinks opening a beer and watching me wash dishes is a masterclass in helping in the kitchen."

He sniffs out a laugh, shaking his head. "Lu, a goddamn pleasure, as always." He moves past me and gives me a wink. "Wyn, I almost forgot. The latest batch needs something—can't quite put my finger on it, but it's close. Mind an old man lurking around to spend some time on it?"

I give him a nod. "Always."

The smile he gives me is one that I won't ever tire of seeing—a proud fatherlike figure who was over the moon when we told him about our plans for the distillery.

He kisses my cheek as he walks by me. "Love ya, kiddo," he whispers. Hearing that from him will never get old.

I move closer to my mother and hit her hip with mine. "Wouldn't mind your input on this batch too."

Her head whips to the side to look at me, just as surprised as I am that I'm suggesting it. But this is as much their legacy as it will be mine. "It's going to be the first official batch of Tennessee whiskey that we'll eventually put out. I could use another opinion."

She smiles. "You know I have lots of those." She waits a beat before whispering, "Thank you." I'm not sure if it's for including her or not making a big deal about her and Tommy, but I'll take it. Tipping her chin toward the cake that was freshly frosted next to her, she says, "Bring that outside for me. I'll bring out some fresh glasses for a little late-night sipper."

The cool evening is welcome, my breath just starting to be visible as I step back outside. When I deposit the cake on the picnic table and glance around the yard, I run my fingers along the edges of my leather cuff. I use it often, when I feel overwhelmed or find myself drifting toward a bad memory. It grounds me, much like the man sprawled out on the grass with my nephew folding airplanes.

"Mom, look at this one soar!" Nash yells out to my sister. "Mom, you gotta see the necklace Julian made for me, it's actually the coolest." He holds out the black leather chain with his orange-colored rock hanging from the center, trying to look down at it.

Stevie gives him two very enthusiastic thumbs-ups as she walks up next to me. "Is your uterus contracting watching that? A sexy-ass man playing on the ground with a kid and making paper airplanes?"

"Not everyone believes that watching grown men play with kids is attractive," Jo says, flanking the other side of me. "There is nothing cute about that thought in the least."

"Bite your tongue, wench. Nash is the cutest human alive," Stevie barks back.

Jo just looks down at her boots and then raises her eyebrows at her. "What was that?" She cups her hand around her ear. "You're forfeiting your turn with the Pradas?"

Stevie flips her off. "You're losing your hearing," she mumbles with a smirk.

"Oh look, it's your father-in-law," Jo says, her voice laced with sarcasm.

"The fuck is he doing still here?" Stevie breathes out. "Should have left by now."

"Its been a little while since we've all had dinner together, maybe he's digesting," Birdie interjects, her chin resting on my shoulder. I tip my head to touch hers as her arms wrap around me. "And I believe your husband invited him."

"Dinner's been over for a while now," Stevie says, and it has both Jo and I looking at each other, knowing there's something going on in that chaotic brain of hers.

"What are we gawking at?" our mom asks, joining the viewing party. She settles a tray of glasses all filled with a shot of something. "You all look like hens on the hunt."

"Mom, what the hell does that even mean?" Jo deadpans.

"You know, hunting for the cock," she says nonchalantly.

"Mom!" I screech out and cup my hand over my mouth, trying not to laugh.

"Jesus Christ—" Stevie says with a clipped laugh.

"Lu, are you kidding me?" Jo grumbles.

But she and Birdie just start cackling like it's the funniest thing in the world. "The three of you girls, my goodness, it's like nobody has ever heard the word *cock* before," Birdie says, catching her breath. "Especially when I know for a fact y'all have enjoyed one a time or two."

Mom mumbles, "Hopefully, more than two."

"Oh my god," I say on an exhale, and my sisters and I exchange the classic side-eye that silently says, *Yes, she just said that.*

"Alright, you prudes, here," our mom says, grabbing the glasses she brought out, popping the stopper off the bottle of whiskey that proudly shows the beautiful logo Jo already made.

"I didn't think I'd have you girls together like this. I thank every goddess in the universe that we can all be together."

Birdie holds up her glass and lifts her chin. She looks at our mother, and they have a wordless exchange, both of their eyes brimming with tears. "To my family, my beautiful girls, my whiskey women, you make me proud every single day."

EPILOGUE

Julian

3 months later…

I SLIDE ACROSS THE BLACK-PAINTED floor on my stool to pull out the design I drafted for this project. It was less than a month after Wyn had officially left her tenured career as a professor when I walked into this building as its official owner. I negotiated the purchase and then drove out to Oregon, packed up my equipment and anything worth holding on to at my place, and put the rest of it on the market. Rumor, Tennessee is home now.

Stretching my hand, I flex my fingers and rub along my palm. The stitches came out and healed pretty quickly, but it left a nice looking scar.

"I was wrong," Wyn said as she ran her thumbs along the reddish-purple mark that stretched along my palm. "I told you that this hand wasn't going to change, that its lines were your destiny." She kissed the scar, and all I thought was being there that night to stop Reed from hurting her was exactly where I was supposed to be.

Protecting her and loving her was always supposed to happen. I wholeheartedly believe that.

"Jules?" Jo calls out from the open wall cutout connecting our two spaces.

"I'm not answering to that. You and Stevie need to knock it off," I yell back as I turn on the buffer, a smile quirking my lips.

"And yet, here you are, answering to it," she calls out.

Downstairs is being renovated into a gallery, making this entire building look more approachable, and hopefully profitable.

I switch on the buffer and run it across once more. If there's anything that I want to shine, it's this. The thin gold band will fit perfectly; I sized her finger while she slept. I knew what stone was going to be hers as soon as I told her the story about it. I just needed to convince a certain asshole to sell it to me. And about three months ago, I made it happen.

JULIAN:

There's an entire block of empty buildings here that are going to waste, especially with a whiskey distillery coming into town, endorsed by Foxx no less. You'd be nuts not to swoop it up. I'll take my name off the bid for it, if you sell me that fucking stone.

RHODES:

Fine, you have a deal. Come and get it.

JULIAN:

Are you fucking with me? That was fast.

RHODES:

Have I ever given off the vibe that I would have time for that.

JULIAN:

My position still stands, I'm not paying in favors.

RHODES:

I think your position is bullshit, but I'll accept the payment you offered with an asterisk that you still owe me something at a time to later be determined.

JULIAN:

Deal, asshole.

He didn't waste time after I picked it up. I glance out across the street and see renovations already underway on the long stretch of abandoned storefronts.

Jo walks by, leaning her elbows on the opening of the half wall divider, looking out where I am. "What the hell is a billionaire doing buying properties in Rumor?"

"He's got nothing else better to do. Billionaires have rich friends, the kind that like to go to art galleries and acquire a bunch of work," I say to her as I focus back on the ring.

"She's going to love it, Jules," she says. Jo's watched me obsess over the design of this for weeks now, but I think she's right.

I hold it up and let the bright light catch the way the gold shines. Fuck, this one came out perfect. I made two others when I wasn't sure I would get the stone I wanted. There were plenty of beautiful gems that I considered for her, but the emerald felt like it belonged to her.

Jo claps her hands. "Okay, I want your knee-jerk reaction to this advertisement display with the pinup and the logo. I want to make sure I didn't just go too over the top here."

If anyone questioned the drive and hard work the Crowne sisters have been putting in, I would come out swinging. Grant and Lincoln Foxx made a trip down to help calibrate their new copper still. The Foxx brothers and Crowne sisters spent nearly twelve hours straight talking through flavor profiles and how they would filter through sugar maple charcoal, making it a true Tennessee whiskey.

Grabbing my bag, I lean against the archway that transitions my space to Jo's.

"What do you think?" Jo asks, biting at her thumbnail.

"She's going to love it, Jo," I say honestly. I don't know how she managed to do it, to change from fine art to mainstream culture and design, but I'm impressed. And I know her sisters will be too.

The youngest Crowne smiles wide, looking at her work and giving it a nod.

I want to give Wyn the things she said she wanted, and not the ones that are just assumed or expected. That's not who we are to each other. Traditional was never a part of our story, and I doubt it ever will be. But I'm going to ask her to marry me anyway.

I hadn't planned to stay in Rumor. A few hours turned into twenty-four. And then twenty-four transitioned into the most important weeks of my entire life.

I think about my dad often, what he would have said if he'd met Wyn in a different time and place, what he would think about the choices I've made along the way. I knew him as best as he was willing to share. A part of me wonders what today would feel like if he never left this town, if he'd stayed and fell in love with the girl, shared a life with a person who knew all the parts of him.

"Is that happening soon?" Jo asks as she moves back toward her canvas.

"Soon," I say with a smirk. *Really soon.* Wyn and her sisters have been pushing really hard to get everything set for the new year, but I think tonight might be a good night for her to take a little break.

Jo smiles. "Not sure if this is too touchy-feely for you—goddesses know it is for me—but I'm grateful for you, Jules. My sister is…" Her eyes tear up as she looks to the ceiling, shaking her head. "Just don't fuck it up," she says with a smile as she points at me.

"Still not into the nickname, Jo," I call out after her as she turns away from the shared space. The most ridiculous part is that I don't really hate it—the idea of having people that folded me in like family and had nicknames for me. I almost forgot what it felt like to have people that noticed when I was around or not. I wasn't planning to fuck up a damn thing, not with Wyn. She's my family now.

My burner phone buzzes in my bag. I had planned to toss it. My plan all along was to leave that part of my legacy behind, but about two weeks after Reed had officially never wandered up the embankment of the river, Wyn said to me, "*Whatever it is you decide to do, I'll support you. If the only thing you have room for in your life is making beautiful jewelry and me, then I won't complain for a single second.*" She drew along the scar on my palm and added, "*But, if you wanted more, if that legacy your family built is still something that you see value in continuing, you have my approval. If you want it.*"

Eventually, my family's legacies would die with me. But having Wyn's blessing to make my own decisions when it came to the cleaning business meant more than I realized. I wasn't ready to be done with it. After everything that happened, I know there are people I trust who would benefit from having access to my skillset—my soon-to-be family, included.

Wyn

THE BEAUTY OF WHISKEY IS that the rules are more flexible when it comes to aging. But we want at least two years and then another seven months in finishing barrels. For now, however, we're in a waiting game for that batch. This younger batch, which had been barreled when I wasn't here, isn't hitting right.

"It's the emulsification." I lean against the edge of the bench, trying to figure out what the hell is wrong with this batch. Frustrating doesn't even begin to explain the feelings I'm having.

"It's not the char on the barrels?" Tommy asks, taking another sip from the whiskey thief. "Wyn, I'm telling you, it was decent when it went into the barrel." He looks up at me as I think about how to turn this around.

"Jack and Coke is the state drink," I state.

He laughs out, "Yeah, for good reason."

I smile, because I know flavors and this one actually has potential.

"What if we have our own take on it?" I thought about the soda barrels that Moonie's always rolled in when we were growing up—a classic cola and a black cherry soda that came from a place up north in Connecticut. "We finish this blend in classic cola, infuse it right into the whiskey. It'll salvage this batch and could roll out in early summer."

He nods slowly, mulling the concept over. When I shared with Tommy about wanting to take this place over, it was part permission and part blessing I was seeking. He gave both.

I glance at our logo that Jo had designed. The way the *W*'s intertwine, making the shape of a crown was a brilliant idea. Whiskey Women Distilling has moved quickly in a few short months. We'll kick off officially in the new year, and then in the spring, we'll finally be able to stock shelves and open the doors to our tasting bar.

It feels like I've found a purpose—not that I hadn't felt it before, but this time, it isn't for anyone else. Some days, it rivals graduate students and lab work, but I love every minute doing this. I'm not trying to prove a point or hide away from my family. This time, it feels right. Whiskey was always the obvious common denominator that I ignored or just wasn't ready to see beyond something to play around with or pour.

Tommy drums his knuckles along the top of the wood barrel he's leaning on. "I think it's a great idea, Wyn." He stands to his full height and says, "Alright, I'm going to head to the stables for a bit. Promised Nash I'd take him for a ride in the morning, which means I need to stock the apples and peppermints, otherwise he thinks the horses are sad about not getting snacks."

I snort out a laugh. That sounds exactly like something Nash would say.

A text from Julian that came in three hours ago waits for me when I lift my phone. I had a habit of getting lost in what I'm doing while I'm out here. The late afternoons are when Tommy comes out and helps me solve any issues or to experiment with things that Stevie and Jo glazed over about.

JULIAN:

I'll meet you at the distillery around 7 tonight. Don't go home without me. Love you.

I smile. *Home.* I love the life we're building. Home is just a short walk down the hill. We drove out to Oregon shortly after I put in my resignation to the university. I packed up my office, and that same night, we got in his Bronco and drove out to the Northern Pacific Coast, packed up his rather expansive studio space, and put his oceanside place up for rent.

I'm not sure how much time passes when I look up from work again. I stretch my neck and squeeze my eyes shut, listening to Stevie's latest podcast episode finish and glancing at my phone. It's nearly seven, and I got lost in work. It's become our habit—work a bit late, make dinner together, and then either spend time out here or at Julian's studio. We both care about what the other does, what we want to accomplish. Some nights, it'll be relaxing on the chair together and listening to music, or grabbing dinner with my sisters, but Julian doesn't just fit into my life; he helped shape it.

A paper airplane lands next to me on the bench, making me smile. He's here just like he said he would be. When I pick it up and turn it in my hand, I realize this clean, pointed fold wasn't a quick one. It took some time. I turn around and find him standing against the sliding doors, feet crossed at his ankles and hands in his pockets.

"I have something to show you," he says with a smile. He cuffs a piece of his hair behind his ear and meets me halfway to the door with a kiss.

"Is it a slice of cake? I haven't eaten anything since lunch."

He slides the door open and the cool air hits me. A reminder that while technically the winter solstice already happened, the weather in Rumor is on a delay. It won't get cold enough for me to consider it winter until we're well into February. He brushes his fingers against my palm and intertwines them as he says, "I'll get you a slice of cake. Your mother dropped something off in the refrigerator earlier. I still don't understand how she gets in the house to do it—"

"Do you really think a door code, or even a lock with a key, will keep her from where she wants to be?"

"Fair point," he concedes with a chuckle.

"She has guidelines. No entering between the hours of nine p.m. to nine a.m. It was my stipulation when I first decided to live so close to her and Birdie."

He squeezes my hand and brings it to his lips, kissing the top of it.

"Wait, you already stopped home—?"

But he doesn't answer, just looks ahead of where we're walking, and with a tilt of his chin up, I follow his gaze.

My chest warms as my hand comes to my mouth as I try to work through what I'm seeing in front of me. Dozens of strands of white lights are strung up around the garden space.

From one end to the other and all along each raised garden bed he's been building.

It looks like a version of Birdie's garden.

I snap my eyes back to him, tears welling. "What?" I let out a laugh. "When did you do this?"

He shrugs as we walk closer. "Found time for it when you were busy. Most of the lights, though, I did today. Tommy helped keep you occupied for me."

My chest warms at that. We walk through the arched trellis wrapped in small lights, and I take in the details that are spread out around me. All along the center walkway that's been redone and, apparently properly this time, with uplighting that shines from the newly installed pavers. I knew he was working on making this more manageable for the springtime, but I didn't realize he was doing all of *this*.

Blooms are limited this time of year, with only a few plants of witch hazel, winter jasmine, and purple kale. The walkway has at least a half dozen oversize cement pots filled with rosemary bushes. It's faint, and even with all of the rest of my senses being filled, I still catch the calming scent of it. The makeshift fence that outlines the space has arborvitae trees planted and decorated with larger patio bulbs. He knows how much I loved Birdie's garden and how terrible I've been at doing this on my own. This is so far beyond what I could have ever done myself. It's like he took the dream right out of my head and made it a reality.

Along the walkway and landing leading into the house are glass garden balls that look like lit bubbles, and just to the left is the outdoor fireplace that he's been working on. Stacked with wood along each side, the center is lit and roaring.

"There's plenty of space to plant what you'd like in the spring. I only added in a few things that Birdie mentioned you liked and wouldn't die this time of year."

"It's beautiful, " I whisper, feeling breathless. I give him a teasing and leveled look. "Are you trying to romance me, Julian Colton?"

He steps closer and kisses my forehead. "Something like that," he says as he walks past me and up the stairs.

I laugh, remembering the last time I said that to him. Shaking my head, I bat away the few tears that have fallen. I'm overwhelmed in the best way possible. This isn't just a gesture, this is time, and he listened.

With his hand on the door, he smiles at me, letting the quiet evening linger. Or maybe he's taking in the moment too. He does that often, lets the quiet linger and just watches. He's an observer, taking in the bigger picture before focusing on the details.

"You told me once that when you were young you didn't think about having the usual things like a big house or a husband, but you did want a garden..." He nods to the garden he built around me. "And a dog..."

I stop moving for a moment. *He didn't.*

But when he twists the handle to open the back door to our place, out comes a caramel-brown puppy. The ball of fluff barely makes it through the threshold before he tumbles out the door, skipping the first two steps and running right to me. My eyes are so blurred with tears, I can barely see as I pick him up under my arm and pet his warm white furred belly. I couldn't guess what breed or how big he'll be, but I don't think I've ever been more excited in my entire life.

"Oh my goodness, hello."

When I look back up, Julian says, "You read my palm once. Told me that I would have one great love of my life. I don't think either of us would have thought at that moment that it would be you."

The puppy squirms in my arms and tries to lick anything he can get near, but I can't take my eyes off Julian as he steps closer.

"Julian, what are you?" I shake my head when he crouches down in front of me, getting on both knees.

"I love you. That's the one thing I know and can guarantee won't change," Julian says with emotion coating his words. "You're it for me, Crowne. I don't need more time to know that I want to spend as much of it as I can with you." His hands run up behind my thighs as I look down into his hazel eyes, knowing everything he's saying is as honest as it gets. "This question, and request, is selfishly for me."

I let out a shaky breath, wanting more than anything to hear it.

He reaches into his back pocket and pulls out the most beautiful emerald ring. The band is so thin that it makes the size of the emerald look even larger than it already is. There isn't a doubt in my mind that this is the stone he told me about.

"Will you marry me, Wyn?" he asks in his deep and confident voice. It only wavers when he adds, "You're my family, my partner, and I'd like to be called your husband. I can see all of this life with you."

I try to take a breath, my chest so heavy with emotions, and my heart so damn full. It's more than what I've allowed myself to want. I look at the garden he's built for me, the way he's shown up, protected, cared for, loved me so fully…

The puppy makes a yawning sound and lets out a bark, making both of us laugh.

Tears fall as I look at the man on his knees in front of me. I swipe my thumb along his cheek, just above the scruff of his beard. His eyes close at my touch.

"Crowne, I swear the way you make me work for it," he says teasingly as his lips tilt into a smirk. "What do you say, do this with me, walk down an aisle, make some promises, live happily ever after?"

Smiling, I take in a breath, and on the exhale, remember to *be brave.*

"Show me."

The End

THANK YOU FOR READING RUMORS & WHISKEY!

If you loved the romance and suspense of Wyn & Julian's story, then get ready for the youngest Crowne sister. Jo's story is next in *Scandals & Whiskey*!

BONUS EPILOGUE

If you want to see what's happening beyond THE END in Wyn and Julian's life, you can find their bonus epilogue at victoriawilder.com!

ACKNOWLEDGMENTS

This book was a helluva ride and challenged me in ways that I haven't experienced yet as a writer. You'll see the word *support* below written a lot, and that's because it takes a lot of it to bring my books out into the world. I am lucky enough to have a team of people behind me, next to me, lifting me up and cheering me on.

To my editor, Mackenzie, this makes nine books together! Holy shit, how is that possible?! Thank you for seeing the big picture and for pushing me to do better with each story. This book challenged me in ways that had you operating as more than an incredible editor, but a therapist and friend. Thank you for talking me through all the lows and for helping to find ways to make even my most ridiculous ideas work and flow. Cheers to this new series!

To my agent, Lesley, seriously, how did I get so lucky?! Thank you for cheering me on, championing my work like a fucking force, and for helping me to navigate all of the incredible possibilities. I am so grateful for you.

This is the first book that I'm releasing as a hybrid (independent and traditionally published) author. And BOTH of my publishing teams, Bloom in North America and Atria in Australia, New Zealand, and the UK, are made up of some incredibly creative and brilliant minds who have all been such a pleasure to work with. Thank you for welcoming me, working with me, and for helping to bring this story to readers.

To Allie, my editor with Bloom, thank you for your unwavering support and for believing in this series even before words were on the page.

To Anthea, my editor with Atria, I feel so lucky to be working with you and to have you in my corner. Thank you for your constant enthusiasm for my stories.

To my amazingly incredible PA, Amy, thank you for *everything*. From brainstorming to beta-reading, keeping me organized when I'm head-down writing, and all of the things in between. I feel so lucky to have you on this wild ride with me. Here we go!

My beta readers are a team of total badasses who each helped to make this story even better, from the broad strokes to the small bits. To Laura and Kate: your notes and big-picture thoughts are invaluable to me, and your gut checks have only made this story better. To Kelsey: your brilliant STEM mind and comments throughout the suspense were exactly what this story needed. To Jill: your keen eye for detail and for making sure I'm being mindful and taking proper care of my readers are all so helpful. To Sierra: your instincts for hooks and swooning at the heart of the story. And to Nicole: thank you for loving all the spice (and, yes, I shaved off some) and for the hawk-eye level of detail. I feel so grateful for your time and attention. I adore each of you and could not have asked for a better team!

To Lemmy, thank you for making everything pretty! From all of the creative content to the PR support along the way, thanks to you and your crew at Luna Literary for helping to bring my books to so many readers.

A massive thank you to Colby, who guides my TikTok adventure (and fixes it when I mess up the algorithm).

To my ARC Teams: you are incredible! Thank you for

reading and taking the time to not only hype this story, but to add your creativity to all of your social posts. I feel lucky to have readers, never mind the kind that want to read what I write early and then hype the hell out of it.

Thank you to Samantha Brentmoor and Connor Crais for being such powerhouse narrators and working with me. Having you both kick off this series as narrators of this story motivated me to write some banger lines that I know will hit even harder on audio. Thank you for lending your voice to my words.

To Julia Connors and Jenn McMahon, my sprint crew and sounding boards: you're both the most supportive women. Thank you for keeping me accountable and building me up when I so desperately need it. I am so thankful for you. LFG!!!

Thank you to my family—

Blair, I will always write this in my acknowledgments now—With a hand enthusiastically raised, "We stole a car!" Thank you for the brainstorms laced with snorting laughs and exaggerated hand gestures; for shipping so many books and trekking to events with me. Thank you for telling me to slow my roll and for making sure there's always a movie quote or dance-it-out moment when necessary.

To my mom, who is my biggest fan: I know you will devour this book in one sitting. It makes me insanely happy to know it's my book you're reading at the kitchen counter. I love you. And thank you to my dad, who will only crack this book for the dedication and acknowledgments (keep it that way, Charlie). Thank you both for being the kind of cheerleaders every kid, no matter how old they are, deserves.

To my kids, someday, when you're older, maybe you'll read these stories. Maybe you'll slam them shut or devour them in one sitting. But, either way, you'll finally see what all those Post-it notes and chaotic whiteboard scribbles were for. And ultimately, your mom fell in love with what she does for a living. Thank you for loving me along the way. I love you both so much.

To Mr. Wilder, thank you for the big and the little things. You are always the best thing.

ABOUT THE AUTHOR

Forever a hopeful romantic, author Victoria Wilder writes contemporary romance with deliciously witty and wild characters. Her stories merge small-town with romantic suspense that feature swoon-worthy men and fierce women who aren't afraid to ask for what they want.

She's an East Coast girl living in southern Connecticut with her husband, two kids, and Yorkie, Linus. She's always chasing the next season and believes in romanticizing whatever you can along the way. You'll always find her either reading, writing, or ready to dish about movies and books.

instagram.com/authorvictoriawilder
tiktok.com/authorvictoriawilder
facebook.com/victoriawilderauthor
bookbub.com/authors/victoria-wilder